As if it wasn't enough to have nightmares, he suddenly realized these were more than just bad dreams…

Dave read the story twice, feeling dread. He should feel distant, uninvolved. The crime didn't happen on campus or in the town of Princeton. Not even in Norwich. He didn't know the victim. It was unfortunate and heinous, but what did that have to do with him?

Dave jerked, his body shaking. Two puzzle pieces fit together—his fear and the carnival killing. He feared the carnival murder because it was like his brother's and Carter's—the same modus operandi. Repeat criminals tended to do things the same way, picking the same types of victims, the same locations, the same way of entering. Didn't Ted Bundy pick similar girls? Didn't Son of Sam, Dave Berkowitz, choose the same locations where lovers parked? Didn't Gary Ridgway, the Green River Killer, prefer strangulation? If it was the same MO, could it be the same killer?

Dave re-read the paragraph on how the carnival worker had died. The phrasing about repeated blows to the face, even after the victim was surely dead, was exactly what had been written about his brother's death.

One other detail finally hit him. Shocked, he realized he'd dreamed about the carnival murder on the same night it happened. He'd gone to sleep before midnight and the kid was killed just after midnight. It wasn't precognition he was afflicted with. It was co-cognition.

Did clown-colored mushrooms spark the gruesome murders? Will his memories of the murders save him or kill him?

At age eight, Dave Austin witnesses his brother's savage murder in rural Norwich, New York, but amnesia suppresses the memory, and the killer escapes. Locals suspect an itinerant, a pedophile, or a disturbed friend maddened by psychedelic mushrooms. When Dave starts college, pressures at Princeton and alcohol elicit dreams, each one revealing a bit of memory. Then come visions as Dave senses the killer return. Images of teenagers killed where his brother died precipitate a crisis, and David returns to Norwich to find his dead brother's friend, a disturbed witness who knows something. Dave's appearance alarms his psychiatrist, the officers who hadn't solved the case, and especially the killer, who knows he should not have let the young Dave escape. Now the killer must correct his mistake. When a crazy farmer invites Dave to learn the killer's name in the Clown Forest at midnight, how can he resist? He may learn what he needs to identify the murderer—if he gets the truth, and survives.

KUDOS for *The Clown Forest Murders*

"A thrilling read, full of smart wonders as prehistoric spores menace a rural New York population—or is there something more, something demonic?" ~ Jerome Mandel, P.E.N.-UNESCO International Short Story Competition winner, author of *Nothing Gold Can Stay* and *Covet the Oven*

"Set in upstate New York, *The Clown Forest Murders* is a novel that would make Washington Irving proud." ~ Tom Hooker, award winning fiction author and poet

"These authors weave a satisfying mystery that keeps you guessing and will not disappoint." ~ Frank B. Robinson II, author of *Thirty Days Hath September*

"Both a chilling psychological thriller and an intriguing mystery, the story will keep you turning pages from beginning to end." ~ *Taylor Jones, The Review Team of Taylor Jones & Regan Murphy*

"*The Clown Forest Murders* is a combination mystery/thriller that is fast-paced, intense, and chilling. You won't be able to put it down." ~ *Regan Murphy, The Review Team of Taylor Jones & Regan Murphy*

ACKNOWLEDGMENTS

This novel is a collaborative work whose story was conceived by one of us (ACB) and honed into its mystery format by the other (RRB). The authors must acknowledge contributions for details in both the major settings of Norwich, New York, and Princeton, New Jersey. Tony Morrow provided input on the outdoor life, including hunting, rifles, and knives. Marcia and Bill Born gave color about Norwich of old and new. Princeton alumni Graham Doran, Rob Crawford, and Shepherd Pryor V offered information on Princeton of the 90s and inspiration. Sean Ryan made suggestions on the opening. Tom Hooker, Rob Jacoby, and Lenny Bernstein, members of the Appalachian Round Table writers critique group, reviewed, in a weighty fashion, plot, and craft. Writers of the Blue Ridge Writers Group also contributed input on various chapters, as did prose authors of the Great Smokies Writer Program of the University of North Carolina Asheville. Dr. Michael Hopping consulted on medical diagnoses and treatments. Sherry Brooks served admirably as a beta reader who ferreted out glitches. For all those who helped in this project, the authors are grateful.

The Clown Forest Murders

A. C. Brooks & R. R. Brooks

A Black Opal Books Publication

DEDICATION

*This novel is dedicated to Princeton's Class of 1997 and
Class of 1966, to family who encouraged creativity,
and to the memory of Patrick K. Brooks
and all those struggling with mental health challenges.*

Chapter 1

Fireworks

July 1983, South Plymouth, New York:

On a bright, sunny day, eight-year-old David Austin set out after lunch with his older brother Scott on a great outdoor adventure. They hiked up the hill beyond their ranch-style house, joined by a friend, Carter Shuman, who carried the reason for the outing, a brown paper bag filled with fireworks left over from Fourth-of-July festivities. The warm weather with afternoon highs projected in the eighties, above average for central New York, meant the boys wore shorts, tee shirts, and ball caps. David, a handsome kid with an eager, smiling face, already had a summer tan, thanks to the YMCA soccer league he'd joined at the end of the school year.

They'd reached the first clump of bushes in the unused sheep field, now owned by the Austins, when Carter stopped. "Do we have matches?"

"Crap!" Scott said. "David, you go back. Grab some and don't be obvious about it."

David wondered why he was old enough to sneak matches when he'd been ruled too young to handle fireworks. Didn't seem fair, just because Scott and Carter were twelve, but the assignment made him feel important. He got back into the house without encountering Mom and found matches in their usual place on the mantle. Both small boxes of wooden ones and books were there lying loose—the jar that usually held them had crashed to the floor during a minor earthquake and had not been replaced. He grabbed three boxes, thought a moment, and added several matchbooks. He'd made it to the back door when his mother, Chella, materialized.

"Where are you off to?" she asked.

Sure that his mother had once been a cop, David fisted the loot and shrugged. "For a hike with Scott and Carter. They're waiting."

He darted out the back door and through the gate in the chain link fence, knowing he was watched. He dove behind the first big redberry bush where Scott and Carter crouched. David presented the matches, proof of his skill and worthiness to be included in the secret outing.

"Good job," Scott said as he pocketed the keys to fire. He smiled and continued, "You really are grown up. I'm sorry I didn't include you in the pool game at your birthday party right from the start. Brothers should back each other." He hugged David and, positioning the Yankee cap over his brown crew cut at an angle, led the way up the hill.

David was already happy to be with the twelve-year-olds in an activity that had to be kept hidden from parents. Now, with his brother's words, he was thrilled. Ever since the start of second grade, he'd become an outdoor kid, mostly trailing his brother, regardless of the season. In the fall, he raked leaves, stacked firewood, and tried school soccer. In winter, the skiing he endured as a first-grader became fun. Spring meant playing in the icy creek, something else kept secret from parents, especially when Scott had to pull him from the cold water and sneak him into the house to dry off and warm up. Now in summer, he hiked or biked wherever the older boys went. Really part of the gang.

Carter had discovered the bag of sparklers and firecrackers in the closet he shared with his brother. A bit more searching had led him to the good stuff—snakes, rockets, and cherry bombs—that were hidden in the dresser. Neither hiding place showed much imagination, and, to Carter, both were the equivalent of laying gold on the bed with a take-what-you-want sign. Like a good brother, he accepted the invitation and confiscated the whole cache, probably figuring he'd get punched but sure his parents wouldn't be told. The punching might not even happen, for Carter was strong and almost as tall as his fifteen-year-old brother. As he told David and Scott, his brother had likely already forgotten about the leftover fireworks.

Scott chose an isolated spot for the noisy event. A good distance up the hill above the Austin neighborhood stood the falling-down Sugar Shack, once used to boil maple syrup but now a wooden heap. It was a favorite campsite for teenagers, who'd marked the spot with a fire pit and empty beer bottles and cans. These things would be the perfect launch vehicles for lit firecrackers.

To get there, the boys climbed a path that traversed fields above the abandoned sheep pasture. The Sugar Shack site perched above a ledge that looked over a slope to a graveled tractor path. Beyond that lay a fenced-in field and then dark woods. To David, the stand of trees was mysterious, and he'd visited it only when he was with Scott. The slope above the shack was littered with gray boulders that reminded him of tombstones, and he thought of it as a cemetery.

Last fall, the three boys had wanted to explore the woods below. They climbed over the first fence and were heading toward the second when a great monster appeared: a bull came out of nowhere, snorting, and shaking its massive head. The boys screamed and flew back through the wire barrier, Scott tossing David over the fence before he saved himself from what seemed to be a charging beast. In fact, it was only a mildly interested bovine meandering toward them. David had bull nightmares for a week after that, and though he hadn't seen the creature for a while—he'd checked more than once, even when snow was on the ground—there was no way he was going back over the fence.

David reached the Sugar Shack first and found John Redford waiting. A big, muscular, flat-faced kid near thirteen, John had been his brother's friend for a year or so. He didn't live in the neighborhood, but had attached himself like a hungry leech, one not easily shed. Even in the heat, he wore the usual oddball western clothes, all in black including a wide-brimmed black hat and kerchief that fluffed out around his neck and made his humungous head seem even bigger. David's mother said that John reminded her of Hopalong Cassidy, whoever that was.

When Scott and Carter arrived, John pointed at David. "Why is the squirt here?"

Once David had overheard his mother say that John might become an actual bully if he had more wit and ambition. David wasn't sure what that meant, but ever since, he'd pegged John as a bully. He fit the mold, having grown an inch or two in the past year and put on weight, which somehow gave him the power he needed to pick on a small target: David.

"I invited him," Scott said.

"He's got the matches," Carter said, as he pulled the fireworks from the bag and laid them side-by-side on a flat rock. The boys watched as if they were eyeing the contents of a pirate's treasure chest where red and blue wrappers took the place of rubies and sapphires. Scott added the matches and picked up a bottle. David chose a cherry bomb, intending to give it to his brother, but John grabbed it.

The big boy lit the fuse, dropped the bomb into a can, and tossed the projectile high over the ledge. When it exploded in air, he whooped and then bent forward as if he'd been shot. "Shit."

"What happened?" David asked.

"I have to take a dump."

"Unbelievable," Scott said. "Take your smell far from here."

"And we don't want to watch you," Carter added.

John maneuvered past the ledge and down a path toward the fence. A small bush might have served, but the chorus of juvenile ridicule from Scott and Carter drove him farther, over the fence and toward the trees. The mockers then came up with a dire litany of evils that might befall him. First were snakes, poison ivy, sumac, and oak. Then, as if gaining a head of steam, they imagined rabid foxes, a maddened black bear, and of course, the bull. As John scrambled to find privacy and relief, they'd yelled about a movement in the trees, hitting the big kid with the scariest of threats, that of the unknown. With a wave of his middle finger, John disappeared.

Scott dropped a lit firecracker into the beer bottle and heaved it over the ledge toward the trees. What sounded like "assholes" followed the explosion.

"Are we supposed to wait for him?" Carter asked.

"No one said anything about waiting." Scott struck another match.

In the afternoon heat, David watched snakes uncoil in a slow burn and enjoyed the one rocket. Scott and Carter bickered over how to stuff bottles and cans with lit cherry bombs and firecrackers. Exploding bottles and cans flew over the ever-darkening gully and entertained them. Although his brother wouldn't let him light anything, David was allowed to throw several projectiles after they were lit. It was like being an important member of the tribe.

John did not return.

"John is an idiot for missing all the fun," Scott said when half the firecrackers had been used.

"Yup," Carter agreed.

John had been gone for over an hour before David thought of him again. His brother and Carter seemed to have completely forgotten John.

Scott picked up the last three firecrackers and took a rubber band from his pocket. He wrapped it around the three to form a fat one. David handed him the quart-sized beer bottle with a broken neck. His brother lit the super firecracker, dropped it into the bottle, and heaved it high. The burning fuse lit the brown glass as it sailed over the shadowed ravine and plunged toward the tractor path. It exploded with a satisfying pop and reverberation that made David smile. The echo died and the boys, sweaty in their shorts and polo shirts, retreated to the fire pit.

"Where's John?" Carter asked. "He should have come back long ago."

"Like an hour ago. I bet he messed his pants and had to go home," Scott said.

"Maybe he's hurt," David said.

The three sat on logs that formed a circle. Without the noise of firecrackers and the laughter of the pyromaniacs, the hillside was silent. Minutes passed and no one spoke until crows, sounding indignant, cawed from down the hill.

"Is that him?" David went to the rocky edge and eyed the forest as birds repeated their complaint. Nothing moved below the ledge all the way to the tree line. Beyond that it was dark. "Where do you think he went?"

Scott came close. "Who knows? Probably so embarrassed about messing his pants, and so pissed off at us for riding him, he headed home. It's getting late, and he's a big pussy." Scott kicked a piece of half-burned wood.

David stared hard into the trees. When he caught movement—or thought he did—his mind filled in details, and it became a figure about John's size. Then it was just shadows in spaces near low-hanging branches. But it did seem to move. "John, is that you?" he called and, when there was no answer, said in a quiet voice, "Should we make sure he's all right?"

"He could have fallen down and twisted something, I suppose," Carter said. "Maybe he yelled himself hoarse while we were blowing up shit."

"Fine," Scott said. "We'll look for him."

Chapter 2

A Killing Field

The boys trekked down the hill from the ridge through waist-high summer grass toward the fence. David followed his brother across the graveled tractor path, feeling the late-day sun warm his back, even as the air wafting to his face from the glen below seemed cold. At the barbed wire barrier near the bush that John first tried to use for privacy, David smelled something unfamiliar. It wasn't a dead animal—he knew what dead squirrels and rabbits and even deer smelled like—more an odor of decay and mold. He shivered.

Checking for the bull and seeing no horned creature, he slipped through the wire strands after Carter and Scott. No one spoke as they crossed the "bullpen" and approached the trees. They peered over the second fence into pines, undergrowth, and gloomy darkness.

David went around a small bush tangled with grapevine to see into another part of the woods. Three crows leapt into the air, screaming, and flapped up the hill under the gaze of a red-tailed hawk circling high above. He plucked a tuft of black cloth from the barbed wire, reminded that John always wore black.

David peered into the dimness of the trees, saw a snarl of low branches and briars that acted like a curtain. The sickly odor was strong here, and it drove him back.

Scott broke the silence the crows had left behind. "The asshole must have gone home."

"Hope he didn't miss all the fun just because we scared him," Carter said.

Scott snorted. "Hard to believe a guy who's bigger than most seniors could be scared of anything in those trees." He raised his voice. "John, you in there?"

A tree creaked, nudged by a rogue wind gust that briefly ruffled high branches.

"Hey, Big Bad John!" Carter leaned over an old post, careful not to touch the rusty strand of barbed wire stapled to the top. "If you're in there and you're hurt, you've got to make some noise so we can get to you. Otherwise we'll figure you took your fat ass home or got eaten by a bear."

David listened, sure they should be able to hear a yell or a stick banging against a tree. He expected something, at least normal forest sounds, like a chirping bird or a fussy squirrel, but all was silent. Even the wind that lifted his hair should have shifted the branches. Nature's quiet meant they should be able to hear a cry for help.

"Must have gone home," Carter said. "Probably in front of the TV right now, stuffing down chips and hoping the washing machine cleans his crappy shorts before his mom comes home."

Scott laughed and pointed to the fence line. "Let's stay on this side along the trees. No use fighting our way through that tangle."

Or through the dark, David thought.

The boys followed the forest edge to the fence that separated the bull field from where sheep used to graze. They crossed the barrier into waist-high grass and walked the fence line down a slope along the edge of the trees. At every other fence post, they paused to shout into the woods. No answer.

"I don't think he's in there," Scott said.

"Screw him. I'm going home," Carter said.

David thought that was a great idea and scooted ahead

away from the woods. Downhill another fence loomed, and he would have to cross it, but then the trip would be easy. He was thirty yards ahead when the sounds came.

A thump and a sharp yelp stopped him. He turned to see his brother and Carter higher on the hill. Carter was on his knees, one hand grasping the back of his head. The boy was moaning as Scott bent over him.

David climbed toward Scott who seemed to be looking up the hill. There a black figure stood with its back to the sun, the face dark and hidden by a brimmed hat. The shadowed face showed a slash of white. Was it a smile? There was something wrong with the smile. Whoever it was wore a ripped and hanging shirt. He thought it was John, but then the figure looming above them seemed too big. As David watched, a thick arm tossed a rock up and down. Up and down.

"What the fuck are you doing?" Scott yelled. He took a step toward the figure, placing himself in front of David, who'd closed the distance between them.

The arm snapped forward and flung the stone. Scott dodged, but the rock clapped against his cheek hard enough to snap his head back. David saw a spray of blood.

As if it were a game, the attacker picked up another weapon, one of the long flat jagged pieces of slate David played with, pretending they were knives. Whatever or whoever it was advanced toward them.

His face ashen and bloody, Scott turned to David. He pointed a red-stained finger at his brother and screamed, "Run!"

But David stood with frozen legs and a frozen mind, sucking air in spastic, shallow pants, never taking his eyes from the big black figure. He heard thumping footfalls and saw the raised arm, the dagger-shaped stone, the smile. Maybe eyes. The head seemed immense, surrounded by a black halo, and the chin seemed long. The beast ignored Carter and came toward the dazed Scott. The stone slab descended, and Scott raised his hand. The rock crashed into his forehead, and Scott crumpled forward, a crimson veil over his face. He didn't move.

The thought exploded in David's brain. Scott was dead.

Carter struggled to his feet, his face smeared with blood and his eyes wide. He had always been the biggest, the strongest, and the bravest. Now David saw tears as Carter began to scramble toward him.

"Run, run, run," he hissed.

The killer struck Carter, smashing a rock on his head. The boy twitched and fell.

Instinct told David to flee, but a deeper instinct drew him toward his brother. He had to help. Scott couldn't be dead.

The creature, its claw-like fingers extended, whirled and lunged. Hard nails sank into David's shoulder. The boy screamed and ripped at the hanging flap of the monster's shirt. His fist punched into the beast's crotch, and the thing roared. Its grip relaxed, and David fell back clutching a piece of cloth.

He rolled, came to his feet, and ran toward the trees, diving and sliding under barbed wire. He stumbled past trunks and branches down the slope into a depression where, panting and straining, he slipped on a smear of wetness. He fell, scattering liver-brown and blood-red button mushrooms and just missing a slab of rock. Warm air touched his face and, reaching out as if the caress would erase a bad dream, he relaxed his balled fists.

The snap of wood brought him to his feet. He dared not look. He tore off, flailing his way over the sunken rocky ground. Branches crashed against him, scraping his arms and cheeks, but he felt nothing. He burst from the woods and dove under a fence into tall grass. He couldn't hear steps behind him but ran faster. Tears blurred everything, and his breath came in gasps. He ran by instinct alone, found his house, and tumbled into the back yard. Hysterical, exhausted, and in shock, he lay on the ground and sobbed.

Chapter 3

The Party

May 1983, South Plymouth, New York:

The murder of innocents demands accounting. But sometimes the cause is obscure and the killer is protected, free and unpunished. This was so for the killings near the patch of upstate New York forest that became known as the Clown Forest. Its name referred to the fast-growing, large mushrooms that sported vibrant colors and resembled clowns with their wide ruffled collars and bushy hair of many hues. Theory had it that the fungi arose from ancient spores held underground for years until the earthquake.

The tragedy of murder resides, not with the victims, but with the survivors who must deal with the aftermath. Like David Austin, the second son of Chella and Trent, born in Norwich, New York, and raised outside the city in South Plymouth near the Clown Forest. Two months before the event that would mar his life, he was a happy, above-average child who longed for his eighth birthday, sure that this meant passage from little kid to kid.

In preparation for that event, the blond-haired boy watched his mother crack the third egg with a knife and plop the clear and yellow innards into a depression atop a cone of Duncan Hines cake mix. A slight tremor shook the liquid, but David figured he'd jostled the table to get a better look. In fact, it was a minor shift in a deep fault, and like the effect of quakes on real volcanoes, it made the cake-mix mountain dump yolky lava down the dry powder slope. Stainless steel hand mixer blades whirled and gently descended into the powder, destroying the yolks and converting the mix to batter, the essence of his favorite golden cake.

"Can I have the mixer blades?" David asked.

His mother nodded. "It's your cake."

"Save the bowl for Scott."

∽∾∽∾

A day later, the cake remnant stood on the dining room table amidst yellow crumbs and smeared white icing. Used red paper plates and plastic cups ringed the lone pastry sliver as David sat clutching a gift. Shrinking blue and white balloons, wads of clown wrapping paper, and yellow ribbons were scattered on the rug. From the basement stairway came the crack of pool balls and a whine of "It's my turn." David sighed. Although his brother had objected, Scott's friends wanted to play pool without the younger boy.

He ran his hand over his brother's present, a red book with silver-edged pages, and felt the white embossed title with his fingertips. He pushed plates and napkins aside and lifted the mini encyclopedia of science onto the table and opened it. Stiff with newness, the volume resisted lying flat. He held it open and breathed in smells of ink, new paper, and glue. The Table of Contents held all sorts of neat stuff—from dinosaurs and diving to elephants and earthquakes, from glaciers and meteors to planets, stars, and volcanoes.

He turned first to earthquakes. The teacher in his school's gifted-and-talented program had explained plate tectonics that caused earthquakes. Students even made a model with gelatin to test how houses made of blocks, paper, or sticks held up when the "earth" swayed.

The teacher said that earthquakes could trigger volcanic eruptions. So David looked at that topic in his book. Crisp black text beside a color chart listed the biggest eruptions, most of whose names he knew. The last project his group had worked on was a volcano. Two years earlier, David had watched his brother make a small volcano. It didn't have much lava, but the firecracker blew the top off. The one in school would be better.

He read of Italy's Vesuvius eruption in AD 79 and stared at the black and white picture of the Garden of the Fugitives, plaster casts of Pompeii's victims—six adults and two children—frozen in curled death. His brother would want to see that.

He turned the page and his breath caught. There was the photo of a gritty cast of a dog on its back, forelegs stretched out, rear paws drawn up, mouth parted. The poor animal had been chained to a front gate and left behind as its owners fled the hot ash from Vesuvius.

His finger moved down the list of other volcanoes as he looked for big killers. Indonesia's Krakatoa killed thousands. But the winner was Toba and its aftermath, which wiped sixty percent of humans from the planet. His eye went back to the picture of the dog.

"You stink. Let me break," Scott said from downstairs. A moment later a crash of billiard balls was followed by the clunk of one hitting the tile floor. A chorus of laughs ensued.

David looked toward the stairs, waited a moment, and returned to the book. He read how the Vesuvius eruption was preceded by clusters of earthquakes. "Why didn't they take the warning?" he asked no one. He went to the earthquake section and studied the color picture of a globe covered with jagged plates floating over a molten core. Volcanoes were strung along the boundaries between the crust pieces.

His brother came into the dining room. "It's your turn to play pool. You can take my place. I'll watch."

"Okay. I'll be right down."

"Good. You'll love the game we picked. Because it's your birthday."

David scrunched his brow, confused.

"It's eight ball," Scott said, "and you're eight." He headed for the basement.

David closed the book and stood. A yellow cake crumb clung to the cover. He blew it off and hurried into his bedroom. On the desk was his knapsack. He shoved the book in. He wanted to show the kids at school the cool gift his brother had given him.

༺༾༿

The next day, David showed the book to his resource teacher, who made up an on-the-spot lesson from the volcano section for the gifted-and-talented group. Then it was time to finish the volcano project. On a small table in the activities room stood their creation, a clay and papier mâché mountain, hand-painted mud brown, cement gray, and vomit green, and stuffed with baking soda and another mysterious mix the teacher had furnished. The cone-shaped top sat on a rubber stopper that had been loosely plugged into the tube from the lava reservoir. The five students pushed back chairs and clustered. David moved the little gray plastic buildings closer to the black indentation that would funnel the lava. He added two human figures from his electric train set. Then he placed a third piece, a small brown dog.

"Time for the eruption," the teacher said. He carried a big syringe filled with clear liquid.

"Wouldn't there be an earthquake, maybe a few, before it blows?" David asked, as he grasped the edge of the table and shook.

The teacher nodded. "Absolutely. Sometimes days or

months before a volcano explodes there are clusters of tremors or earthquakes. Anyone know why?"

David opened his mouth, but the bossy girl from another class, shot her hand up. Her name was something with a "J" like Jerry or Jilly. David thought of her as Ponytail. The teacher smiled at her.

"Because volcanoes occur where big plates meet," she said, "and when they shift, the ground shakes." She glanced at David. "And the edges are where the hot stuff gets to the surface."

"The borders are called fault lines," the teacher said as the wall clock clicked its five-minute warning. "Now for our own not-so-hot stuff." He stabbed the needle into a rubber gasket under a lichen bush at the base of the mountain and depressed the plunger.

Nothing happened.

David shook the table and a gurgling sound arose. Seconds later, the sound moved up the throat of the volcano. With a pop, the cone atop the mountain flew off and bounced down the slope. Lava dyed red with food coloring bubbled out the top and began a slow descent toward the doomed villagers. The cool blob swept houses aside and covered the small people, but before it engulfed the dog, David snatched the creature away. The youngsters cheered and clapped.

Except for Ponytail, who asked, "There aren't any faults around here, are there?"

"Only the Ramapo fault," the teacher said. "And it's pretty quiet."

⌘

At these words, the plates of the Ramapo fault two hundred miles southeast of Norwich moved enough to send ripples into central New York. The little quake, one of thousands each day around the globe, was hardly noticed, but the movement reached a hillside behind the Austin house and released gas into a chamber near the surface. The gas filled a vault encased in slabs of stone, a cool and dry crypt that had lurked silent and dark for millennia. Once, air had wafted into that cavern over a layer of earth and decaying organics, and chemical-rich water had dripped from above. Nature filled the space with a species that needed no starlight to prosper. When the tomb was sealed, trapped spores, still alive, began a long vigil.

David and his fellow students didn't notice the first quake, but a month later, at the start of summer vacation, most Norwich residents were very aware of the second quake. A quarter inch jolt along the Ramapo fault shook central New York, including the Austin house where David watched a ceramic jar topple from the mantel, breaking and spilling boxes of matches.

The earthquake lasted seven seconds and released enough energy to crack the rock protecting the spore cave. Gas and water exploded from the cavern with a sharp hiss. Pent-up vapor roared through the fissure and sprayed high across trees and over remnants of the slab guarding the cavern entrance. The fungal spores rode the liquid into a natural bowl-shaped depression where oily pools formed on the forest floor. In the late-spring warmth, they germinated, and days later, the area was thick with mushrooms—hardy, seductive, and rich in mind-altering compounds.

That would have been inconsequential if no one had wandered into their habitat. But someone did.

Chapter 4

Fungus

June 1983:

On the day the larger earthquake struck central New York, Ed Malone sat atop his tractor surveying the hay he'd harvested in his field near the Austin house. He wiped a cloth over his thick neck and black hair in the late spring sunshine, knowing Mary would be ticked when she found out he'd swiped a kitchen towel as a sweat rag. *Just one more thing for her to bitch about. She oughta show a little more appreciation for what I have to do to earn a buck.*

His father had faced the same problems with Ed's mother. The two argued constantly, and Dad hit her. Knocking people, including his wife, around was what he did. If the bastard hadn't died in that freak hunting accident, his chest pierced by a nine-inch deer tine, eventually he would have killed her. His mother's second husband was a pansy, for which she'd probably felt lucky.

But Malone was not his father, and Mary was not his mother. When Malone slapped Mary the first time, the woman slapped back. *Damn her.* Then she grabbed a knife and chased him from the kitchen.

Now their conflicts were mostly verbal.

The earthquake put a stop to his domestic musing. He

twisted in the tractor seat to find the source of the rumble, his biceps stretching the sleeves of the coal-black tee shirt he always wore. If it wasn't dark blue. Dark was his color. The outdoor work of a dairy farmer had hardened the man's muscles. He eyed the southwestern edge of the field where a hill rose abruptly, a part of his property he rarely checked. Trespassing kids played up there. Today all was quiet, but summertime would bring the shouts from the spawn of careless parents in new homes sprouting like weeds beyond his fields. Lucky for the damn kids, he rarely kept the bull in the pasture above the trees anymore. Nothing seemed amiss, and he wondered if he'd imagined the noise.

He closed his eyes, savoring the sweetness of mown hay in the warm morning air. *Maybe Mother Nature isn't always a bitch.* As soon as the thought was complete, a crow flapped from the hillside trees with a harsh, portentous squawk followed by an earth-growl and movement.

The vibration, abrupt and violent, set the John Deere swaying, rocking on the giant rear wheels. Malone rolled from the tilting seat and landed hard—shoulder first. His breath whooshed out, and his foot twisted in a tire ridge, sending pain that dwarfed the discomfort in his shoulder.

"Damn, damn, damn." He punctuated the last by smacking the offending tire.

The horse—which he kept only because his daughter liked to ride, or thought she did—was spooked by the quake and paced nervously at a nearby fence. At the sound of Malone's voice, it shook its head, snorted, and bolted.

The earth answered his cursing by shifting again, causing the ground to sway just as he regained his feet. Malone grabbed the tire and waited for quiet. "What the—that's the second quake in a month," he said to the tractor.

Maybe because he was a farmer and more attuned to the land, he'd felt a small quake in late May, even though no one else had. Except for David Austin, who'd seen the egg shimmer atop the cake-mix volcano.

When Malone told his wife about it, Mary had called

him nuts and blamed it on the bourbon in his hand.

Wincing with pain, he hoisted himself onto the tractor and was about to crank the machine when a hiss dragged his gaze up the hill. The sound magnified until a plume of mist rose sunward, arcing over the pines, glistening in the morning sunlight. Little water existed in that area, nothing to account for the shooting spray, and Malone wondered if the quake had released a new spring. He wanted to investigate immediately, but the pain in his ankle squelched that notion and sent him to the house in search of an ice pack.

Aspirin and icing helped his minor ankle swelling, and hours later, Malone decided that walking might keep it loose. He liked to hike and would get out when he could— not only during hunting season, but whenever the cows gave him time off. It was a good way to escape from Mary and her pressures and to check for the best places to hunt. He maneuvered gingerly out the rear door and down the porch steps.

Mary appeared from nowhere. "Where are you going?" she asked, hands on hips.

He didn't feel like explaining the new spring, so he ignored the question and headed for the barn where the four-wheeler was kept. His son used it last and, to Malone's amazement, left it with plenty of gas. He was further amazed when it started immediately. As he roared from the building, Mary was still watching from the porch, and that made him feel good. *Let her wonder.*

He parked near the fence at the edge of the field he'd been haying. Taking care where he put his injured foot, he climbed the slope alongside the woods until he was above the eruption site. He entered the pine trees whose needles were still damp from the mist, and began to search for the source of the moisture, taking time to check for signs of deer, expecting to hunt there in the fall. Today, heat and gnats made the hike uncomfortable as he picked his way past briars, hemlock, and spruce. Sunlight, filtered by the arch of firs, slashed cathedral patterns across the duff to reveal evidence of the spring as pools and rivulets in the rotting leaves.

Despite his subpar ankle, Malone had no trouble stepping over fallen branches, roots, and rocks. Until he found a clump of wet pine needles in a dark space on a slope. His foot went out from under him, and he fell on his backside, sending a scatter of grit downhill. Chilled despite the sun, Malone rose and circled, examining slabs of broken rock. Near one massive piece, a hole framed by a collar of wet stone caught his attention. He leaned over the man-sized opening feeling heat on his face, the opposite of what he'd expected. A breeze moved a branch, and a shaft of sun dove into the hole, allowing him to see a substantial cavern. The vision was brief, but the odor of mold made him think of his dead father. His old man had been dead two days from the deer attack when they found his body.

Malone shrugged off the image and followed the rivulets a short distance into a bowl-shaped depression. The purple-brown water formed oily pools rimmed with eerie halos of tiny ocher fungi. He stared as the pinpoint mushrooms appeared to change colors, the dull grayish caps now flashing with reds, oranges, blues, and yellows. As mesmerized as a kid in a candy shop, he sank onto a rock and rubbed his eyes, blinking, trying to focus, sure that what he saw in the weak sunlight was an optical illusion.

But the prism of colors became even more bizarre, the hues now blending in spirals and swirls, forming pinwheels and petals, and morphing into twists, stripes, and whorls, patterns that made Malone dizzy. He breathed deep and slow, trying to calm his mind. He held his eyes closed for several seconds. When he opened them, the multicolored fungi had grown and now flashed with gleams of ruby, sapphire, and emerald.

Lightheaded and disconnected, he struggled to his feet and grabbed a tree for support. A compulsion to put his hand on the toadstools came tinged with fear. Malone knew mushrooms as harbingers of decay, consumers of old wood, something one ate from the wild only if knowledgeable. *Else stick with the grocery store kind.* He certainly had never seen this chaotic type before. Perhaps these mushrooms, so unlike the white buttons found in the supermarket, were toxic, or even lethal. But he didn't want to eat them, just touch them. *How could that be dangerous? Then why am I afraid?*

He reached to the nearest puddle, stretching his fingers toward a flashing fungus, hesitating when he noticed the growth. In minutes, the mushrooms went from the size of nailheads to as big as dimes *Has it been only minutes?* He checked the sun's position. *Maybe I'm just closer.*

As he went to pluck the nearest mushroom, he saw red spikes, short spicules guarding the cap. Why hadn't he noticed them before? *They're red, dammit.* He bent his head to the ground, pressing his ear to the duff, and eyed the stem under the little bristled umbrella. No spikes. His fingers slipped under the cap, pulled the mushroom from the brown muck, and brought it close to his face. "Just a mushroom with purplish gills under the hood," he said.

Then the smell hit him, a pleasant odor of the familiar, some sort of food. Another sniff and it came to him—honey-glazed ham, maybe a bit past its prime, but not disagreeable. His tongue traced the line of his lips as the mushroom began to quiver and then vibrate. Malone willed his hand not to move. Still the damn thing wiggled, now faster, a pulsing throbbing, intensifying until it exploded, the umbrella contracting and flattening, emitting a spray of dark particles. Malone jerked back and sucked in air. He sneezed, three times quickly, the third so violent he dropped the mushroom and stumbled backward, catching his bad ankle on a rock, flopping into a cluster of fungi that hadn't been there a moment ago. He felt the sting as spikes scratched his arm and saw a thick cloud of spores arise as the toadstools blew apart. Malone rolled, got to his feet, and skirred from the depression.

Confused, unsure if he was supposed to go uphill or

downhill, he scanned the area and panicked, choosing to limp down the hill, his eyes watering and his lungs pained. A faint, high-pitched noise rose above the sound of his footfalls, and it took a moment before he realized the source of the sound: he was whimpering.

Chapter 5

Wolf

Hours after Malone's departure, a gray wolf wandered into the same depression. New York was not supposed to have wolves, although there were unconfirmed sightings. This old predator, with prominent ribs, a white muzzle, and a dull coat dotted with mud and burrs, may have been one source of those reports. He'd probably made his way south from the Adirondacks, seeking warmer weather and easier food.

The animal hadn't eaten in over a day. Age and cataracts made it a scavenger, an outcast from the pack. Forced into the foothills, it subsisted on road kill and dump scraps. Now, at dusk, it smelled fresh blood that drew it to the place where the mushrooms grew. In among the crowded trees, the wolf found the crushed carcass of an unlucky rabbit killed by flying rock.

The canine eyed the odd-colored fungi and hesitated, sniffing for danger. Hunger drove it to the bloody rabbit. It pawed away the rock and clamped the meal in still-strong jaws. It ate slowly, crunching through the light bones, happy to enjoy a meal un-pestered by passing cars or bottle-throwing humans. At the rabbit's haunches, the wolf snared a nearby pink toadstool and tasted the burning. The animal shook its head but swallowed, driven by hunger for fresh meat. When the wolf had reduced the rabbit to stray bits of fur, it sat, ears alert to new sounds carried over the silent hill, a clucking and a fluttering of wings. The wolf licked black lips and left the forest to investigate.

છબછ

Malone stumbled home and skipped dinner. Refusing to answer Mary's questions, he spent the evening on the porch in an Adirondack chair, sipping Jim Beam. Hours after dark, when the house was quiet, he limped to bed and turned on the television. Feverish and agitated, he repositioned his swollen ankle and arm as the final strains of the *Cheers* theme played on TV. In the screen's flickering glow, his breathing slowed, and he began to doze. Mary clicked off the set, and she, too, gave in to sleep.

The first deep bark did not disturb them. Nor did the second. It took a cacophony of terrified chickens and barking dogs to jolt Mary awake.

"What in God's name is that?" she hissed as she sank her nails into her husband's already-scratched arm.

Malone shot up and smacked her hand away. He listened to the continuing ruckus. "Something's spooked the chickens, maybe a fox or a neighbor's dog. Damn it. I'm sure I locked the coop this evening." As he felt for his shoes, a thump came from his son's room. He stood and turned to Mary. "You and the kids stay here. I'll scare it off, whatever the hell it is. If it's a fox, it'll run as soon as I flip on the light. A dog will run when I go out. Else I'll let Nelson loose on the sonofabitch."

"Better take the gun, in case it's rabid. Like that Cujo dog in the movie."

The racket of chickens and barking dogs grew louder.

"You waste too much time in front of the tube." Malone slipped on his robe and grabbed his Remington 870 pump shotgun from the closet. "Go to sleep. I'll be back in a minute."

He limped down the stairs, reaching the kitchen as a high-pitched yelp came from the backyard. Malone's three dogs slept there. The beagle Fred never did anything more aggressive than bark. The two hounds, however, weren't cowards and would have had no trouble scaring off a neighbor's mutt. Strange there were no deep barking sounds. Perhaps they'd run the intruder off and chased after it. *Then why are the chickens still squawking?* It pissed him off to think that his chickens had been terrorized and would quit laying for weeks.

At the kitchen door, Malone flipped on the porch light and peered through the windowpane. Motion near the house caught his eye. *Probably Fred darting under the deck.* His hounds were not in sight, but he heard a deep growl followed by a chopped-off scream, and then silence. He started to open the door, stopped, and backed into the kitchen. In a drawer, he fumbled with the ammo brick and grabbed three buckshot shells. He loaded one in the chamber and two in the magazine of the Remington.

"What is it, Dad?"

Startled, Malone turned to find his son Jason at the kitchen door. "Why are you up? Stay upstairs with your mother and sister."

He hobbled out the door into cool air and down the two wooden steps.

Clouds hid the moon, and a breeze made him bunch his shoulders. Fred crept from under the porch and yelped. Malone shoved him away, and the dog retreated, whimpering. From the chicken coop came a mixture of muffled squawks, thumps, and growls. Cradling the gun, Malone made his way to a post in the shadows and flipped the switch for a light near the coop. Nothing happened. Cursing, he remembered that the floodlight had been on his list of things to repair over the winter, another chore undone.

"Get out of here, whatever the hell you are!" he screamed as he moved to the closed gate.

The hounds could jump the fence, and he wondered

where they were. Nelson, who'd grown up with his son, never let a fence keep him from accompanying the boy on outings. The thought that either dog might be hurt brought new anger and a tinge of fear.

"If you've hurt my dogs, you're gonna meet the business end of this shotgun!" he said, as the gun barrel shook.

He approached the nest house in the near darkness and heard the commotion of flailing chickens. An odd, feral smell drifted his way. Fred had come to the open gate and stopped there, still whimpering. Abruptly, all went quiet. Malone couldn't see anything on the side of the structure and was cursing the lack of a flashlight when a light came on. Someone in the house had the good sense to turn on the lamp near the walk. The illumination revealed pushed-in chicken wire and his dogs. Nelson's throat was ripped open. Inside the fencing his other hound was on the ground, bloody and still.

Malone cursed, sucked in his breath, and approached the coop door.

Chapter 6

Combat

Malone inched toward the coop that had grown ee-rily quiet. Its plywood door was ripped in two, one part folded to the side on a twisted hinge, the other on the ground with the broken latch still attached. *One big, effin dog*, he thought. A cool breeze sent a chill through his thin bathrobe and brought something else: the tang of blood. He forced himself forward.

The walk light illuminated the inside of the coop where chaos reigned. Nesting boxes had been scattered and blood-spattered chicken feathers swirled above wings, legs, and heads. A bird with half a leg flapped toward a high perch where three chickens sat frozen. He shivered, looking left and right into darkness. As he stepped closer to the gloom, something big and dark lurched toward the opening. A growling blur exploded at him.

Malone yelped and fell back, banging the rifle stock on the ground. As the wolf leapt, he squeezed the trigger. The pellets sprayed wide, rattling a tree branch, but one passed through the animal's ear. Then for a moment, the night was silent.

As Malone struggled to his feet, the wolf righted itself, shook its head, and glared. Things seemed to move in slow motion: the moon escaped the clouds and spilled blue-white light on the chicken enclosure and revealed the creature with malevolent yellow eyes, snarled black lips, and bloody fangs. It made no sense, but Malone let his mind wander, imagining Nelson chasing a Frisbee and playing with Jason. The wolf growled, and Malone snapped back to the present. *Nelson's dead, killed by the thing before me.*

As he pumped another cartridge into the chamber, the beagle whined somewhere near the house. The wolf sprang, and Malone pulled the trigger. The predator fell with a gurgled yowl and didn't move. Malone's shot had missed the animal's chest, but the hind paw was a bloody stump. Malone moved in for a closer look, and the wolf jumped, jaws snapping. The farmer jerked back, smacking the barrel against the creature's side as its fangs raked his forearm.

Malone seemed to lose his hearing. There was no sound from Fred and nothing from the chickens. He shook his head, and the silence was replaced by a head-pounding roar. His slashed arm was on fire, and he was sweating, not from exertion, but from sudden, consuming fever.

The wolf staggered up on to its three remaining paws and Malone fumbled to pump another shell into the chamber. Even maimed, the wolf was faster. It lunged, thick claws ripping his robe and raking his shoulder. Pain staggered him, and the wolf fell against the chicken wire. Ignoring the agony in his arm and shoulder, Malone fired again at the quivering beast.

Blood exploded from the chest wound, and the raging noise in Malone's ears subsided. He could hear chicken squawks and the dog's keening. With a racing heart and gasping for air, he stepped toward the wolf and nudged it with his foot. As if spurred on to one last effort, the wolf coughed up a clot of tar-black blood and opened its jaws.

"What the hell?" Malone pumped the shotgun and squeezed the trigger. Nothing happened. He'd already used the three shells. Lifting the Remington by the barrel, he said, "This is for Nelson, you bastard." The stock smashed into the wolf's head with enough force to shatter bone. Bits of fur, skull, and brain clung to his weapon when Malone yanked it up. "Bastard!" The word sputtered from his mouth. Again he crashed the weapon onto the already mutilated head.

The wolf's eyes rolled back in its skull, and blood oozed onto the chicken-scratched ground. Malone's vision was tinged red, and a roar again filled his ears. His injured side throbbed as he raised the gun for another blow.

"Stop, Dad. It's dead." Jason stood shivering just outside the chicken fence with his fist balled at his mouth.

Malone froze. His son's words made him see the bloody mess at his feet. The wolf was certainly dead. He dropped the weapon. *What the hell am I doing?* A sense of unreality, a fog of fear and adrenaline, gripped him. His mind refused to clear, and his hands trembled. Despite the chilly night air and ripped bedclothes, Malone felt hot. He managed two steps toward the house and collapsed.

Mary and Jason dragged Malone into the house and laid him on the kitchen floor. By the time the ambulance arrived, Malone had regained consciousness and was angry. At first, he refused to speak with the medical team. Then, in belligerent tones, he asserted he just needed some sleep. The EMTs dressed his scratches and puncture wounds and loaded him, protesting, into the ambulance. Under sedation, Malone spent the night in the hospital.

At daybreak, an animal control officer showed up. Shaking his head at the carnage in and around the chicken coop, he told Mary he was sorry about what happened. His concern for Malone and rabies didn't evaporate, but when he saw the wolf carcass, he grew excited, telling Mary that this was actual evidence of a wolf in New York. He photographed and collected the carcass with care and hurried away with it.

જીન્જી

Days later, Malone woke at mid-morning, far beyond his

normal rising time of dawn. The bedside window showed the sun well above the horizon, but he felt no inclination to get out of bed until he smelled bacon and heard Mary making noise in the kitchen.

The scratches on his shoulder and his arm reminded him of the battle with the wolf. He didn't recall all of what happened, but the picture of his dead dogs filled his mind. It seemed like he had been punished, maybe for how he treated Mary. All his life he'd stuck to the straight and narrow, avoiding risk, sure to tread the tough but safe path, one that held no surprises. *And not much reward, at least compared to the bastards in the new houses. How hard do they work to earn a living?* No way as hard as him, he was sure. And then their snotty kids would sneer at him, call him a shitkicker, when he went to town. How much grief did they give his son? he wondered.

He'd accepted the challenges and dangers of life, believed that hard labor put food on the table, and that struggle produced reward. Not success on a silver platter, but something. If you worked hard enough, you could enjoy a Saturday picnic or, even better, hop on a bus down to the big city to catch a Mets game. His life had been structured: up at dawn and work till dusk. Each April meant rains. Summer meant growing crops, and fall brought harvest. Calves were born, and chickens laid eggs. Except he didn't have many chickens left, and the survivors probably wouldn't lay for weeks. That really ticked him off.

The phone rang, and Malone let his wife answer it. She liked yackin'. Mary's blather about a church picnic drifted up the stairs. He'd slapped her once just for that irritating voice. A twinge of regret made him wonder again if the wolf was punishment for that sin. Maybe.

Still, Mary deserved what she got for aggravating him. A wife should support her man, not bitch about money all the time.

He wasn't perfect, but he didn't deserve any special smiting from heaven. It wasn't as if he'd hit her with something hard, only the back of his hand on her cheek. It would be different if he'd smashed her in the mouth.

Mary pushed the bedroom door wide. "Good. You're awake. Are you getting out of bed today?"

Wrinkles formed on Malone's forehead. He got up every day, so what was the woman talking about?

"You've been in that bed for two days. The doctor said to rest, but I don't think he meant in peace."

"What do you mean?"

"Basically you've been sleeping and hardly eating since the hospital."

Malone maneuvered to the edge of the bed, wincing when he tried to use his injured arm. He didn't remember the last two days or any doctor. But the bandages said he must have seen one. Not remembering scared the crap out of him, but why would Mary lie about such a thing? The last thing he recalled was shooting the damn wolf and smashing the shotgun butt on its head. He tried and couldn't bring to mind anything after that. Was his mind damaged by the wolf encounter? More likely, it was whatever the damn doctor gave him in the hospital. That had to be it.

"I'm getting up. And I'm hungry."

"Good." Mary didn't leave. "You've been babbling in your sleep."

"Yeah? 'Bout what?" He maneuvered into underwear and jeans.

"About wolves, punishment, evil, sin, and Nelson. It was crazy talk. Made no sense."

Malone considered that as he pulled one of his tee shirts from the drawer. It was either midnight blue or black, he wasn't sure, but it had a stupid logo on it. Mary had bought it to support some dumb cause. At least she got the color right. His arm was loosening up, and he was able to get the shirt over his head, frowning at the notion of Mary sitting on the bed listening to his private thoughts and having a good laugh. Probably give her something to blab about to the church biddies. "So what? I was probably dreaming."

Mary shook her head. "You never dream and, even if you do, you don't talk in your sleep. Here's the really weird part: you were crying. Like a kid scared of the monster in the closet. I've never seen you shed a tear, Ed."

"Sounds like bull to me." He sat on the bed, closed his eyes, and took several deep breaths before he felt calm again. When he grabbed his boots, something on the edge of the sole caught his eye. He brought the boot close and examined the grayish fleck. It was soft and came off easily: a bit of mushroom.

He flung the blob to the floor, his mind filling with a vision of the flashing colors in the misty forest. *The mushrooms are as natural as tomatoes in August, right?* The hell they were. What about the wolf, he wondered. With no evidence, Malone jumped to the conclusion that the mushrooms and the wolf were connected, a linked evil, something abnormal and sinister that had almost killed him. What really frightened him was the conviction, based on nothing but a feeling in the pit of his stomach, that the evil had more in store.

"Why are you telling me this crap?"

"I think you should see that psychiatric doctor in town. Just to talk." Mary headed to the door. "I've put your antibiotic pill by your juice."

"Ain't takin' no pills. What's for breakfast?"

"A mushroom omelet."

Malone shuddered.

Chapter 7

The Hiker

July 1983:

The morning of the murders, a hiker ascended the grassy hill above the Austin house alone, climbing up to and beyond the Sugar Shack. Jeans protected his legs from the briars and wire fences, and a comfortable tee shirt suited the warm mid-morning temperature.

Strong and fit, the big man liked long walks in the woods. They gave him time to clear his mind and to master the anger that seethed just below the surface. To be angry about what happened so long ago was silly and, even though it festered within him like an infected thorn, he'd always been able to control it. Control was important, essential for functioning in society.

He made it to the top of the incline, rising several hundred feet and covering three miles. The path required crossing several barbed wire fences guarding fields no longer used for either livestock or crops. He liked overcoming obstructions, traveling alone where few went.

On a log in a clearing, he sat and ate his lunch. In the slight breeze that rippled gently through the long grass, his mind strayed to the forbidden subject. Whenever he let down his guard, his physical ailment wormed into his head. Most of the time, he managed to suppress the memories of how he'd been injured as a twelve-year-old, but the more he relaxed with physical exertion, the more his guard fell. As water flows downhill, his thoughts trickled to what had happened, flowed faster, and gushed to anger. Controlling the anger was never easy, but being this close to the woman who caused his injury so many years ago made it tougher.

He made sure he left nothing behind and trekked west of the ruins of a maple sugar distillery and the fenced field below it. He descended the hill and entered the stand of trees below the field that once contained Ed Malone's bull. In the distance, he heard voices—boys talking in their brash, boasting way, annoying sounds that rekindled his memory. Pops like small explosions interrupted the inane chatter.

He'd been bullied as a kid and made the object of taunts and physical assaults, probably because he was smarter than other kids his age. He was also a momma's boy, and—now he could admit it—a crybaby who lacked skill in dealing with his peers, the perfect storm of traits that invited bullying. The abuse became worse when he went through puberty, for his tormenters decided to use sex for torture.

The hiker shook off the memory as he wandered to the edge of a depression surrounded by large pines. The area seemed odd, wetter than it should be and with a smell of mold. Needing more distraction, he decided to explore, descending the slope, hoping it led to something interesting. But the attempted distraction failed, for again he heard the annoying boyish voices laughing. Now they were above him on the hill.

Then he found the distraction: toadstools, hundreds of them, the likes of which he'd never seen before. In the light filtering through the trees, the fungi twinkled in a spectrum of colors. He stopped, trying to interpret what he was seeing and to remember what he knew about mushrooms. As he breathed slow and deep in the slanting rays of sunshine, the colored fungi mesmerized him, sending him into a fugue. That was broken when he heard the boy voices coming closer, stopping and calling to someone in the trees.

His mind jumped back two decades to a hot afternoon in an isolated field. Three bullies—two big boys, one an older teenager, and a girl who was the ringleader—dragged him and another smaller boy, who was as much a target for their abuse as he, into a secluded corner of the field. The other victim whimpered as they were shoved behind high bushes, and the torture began.

"Pull his pants down," the girl said. "I want to see what he's got."

The bigger bully held him while the other pulled down his jeans. He screamed, but the girl just laughed as he was exposed. She came close.

"What a weenie." She turned to the other whimpering victim. "Touch it. See if it gets bigger."

The bullies repeated "weenie, weenie" like a mantra and made sucking sounds. They pushed the smaller victim toward the exposed penis. The boy swiped at tears now rolling down his face.

She slapped him. "Do it."

The hiker remembered how mortified he'd been when the crying kid wrapped a hand around his organ. He was even more shamed when he became erect.

"Suck on it," the bitch commanded.

It happened so fast. The mouth on his penis, the feeling, his excitement and chagrin, and the sudden ejaculation, spilling semen into the whimperer's mouth. His fellator croaked something and clamped down. Pain exploded, he screamed, ripped the kid's shirt, and collapsed into blackness.

He'd awoken alone, still exposed, clutching a tee shirt to his bleeding organ. They'd run, leaving him. His flaccid penis was covered with blood and felt sore, but the flow was stopped by the cotton shirt. He pulled on his pants and, crying, limped home. He knew he couldn't tell his mother. It would be too embarrassing, and she'd blame him. So there was no doctor and no police report. Later, when he realized how difficult it was to get an erection and how ugly the scar on his organ was, he blamed the girl and her filthy, foul-mouthed boys.

Now, the hiker tried to calm himself, but the boys wouldn't let him. Their calling into the woods denied him the serenity he needed. They were near him now. He kicked at the damn mushrooms, scattering red, brown, and yellow caps. Black dust rose from the caps, drifting on an updraft. The hiker sucked air, and a new feeling gripped him. The anger he'd controlled before was far stronger, more akin to rage.

The voices seemed closer, yelling for something. Definitely young boys. Pubescent boys, the kind who would put things in their mouths.

The hiker climbed up the slope and out of the trees.

Chapter 8

Earlier that same day, Jack Pfeiffer, a rugged, muscular six-footer, had gotten a call at his Norwich auto repair shop. The caller was his wife's too-friendly friend, a blonde divorcee named Debra who looked and sounded like Deborah Harry, the sultry lead singer of Blondie and one-time Playboy bunny. Pfeiffer lusted for Deborah and loved her singing, too. He had recordings from her days with the folk rock group, The Wind in the Willows, and the all-girl band, The Stilettos. Andy Warhol's painting of the singer plastered one wall of his shop office, and Robert Mapplethorpe's portrait hung opposite.

Divorced Debra had a car problem and wanted service. She lived in one of the houses built above the Malone farm in South Plymouth, off the road that passed the dense woods, the bull pasture, and the Sugar Shack a mile or so away. Business was slow, so Pfeiffer was able to do the house call early.

It didn't take him long to coax the balky Chevy Camaro to life and get it running well enough to have it driven to his shop. It needed new plugs and points and maybe a carburetor. That's when he made the mistake of agreeing to a drink, which became four, maybe five. And then he'd provided free bodywork for the lonesome lady. Just as a goodwill gesture and sound business practice. Debra didn't seem to mind the beer gut he'd developed. Sometime late morning, he found his pants and left. He drove a short way and had to stop to take a whiz.

After he tended to nature's call in the woods, he didn't know what happened next. He woke late in the day surrounded by trees, hat over his face, shirtless, on the ground, covered with crap: leaves, pine needles, and scummy white stuff. He apparently hadn't napped in the truck. In fact, it was nowhere in sight.

A stream nearby allowed him to clean his muddy hands. He wiped the mess from his face, arms, and pants and staggered in the direction where he thought he heard the sound of a passing car. Tucked in the trees with its front bumper nestled against a bent sapling was his black pickup. He grabbed a clean shop shirt and slipped it on as he assessed the situation. Luckily, the rear tires had a solid perch, and the slope was minor.

The bigger problem was why he couldn't remember how the truck got where it was or what he'd done for the missing hours. The sun was low in the west. Had to be hours. His wristwatch was missing—probably left it next to Debra's bed of sin. He didn't think he had that much to drink and certainly had never suffered a blackout before. Maybe he'd remember later.

He maneuvered the vehicle back from the tree and onto the road. As the sun hovered above the western trees, he drove along Route 23 toward Norwich, his mind still buzzed, trying to remember something. He glanced several times at his square jaw in the rearview mirror and smoothed his black hair, knowing he looked like hell. When a cruiser with its lights flashing passed, he almost pissed his pants. If they stopped him now, he might be given a breathalyzer test. It had been a couple of hours, and he's had only three or four or five drinks, but who knows what could still be detected? He'd have more points on his license. Maybe lose the right to drive. Without a license, he was up shit's creek.

Another cruiser whizzed by. Pfeiffer wondered if more

were coming and figured it was prudent to get off the road and wait. There was a pull-off ahead where the gravel parking area fell below the road surface. Not enough to hide the pickup, but at least he would be less obvious if any other cops cruised by. He turned into the space and, in his half-aware panic state, almost missed seeing the thing in the three-foot-deep ditch off the gravel.

In the slanting light, it looked like a big bag or maybe an animal, but then it moved and flashed white skin. Pfeiffer got out and approached cautiously, shaking his head and blinking to clear his vision. In the drainage gully, a boy of middle-school age sat with arms circling his legs. His head rested on his knees, and he was shirtless with something brownish smeared on his chest and arms. Like the mud Pfeiffer had washed from his own hands.

The boy rocked side to side and seemed to shiver even though the temperature was still near eighty. He whimpered in tones ranging from a high whine to a low growl, and dribble moistened the corner of his mouth.

Pfeiffer stopped several feet away, near the stone picnic table. "You all right, kid?"

There was no answer, but the sound changed, becoming rhythmic and throaty, even like a chuckle. Not a funny chuckle. Inclined to mind his own business, Pfeiffer backed up, not sure what to do. He probably had forty pounds on the kid, but had no intention of trying to handle someone who might be injured or, based on the odd sounds, probably crazy. Not one as large as this. "I'll be right back, kid. Just stay put. I'll get some help."

The boy's head turned to followed him, his eyes showing just pupil.

Black as joint grease, Pfeiffer thought, swallowing. He sprinted to the truck, shoved the key into the ignition, and powered his CB radio. He dialed channel nine, the emergency channel monitored by the Chenango County Sheriff's Office, and requested assistance.

The dispatcher wanted his name, but he ignored her

question and reported the boy in the ditch, giving the approximate location. He denied knowing the kid's identity or his condition. The woman again asked for Pfeiffer's name, and he didn't answer. After a pause, the woman promised to send a car, adding that it wouldn't be long.

"Holy crap."

"What was that, sir?" the dispatcher asked.

Pfeiffer unkeyed the mike, started the truck, gunned it onto the highway, and headed toward South Plymouth. He didn't want to meet the sheriff's office car coming from Norwich and hoped the ones he'd passed were too busy to take his call. He'd use Country Club Road and find his way back to Route 12. It was clear that he couldn't hang around even if he were sober. If it got out that he'd found some kid late in the afternoon, his wife would ask questions. Such as why he was so long in getting back from the Camaro lady. He really had no answer, but he didn't think that falling asleep in the woods—if that's what happened—was enough to keep his ass out of trouble.

Chapter 9

Rob Moore

Sheriff Rob Moore was an ex-military man who'd grown up in Norwich and gone into police work after his four-year army stint ended fifteen years earlier. After serving for fourteen years as a deputy, he decided to run for sheriff and had been elected the previous fall. As sheriff, he spent most of his time giving his staff their assignments for traffic control, warrants, witness transport, and only occasionally for bar-related fights and domestic violence. Directing others didn't require extra hours, and that allowed time to maintain his athletic fitness by hiking, mostly in the Adirondacks and on the Appalachian Trail. He'd chosen a short local outing that day, and had just returned home when the call came in from his dispatcher.

Moore listened as the woman rattled off the facts that had the sheriff's office in turmoil. Trent Austin had called about his missing son, wanting help because he couldn't leave his younger son. Deputies had found two boys, both dead from head trauma. The location was a couple of miles beyond the city limits but within Chenango County and therefore his territory.

The deaths would make for an enduring news story, Moore knew. One murder in a decade was a rarity in Chenango County. Two murders were unbelievable. He told his dispatcher he had to clean up and would be in ASAP. After a shower and shave, he donned his uniform and drove to the office in the center of Norwich. There he was getting ready to join his deputies at the scene when the call came in about a child in a ditch.

"I'll take this one, Tucker," he said to the only deputy left. "You can stay here and man the phones. In case the men need some kind of assistance."

Jeremy Tucker put his hat on. "Not a good idea, Sheriff. Kid was described as 'big.' Let the civilians take care of the phones. Besides, there's only one car left, and it makes no sense to leave me here without a cruiser."

Moore frowned. "Fine. Let's go. But I'll handle this."

They drove out of Norwich west along Route 23. At the reported location, they found the gravel pull-off empty. Tucker got on the radio to confirm they were in the right place.

"This is the spot," he said to Moore. "Guy said he saw a kid in that ditch over there."

"Wonder why he didn't stick around, the caller I mean." Moore lifted his two hundred pounds from the cruiser. "How far do you figure we are from the murder site? Three miles maybe?"

"'Bout that. You think this kid's connected? A witness or something?" Tucker smoothed his hair and adjusted his cap.

"Maybe," Moore said. "We really don't know much at this point. We haven't had any reports of a missing kid, have we?"

"The only call we got today was from Trent Austin, father of one of those dead boys. God help him."

"Yeah, right. I know the wife," Moore said, as he spotted the chuckling boy twenty feet ahead of the car, in the depression bordering the parking area. "Check with dispatch to see exactly how this was reported, and I'll see to the kid."

Moore approached the boy, who was rocking and mumbling and didn't acknowledge the sheriff's arrival. Seemingly caught up in his own world, he continued to make unintelligible sounds. Moore couldn't make out any words as he stepped near. He surveyed the boy, seeing no obvious injury and nothing unusual in the vicinity.

"What's the problem, son? Are you injured? Can you tell me what happened?"

The boy spoke, but only a few words were understandable. "No, I don't want to do it." The boy seemed to shrink closer to the ground.

"You don't want to tell me?" the sheriff asked. More mumbles. "What's your name?" Only unintelligible sounds. Moore reached out and placed a hand on the boy's shoulder. "Everything's all right. Can you stand up?"

The sound stopped, and the big head rotated. When their eyes met, Moore saw confusion, but beneath that lay something unexpected, a look of darting fear. He'd seen that look in the eyes of women and children held hostage by men twice their size. He remembered those domestic violence calls as the scariest of his career. A drunk swaggering in his wife-beater shirt with a gun or knife could explode into a killer.

The boy seemed to comprehend his surroundings for the first time and cringed into himself. And then the fear-filled look vanished, replaced by what could be anger. His jaw thrust forward, and the brow contracted. The big pupils shrank, and red veins spider-webbed the marginal whites.

In an instant the kid went from cringing to grabbing Moore's arm and exploding upward. His hands were strong, and one went to the sheriff's neck. Then he clamped both hands there and began to squeeze. Large, almost as tall as the sheriff, with the body of a football lineman, the lost soul was now an assailant.

Surprised, Moore acted by instinct. He brought both forearms up sharply, driving the boy's hands from his throat. At the same time, he stepped forward and used his weight to push the attacker backwards and off balance.

The shirtless boy tried to keep his footing on the bank of the ditch but slipped and fell onto his side, and Moore dropped to pin him. Tucker clambered into the ditch and forced the boy's arms behind his back. Moore cuffed him. With his face in the mud and grass, the boy relaxed. The sheriff and the deputy exchanged looks.

Moore pressed the center of the boy's back. "Take it easy, kid. You're not going anywhere. Whatever the problem is, we'll sort it out." A shiny green fly buzzed near the pair. Moore waved it off and pulled the captive upright. "Tell me your name."

The boy looked around and settled on Tucker's hat. He stared for a moment and said, "I didn't do nothing." His head slumped forward.

Moore and Tucker half-carried the stumbling boy to the patrol car and slid him limply into in the rear seat.

"Why are you here, son?" the sheriff asked. He got no answer. Moore brushed the dirt from his knees, slipped into the front seat, and said, "Tell dispatch we've got the kid and will take him to the hospital."

Tucker examined the boy's body. Scratches streaked across the muddy chest, deep red cuts in sets of three. "Shouldn't we have the crime scene tech meet us at the hospital, just to get samples of the blood on his skin, just in case some of it isn't his?"

Moore agreed and Tucker made the call.

✂✄✂

During the trip to Chenango Memorial Hospital, the captive sat quietly in the back of the cruiser. The sheriff alternated between eyeing the road and glancing in the rear-view mirror, watching the boy's head flop slowly back and forth, his eyes empty, his face expressionless. The darkness in his face had faded. Whatever had propelled him to violence seemed to have vanished.

"He seems to be staring at something," Moore commented.

At the ER entrance, an orderly had a wheelchair ready and took the boy, cuffed to his conveyance, to a treatment room.

"Wait for the tech," Moore said to Tucker "I'll see what the doc has to say."

The ER physician, a bulky dark-skinned man with intelligent eyes, returned to Moore after the examination. "The patient has a cut and knot on the back of his head, but no broken bones. He doesn't seem quite aware of his circumstances. We'll check his blood work and observe him, but aside from being scratched and dirty, he seems physically to be in pretty good shape."

"That's it?" Moore asked.

"There's one other finding, Sheriff," the doctor said. "There was an abrasion on the penis, at the lower edge of the glans."

Moore waited.

"The head of the penis."

"What could an abrasion mean?"

"Could be evidence of sexual assault."

Moore frowned. "Or he could just whack off a lot. Kids do that, you know."

The technician from the sheriff's office collected samples of the skin smears and did routine swabs for sexual activity. The patient remained quiet with his eyes shut. When the guy was done, a nurse treated cuts on the chest, face, and arms, asking her patient in a conversational tone a litany of questions about his name, parents, where he lived, what school he attended, and who his friends were. She got no responses.

The sheriff listened and watched, and when the treatment seemed to be over, the doctor returned.

"So there's nothing seriously wrong with him?" Moore asked.

"He might have a concussion. His unresponsiveness might be due to some shock. We'll keep him here while you find his family, and I'll order a psychiatric consult."

"He could be violent," Moore said.

"We handle drug overdose patients all the time, including users of amphetamines and other stimulants." The doctor tapped on a clipboard with a thick finger. "I'll order restraints and close monitoring and have Jim Caruthers, the on-call psychiatrist, look at him. He has a number of young patients and can decide what treatment, if any, the boy needs."

Moore nodded and then turned to the patient. "What happened to your shirt, son?"

The boy's eyes remained vacant, apparently focused on chrome trays and boxes of latex gloves.

One of the trays contained discarded cotton balls used to clean his scratches. When he apparently noticed those, he turned away.

"I'll have my deputy stay until you transfer the patient to a room," Moore said.

Moore found Tucker pacing in the hall and waved him over. "I'll take his picture and get it printed. One of the school principals will know him. Have the men at the murder site keep an eye open for a kid's shirt and then check the area where he was found."

"He's tied in with the death of those boys?"

"Maybe. If his shirt is there. Or the blood on his chest isn't his own."

Tucker looked toward the treatment area. "How old do you figure he is? Twelve, maybe fourteen?"

Moore studied the patient. "About that. But I don't have kids. We'll know for sure when we ID him. More important is why the violent outburst. Maybe the psychiatrist can find out what's bothering him."

"And if he had anything to do with the death of those two boys. Of course, his being near the site could be a coincidence."

"Right, but I don't like coincidences. Stay here until they've got him secured in a room." Moore left to get the camera.

❧❦❧

The principal of the local Christian school readily identified the unknown patient as John Redford. Redford had no history of problems with the law. No missing shirt was found. The blood on his body was of his type, and the quantity was consistent with his wounds. His mother didn't know where her son was that day, but she admitted that Scott Austin and Carter Shuman were boys that John knew.

His younger sister claimed she'd been with her brother all day until maybe an hour or so before they found him in the ditch.

Chapter 10

Reggie Peckrough

Reggie Peckrough heard the phone as he pulled his pickup into the empty garage bay. Whoever it was would have to call again, because the new answering machine was still in the box. He poked the remote to close the overhead door and waited till it thumped down before getting out. The phone gave up as he pulled the plastic sheeting off the driver's seat and carried it to the garbage can, which was lined with a new, black leaf bag. The sack wouldn't get anything else, and he'd squish it down to size before it went into one of the clear bags accepted by the landfill. God help him if he tried to sneak something recyclable into the dump. Since no one would check inside a small black sack, it even seemed possible to discard body parts and still follow the rules. If they were chopped and diced and neatly wrapped.

He wiped his hands with a rag and tossed it into the can. The phone started again as he opened the kitchen door. He stepped to the sink and rinsed his hands, wondering if the caller might be one of the women who were always talking to him during downtown walks.

They were attracted to him—how could they help themselves? At six-feet-two with a broad chest and muscled arms, he cut an imposing and easily recognizable figure on Broad Street, the shop-filled, main thoroughfare of Norwich, where he liked to take his constitutionals. By striding with a long gait, a confident air, and swaying his shoulder-length hair, he surely added to his attraction. When he grew a black beard that he thought made him scary, the girls in their twenties came at him like mosquitoes at a nudist camp. When he started coaching soccer for the county recreational department, the mothers in their thirties spun webs about him. He liked the attention.

He picked the phone from its cradle. "Hello?"

"Reggie, this is Ellie. John is in the hospital. The sheriff found him along a road outside of town. He has some scratches and a bump on his head, but he seems okay. At least physically. But he's acting strange."

The call shocked him. He knew John well as one of his soccer players and a fellow hiker, and the boy seemed fine when he'd last seen him. Now he was injured and in contact with the cops. Not good. As for why Ellie, a divorcee with a daughter five years younger than John, was calling him, that was a different matter. He'd coached her son in soccer and, as a result, befriended Ellie. But he wasn't her special friend, the kind you'd call about a medical event. Now that he considered it, she had been bubbly warm when she invited him to dinner. She'd tried to get him to talk about himself, which he'd declined to do. That tactic probably only fueled her imagination.

Other women were always asking him questions he didn't want to answer. Since no one knew where he came from, and how, without a job, he had money, they could let their imaginations create his past. Perhaps mystery added to his desirability. The popular theory made him the beneficiary of a trust, claiming he was one of the Peckroughs of Auburn, owners of a large tract of land on Route 20 west of Cazenovia.

"Calm down. What happened?" Peckrough listened as Ellie filled in the few details she had, including the fact that Sheriff Moore claimed he'd been attacked by her son when they picked him up along Route 23.

This is not good. "What did John say?"

"Nothing"

"He didn't say where he was today?"

"No. He's just quiet."

Peckrough considered what that might mean. He didn't want to get dragged into this, but knew he might. He was, after all, John's mentor. When the boy showed great interest in his collection of Indian pottery, hammers, arrowheads, and spear points, he'd wanted to start his own collection. Peckrough taught John how to chip obsidian, chert, and flint arrowheads, and he took to it immediately. The boy was so enthused he got his teacher to invite Peckrough in to lecture on New York Indians, and that had led to invitations from several middle schools in the area. Then there were the outings last summer in search of artifacts. They didn't find much, but under Peckrough's guidance, John had at least learned what to look for.

Soccer was another connection to John. Peckrough knew the game well and had an ability and willingness to teach the sport. His other vehicle, an eight-passenger Dodge van, made him the ideal coach. He could pack almost a team of ten-to-twelve-year-old boys, as well as coolers and a net bag full of soccer balls.

Peckrough heard Ellie say the kid attacked the sheriff. He wondered if that were true. Didn't seem credible, but the woman never struck him as prone to exaggeration. If they asked him how John behaved on hikes, he would say he'd never seen any signs of aggression. If they asked about soccer, he would say John was a big kid, not real fast, but one who never acted the bully.

"Did John mention me?" Peckrough asked.

"No. He didn't even give his own name."

With the phone tucked between his shoulder and ear, Peckrough ran water onto the towel at the kitchen sink. He wrung it out and wiped his face. "So he'll be released?"

"They want a psychiatrist to check him."

"Why, for God's sake?"

"I don't know."

Peckrough sighed. "That sounds serious. Where did the police find him?"

"A few miles out of town toward South Plymouth. He has friends in that direction outside of Norwich," Ellie said.

Peckrough stared at his muddy boots and knew he'd have to mop the tile.

"Reggie, are you still there?"

"Yes. I'll come to the hospital. But I need to take a shower first. Give me a half hour." He decided to also trim his beard. "No, make it an hour."

cↄeↄ

Peckrough arrived at Chenango Memorial Hospital to find Ellie still in a treatment area with her son. The thirty-five-ish woman had maintained a slender build, despite having two kids. Her tousled reddish-brown hair framed a pretty face with high cheekbones. The hair looked as if it had missed its daily brushing. He thought the natural state gave her a wild look.

She looked up as he neared the curtained alcove and waved him to the hallway. "Thanks for coming, Reggie. I just…I just needed someone here to help me deal with this. We're still waiting for John to be admitted and for the psychiatrist to show up. I convinced the deputy to leave me alone with my son, but John won't say much about what occurred. Nothing like this has ever happened to us before."

"Maybe he doesn't remember what happened. Or he's embarrassed about something and needs a man to talk to," Peckrough said. "Why don't you go to the cafeteria for a cup of coffee and I'll give it a try."

Ellie seemed doubtful. "I suppose it couldn't hurt. Don't expect much and back off if it bothers him." She stared at her son for a few moments and left.

Peckrough went to John's bedside. The boy's wrists

were loosely secured on the bed rails with straps. John shrank away from his new visitor and seemed to study the ceiling.

"How you feeling, John?" Peckrough began.

John rotated his head, blinked, and focused on Peckrough. "No. I don't want to." He arched his back and cringed away.

"It's all right, John. You're safe now. Can you tell me how you got to where the sheriff found you? Do you remember where you were this afternoon?"

When John didn't answer, Peckrough said, "Well, maybe you're not thinking too clearly right now, but that will change. Just remember that you don't have to say anything that makes you uncomfortable. They can't force you. And don't talk about imaginary things. That will just get you in trouble. Just relax and soon you can go home. Hang in there." He was about to pat John's arm, but stopped himself.

Peckrough turned to leave and found Deputy Tucker looking at him. The men eyed each other.

"He didn't tell me anything," Peckrough said and headed for the cafeteria.

Chapter 11

Ed Malone

The morning after the murders, Malone sat in his usual booth at the Bluebird Diner, the favorite breakfast spot in downtown Norwich for those who didn't want to eat with Ronald the Clown. Steam swirled from his coffee mug as merchants with free time before stores opened filled the place. Mothers who'd dropped kids off at school and wanted to avoid housework occupied a large table in the back beyond the row of booths.

At a counter, patrons sat on plastic-covered stools facing the kitchen window where the cook did his thing. He clipped paper slips with orders for French toast, pancakes, and egg concoctions to a circular wheel at eye level and, with regularity, slid full plates under infrared lamps. Waitresses picked up and plunked down the chow, refreshed coffee cups, and sometimes smiled.

A hired hand was milking Malone's cows, and the guy might have to continue that chore, for after his encounter with the wolf, the dairy farmer had lost his enthusiasm for work. He preferred being around people and usually liked the buzz at the Bluebird, but today he felt awful and didn't know why.

It had been weeks since the wolf attack. The negative rabies test had been the only good thing about the bloody affair. He'd spent several days resting but had ignored the prescribed oral antibiotic. He'd paid a price for that with a fever.

He pulled the plastic bottle of pills he'd just picked up and shook it, resolved to take all the meds as the doctor ordered. The doc said his arm and chest had mostly healed. His arm was weak, maybe permanently, but he could still do farm work—if he wanted to.

More than once, he'd awoken sweating, the image of the demon-possessed wolf vivid and threatening. He trembled when he thought of returning to the woods to see if the iridescent mushrooms were still there. Now, stirring his brew and waiting for his Danish, he practiced the calming exercises Dr. Caruthers had given him and willed himself not to think about fungi or the wolf. He forced himself to repeat the doc's silly mantra, "Everything is normal. I am fine."

By the tenth repetition it became, "Nothing is fine. I am doomed." He gave up and went back to thoughts of earthquakes, mushrooms, and a mad wolf, convinced they were all sinister forces out to get him. These thoughts were not new, and they could not explain the feeling that incapacitated him today. Fear—that was it—of what was coming, though he couldn't say exactly what it would be.

A busy waitress delivered Malone's pastry and refilled his cup. He sliced the Danish, smeared sections with butter, and ate slowly. The Bluebird bustle abated as customers ate their meals, paid their bills, and left. Store owners went to open up. Soccer moms disappeared, perhaps to do some laundry before lunch dates and afternoon bridge. Malone usually left at this time to tend to the never-ending farm repairs: tractor service, barn work, painting, and fence-fixing. But today he stayed seated and took a third cup of coffee. He had a strange feeling that something bad had happened, something he was part of.

His attention strayed to the two waitresses standing within earshot. They wore the standard Bluebird blue uniforms adorned with aprons that had started out crisp and white but now were moving toward limp and spotted. They chatted behind the checkout counter, a glass case filled with pastries—from simple maple-glazed donuts to bear claws to nut-strewn Persians. The last-chance sales-trap as you paid your bill. Normally, Malone wouldn't eavesdrop, but he needed something to distract him, to fill his head with local gossip. Besides he knew both women, and that sort of made it okay.

Jackie, the older one, rested a hand on Elizabeth's arm as she spoke. From the look on Elizabeth's face, this story was worth hearing. Malone slid closer.

"The poor boy was hysterical when he came to the ER," Jackie said. "He was scratched up—must have gone right through a pricker patch—but the real problem was his head." She smoothed her gray-streaked hair. "It was like he had something bad inside that he couldn't let out. Thank goodness he made it to his back yard, and his parents were home."

"This was the brother of one of the dead boys?"

Malone jerked back, but the women didn't seem to notice.

"Yes. The fella's older brother and a friend were killed," Jackie said.

Elizabeth wiped her eyes. Malone knew she had two children.

"How old were the dead boys?" Elizabeth asked.

"Twelve," Jackie said.

Elizabeth gripped the counter. "Who would do such a thing? Had to be a madman, right?"

A mad man or a mad animal, Malone thought. Where did it happen? He had to find out. He stood, grasped the table to steady himself, and fought dizziness as he navigated to the display case.

"You don't look so good, Ed," Jackie said. "Are you feeling okay?"

"Who was killed?" Malone leaned on the top of the display case, his knuckles white, clutching his breakfast tab. As he fumbled to pull a ten from his wallet, he felt warm.

His voice had sounded loud. He willed himself to relax.

Jackie plucked the bill from him. "Don't you read the newspaper? Scott Austin and Carter Shuman, according to the Binghamton paper."

"Not an accident?" he whispered, barely loud enough for the women to hear.

"Not a chance. Cops are looking for a killer," Jackie said.

"And the young boy you spoke about?" Malone leaned forward, backing Jackie up.

"David Austin. Poor boy went crazy."

"How would you know that?" Malone asked.

Jackie hesitated, as if deciding to reveal something else. "My sister-in-law is an ER nurse. She said he was screaming that he didn't want to touch the mushrooms. It made no sense."

Malone's eyes widened. He turned pale and started to tremble. In a breaking voice, he asked, "Where did this happen?"

"Out your way, toward South Plymouth, a couple a miles west of town off Route Twenty-Three," Jackie said. "Not far from your place. I'm surprised you didn't hear the ruckus."

He ignored his change and hurried to the door where he plowed into Reggie Peckrough.

"Slow down, Ed, before you hurt yourself," Peckrough said, grabbing Malone's arm.

Malone eyed the man. "Get the hell out of my way."

Chapter 12

Jim Caruthers

Dr. James Caruthers was the psychiatrist on-call on the day of the murders. He saw David Austin in the hospital and quickly determined that the boy had suffered a traumatic event. The doctor probed gently, but could elicit no details from the patient. He suspected even then that the brain was suppressing the memory of what happened, a coping mechanism designed to protect. He completed his exam, prescribed a sedative, and arranged for follow-up visits.

The parents, Trent and Chella, stunned by the death of one child, now had to deal with a traumatized son. The parents needed more help than David did, but that was best provided by family and their pastor. Caruthers made the first calls to gather the support group they needed to survive the crisis.

He also saw John Redford at the hospital, and that patient was a different story. He had superficial arm and chest wounds and may have hit his head, but had no signs of concussion. He was unresponsive to questions, but began to display the same symptoms Sheriff Moore reported: repeated rocking motions and nonsense vocalization. Redford never said anything about the killings. Concerned that his patient may have suffered a break from reality and might pose a threat to himself or others, Caruthers ordered his transfer to a psychiatric hospital for observation, evaluation, and treatment. The boy's mother had at first been resistant to the idea, but after consulting a family friend, she accepted the doctor's recommendation.

On the transfer order, Caruthers indicated a tentative diagnosis of schizophrenia. He listed the behaviors he considered adequate for involuntary hospitalization, but with the mother's consent, the admittance would be voluntary.

⁊

A day later in the morning cool, Carruthers sat over a breakfast of juice, toast, and yogurt on the wide front porch of the brick house that served as his residence and psychiatry office. Tall hedges provided privacy for both him and his patients on the property located a half block off Broad Street. The shielded driveway led to parking in the rear where patients could leave their cars and enter the back door unseen.

Caruthers's practice offered psychiatry services to a variety of clientele, including juveniles, teenagers, and adults. He was a local boy, raised in Oxford, a town smaller than Norwich less than ten miles south on Route 12. At age eight, good fortune befell him—the New York State Correctional System took away his abusive father. The man had made the mistake of killing his mistress and getting caught. Caruthers was raised by his mother, a woman of strong religious convictions who required daily Bible-reading, prayers before meals, regular church attendance, and denial of all things sexual. Getting away from her was one of the rewards of attending college, followed by medical school at Stony Brook and postgraduate training in New York City. He'd returned to Norwich for two reasons: he loved living in central New York State, and the area lacked a psychiatrist. That his mother now resided in Norwich was a burden he just had to bear.

He found himself thinking how best to treat the Austin boy and whether the fact that he knew Chella Austin was a problem. They'd been able to work together smoothly on a hospital committee. There was no other local psychiatrist, and he really wanted to monitor David and his apparent amnesia. Whereas the Redford boy might not be connected to the violence—that issue and the patient's problems were now in the hands of the staff at Riverbend Psychiatric Hospital—David Austin was clearly linked to what befell his brother and friend, and that was the cause of his lack of memory.

Caruthers stared at the white wicker table and the matching chairs with thick floral pads—his mother had chosen them. She'd also picked the flower-filled glass vase he'd pushed aside to make room for the breakfast tray. His taste did not run to flowers or white wicker, so when the chair made stress noises as he shifted his weight, he smiled, taking the squeak as a reason to replace the set. Twenty minutes later, he was sipping a second cup of coffee when the office phone rang.

He got to it on the fourth ring and listened to Ed Malone speaking in a distressed voice. Malone wanted an immediate appointment. Caruthers knew his story: after his encounter with the wolf, farmer Ed was convinced that an evil, supernatural force was out to get him. Caruthers wondered if there was a new problem as he eyed his calendar. "If you get here promptly, I can fit you in, Ed. Where are you?"

Caruthers waited for the answer before he made an entry in the appropriate time slot. "The restaurant is only a few blocks away. Maybe you should walk, Ed. It might be calming."

The doctor went to the porch to gather the remains of breakfast, thinking about why Malone's statement bothered him. The man claimed the evil force manifested in the wolf was tied in with yesterday's murders.

Caruthers reviewed what he'd learned about the crime from treating the two young patients at the hospital. Nothing really. David Austin had no memory, even if he'd witnessed something.

His parents knew only that the boy was hysterical. They thought that David may have seen his brother and a friend killed, but they didn't even know that for sure. There was no hint from David about anything that couldn't be explained by human malice.

John Redford said nothing about the murders. He too may have suffered some trauma, but that didn't necessarily involve the murders, even though his mother admitted her son had hung around with Scott and David Austin. That might be a coincidence, but it was the kind of thing that the police tended to zero in on.

Now Ed Malone, who owned a farm near the murder site, was upset enough by the deaths to require his time. The doctor re-centered the flowers and took his breakfast tray inside.

When Malone arrived, Caruthers asked him to wait one moment, hoping the special calming features of the waiting room—the bay window framed with white gauze curtains, walls and furniture in earth tones, and the soft music— would help settle the patient. It didn't, and Caruthers ushered him into the office. Once seated, the farmer twitched and seemed intent on strangling his baseball cap.

"Ed, you need to relax and take control," Caruthers began. "You can do it, Try the exercise we used last time. Close your eyes, and take deep even breaths. Let your hands go limp."

Malone followed instructions and when he opened his eyes, Caruthers thought the man seemed less agitated. Slowly his patient put the Mets hat on his head.

"So, what happened?" Caruthers asked in a concerned tone.

"The killings west of town. The two boys. They were attacked. It's horrible."

"It is horrible, but what does it have to do with you?"

"It could have been another insane creature, just like the

wolf." Malone glanced around the office, refusing to meet Caruthers's eyes.

"We've discussed the wolf, Ed. It was acting in an unusual manner, but we agreed that it may have been poisoned. There's no reason to believe that the animal was possessed. How did you hear about the murders?"

"A waitress at the Bluebird. She got it from an ER nurse who was there when they brought the brother in."

Caruthers wondered if he'd seen that nurse and if she should be cautioned about talking about patients. "And do the police think an animal could be involved?"

Malone shook his head. "The boys were hit with rocks. I didn't say it was a forest animal. I said a creature. A man is a creature."

Caruthers tapped a pencil on a pad. "Even if we have a murderer at work here, why is this upsetting for you?"

Seconds passed before Malone answered. "The boy mentioned mushrooms. I bet the killings happened not far from where I saw the colored ones."

Malone's statement stopped Caruthers. His patient had talked about the garish fungi before, but the doctor had not heard David Austin mention them. If Malone and the blabbing nurse had heard correctly, the fungi connected Malone and David Austin, and that could be significant. Even if their mental conditions seemed quite different.

"*If* you saw colored ones," Caruthers said.

When Malone reported his encounter in his first session, Caruthers had suggested that the colors might have been imagined in the dim light of the trees. He waited for his patient to say more.

Malone stood and walked to the big window that looked out on the rear yard. Without turning around, he said, "They could have caused things."

"How?"

"Just like you said with the wolf. By poisoning people."

Caruthers had to admit the logic of his patient's reasoning, especially since mushrooms were known to produce potent hallucinogens. "But something else is bothering you, isn't it?"

Malone's head fell forward, and he answered in a whisper. "I can't remember where I was yesterday."

That caught the doctor's attention. Amnesia was a new symptom for Malone, but David Austin had a form of amnesia. And even the Redford boy seemed to have lost track of where he was yesterday. Caruthers waited for Malone to elaborate, and when nothing came, the psychiatrist asked, "Do you remember the start of the day?"

Malone shrugged. "No."

Caruthers eyed his watch. "You seem calmer now, Ed. I'll write you prescriptions for an anti-anxiety drug and for a sedative. I want to follow up on your memory loss." He checked his calendar. "Can you come back next Tuesday?"

The appointment was made, and Caruthers wrote the scripts. He told Malone to call him if he did not feel better and walked the man to the front door.

After Malone left, Caruthers stroked his two-week growth of beard. It wasn't working out and would have to go.

ೞೞೞ

Before Malone returned on Tuesday, Chella Austin brought David for his follow-up visit, the first of many sessions for the rest of the summer. Caruthers's first task was to help David deal with the shock and grief of his brother's death. Primarily with talk, he was able to ease their immediate problem. Trent Austin had declined his invitation to come in.

Over the course of months, Caruthers probed David for memories of that fatal day. David recalled only the fireworks and the hospital. There was nothing about the murders, either the time leading up to them or the time subsequent.

Caruthers diagnosed psychogenic amnesia, with memory deficits surrounding key events. Significant psychological trauma could explain the condition. This was the first case Caruthers had encountered of what is also called hysterical post-traumatic amnesia, and it fascinated him. He explained to the Austins that memories had been suppressed by a brain trying to protect itself from something painful. Memories were stored, but the retrieval process was blocked. Occasionally, with the passage of time, they surfaced on their own.

Chapter 13

Parker Holmes

August 1983:

Detective Parker Holmes of the Norwich City Police Department strode into the conference room at the sheriff's office and frowned when he found it empty. Holmes was a compact man, a bit red in the face with a short haircut. From certain angles, he resembled Jack Webb, an impression supported by his tweedy sports coat and narrow black tie that gave him a Joe Friday look. He placed his zippered leather case on the table, slipped off the coat, and sat, wondering what Sheriff Moore had on his plate that could be more important than these murders. *Always seemed a bit of an odd duck*, Holmes thought as he opened his case, extracted sheets of paper and a yellow pad, and created two piles. At mid-morning, the old window-unit air conditioner was grumbling and losing the battle against the early August sun baking the east-facing windows.

Rob Moore swept in with a cup of coffee and pointed to the coffee pot on a side table. "Help yourself. It's fresh."

Holmes went to pour a mug and, still standing, asked, "So where are we?"

"Basically nowhere. We have the reports from the medical examiner and the state crime lab. The autopsies confirmed what was obvious: the two boys died of blunt force trauma to the face and head. The lab guys found a partial shoe print in some dirt, large and probably from a male shoe. Maybe from the killer, although it could have been left before the murders. One bloody rock had a smeared fingerprint. Looks like the killer wore gloves. A real lack of physical evidence."

"What about the black hair found on the Shuman boy?" Holmes asked.

Moore closed his eyes and sank into a chair. "It's gone missing. Either at this end or at the state lab. We're checking."

"What the hell does 'missing' mean? Your office had custody, and it's not like there was a truckload of evidence to keep track of."

"I know, I know. The chain-of-custody record says we shipped it, but it wasn't logged in at the state lab. We're searching."

"That's a comfort. The one piece of physical evidence that could belong to the killer and you lose it."

"Or it could belong to a sloppy cop on the scene. Hell, I've got black hair."

Holmes held up his hand in a stop signal. "You weren't at the scene."

"I'm just saying…"

Holmes stared at Moore a few seconds. "Given the fact that the shoe print was large and may have been left by the killer, we are looking for a large male who lucked out because most of the ground was grass-covered and didn't have any usable footprints. We'd surmised *that* two weeks ago."

"Correct. Sorry I didn't provide rain to trap better prints."

The two men sipped coffee in unison. The AC noise changed its pitch. Holmes moved a piece of paper.

Moore spoke first. "The use of the rocks as a murder weapon suggests this wasn't premeditated. The killer didn't come prepared with a knife, axe, machete, or mace."

"Nor a gun," Holmes added. "What about the disfigurement—as if he was trying to obliterate the faces of his victims? What do you make of that? Some kind of sexual angle?"

Moore frowned. "How the hell do you come up with that?"

"There's research connecting violence, including murder, to sexual deviation or paraphilia. I have a sheaf of references back in my office. And there's plenty of precedence for linking sex to mutilation. Jack the Ripper killed prostitutes and slashed open abdomens, stealing a uterus here, a kidney there. In the fifteenth century, the French nobleman Gilles de Rais killed dozens or hundreds of kids, mostly young boys. He mutilated them and liked to ejaculate on them." A sheen of sweat formed on Holmes's forehead. He pulled out a handkerchief and wiped his face. "And then there was Albert Fish, the Gray Man, the Werewolf of Wysteria, the Brooklyn Vampire. Two hundred years back, he molested a hundred young boys and killed several. He then chopped them up and ate parts."

"All right, I get it. I can't say I'm buying it, but if that's part of the motivation here, what do we do with it?" Moore asked.

"We've already been looking at locals who might have an interest in younger boys."

"You didn't clear that with me."

"I know this crime happened in your bailiwick, and that gives the Chenango County Sheriff's Office jurisdiction. But it happened just outside the city. Norwich is where the victims went to school and played. The killer may have spent time in Norwich, maybe even lives here. Someone here knows something. All of this brings the city police into it."

"Shit, Parker, I know all that. But this task force is supposed to coordinate. You should have told me about the pervert fishing. Did you find anything?"

Holmes lifted a sheet of paper and studied it for a moment. "We found a few sexual offenders with records. But they either had no connection to the victims, or had alibis, or lacked violent profiles."

"I think it was a transient," Moore said and went to refill his cup.

Holmes ran a hand through his crew cut and played finger drums on the table. "Why would a transient be roaming around in the fields near town?"

"Transients roam around all the time. That's what they do while they're in transit," Moore said with his back to Holmes. "And fields are nice places to take a walk. I hike the hills around here all the time."

"You a hiker? I didn't know that."

"Yes I am. I've covered a lot of miles in the woods, and I'm a card-carrying member of the Appalachian Trail organization. My plan is to complete the Appalachian Trail in three years." Moore sat back down.

"What—on your summer vacations?"

"I may take some personal time."

Holmes glanced at his notes. "But that field is not located near any trailhead. Sounds more like someone who knows the area. And why choose these boys?"

"How the hell do I know? Probably random, just like the weapon choice," Moore said. "Kids in the wrong place at the wrong time. I've got Deputy Tucker going over their activities, friends, and adult contacts. Nothing jumps out."

"What about the location? Anything special?"

Moore positioned himself in front of the air conditioner. "Not that we could determine. That site is near an abandoned maple sugar still. In fact, the boys were at the still before they were attacked. We found plenty of evidence of that: sneaker prints, matches, remains of firecrackers and other fireworks."

Holmes scribbled on his yellow pad. "So we have diddly. Parents lose sons, and we are supposed to find the bastard who took their kids' lives. And we have squat. We need a break, or this killer walks away scot-free. Anything more from Jim Caruthers?"

"The doc agrees that David Austin was traumatized by something. Either the boy found his brother and his friend after the attack, or he witnessed it. Unfortunately, he's blocked all memory of the event."

"Won't that memory come back?"

Moore opened his mouth to respond, but held it as a rumble sounded over the hum of the AC unit. The sheriff's office shared the building with other county services, including garbage collection. County dump trucks inhabited the nearby parking lot. When the noise faded, Moore said, "Caruthers admits Austin's memory may return. Possibly. With time. But he may only remember finding the victims. He may not have seen the killer, and that wouldn't help us. The doc will tell me if anything comes up."

Holmes made a note to talk to Caruthers, who happened to be his brother-in-law.

"The good doctor also mentioned that any memory may be faulty," Moore added.

"Faulty?"

"The kid could invent something up that makes him feel better."

Holmes tapped his pen. "The Redford boy?"

"Another dead end. He might have nothing to do with the murders. Could be part of a separate incident, maybe sex hanky-panky in the woods. There's the sex angle you're hung up on."

"Seems too big a coincidence to swallow, finding another traumatized boy within a mile or so of the murder victims and one who happened to know the two dead boys as well as the brother."

"Coincidences happen."

"I think he was with the boys at some point."

"Maybe, but I don't see how you can know that. And it doesn't mean he witnessed the killing."

The men fell silent. As the air conditioner chugged, Moore stared out the window, occasionally sipping coffee. Holmes studied another piece of paper, then got up, and poured a refill. Both men drifted back to the table and sat.

"You wrestled with this Redford kid," Holmes said. "Could he have done the killing?"

"It's possible. He's big and showed aggression. Unfortunately, the only evidence that he was even there were footprints that might be his, but none were a clear match."

Holmes drank and examined the ceiling tiles. "I bet we have two witnesses—David Austin and this John Redford. But neither can tell us what they saw. I hate to think we have to wait for them to reveal what they know. That could be years. So, do you have any ideas? You're the chief investigator."

"Parker, I've got a bad feeling about this. Smells like a cold case already. Even if it's hot from the oven. We have what may be a random killer unknown to the victims who just happened to be in an isolated place when he showed up. We have witnesses who may have seen something, but who can't report what they saw. It's been two weeks, and we have crap to go on." Moore waited twenty seconds, as if expecting some objection from the detective, before he continued. "I've been wrestling with the way this went down. Seems like random killing, maybe the work of a deranged individual, someone who snapped and went berserk, making motivation not much of a factor."

Holmes leaned back. "But he had smarts enough to not leave evidence behind, to wear gloves, and to escape from the area without being seen."

"Even the insane can be clever or have dumb luck."

"I've checked all over the state for crimes with a similar MO." Holmes pushed a sheet of paper forward. "You're looking at the list of young boy killings in the past five years in the upstate area. Nothing quite like this. If you're gonna kill one kid—let alone two—you do it quickly with a gun or knife. You don't bash brains in with rocks that happen to be lying around."

Moore studied the paper and sighed. "A number of these cases do have a sexual aspect. At least, there was evidence of molestation. But the medical examiner found nothing like that with our victims."

"True. But this trauma was to the head and face. Doesn't exclude the possibility of something sexual in the mind of the killer, especially if that mind is deranged. We should keep that possibility open."

"We need the Austin boy or the Redford boy to remember something," Moore said.

"How do you suppose the killer got away from the crime scene? A vehicle?"

"Probably. There's a road about a mile away where a car or truck could be parked. We collected some tire tracks that looked fresh."

"And?" Holmes said.

"Two different treads. Both common to pickup trucks. If the killer had wheels, he could be in another state already."

Holmes gathered his papers, stood, and folded his jacket over one arm. "Or he could be right here acting as if nothing happened. Waiting to snap again."

Chapter 14

Endicott, New York:

Jim Caruthers had referred John Redford to Riverbend Psychiatric Hospital in Endicott the day after the murders. The paperwork he sent ahead of the patient listed symptoms of confusion, fear, nonsense talking, repetitive movements, and possible hallucinations. These behaviors had been documented by the medical staff at Chenango Memorial Hospital. The law enforcement officers who found the boy also reported the additional symptom of aggressive behavior. Dr. Caruthers suggested schizophrenia as a diagnosis.

Dr. Abul Rahman, the admitting psychiatrist at Riverbend, had studied the Redford report and was inclined to agree. During the admission interview, he found the patient to be agitated, maybe with possible signs of paranoia. He ordered the antipsychotic Thorazine, but Redford seemed to have an allergic reaction to the first dose. This forced a switch to a different antipsychotic, Haldol, which Redford tolerated. The patient had settled into the hospital routine without apparent difficulty.

Over the next few weeks, Rahman saw Redford daily and covered many topics, including where he was, what he was doing, and who he was with on the afternoon the police found him. Although Rahman knew of the murders that day, his primary desire was to treat his patient, not solve a crime. If the doctor found a connection to the killings, it might allow him to address Redford's issues more effectively.

Redford had no answers and became agitated and sometimes angry on being questioned about where he was and what he did on the day he was brought in by the sheriff. Rahman suspected that his patient was hiding something, perhaps a great deal. Although nothing Redford said linked him to the murders, Rahman didn't believe that the boy just happened to be in the vicinity.

When Redford became eligible for visitors, his mother and sister came. They commented that he seemed better, and Rahman agreed. Ellie Redford, of course, wanted to know when her son would be released, but the doctor was not ready to discharge his patient.

After several visits with her son, Ellie Redford invited Reggie Peckrough to an August cookout on her deck. The deck overlooked a sloping, secluded backyard bordered by hedges and arbor vitae.

A woodpecker provided background music with tat-tats in a maple tree as Peckrough grilled steaks to go with salad and corn. He sampled his Manhattan-style clam chowder from a pot on the grill and decided it was a work of art. Ellie accepted a bowl.

"So what's the latest on John?" Peckrough asked.

Ellie had visited John earlier in the day and brought her guest up to date on things at Riverbend. "He's better, but not right. He sometimes sits for hours doing nothing. Then he seems to be afraid of something, but won't talk about it. Rahman wants him to open up."

Peckrough sipped his beer, flipped the steaks, and rolled

the hot dogs required by Ellie's daughter. "What did Rahman say about John's prognosis?"

"Nothing really. It would probably help if John could remember where he was before he was found."

Peckrough moved the steaks to the side of the cooking grate, and Ellie began to dish out salads. The silence was broken when John's sister called from her upstairs room and asked if the food was ready.

"Yes," Ellie said. "Wash your hands."

A squirrel in a border oak dropped an acorn to the deck, and Ellie jumped. "God, I'm so on edge."

"Calm down. This will work out. Maybe I could get John to tell what he remembers," Peckrough said.

"How?"

"Just by being a new but familiar face, a male authority figure, you know: soccer coach, hiking guide, friend."

"Maybe. I'm not sure. I suppose it might be worth a try. John did a lot with you. It might help. Are you saying you'd be willing to go down there?"

Peckrough rolled the hot dogs away from the center grill heat. "Yes. I'd like to see John, to talk to him."

"Rahman has to agree. I'll suggest it to him and see what he says."

"Good. Tell him I can do it anytime. I think we're ready to eat."

☙❧

Rahman said he might allow a non-family visitor after he met the candidate. He agreed to see Peckrough in early September.

Peckrough drove to Endicott as fall took possession of central New York. Trees had given up green camouflage in favor of bolder colors, and curls of smoke rose from chimneys where residents made the first dents in the car-sized stacks of firewood. He was nervous, thinking about what to say to John and how to say it. Most of all, he wondered how John might react.

The morning temperature in the forties forewarned of the coming winter, but by the time he left Norwich, the afternoon sun had warmed the air into the seventies. His jeans and new button-down shirt in a bright color he never wore were comfortable for the daytime warmth and would be fine in the hospital. Out of respect for the rapid chill expected at sundown, he stowed a collared sweater on the seat next to him, just in case the visit lasted longer than expected. *Good to be prepared.*

He parked in a lot bordered by a fence and trees and entered a brick building. When he identified himself to the receptionist, she pointed to the waiting area in the lobby. He watched her make a phone call that reminded him he had to pass inspection by the psychiatrist before he got to John.

Peckrough eyed the lobby motif. He wasn't sure why the color scheme bothered him—it was standard gray institutional décor—but he wanted more blues to soothe anxieties. Like the one he was feeling. He was about to close his eyes when Dr. Rahman arrived and invited him to follow.

The psychiatrist led the way to his office—equally gray and institutional—and offered a chair. The doctor asked questions about how Peckrough knew John, what they had done together, what he thought of the boy, and what the two of them might talk about. Peckrough gave what he hoped were qualifying answers: that he'd met John as a soccer coach and had taken him on hikes in search of Indian relics. He indicated that he was a friend of John's mother and would talk about life as it used to be.

Rahman took a while before laying down some ground rules. A visitor had to meet with John in an interview room with observation facilities. Whatever John said or did would be seen and heard. He should interact normally but should avoid physical contact that might upset the patient. If a topic seemed to bother John, he should steer away from it.

Peckrough nodded his agreement.

Rahman smiled and led the way to a small room with metal chairs and a metal table. The chair cushions and walls were a pale green that created a sense of spaciousness. *Makes the lobby look good,* he thought. Peckrough chose the chair with his back to the mirror that covered one wall. The doctor left and, after a five-minute wait, an orderly in whites escorted Redford in and steered him to the chair on the opposite side of the table.

When they were alone, Peckrough studied the boy he hadn't seen in two months. He'd lost both his summer tan and a few pounds. The weight loss evident in his face made his eyes seem larger. He showed no surprise to find his soccer coach in the room. *Perhaps he doesn't recognize me with the shave and haircut.*

Unsure of the best way to start, he pushed back his hair and, in a rush, said, "How are you doing, John? Your mother said you seemed better, and I can see it. We've been having barbeques on the back deck, and I miss our playing horseshoes. Soon you'll be out of here if you continue to do well." He ran out of steam.

Redford looked around the room before letting his eyes settle on Peckrough. His large fingers drummed on the gray table. "Coach, they think I did something bad. I can't leave until I remember."

Peckrough was pleased to be called coach. "How do you know what they think?"

"The questions Dr. Rahman keeps asking. He doesn't say it was bad, but I can hear what he's thinking."

"Something bad? Like what?"

"What I was doing before they found me. Where I was. But I don't remember." Redford stretched his arms across the table. "It was evil. I can feel it inside me."

Peckrough squinted. "What is 'it'?" When Redford didn't answer, Peckrough went on. "Maybe you're imagining things, John. Do you remember anything? Were you alone?"

"I was...I don't know."

Peckrough smiled. "You'd know something like that. Your sister says you were with her most of the afternoon. Do you remember that?"

Redford shook his head.

Thinking that the specific question was not the best approach, Peckrough tried something else. "Just give it time. Maybe you were out walking and something frightened you, like a bad dream. You probably have nothing much to remember. What else do you and Dr. Rahman talk about?"

Redford stared at the table. "I was scratched. They did it to me"

Peckrough smiled. "I know. I saw you in the hospital. Probably briars."

Redford frowned and shook his head. "The buggers weren't briars." He pulled his arms back and returned his hands to his lap.

Peckrough didn't see how identifying what may have scratched John made much difference. That isn't what Rahman wanted to hear. "Well, if you can't remember where you were and who was there, it could be due to the bump on your head. Just keep behaving yourself, and you will be out of here. Do you want me to tell your mother anything? Anything you need?"

"No." Redford's hand reappeared on the table.

"Cool fall weather is great for hiking. I'd love for us to hike together, someplace new. We'll find more arrowheads." Peckrough felt he'd run out of topics. "I bet you'd like to get back to school. I'll come back to see how you're doing." Then he did something he regretted. He reached across the table and grasped the boy's hands.

Redford's face lost its flat expression, and his brow furrowed. "The evil is sleeping now. But the hunger will come again, and there will be *blood*." The last came out as a shout. He yanked his hands free and stood, kicking his chair over.

ᑲᑭ

June 1984, Norwich:

In the fall after his brother's death, David was functioning well enough to return to school just before Labor Day. Caruthers saw him several times during the school year as he made his way through third grade. Although his patient seemed to be coping, no memories of the missing day emerged.

A problem arose at the end of the term in June, as the one-year anniversary of his brother's murder approached. Chella called for an appointment, saying that David was having problems sleeping. It was affecting his schoolwork, and she expected he'd have trouble with end-of-semester tests.

Caruthers fingered one of the collar buttons on his dark blue shirt as he checked his calendar. He said he could see them at five, if that was possible. "There's no reason to deprive a young man of needed sleep," he said.

☙❧

When Chella and her son came into the office from the waiting room, Caruthers noticed that Chella now wore her black hair in a pageboy cut and seemed more intense than usual. She sat opposite her son and rubbed her forehead. David was motionless.

"David, I want to talk to your mother alone first," Caruthers said. "Can you give us a moment? There's a new issue of *National Wildlife* in the waiting room. It's got a piece on polar bears."

The boy rose slowly, as if he bore something heavy, and trudged away.

After he'd closed the office door, Chella said, "He's not doing well. He's worse than last month."

Caruthers tilted back in his expensive, executive-leather desk chair.

The woman seemed older, the pain of having lost a child written on her face. "At the anniversary of a loss, it's not unusual to feel renewed grief. How is he worse?" Caruthers asked.

"He's still afraid to be alone and hasn't been able to make friends."

"Those behaviors have been present for the past year," Caruthers said. "Has there been something different?"

"There are dreams."

Caruthers came forward and leaned over his desk. "About what?"

"I'm not sure, but it seems to have something to do with the back of our property. You know he hasn't dared go there. Maybe you could get more details from him."

"All right. Why don't you send him in alone? Maybe he'll be more comfortable that way."

David came in, still sagging, and sat, staring at his sneakers. He studied the doctor's desk.

Caruthers gave him a chance to speak first, but he remained silent. "What are the dreams about, David?" he asked in a soothing voice.

The boy lifted his head with apparent effort. "It's only one dream. I'm in the field up behind our house, and I feel afraid."

"What makes you afraid?"

David shrugged. "Don't know. I just feel it."

"Are you alone?"

The boy hesitated as if he'd never considered that possibility. He picked a bit of lint from his pants. "I'm not sure. I think I am."

Caruthers tapped his pen on a notebook. "What else do you remember of the dream?"

David hugged himself as he spoke. "I'm in a field and it's very sunny. I look up but the sun blinds me. And then I start running and running. I have to get away. And I'm scared."

"Is someone chasing you?"

"Maybe."

"Who?"

"I don't know."

As Caruthers checked the boy's vital signs, he assured him that dreams were not unusual and went over how school was going and whether there was more he wanted to discuss.

"There's really nothing else," David said.

"Fine. Why don't you send your mother in, and you can finish with that magazine."

Chella came back in and got right to the point. "Couldn't this be the start of a resurfacing memory, Jim?"

"Maybe, but that doesn't mean the memory is accurate."

"But the dream is preventing David from getting sleep," Chella said. "And the fear makes him less able to deal with school. Isn't there something we can do? I've read about hypnosis being used to recover lost memories."

"Hypnosis has been used, but it doesn't always work. If David could access his repressed memory, it might not be good for him. What recovery he has made from the trauma of that day a year ago might be lost. There's also the issue of the police. They want David to remember something that gives them a lead on the murders. Anything. I've held them off, but it's been a year, and they seem discouraged. If we tried hypnosis, they would want to be present with their own expert, and that alone might be disturbing for David. For now, we should give him a chance to talk about his dream and see if it changes or becomes more detailed."

Caruthers was about to schedule another appointment when Chella made an unexpected announcement. Trent Austin, her husband, had gotten a job offer in Cortland, New York. "We're moving there. It will get David away from that house and the damn field."

"Cortland is only an hour away."

"Trent doesn't want him in Norwich."

Caruthers suspected that was important for Chella as well. She didn't make another appointment, and the doctor did not have a chance to explore the dream or to try hypnosis.

Chapter 15

Release

December 1986, Endicott, New York:

Whatever knowledge John Redford had about where he was and what he was doing on the day of the murders remained hidden. He stayed at Riverbend as a patient with a diagnosis of schizophrenia and paranoia. There he might have lingered, except for what emerged as new and problematic behavior when Redford was sixteen. The change occurred while Dr. Rahman was on a pre-Christmas vacation in the British West Indies.

On his return late in the day, Rahman arrived at the hospital to find his resident, Mark Elderin, standing outside Redford's door. In white pants and jacket, Elderin portrayed a puzzled Pillsbury doughboy as he looked through the small observation window.

"Evening, Doctor," Rahman said, reaching for the chart. "Is there a problem?"

"Not a problem. Just a change. How was your trip?"

"Excellent. I sat on the beach, played golf, and sampled umbrella drinks and exotic island cuisine. Also exotic ladies. I'm fully relaxed and rejuvenated." Rahman glanced through the wired glass. "How's John doing? What is the change?"

"New symptoms. He complains about smelling something odd then becomes quiet. In between these episodes, he vocalizes nonsense. Last evening, there was posturing, and we restrained him to prevent injury."

At the intersection down the green hallway, a nurse pushed a medication cart past. As the rattling sound faded, a voice from Redford's room uttered a few words. Rahman listened, raised a finger to his lips, and tapped. "Interesting. When he arrived, his file noted nonsense vocalization as a symptom. That's a behavior consistent with schizophrenia."

Elderin nodded. "When he's talking, he uses words and pauses, as if he's listening to someone and repeating it word by word."

"What does John do when he's not speaking?" Rahman asked.

"Nothing. He seems quite normal. But his cycle of smelling, quiet, odd body positions, and talking recurs. He's more vocal than before. Even when he attacked that medical student last year, he was quiet about it. Sometimes he screams about monsters—that's new. When attendants tried to calm him down, he went ballistic. Kicking and biting. As if the medication had no effect."

Rahman peered through the window. The bare walls reminded him that his patient had refused any gifts of posters or family pictures offered by his mother and sister. Nothing decorated his walls. Hospital art classes encouraged work to express a patient's feelings. Often the artwork adorned a patient's room. John liked to paint rather garish, multicolored abstract images of buttons, sometimes supported by cylinders, but he never explained the pictures and never posted them.

Rahman scanned the entries in Redford's chart. "Looks like he was dosed several hours ago to get him to sleep. Doesn't seem to be working. Let's have a look."

Elderin fumbled with his ring of keys, unlocked the door, and swung it open. A slow rumble of Redford's words filled the hallway.

Rahman moved to the bedside and checked the straps

that secured John's ankles and wrists to the metal frame. John's eyes stayed closed as he clenched and unclenched his hands in rapid succession. His feet kicked at the sheets with what seemed like bicycling movements. His brow furrowed, suggesting deep concentration, and he became quiet. Possible words, some whispered, some roared, came from him, but Rahman could decipher only bits.

"He shouldn't touch it…" John said.

"That I understood," Rahman said.

"The bastard got what he wanted. I'll tell him to come, and he'll scream because that's what has to happen," Redford continued.

Rahman imagined a scene from *The Exorcist* and regretted it. John didn't deserve that label. And certainly his relatives didn't need the image.

Some relatives stopped seeing patients. Twice-a-year visits would become once-a-year. Once-a-year became every other year. He'd heard relatives remark that a loved one had become a lost soul. And then they would stop coming, continuing to execute the necessary paperwork remotely or severing all ties. At that point, the patient effectively became a ward of the state, even without a judicial ruling. And then Rahman would lose hope.

But in John Redford's case, his mother and sister continued regular visits. They would sit and listen if John was in the mood to talk. In the first year, he sounded like any ordinary boy, excited about baseball, football, and soccer. He'd relate what he was learning in his high school equivalency courses.

With the passage of time, John assumed he would be getting out soon. He wanted to hear about plans for the future. What the family never talked about was what got him into the hospital in the first place.

Reggie Peckrough also showed up every few months. Unlike the mother, he focused on what got John into Riverbend, on what John did in therapy, and on whether anything was coming back to him about that day when he was found in the ditch. Peckrough did not get any more information than Rahman did.

When Rahman laid his hand on the boy's shoulder, the young man didn't flinch. His words—more a stream of consciousness—continued.

"How are you today, John?" Rahman asked.

"…whatever it takes, I just want to try once and for all, and we'll see where things end up…and they'll all find out…I've got to go and take them and make them see what I see and then they'll know, and I'll have to twist them until they understand…"

"Who are 'they,' John?" Rahman lifted John's arms. "Who needs to understand?"

Redford quieted, and Rahman turned to Elderin. "Is this the same dialog he's been having?"

"Sounds clearer, but the content is about the same. An urgent warning and need for action. Stopping someone from doing something but wanting them to do something else. None of the staff has been able to make sense of it. He keeps mentioning 'they' and 'them' and people who'll finally know something. Then there are references to physical violence. With paranoia, 'them' and 'they' aren't unexpected."

"John does have some violence in his background," Rahman said. "So that is not entirely out of character. What's new is the degree of vocalization."

"…dirty fuckers the whole lot of them, screaming and crying and not knowing they got what they get and that's right for everyone…" Redford's hands grabbed the sheet, lifting it and letting it drop. He repeated the action.

"Should we be doing something more?" Elderin asked. "I reviewed his record to see if anything the staff did or said provoked this change. There's a note about an allergic reaction to Thorazine three years back, but I confirmed that he wasn't given that drug."

Rahman considered this response for a moment. He leaned forward and raised one of John's eyelids. He trained his pen light on the eye. "Interesting." He raised the other eyelid. "Look at this, Doctor."

Elderin did so, and his mouth opened. Redford's eyes were both fixed off to one side. "He's having a seizure."

"Exactly."

"Seizures are of short duration. This behavior has been too long."

"There are reports of prolonged symptoms with seizure disorders," Rahman said. "The reaction to Thorazine may not have been allergic, but exacerbation of a seizure. Let's get an electroencephalogram right away. I believe we have a misdiagnosis."

Elderin left the room.

Rahman put his hand on John's shoulder. "With the correct medication, status epilepticus is controllable. You may become functional enough for release, John. That's our goal, after all."

⌘

During Redford's incarceration, Rahman received several calls from Chenango County Sheriff Rob Moore, asking how the boy was doing and whether he'd recovered any memories of the day he was found. Rahman let Moore know that no information about that day or about the murders of Scott Austin and Carter Shuman ever came from Redford.

It was hard to tell how that information sat with Moore.

Rahman phoned Moore to tell him that John Redford was about to leave Riverbend.

"And he will live at his mother's house?" Moore asked.

"Correct. He's still a minor."

"Right. And this kid never said anything that would even place him with the victims on the day of the murders? No hint?"

"None."

"You grilled him directly on the subject?"

"We don't grill, but we did cover that ground," Rahman said.

"And he never said anything about a stranger or a vehicle that might be a lead?"

"I'm sorry, Sheriff. He uses a masculine pronoun but not in a context of killings. I suspect that John Redford has no connection to the murders." Rahman could hear over the phone what sounded like a pen thumping on paper.

"You may be right, Doc. I've always thought it was a transient that committed this crime. Someone we'll never see again because he has nothing to do with this community. We checked New York and surrounding states for any killings of minors and found none with the same MO. We interviewed everyone in the vicinity who had any hint of violence or sexual deviation in their past. We found nothing. This is a cold case."

Rahman was surprised. "I thought you said there was nothing sexual about the attack on the two boys. They were beaten about the head and face with rocks, right?"

"True. The sexual angle is something that a Norwich detective brought up."

"What about the young brother—wasn't his name David? I heard he may have seen what happened."

"If he saw anything, he can't remember it."

Rahman heard the sound of a chair being shoved back.

"Let me ask you a question, Doc. What's the chance that a memory might resurface after a number of years?"

"It could happen."

"Come on, Doc. You're the shrink. Wouldn't the passage of time make any memory unreliable?"

"It's possible that a memory could be garbled, but it could also be spot on. You'd need physical evidence to corroborate. And that's more your field, Sheriff."

"How about hypnosis for bringing back memories?"

"It's been tried with success in eliciting repressed memories, but the memories could still be false or distorted."

"So not very useful as evidence," Moore said matter-of-factly. "Well, thanks for the call, Doc. Maybe the Redford boy will think of something germane once he's out in the real world again. If you hear anything, let me know. The murder case remains open. The families, of course, never forget. And neither do I."

☙❧

The EEG confirmed John's seizure state, and he was diagnosed as suffering from status epilepticus. He responded to a benzodiezapine and had no more seizures. Although he never said anything about what might have happened to put him in that ditch, his mental state and effective treatment warranted discharge. Redford's incarceration had begun the day after Scott Austin and Carter Shuman died and had lasted over three years.

His departure was witnessed by a staff psychiatrist, a nurse, and his mother, who provided the ride home. Only when Redford was safely in the car and leaving the snowy hospital grounds did he smile.

Chapter 16

Graduation

June 1993, Cortland, New York:

The Austins had moved to Cortland in the summer of 1984 in an attempt to escape. For Trent Austin, David's father, it meant a chance to get away from the malignant memories in Norwich where he, Chella, and David were known as the secondary victims of Scott's murder. Pastor, congregation, co-workers, school teachers—all saw him and his family with eyes of pity. In some ignorant eyes, Austin was a suspect, the monster who killed his own son.

Cortland, a larger town west of Norwich, provided a job and a new life. He soon realized that the move was a good one. Dave—his son stopped being David in the fourth grade—accepted the transition, made easy by the similarities between the new home and the old. So much was the same: a landscape of hills and farms, a climate of mild summers and cold, snowy winters, and more cows than people.

A few days after starting in the Cortland school, Dave came home excited. He rushed in after classes and shouted, "Mom, guess what."

Chella stopped unpacking a carton of knickknacks. "I give up. What?"

"Guess what the mascot of the Cortland sports teams is."

"The cow."

"No, it's the Purple Tigers."

"I don't think I've ever seen one. And why is this great news?"

"It's almost like Norwich. You know, their mascot is the Purple Tornado."

∽∾∽∾

Trent heard this story and had to accept the notion that being purple made Dave feel at home. He made sure his son's room was painted a shade of purple.

Caruthers had recommended Dave continue with psychotherapy, but Trent decided on a wait-and-see approach. Norwich was close enough that Chella could take their son back to Jim Caruthers if needed.

As a family friend, the doctor kept in touch, always asking how Dave was faring and if the dream had changed. Occasionally, during the winters of grade school and middle school, Caruthers invited Dave to ski with him at Greek Peak, a major ski area not far from the Austin house. Trent had been the one to get Dave started with skiing. His son loved the sport and jumped at the chance Caruthers offered for free lift tickets and pizza. As far as Trent knew, his son had no memories of the events on that July day when he was eight years old. The closest anything came to surfacing was the unclear dream that started when he was nine, the one he described about being in a sunny field and afraid. As long as his son could cope with the occasional dream and headaches, and as long as he continued to do well in school, Trent was sure he'd made the right decision.

Caruthers seemed satisfied and did not bring up Chella Austin's suggestion about trying hypnosis. Benign neglect seemed to work. Dave still had dreams, but he coped and prospered.

∽∾∽∾

Nine years passed and in June 1993, Dave completed high school with an excellent record and was headed to college. On high school graduation day almost a decade after Scott's death, he should have been in a celebratory mood. Instead, he felt uneasy, anxious to get the ceremony over with. Dressed in a purple gown with gold trim, he joined friends at the football field. Three boys, swimmers like Dave, slapped him on the back and bellowed greetings. Four girls of their inner circle, standing taller than usual in heels, nodded and fussed with mortarboards and stray hair wisps. Dave forced a smile and scanned the stands where his parents were settling.

As school bigwigs took seats, the school band worked its way through "Tomorrow." Dave lined up on the track with other seniors, ready for the entrance parade under a bright sun. A slight breeze pushed strands of white clouds across the sky. *An ideal day*, Dave thought, *except that they still don't know who killed Scott.*

The band switched to "Pomp and Circumstance," and the graduates marched to their seats. Dave felt clumsy as he tried to keep step to the cadence of the traditional song.

He had no reason to be anxious. He'd been a top-notch student, lettered in swimming and soccer, and still found time to refurbish a city playground. He'd aced math, science, and literature courses and scored high on the math and verbal sections of college entrance exams. College applications had produced acceptances from half a dozen top schools, including Dartmouth and Princeton. He'd had no problem choosing Princeton after a fun-filled, beer-party weekend. The Dartmouth visit featured melting, man-high piles of snow.

The superintendent was thanking parents and relatives for their support when Pete, a fidgety kid on his way into his father's auto business, leaned close to Dave. "Do you know what you're gonna say?"

"Nah. I'll just wing it." He'd been working on the salutatorian address for a month, writing it out, shortening it, lengthening it, ripping it up, and starting all over. He hated the thing.

"You warm up the parents," a tall blonde girl whispered, "and I'll leave them cheering for all their wonderful kids." Tracy, the valedictorian, had been Dave's academic competitor, beating his grade point average by a hundredth of point. She put her hand over Dave's and squeezed. "I know you're thinking of your brother. I can see it in your face. I'm sure he's watching today."

Dave, surprised there was anything in his face, tried to smile, kicking himself for talking about Scott in Tracy's presence. He noticed the girl's fingers, long and elegant, her nails polished in a light pink, and thought of little hooded snakes.

A dun cloud hid the sun, casting a shadow over the senior class but leaving the bleachers in light. He found his parents in a middle row. Above them sat a flat-faced, chunky guy who seemed to stare sphinx-like in his direction. Dave glanced away, but try as he might, he had to look again. The man's expressionless face, still aimed at him, seemed familiar.

His mind churned to come up with a name.

"What?" Tracy said.

Dave brought his hand to his mouth. "Nothing." More churning and he glanced again, imagining the face much younger. The fellow took off his baseball cap, and the red hair triggered the memory.

It's John Redford, Scott's friend. He remembered that Redford had been hospitalized after Scott was killed, but had no idea what had happened to him. *Why is he in Cortland? Why is he staring at me?*

An older broad-shouldered guy in a dark blazer, white shirt, and red tie sat next to Redford and also seemed familiar. The man pulled a white handkerchief from his jacket pocket and handed it to the redhead.

They know each other. Dave's head started to ache. He examined his note cards without seeing them and searched for some wisp of memory about the man. A poke in his leg focused him.

"Wake up. You're next," Tracy said.

At the podium, Dave placed the file cards before him. Although he'd earned a reputation for pranks and foolishness as a high school student, this wasn't a time for either. His words came slowly, his voice catching as he dedicated the address to his brother. He scanned the audience looking for his parents, but all the faces were a blur except for one—John Redford's.

Then a third man caught his attention. A dark-haired guy with hard eyes and narrow lips, eyes black as new tires, sat in the front row.

Dave's heart beat faster, and his temples throbbed. *Of course, he's looking at me. I'm the speaker.* He cleared his throat and found words that advised his classmates to cherish those around them while they could.

Still the black-eyed man watched, grinning.

Suspecting he'd also seen this person before, Dave fought to focus on his speech, his voice. He mentioned the excitement of the future and ended like an army recruiter as he urged his classmates to use the gift they had been given to be the best that they could be. The man in the front row did not clap.

Tracy followed, but Dave heard nothing, struggling to keep his eyes away from the disturbing face. He hardly paid attention as the principal announced awards for academic achievement and scholarships, several of which were Dave's. Diplomas were handed out alphabetically, and the band played the school song. When it was over, graduates, less organized on exit than entrance, strode along the track, robes flowing behind them as banners.

At the end of the football field, Dave waved to his mother and father. His father held up a camera and pointed to the front of the school.

"Be there in a moment," Dave called. He shook hands with classmates. Close friends, many of whom were also heading to college, got hugs. As he turned to join his parents, a touch on his arm made him jump.

"Nice speech, Dave. I'm Ed Malone." The front-row gazer had a creased face with a sun-baked appearance. "You probably don't remember me, but I knew you in Norwich." Malone examined Dave, as if expecting some sign of recognition.

"That was a long time ago," Dave said.

Malone smiled, showing brown teeth, and continued. "Your talk was inspiring. Made me think of the tragedy with your brother. I happened to be passing your house that day when the police arrived. I heard later you couldn't tell anyone what happened. Just horrible. A real shame the cops never found the killer."

Dave wanted to punch the guy. Why the hell would anyone ruin the day by bringing up stuff he didn't want to hear? If Malone was someone he should remember, seeing the guy did not make it so. Perhaps, he was locked somewhere in the memories that Dr. Caruthers claimed he was hiding. Dave just wanted to get away from the man.

"So I just wondered how you were doing."

"I'm fine. Why are you here, Mr. Malone?"

"Oh, just a coincidence. A nephew is graduating."

"Who?" Dave asked.

"Not someone in your circle, I'm sure. You're an athlete, the second in the class, off to college. That's great, and I'm sure you'll do well. I hope the future is better than the past."

The scruffy Malone backed off and disappeared into the parking-lot crowd. Dave stood open-mouthed, a bit stunned. The encounter made him uncomfortable. He didn't believe that Malone had ever been near his Norwich house or "knew" him, whatever that meant. And Malone hadn't told him the nephew's name. His class had no Malones.

Chapter 17

Lunch

Two months later, it was time to pack for college. Dave took a break from stuffing clothes, books, music, and his lucky GI Joe figurine into boxes and joined Jim Caruthers for lunch. They met at a local diner just off Route 23, the same road that went through Norwich and continued east to Oneonta.

Dave parked and followed an ancient gentleman with a walker up a ramp. He held the door and stepped after him into an over-cooled, shiny eatery. Counter stools were filled, mostly with trucker types, but a rear booth was open and would provide the privacy they'd need. Five minutes later, Caruthers joined him.

In the ten years he'd known Jim Caruthers, the doctor's appearance hadn't changed much. The big man spent his days in an office, but he put in enough time outdoors to give him a rugged, healthy look. He still had a full head of hair and was his usual neat self in jeans and a dark blue lumberjack shirt. As the doc slid into the booth, Dave wondered why he'd never married.

Caruthers dropped a spiral-bound notebook on the table. "Good to see you again, Dave. I'm heading over to Cornell for a seminar and couldn't drive past without saying hello. How have you been?"

"About the same. I manage."

"Headaches?"

"Occasionally. No big deal. Just a dull pain that ebbs and flows. Not like migraines."

They ordered sandwiches and drinks. Caruthers waited until the waitress retreated before he asked, "How about that new thing, the scared feeling that comes with the headache outside the dream?"

Dave had to think about the last headache. "Actually, the fear comes before the headache starts, but it hasn't gotten worse. Still think this has to do with memory?"

The psychiatrist's deep voice quieted a notch. "Could be. Something you don't want to remember."

"Maybe it's better not to remember."

"Perhaps, but headaches aren't trivial." Caruthers opened his notebook and glanced at a page. "I wanted to follow up on something we talked about before, namely the last time you remember being outdoors with Scott."

Dave hadn't been able to see himself with Scott when Caruthers first asked this question and hadn't thought about it since. Now, he studied the placemat, letting his mind take him back. When a large, white-faced Coca Cola clock buzzed the quarter hour, he said, "I remember that Scott and I were in the woods behind our house, but it wasn't on that day."

"What happened?"

"We discovered a place in the trees with massive slabs of rock. There was a black opening with some kind of deep hole underneath. We couldn't move the rocks, but we felt a blast of warm air. We dropped rocks into the dark hole and heard the echo from deep below. I remember that Scott wanted to hear what firecrackers would do."

Caruthers jotted a note in the pad. "What was so special about this hole?"

"Scott said it might be a cave, maybe as big as Howe Caverns. You know, that tourist spot a farmer found when he saw his cows cooling themselves around a hole in August? Not the same 'cause this one had warm air. Anyway, we decided to get the firecrackers."

A heavy eighteen-wheeler rumbled past outside, shaking the diner windows and rattling Caruthers's coffee cup. It also rattled Dave's brain. "But we never got a chance to drop them in."

"Why not?"

"The ground began to shake. Really hard for about five seconds. Both of us fell. When things quieted, we got up. The hole was spewing crud—dark water and wet leaves. Scott grabbed my arm, and we ran back home. I remember now that it was the first time I'd ever seen Scott afraid."

The food arrived, and they ate, talking about less serious stuff, like how great it was that Princeton dorms were coed and whether winter in Princeton would be better than in central New York. After finishing half his ham and Swiss, Caruthers said, "That quake was probably the one connected with the Ramapo fault. If it shook that hard, I can probably find the exact date."

Dave sipped his drink. "I don't see how the earthquake has anything to do with Scott's death."

"Maybe nothing. Is this a memory you had before?"

"I don't think it was a *repressed* memory, if that's what you're asking. I just hadn't thought of it until now."

Caruthers closed the notepad. "Well, your life is about to change. Princeton will not be high school. There'll be different kinds of fun and different pressures. Most everyone you meet will be in the top ten percent of their high school class. That's the competition. When you get there, you'll immediately be three weeks behind in assignments."

"So I've heard."

"I'd like to touch base with you there. It's only a half-day drive from Norwich. What I'm saying is that you can always call me. If anything comes up, or if you just want to shoot the bull."

Dave smiled. He wanted nothing more to do with shrinks.

Caruthers put a bill on the table. "I sense that you may be starting to remember things that happened ten years ago. That can be good and bad. If you do uncover memories, you need to realize something. Your memory could be a threat to the murderer. He's still out there, and he may be keeping an eye on you. Be very careful who you talk to and what you reveal."

The image of Ed Malone filled Dave's mind. He opened his mouth, but no words came out.

"Have some dessert. I have to run if I'm going to get to Ithaca in time for the seminar on amnesia."

Dave watched his psychiatrist leave then decided against the lemon meringue pie. He paid the check and realized his head hurt. When he reached his car, he caught movement in his peripheral vision and turned. A figure stood near the line of trees at the edge of the parking lot. A splash of red made him think of John Redford. Dave rubbed his eyes, looked again, and saw nothing. He hoped he wasn't getting paranoid.

✥✥✥

Back in his room, Dave sat on his bed staring at the scrapbook he'd kept for ten years. He turned the pages slowly, looking at the faces he'd clipped from magazines. All were men—athletes, movie stars, models, and many anonymous figures. They all had things in common: a coarse roughness, good figures, and darkness. They were all big. Dave wasn't sure why he collected the pictures and kept them neatly pasted in a book without any words of explanation. He knew they didn't remind him of his brother because Scott never had as much life as these men had. Dave kept the book hidden because he didn't want to explain it. He couldn't explain it.

He picked up a black felt-tipped pen and made the first mark on the smiling face of an overly masculine clothing model. He sketched a beard, something full that made the face broader. He moved to the next image and did the same. After decorating each picture with black facial hair, he dropped the marker. He grabbed the scalpel from his biology lab kit and stabbed the picture of a cowboy in black. Back and forth the razor-sharp steel moved until he'd sliced through the scrapbook page beneath. More pictures were mutilated, casting shreds of paper onto the floor and the bed. At last, with his head throbbing and his arm trembling, he dropped the blade and fell onto his pillow.

Chapter 18

College

September 1993, Princeton, New Jersey:

Just after Labor Day, Dave sat in the back of the Austin family van amidst boxes, luggage, and two monster speakers as his father drove and his mother navigated to Princeton for the start of his freshman year. He tried to relax and enjoy the signs of late summer—fields crowded with browning corn stalks, clusters of yellow school buses, and football players in helmets and shorts. Reds and golds already painted the tree leaves of upstate New York. Despite the sparkling weather and the anticipation of Princeton, Dave remained under the cloud he'd felt since leaving Dr. Caruthers.

They reached Princeton in late afternoon. Dave was dropped off on University Place and sent to find where to check in. The Austin van headed with a clog of cars to a parking lot south of campus. Dave walked to the registration site near the power-generation complex, appreciating what he saw of the Gothic campus: grass and abundant trees, open fields, slate paths, and old and new buildings that blended nicely.

Ivy-covered classic stone buildings sheltered by venerable trees bore cornerstones naming, he assumed, generous alumni. Newer rectangular dorms had young trees and cornerstones with the year of the donor class. He couldn't decide which he liked better.

Throngs of freshmen and their parents, grandparents, siblings, and assorted kin milled about, laughing and chatting, carting boxes toward dormitories. Here and there, Dave spied gentlemen in black blazers, tan slacks, and ties with regimental strips of orange and black, the college colors. He would learn soon enough that these were proctors, University officials in charge of order and decorum, a necessary counterforce to the chaos of students.

Dave returned with a room key and directions to his dorm. His father found a spot for the van behind a freshman quadrangle, two dorms facing a flagstone courtyard with a large sycamore in the center. The brick-faced dormitories that formed two sides of the space and a matching dining hall with lots of glass pleased Dave as he imagined himself absorbing knowledge on a wood-and-wrought iron bench in the ivy garden.

His second floor room in 1942 Hall looked out on the courtyard. There, a tallish girl in jeans and a polo shirt emerged from the east-side dorm. She stroked her auburn hair and pulled it behind her back as she examined a collection of cartons and suitcases as if to decide which to pick up first. When she glanced about, Dave imagined a plea for help and, like a bee first to spy a new bloom, he darted from his room. Halfway down the stairs, he slowed to maneuver past his father.

"Where do you want the computer?" his father asked.

"On the desk in my room—I just put a box there. It's the desk near the window."

"It will be cold in winter."

"There's a radiator." Dave jumped down two steps to the landing.

"Where are you rushing to with more energy than you've shown all day?"

"To help move something."

Outside, he stopped to compose himself. The girl was

still eyeing boxes when Dave moseyed up. "Can I give you a hand?"

She squinted at him with blue eyes set in an angular face. A shaft of sun changed her frown to a smile, and as if suddenly realizing he was the perfect tool for her project, said, "How nice of you to offer, Dave Austin."

Dave's face paled. He sputtered, stopped, and breathed deeply. "How do you know my name?"

Her smile widened, and she held out her hand. "I'm Jennifer Ensing, and if you manage to get that big carton up to my room, I may tell you how I know who you are." She pointed at the price of more information.

He had the eerie feeling Dorothy must have had when she landed in Oz. At best, he'd hoped to meet a good-looking girl, probably only to learn that she had a boyfriend at Rutgers, a guy who happened to be a wrestling champ with a car. He wasn't ready to deal with another mystery, but Jennifer was pretty, so he hoped there would be a simple explanation. As he hoisted the box, his father appeared across the courtyard and watched for a moment. Having apparently figured out what was unfolding, Trent Austin shook his head and left in the direction of the van.

Jennifer led the way up two flights of stairs and into a room with a bunk bed and two desks. Dave deposited the box on one of the chairs. There was no sign of another occupant.

As if sensing the question, Jennifer said, "My roommate is on an orientation camping trip and will be in tomorrow. And my parents are at the financial aid office. So I really appreciate your help with that big box. I didn't want to endanger my elegant nails by lugging that heavy thing up here." Jennifer held out five fingers with short unpainted nails.

It took Dave a second to get the joke, just enough time to leave him feeling dull and stupid, but he recovered. "Very wise of you, Jennifer. So where is my reward?"

"What do you mean? We barely know each other." Jennifer flashed the magic smile.

Dave laughed. "But you know me. Tell me how. No excuse. Deliver or I report you to the student committee on promises. Tell me how you knew my name. Have you been following me for years?"

"I've often considered stalking as a hobby, but that would hardly be necessary. You haven't been anywhere but in Cortland. I was at your high school graduation watching a friend get her diploma, and she pointed you out. I heard your speech. Nicely done, by the way."

"So you're not from Cortland?"

"No, but neither were you, originally. I come from a small town not far from Norwich, your real hometown. Cory, my friend, gave me your history."

"Cory? As in swim-team Cory?" Dave asked, dumbfounded that Cory's confidant was Jennifer but no longer surprised that she knew him. He and Cory had once been an item.

"She's the one."

"So where are you from?" Dave asked.

"Guilford. Some of us from the outskirts got into college. Part of the Princeton diversification agenda, no doubt."

"Well, this is a super fine college to get into, ma'am," Dave said in his John Wayne drawl. "You being from the outskirts and all. I'm sure they have remedial programs to ease your entry into these hallowed halls."

Jennifer stuck out her tongue.

Dave smiled with a suspicion that he'd seen this girl somewhere before. Maybe at a soccer match. He had memories of playing soccer on a Saturday in Guilford. Maybe he'd seen her at graduation. She could have sat near John Redford or Ed Malone.

"We'd better continue with the toting of bales and moving of barges," Jennifer said. "I can handle the small stuff myself. Wasn't that your father I saw looking your way?"

She led him to the door and down the wide stairs now clogged with girls and parents.

"If you're all right with the rest of your stuff, I'll help my mom and dad with mine," Dave said when they got outside.

"I'm fine. Maybe I'll see you in the dining hall tonight." She used the same elegant fingers to shoo him toward his dorm.

Dave wandered back, thinking. Maybe she just had a face that resembled someone else he knew. Maybe she'd visited Cory in Cortland. A close friend, no doubt. Why else would she travel to attend a high school graduation? He'd have to ask where she'd hung out during those visits.

He stopped before his entryway and turned back. Jennifer had disappeared. Why hadn't she said anything about his brother? Shouldn't there be the usual expression of sympathy, since she'd heard what he'd said at graduation? Cory certainly knew about Scott's death and would have told her. Yet Jennifer had said nothing. Maybe it was something she was uncomfortable with. The fearful feeling he'd had since the last meeting with Dr. Caruthers crept over him, but he shook it off. *No reason for paranoid thinking.* Jennifer was nice and good-looking and could be his first college friend. He decided that the day was gorgeous and the campus stunning.

Chapter 19

First Date

Dave entered his dorm room to find a tall kid stowing books on the desk bookshelf. His wind-blown brown hair and eager face reminded Dave of a young Indiana Jones.

"Howdy. Todd Jensen of Lansing, Michigan," he said, flashing a smile.

"Dave Austin of Cortland, New York. We already have something important in common: snow tolerance."

Todd was happy with the desk near the door but insisted on the lower bunk. Dave agreed. Being shorter, he was less likely to bang his head on the ceiling in the top bed. They covered the usual stuff in short order: how they'd chosen the college, what they might major in, and what extracurricular stuff they would do. Dave was pleased to learn that Todd had a car, the key to all sorts of adventures.

Both sets of parents entered together and introduced themselves. Dave hugged his mother and father and received his father's advice to stay out of trouble. Todd's father recommended that they make good use of their time and not squander the vast amounts of money spent on their education.

Mothers kissed and said good-bye. Chella Austin reminded him to call. Both boys assured their parents that their only interests were in the acquisition of knowledge.

And then they were alone in the heady freedom that was college.

Todd immediately changed into white shorts and a white polo. "Study, study, study is my mantra," he said as he laced up his sneakers. "And right now, I am off to study how to serve a tennis ball down the center line at over a hundred miles per hour." He departed with a tennis racket and a can of balls.

"Have fun. Don't miss feeding time." Dave called out the door. He began to arrange his desk and was emptying a carton of books when the phone rang.

"Den of iniquity, Dave speaking," he greeted.

"Sounds like you're settling in," a familiar voice said.

"Dr. Caruthers, good to hear from you. How did you get this number?"

"University operator. Quite accommodating. I just wanted to see how the arrival at Princeton went. I had the date marked on my calendar."

"Went fine. Still is fine. Ask me after I sample the food. I even met someone who knew me."

"Someone from Cortland?"

"She has a friend in Cortland. I know the friend who apparently told my story after the graduation speech. The girl I met is from Guilford. Small world."

"Quite small. She wouldn't happen to be a looker, would she?" Caruthers voice had a smile in it. "I detect a level of enthusiasm in your voice that is connected usually with limbic excitement—as in boy meets girl. What's her name? I know some people from Guilford."

"Jennifer Ensing. She has reddish-brown hair, blue eyes, an alluring smile, and a model's body. But I hardly noticed."

"Name doesn't ring a bell. Well, enjoy the adventure. Use good sense in discussing things from the past."

Dave knew exactly what things Caruthers was referring to. It wasn't the first time he had cautioned about dealing with his past. If his underlying problem was failure to remember, you'd think that talking about it might bring memories to the surface. Has to be with the right listener, he figured. The call ended just before "Have I Told You Lately" began playing from a room down the hall. Dave went to meet his neighbors.

ͽϾͽϾ

At dinnertime that evening, Dave found Jennifer in the dining hall. She wore a black and orange sweatshirt and khaki shorts that showed off long, tanned legs. He introduced her to Todd, who spied someone he knew and left them alone to eat fried chicken, rice, and string beans.

"I met two other guys in my dorm. Named Colin and Jabe. Seemed cool. They stopped by to introduce themselves, and then left to have dinner with their parents," Dave said.

"Are they cute?"

"Not your type."

"How would you know?"

"You like helpful types, as in lift-that-box helpful."

The food was good, and a day of moving packages and arranging rooms had sparked an appetite. For dessert, they ate soft ice cream—she vanilla, he strawberry—in a cone. They talked about the weather of upstate New York, soccer, and why they'd chosen Princeton over other possibilities.

"Does your phone work?" Jennifer asked. "Mine is dead."

"Ours is good. I even got a call from outside this afternoon."

"Outside, as in not on campus?"

"From Norwich in the wilds of central New York."

Jennifer sat back, her brow furrowed. "Really. You still know someone there?"

"Just a family friend. Dr. Blue went to school with my mother."

"Dr. Blue? As in Code Blue?"

"That's just my nickname. He loves that color. Wears blue denim, blue shirts, blue ties, blue jackets. Deep dark blue."

"Was he your family doctor?" Jennifer pushed her tray to the side.

Dave hesitated and shrugged. "Sort of. Really a family friend."

"Is he a GP?"

The question struck him as a bit odd, but he answered. "Actually he's a psychiatrist."

"I always wanted one of those on call. Hope you didn't talk too long. Those are billable doctor minutes. I know how the system works."

"Hey, he's just a friendly guy."

"Right." Jennifer stood. "Well, we have a big packet of orientation materials to go over, including the process for course registration, so we'd better get to it."

"Okay. I guess I can't start college by goofing off the first night."

"I'm sure it's been done, but I'm gonna be good."

They carted the trays to the kitchen window and left the dining hall. As they were about to part, Jennifer said, "Speaking of doctors and bills, I heard they have a pretty comprehensive health service on campus, and it's free. Do you know anything about that?"

"Nope."

Jennifer let a group of students pass before she added, "Everything from birth control to psychological counseling. Just so you know." She flipped up the hood of her sweat-shirt and headed toward her dorm.

Dave stared. Did she bring up counseling because he said he knew a psychiatrist? Did she think he knew Caruthers because of his brother's death? Again, he imagined Cory blabbing about things that shouldn't be blabbed about. Clearly, Jennifer knew a bit about his life story and figured he might need help. How nice. Every girl wants a psycho boyfriend. And what did she mean when she said she knew the system?

Chapter 20

A Gathering

October 1993, Norwich:

After the murders, rain became scarce in Norwich, almost as if nature refused to wash the blood-soaked ground. Two years of drought forced the mushrooms to retreat. The surface manifestation of the organism disappeared in the hot dry summers and extra cold winters. Beneath ground, however, the source fungus, the mycelium, persisted. Just as it had done for millennia, sealed in the cavern, it survived and waited for better days.

The year Dave started at Princeton brought perfect conditions for fungi. A warm summer with frequent rains revived the subterranean organism and Technicolor mushrooms again filled the forest glen. Each fungus formed spores furiously, as if making up for lost time. With regularity, mushroom caps exploded millions of germ cells into the air. The spores entered any who wandered close and rekindled behaviors that had lain dormant for a decade.

Ed Malone, who'd run a dairy farm near the Austin house and who'd encountered the strange mushrooms on his property ten years earlier, now lived alone in a rented trailer in a park on the outskirts of Norwich. The price was perfect for the mostly unemployed Malone, for the landlord was willing to pay him for maintenance work with free rent plus a little money. Not long after the wolf attack and the murders, he'd been forced into this arrangement when his wife divorced him and the bank foreclosed on the farm. Instead of having to deal with balky tractors, muddy cows, and brainless chickens, he made a living replacing outlets, snaking clogged drains, and tarring roofs. That produced enough money for bread and beer.

He'd considered relocating to some place where no one knew he was a failure at farming and marriage, to where people had not heard Mary blabbing about his slapping her around. *What the fuck was that, anyway? I hardly touched her, the dumb bitch.* But he knew Norwich best, had been raised there, liked the setting and climate, and refused to be driven away. And he wanted to see his kids, even if it was only from a distance. The judge said he couldn't get closer because he had developed a drinking problem. *More bull.*

Malone did drink beer and harder stuff, but he considered his consumption moderate. In fact, he had no beer gut and was still strong and quick for a man in his forties, despite the cigarette addiction. He confined his bar visits mostly to weekends or when thoughts of the wolf and the evil it represented hounded him. Recently, he'd spent a lot of time in the tavern—for, as the mushrooms filled the woods, dark thoughts filled Malone's head.

෴

On Friday evening, the official start of the weekend by Malone's reckoning, he occupied a stool in a friendly bar. The day was reason enough to drink. But he had another: he felt the evil permeating the area like a tainted mist.

"Hit me again," Malone said to the bartender.

The server, a wide-body guy in his mid-fifties who'd bought the dive of a bar a year back, scratched a hairy, tattooed arm and raised an eyebrow. "Don't you have to work tonight?"

"What the hell business is that of yours?" Malone poked a finger at the ten spot he'd dropped on the bar. "Give me a drink."

The bartender, apparently used to surliness in patrons, shrugged and refilled Malone's shot glass with Early Times and his beer glass with Genny.

Malone was due at the carnival in Cazenovia, a small town less than an hour north of Norwich, but his job didn't require sobriety. The show had arrived as usual after the first frost and set up on a site near the lake. Malone got hired as a janitor. He worked alone, cleaning rides and the public areas near games of chance and food stands. And there was always mess. Families, teens, and loners crowded the carnival every day and night of its week-long run, all eager to enjoy the mild weather of Indian summer before the onslaught of subfreezing mornings and persistent snow.

For Malone, it meant temporary work, the unskilled sort he loved. He could handle simple manual labor at a carnival even with a few snorts under his belt. It was work done after midnight, after closing, and that suited his normal schedule just fine. He'd shed the rise-at-dawn life of a farmer and become a night owl. An owl with a broom and a shovel. Quite a comedown from driving a big tractor pulling a plow, a reaper, or a harvester. That was a loss he still blamed on the evil force behind the damn wolf. He just had to control himself until the carnival closed up and moved on. Hold on to the job, get some money, don't mouth off to the boss man, don't pop the guy. He so much wanted to kick the asses of the shitty kids who dropped their shitty crap all over the shitty carnival where he had to clean.

Malone finished his whiskey and said, "Sorry about mouthing off, Mack. Sometimes my mouth does its own thing."

"Yeah. Right. Lately more than usual."

Malone felt for the flask he carried in his pocket. He'd filled it with Jim Beam in his trailer. It would be his midnight belt, something to calm his nerves and keep the demons away. He zipped up a hooded sweatshirt and went to his truck.

℘℘℘

Reggie Peckrough, one-time youth soccer coach and hike leader, was also getting ready for the carnival, just as he'd done every year since his return to Norwich. He was the convivial sort, after all, and liked all kinds of celebratory gatherings. Watching young people having a good time turned him on and made him feel a part of the community.

He'd been driven out of Norwich by Mrs. Ellie Effin Redford and, now that he was back, intended to enjoy himself fully. The Ellie thing still grated. Not long after the Austin-Shuman murders, while he was still visiting John Redford at Riverbend, Ellie's moon-faced gaze had turned on him filled with romance. When she'd pushed him on whether he reciprocated her feelings, he told her he had no feelings for her. It wasn't as if he didn't appreciate women, just not Ellie. He said nothing about his sexual preferences, but the suspicious bitch let her imagination take hold and jumped to a conclusion. She passed very rapidly from lack of comprehension to imagined understanding and disbelief, and then to anger.

"You mean you're queer? A fucking queer?" she'd yelled. "I've wasted two years on you, you pretty-boy liar. Get the hell away from me."

Then she started yelling about her son and how she didn't want Reggie near the boy, even though John was still securely locked up in Endicott. Did she think he molested him in the hospital visit room before the one-way mirror?

Peckrough knew the bitch would blow up her motherly concern to cover every soccer kid and every young hiker he'd ever talked to and would blab her suspicions. Not that she had anything but her half-baked feelings to go on. Small towns didn't need proof of innuendos and rumors.

Time to take a vacation, he thought.

He left and stayed away, hiding, for five years. He wasn't sure Ellie had talked, but women always did. Like a re-corked champagne bottle—just shake 'em up, agitate 'em, and they're sure to blow.

When Peckrough heard—finally and well after the fact—that Ellie had left town, he decided to return. For a couple of reasons. He liked Norwich, a perfect place for him, large and diverse enough that he could blend in. He couldn't coach soccer and lead youngsters on hikes again, but there were other communities for him. He also wanted to contact John Redford, just to make sure there weren't any new memories disturbing him. Redford had moved to Norwich to live on his own. When Peckrough figured enough time had passed for any Ellie fallout to dissipate, he returned.

His new landlord had gossip to share along with the key to his rental house. "Musta been right after you left," the man said. "The woman took up with a chemical engineer."

Peckrough imagined she'd had potential husband number two waiting on the side and brought him on stage to fill the role she'd had in mind for him. Undoubtedly, she shacked up with the chem dude immediately after she got rid of what she called the queer soccer coach.

"She had a For Sale sign in front of the house a month later," the landlord said. "Mrs. Redford and her daughter went to live somewhere east of here. Seems I heard she married the engineer guy sometime before her son was released from that there mental place in Endicott. Yeah, that's right. Took him with her to her new home. When he got to be eighteen, the boy came back here."

None of that surprised Peckrough. Ellie was obviously hot to trot and had marriage at the top of her agenda. *Mission accomplished*, he thought. *John must have been still a minor when she took him from the hospital. With a new cock ruling the roost, could you blame John for wanting out as soon as he could leave?*

Peckrough figured Ellie had spoken to someone about him because the Norwich cops wanted an interview on his return, even though he'd been questioned before. He couldn't give an alibi for the murders back then, so how could the cops expect one five years after the crime? He was cooperative and explained his reason for leaving as a romance gone bad with Ellie Redford, claiming that she'd broken things off. It became clear that they had nothing to pin on him.

Peckrough had repainted and redecorated to create his sanctum and now stood in his scrumptious bedroom drying from a shower as he fingered a chartreuse tee shirt. He'd always liked fine clothes, especially ones that felt good against his skin. In fact, once he'd been outed and ostracized by the "good" people of Norwich, he'd decided to flaunt being different by trying cross-dressing. *Screw these rednecks*, he thought. He found he liked wearing women's garments and the looks he got.

The open drape allowed light of the half moon to give the room a dramatic glow that really made the shirt attractive, but he decided against anything flamboyant for the carnival. Not that it would be seen under his jacket, but no point risking attracting attention at an event where roughneck yahoos were looking for an excuse to kick butt. Best to be unnoticed.

Peckrough chose the dark denim and a dark hooded jacket. He'd had them forever—was it ten years? But they'd do fine with a black shirt for a much-needed night of fun.

 დოდო

John Redford had spent an uncomfortable year at his mother's new house, one he'd never known growing up. The brainy, anal dude his mother married seemed hostile, maybe afraid of John who, by then, was about full grown with a mysterious history. John never spoke of the past or of his psychiatric treatment, and that silence didn't endear him to his stepfather. The dark cloud hovering over him probably fed the guy's anxiety.

If the hostility was fear, John could sympathize with that, for he himself felt fear.

The chemical engineer was a take-charge, problem-solving sort and found John a job and a place to live in Norwich. Jack Pfeiffer ran an auto repair shop and seemed to take a special interest in him, claiming to remember him from newspaper reports that linked him to the Austin-Shuman murders. Pfeiffer knew he'd been in Riverbend and seemed sympathetic, not only giving him the job but training him personally to tinker with cars.

Another thing happened when he settled in Norwich. Reggie Peckrough made contact. Surprised, uneasy, and not needing his old soccer coach in his life, he told Peckrough to leave him alone. But when Coach offered to buy dinner at a decent restaurant, John changed his mind and accepted the invitation, despite the bad feeling it gave him and regardless of what his mother would think. The food was a surefire temptation for someone living in a one-room shack where cooking meant heating Vienna sausages.

Peckrough had picked a bar and restaurant on Route 12 south of Norwich. John arrived early and sat in an isolated booth, not hard to find since it was early and the dining room was empty. The waitress brought bread, and John was working on his second dinner roll when Peckrough arrived.

"You're looking good, John," Peckrough said. "How are you feeling?"

"Fine. I guess."

They ordered steaks, baked potatoes, and salads. Peckrough sipped a beer and Redford a soft drink, neither speaking until after the salads arrived.

After the waitress left, Peckrough asked, "You guess you feel fine? What does that mean?"

"Sometimes I remember things I don't want to remember."

"About what?"

"That day when it happened."

"In the woods?"

John grabbed another role and didn't answer.

Peckrough stared across the table as their meal was served. He added butter and sour cream to the potato, cut into the rib eye, and tasted it before continuing the conversation. "So you don't remember exactly where you went or how you wound up in that ditch hours after the murders?"

John chewed on a piece of steak. "Nope."

"Remember anything else?"

"Nope."

"But nothing happened to you, right?"

"Don't know."

John was confused. Peckrough had asked questions throughout the dinner and a lot of them made little sense. But Coach seemed happy with the answers he got.

In fact, this had been the first of several dinners together. Over time, Peckrough took John out to restaurants and even cooked for him at home. Always there were questions— gentle and oblique—about what happened in the woods. John began to view Peckrough as a pain in the butt, always asking about stuff that happened ten years ago. Even if he remembered some details from that day, John did not want to talk about it.

In the fall, when John said he'd been having trouble sleeping, Peckrough urged him to take a break from routine and to have a good time. He suggested the Cazenovia carnival as a good place to start. The more John thought about it, the more he liked the idea. Luckily, his boss sometimes let him borrow cars with the understanding that he was road-testing the repairs he'd done. On Friday of carnival week, he had an old but sweet black truck.

He slipped the knit ski cap over his red hair, grabbed a dark fleece, and headed out of his shack to the truck. Maybe he'd find someone to take a ride with him.

Chapter 21

October 1993, Cazenovia, New York:

He'd held it in control for years, keeping it hidden, playing a role, acting nice, pretending he was just a normal guy. No more. This change had come over him only after he'd stumbled into the mushrooms, but he did not recognize the connection. All he knew was that the thing within him had re-awakened the hot memory of what had happened to him and a need to strike again. He could no longer contain the demon and felt a certain thrill at the prospect of freeing it. It was more than a thrill, it was a sense of power. He could feed the beast and remain free, just as he had after the first killings, a decade past and long forgotten.

His first target, the child of Chella, was easy to pick. What he needed now was a new target, one of a certain age. Vulnerable, of course. Hunting at a visiting carnival filled with transients was perfect. Lots of strangers, lots of young, deserving prey. All were perverts, all guilty of disgusting, filthy behavior.

In the dark on a cool fall night, he parked in the dimness near the trees, a hundred yards from the carnival entrance. He sat as the truck engine ticked to coolness, listening to the distant calliope and rumble of crowd voices. Halloweenish green, yellow, and red lights danced along the lakeshore and stretched skeletal fingers on the glassy, black water.

Time to hunt. In black clothing, with a cap pulled low, he slipped unseen onto the grounds from the lakeside. Staying in a shadowy periphery, he eyed people as they played games, ate hot dogs and cotton candy, and queued for the coaster and Ferris wheel. Cooking grease and ozone spoiled the air as young and old wandered by, talking too loudly, laughing over the clang of bells and whirling metal. None noticed him, the nearly invisible, hungry animal.

He eased into the woods that edged the fairground near the restrooms. Clouds dimmed the moon and starlight, creating the darkness where he could turn from the crowds to light a cigarette. With his hand hiding the glowing tip, he let the smoke drift to the still lake waters.

The girls visited the restrooms in pairs, but the boys went solo. He wanted a male, a young one. Not too young. That would mean hovering parents. One alone. He could watch and pick. Someone glancing in his direction might catch the glow of the butt tip, but not much else.

The need burned in him, a hot force that sharpened his mind. A tingle made him shiver. He rubbed his big hands together, eyes closed, imagining the first blow, then another and another.

A young man, apparently just wandering, emerged from behind a food booth. The killer gave him a crocodile stare. He could lure him into the woods, but that would be dangerous. The prey might scream, might be missed quickly. Now that he thought of it, any patron missing before closing could trigger a search. He didn't want to be interrupted. It would be better to wait until the carnival closed at midnight. Then he might find a straggler. *Be patient*, he thought. *Control the rage.*

The teenager, apparently smelling the cigarette smoke, saw him and approached. The boy fished his own cigarette from a softpack and came closer.

"Got a light?"

He could easily drag this thin kid into the woods, but they were too close to the restrooms. Someone would hear. He offered matches, his hand trembling with the desire to smash the pimply face. The teenager didn't seem to notice. The oblivious lamb, so near the lion, struck a match and sucked life from the flame. He mumbled a thank you and left.

The hunter breathed deeply, opening and closing his fist, as an odor of urine from the toilets drifted over him. He had to be patient in picking his victim, but it was stupid to loiter where he might be seen and remembered. He headed for his truck with a dull headache made worse by the screams from the small roller coaster and the yaps of a dog on an estate near the woody lakeshore.

Shunning the lights of amusements and booths, he reached the parking lot where a lone streetlight near the road lit the expanse of gravel. He skirted the edge of the lot and slipped into the woods, stepping quietly to where he'd backed his vehicle up to the trees. When he opened the truck door and slipped in, no dome light came on. He'd pulled the bulb. Thwarted for now in his hunt, he leaned back, gripped the steering wheel, and focused on why he killed. It was for revenge, for what was done to him by kids like the happy-faced, little angels eating cotton candy. The cute little cocksuckers.

At midnight, people herded from the grounds, clomping across the parking lot in small groups, bleating and braying, setting his nerves on edge. Cars exited, turning either toward the village center a mile away or in the opposite direction. Eventually only a few vehicles remained. He sucked on a cigarette until the tip glowed red and, realizing it might be seen through the windshield, lowered it to the ashtray. Angry that no young man walked alone, he became frustrated, worried this wasn't the night. He needed to see blood, but he would have to have a better plan, some way to get his victim alone, a way to escape.

Two old fatties oozed into the last car and pulled away.

He was about to give up and drive off when movement near the carnival entrance caught his eye. A lone figure, a thin kid dressed in jeans and a gray sweatshirt, walked through the arch and onto the gravel. The hunter's pulse quickened, his mouth went dry, and his senses sharpened. There was no other car in the lot. So where was the kid going? The boy continued to the road and turned toward the village. *Probably a worker walking into town. Alone. In the dark.*

The carnival lights faded. First the rides, then the games, then the food concessions. The floods near the arch were dimmed. Only perimeter strings of red, orange, and white bulbs, that outlined the site, and inside security lights, that marked each section, remained lit. The parking lot blackened as he drew the last puff from the cigarette and cast the butt out the window. The red glow bounced once. He slowed his breathing. The anticipation of the hunt engulfed him as he slipped on a pair of black garden gloves. When he turned the ignition key, the truck purred to life and rolled smoothly out of the lot.

Low beams scanned the inky road as he crept along, looking for the light-colored sweatshirt. He caught a glimpse of something bright—the prey—under a distant streetlamp and pressed the gas pedal. He was slowing when flashing red and blue lights appeared in the rear view mirror. Had he done something stupid like driving too slow? Was a brake light out? If he were stopped, there would be no chance for smashing a face tonight. He pounded the dashboard and pulled to the side of the road. A Madison County Sheriff's Office's cruiser sped past.

His jaw unclenched as he pulled back onto the pavement, covered a hundred yards, and saw gray on the opposite shoulder. The sweatshirt shuffled along, head down. He pulled up beside him and called out in what he hoped was a friendly voice, "Need a lift?"

The kid jumped, obviously startled, and his eyes took in the truck from front to back. They settled on the man leaning out the window toward him. He took ten seconds to answer. "I'm just heading into town. I need cigarettes from the all-night place."

"Hop in. I'll stop there. I need a pack, too."

The sympathy of another smoker may have helped.

The young man crossed the two lanes and went around the front of the truck, its headlights revealing a small-boned, blond-headed boy who appeared to be in his late teens. He climbed into the passenger seat and muttered, "Thanks."

"Not really safe walking on this dark road so late at night."

"Safe enough for me."

"On your own, eh? How do you like working at the carnival?"

"How do you know I work there?"

The killer smiled. "Where else?"

"Well, you're right, and that stuff about a circus being your family is a lot of bull," the boy said with a bit of venom. "I'm just an employee."

The hunter nodded and flashed another smile. "Shit. I forgot my cooler back there in the carnival lot. Lemme go get it, and then I'll take you into the village."

Without waiting for a reply, he swung the truck into a U-turn and sped back the hundred yards to the unlighted lot. He pulled the truck up to the woods. Clouds parted and silver moonlight pierced the trees.

"I don't see no cooler," the kid said.

"It's right there in the woods. I was dumping the water out." The man reached down beside the driver's seat and closed his hand around the tire wrench. "Maybe not quite here, but somewhere close."

"Where?"

The bar caught the kid in the forehead. A crack of bone sounded as the head banged back against the head guard. Blood splattered the seat cover. The killer got out and went to the passenger side, yanked open the door, and dragged the limp body from the truck.

He began to feel the pleasure as he lugged the kid into the woods, yards back from the edge of the lot. He laid him on his back and pulled a penlight from his jeans pocket. The beam showed a sheen of blood on the boy's forehead. The killer felt for a pulse. Faint but there. *Too bad the boy is unconscious*, he thought, as he flashed the light to the left and then to the right before he found what he was looking for. Quivering with anticipation, he reached down and picked up the long thin rock, one shaped like a caveman's ax. Then it began.

Again and again he pounded the pointed weapon down on the boy's face, smashing cheekbones and ripping eyes from their sockets. Thuds and crunching were the only sounds in the silent trees. He felt blood splash his face and smelled feces. When exhaustion ended the pounding, the boy had no face. Sticky wetness stained the front of the killer's pants. It wasn't blood.

He took a hunting blade from his pocket, bent down, and lifted the dead boy's blood-soaked tee shirt. He cut the front from its chest and stood grasping the scrap of cotton as the perimeter lights on the carnival grounds finally went out, making the truck invisible.

Back at his vehicle, the killer stripped off the bloody shirt and pants and put them in a bag. He donned his extra clothes. Now, as calm as a frozen lake, he started the vehicle and drove carefully and slowly to his place, to where he belonged.

♥♥♥

The Norwich Police Department received notification of the Cazenovia carnival murder the next morning, as did all law-enforcement agencies in the area. The official document did not provide much more than the newspaper accounts. Parker Holmes read the information twice and decided to walk to the sheriff's office.

Moore was at his desk and seemed preoccupied. He waved Holmes to a seat. "I know what you're thinking."

That caught Holmes by surprise because he wasn't sure what he was thinking. "What's that?" he asked.

"You're thinking this carnival killing is related to the Norwich murders a decade ago, right? You're sure that the killer has returned."

"And you're not? Come on. The MO is the same—death by blunt force trauma caused by repeatedly smashing a rock into the victim's face. The victim wasn't so much older than the Austin and Shuman boys and was of small stature. Cazenovia is less than an hour from here."

"All of which is true, although this victim was five years older—"

"But on the small side," Holmes said.

Moore leaned back in his desk chair. "Parker, it's been ten years. Serial killers don't often wait ten years between their crimes, although there is no set interval. More likely that this is a coincidence."

"That's what you think." It wasn't a question.

"Yes."

"So what should we do?"

"Remember the last similarity you cited, that Cazenovia was near Norwich? True, but it's far enough away to be in another county. It's not in my jurisdiction."

Holmes left, slamming the door.

Chapter 22

The Lecture

October 1993, Princeton:

Dave had visited eating clubs on Prospect Street the night the carnival worker was slain in Upstate New York. By the time the young man was dead, Dave was blitzed on free beer and more than one sip of Jack. His love of booze had bloomed in high school, and he was happy to learn Princeton eating clubs relied on free samples to attract new members. Around eleven-thirty he stumbled back to his dorm without being accosted by a proctor and slipped gently into the upper bunk without, he hoped, waking Todd. In fact, he wasn't sure Todd was even there.

An hour or so later he woke, agitated and grasping in vain for a dream element that seemed new and important. Something violent where he was a witness. He went to the bathroom, disposed of a bladder of beer, and returned to his bed to dream again.

He rose after seven, panting from the same night vision, now grown more detailed. He maneuvered to the edge of the bunk and did a slow-motion fall to the floor. His roomie was gone, so he sat on the lower bunk and held his knees to quiet his trembling hands.

In the occasional dreams he'd had through high school, he was alone and afraid in a sunny field. But this dream was different. It had nothing to do with him. He was an incorporeal observer, watching a figure creep through dark trees. Dull white light, maybe moonlight, and other dimmer lights of red and yellow barely illuminated the black-clad figure. Dave floated above the scene, seeing the man crouched over a figure and doing something bad. Very bad. When the man stood, the red and yellow lights winked off, the moon faded, and a single beam pointed to something white. Mushrooms covered the ground, but they didn't stay white. Christmas colors were everywhere. The spotlight focused on one of them. It moved, the edged reddened, and it became an eyeball.

Thank God he woke at that point, he thought, willing his heart to quiet and the headache not to happen. He surveyed the small room to distract himself from the dream. Green cinder blocks enclosed the space. On the floor lay a shaggy rug that reminded him of a dead muskrat. No wonder people thought they'd scrounged it from a discard pile. On opposite walls stood two desks: Todd's neat, Dave's chaotic. Sliding doors guarded a large closet: Todd's half closed, Dave's open. His side of the room hid things, just like his messy brain did. He had to get a handle on both. He started by folding clothes and hanging them in his half of the closet, continuing until he found his bath bag.

In the bathroom, he stripped and entered the shower, using the wall to steady himself. The water pounded life into him, but even as the room grew warm and steamy, he still felt icy inside.

Unlike his roommate, Dave felt like crap in the morning and struggled to get out of first gear. Even without his usual hangover, mornings were an affront. He was a night person—hell, his eyes were even bigger than average. *All the better to see you with, my dear.* This morning the mirror told him they were also redder than usual.

Todd, the morning person who arose cheerful and alert, the idiot who liked eight a.m. classes, was in the room when Dave returned.

"Morning, Austin." He gave Dave a onceover and added, "As usual you look like shit. Generally your face is a gruesome sight. Today it's worse. Thank God for an eight o'clock class so I didn't have to be here when you emerged from the crypt."

Dave mouthed a fuck you.

Todd smiled. "Well, not everyone is destined to thrive in a tough college environment. Fortunately, I've handled tough things before."

Dave inspected his jeans. Satisfied with their lack of obvious, odiferous stains, he pulled them on. "You're sounding quite ass-like this morning. What do you mean by 'tough'? Like having to screw your cousin?"

"You are a high-class jerk. I went to a selective, college-prep academy, remember?" Todd placed another notebook in his backpack.

"You call that tough? I saw a psychiatrist for years after my brother died. Hell, he's still on my ass."

"Okay, that's in another league." Todd paused as if choosing his words with care. "Is that why you drink all the time?"

"What are you talking about?"

"You're on the street sucking beer every night."

Dave gathered papers at his desk, stopped to gaze out the window. Gold, red, and brown leaves were scattered over the courtyard, and students in fleeces shuffled to the dining hall. The scene seemed peaceful in the flat morning light. "You exaggerate. Beer relaxes me."

"And gives you that tremor in the morning."

Dave stared at his hand and put it in his pocket. "I had a bad dream, and I can't quite get my mind around it."

"A dream. That you remember. Maybe the boozing caused it. You fell from the bed ladder twice before reaching your nest. Probably hit your head." Todd opened his mouth and closed it. When he spoke next, the sarcasm was gone. "I can see it's bothering you. What was the dream about?"

"Hard to say. Some guy in the woods doing something scary."

"And you've had other scary dreams?"

"Yes, but this was different. I was just an observing presence, not a participant. Still scared the shit out of me."

"I've only had six weeks of Abnormal Psychology—the Nuts and Sluts course—so I can't provide professional-quality counsel yet. Maybe after midterms. But my assessment is that you are one screwed-up puppy. Go see the shrink at the health center. It's free, you know. Well, it's not free, but it is prepaid. And your alumni giving will cover it later. Something you will be reminded of yearly for the rest of your life."

"First I need bacon and eggs." Dave donned a windbreaker, grabbed his pack, and headed out the door, figuring he could still make his nine o'clock if he left directly from the dining hall.

When the biology lecture turned out to be about fungi, Dave perked up. He'd seen one in his dream—at least it was a mushroom until it became an eyeball. He should know more about them.

The prof presented the life form as a kind of mystery, a species that diverged from plants and animals over a half billion years ago.

Dave always thought of fungi as plants—he and Scott found them growing in the woods—but the professor set him straight: they lacked vascular elements and chlorophyll.

They didn't manufacture their own food via photosynthesis and depended on living and dead organic matter for nutrition. That put them in their own kingdom, Mycota, and, in the mind of this academic, justified a whole lecture, one filled with colorful slides of rusts, smuts, puffballs, and fungi of jelly, club, and shell persuasions.

Dave learned that the toadstools he'd kicked around as a kid were basidiomycetes, the club fungi. Maybe that was why he loved the topic: the fungi reminded him of a happier time when he roamed with Scott in the back fields and woods, kicking the caps off mushrooms and poking shell fungi from logs and trees.

The prof seemed way too excited when he reached the last topic: the danger in fungi. He started with psychedelic mushrooms, those containing hallucinogens. Then he turned to the poison ones. After touting *Amanita phalloides*, the death cap mushroom, and several others as lethal examples, he ended with an aphorism he'd probably been using for years. "There are old mushroom hunters and bold mushroom hunters, but there are no old, bold mushroom hunters."

The coincidence of dream and lecture with mushrooms made Dave wonder if he had inadvertently heard the lecture topic beforehand, and if that knowledge could have sparked his dream. He hadn't done the required reading, so that couldn't be it. Maybe he was prescient. Or full of shit. Or nuts.

⌘⌘

Jennifer waited on a bench outside the lecture hall. Dave assumed a carefree persona and went to her. He plopped his backpack at her feet and made a picture frame with his hands. His fake camera scanned her from feet to head, taking in a brown beret and a gray U-Store sweater with the required large orange P.

"Nice sweater. Bad hat," Dave said and swiped it off, hiding it behind his back.

"Give that back. What's wrong with it?"

"Should be black or orange, anything but brown." He dangled the beret in front of her.

Jennifer grabbed her hat. "You seem way too excited. What's up?"

"Just a mega-fine lecture. All about fungi." He gestured, sweeping his hands as if gesturing to a congregation.

Her hand went up. "Do not tell me about them. I resist all science. Don't do it."

"Fungi can grow on just about every substrate. The fly agaric mushroom, *Amanita muscaria*, was used by Central American Indians in rituals to cause hallucinations—"

"Stop. Or I'll tell you about existentialism."

"No. Please, no." He covered his ears.

The lecture hall crowd had dwindled to a few, slow-moving students who obviously did not have another class waiting for them. Jennifer squinted in the shaft of fall sun that shone through a majestic sycamore shedding its last leaves. "Glad to see that your appetite for knowledge has been whetted. Have you always had an interest in things that feed on the dead?"

"Not just dead stuff. Fungi are heterotrophs that absorb their nutrients from organic matter. You know, other creatures. Or chemicals. The creatures can be dead, but some fungi feed on living things, like tobacco plants. Hell, they're probably a threat to the marijuana crop. They can eat just about anything. Even been found sipping jet fuel, leading to clogged lines. Think of that next time you fly."

Jennifer put her hand on his arm. "Calm down. What exactly is going on with you?"

Dave's hyper state abruptly vanished, and his face became white. He stared at a black squirrel that stopped on the grass a dozen feet away. The creature seemed to be waiting for his answer. He leaned forward and covered his face with his hands.

"What is it?" Jennifer asked.

Dave hesitated. If he revealed the connection between the lecture and his dream, Jennifer would think he was nuts, or at least weird.

"There's something. I can see it. Just tell me."

Maybe truth was easier than denial. "I had a disturbing dream, the scary kind, and I woke up feeling like I should remember it. Well, I recalled parts of it—I wasn't in the dream, but I could sort of see what was happening. A guy was bashing something, maybe someone, on the ground, and then there were mushrooms. That why today's lecture about fungi is disturbing. It's like there was some connection between the lecture and the dream, like I had a premonition."

"Could be a coincidence," Jennifer said. "And the human brain is always looking for patterns that might not be there."

"I guess. Maybe. You could be right."

"Ouch!" Jennifer jumped up, rubbing her head. A fat acorn had fallen from the towering oak above them.

On a branch about twelve feet above the bench, an empty-pawed squirrel chittered.

"Nice shot," Dave said. The big-capped acorn settled at his feet. "Look. The cap on that thing matches the cap on your head. Same wrong color. Is that a coincidence?"

Before Jennifer could answer, another squirrel darted forward, snatched the acorn, and scampered to the nearest tree.

"So what about this dream of yours?" she asked.

"Dreams are supposed to be in black and white, aren't they? My dream had color—the mushrooms were like holiday lights. What does that mean?"

"Did you visit the street last night? Too many beers as usual?"

"I had one beer after dinner," he insisted. "Just to be social with the members who are trying to recruit me. No big deal. The dream wasn't alcohol-induced." *What a liar I am.*

"Maybe you were sore from soccer practice. The brain uses dreams to dissipate unwanted stimuli to keep you asleep."

"No soccer yesterday. That isn't it. You're ignoring the feeling of fear that went with it." Dave lowered his voice as a group of students sauntered by and glanced in their direction. "Maybe I'd better talk to someone who knows something, like the shrink at the infirmary. That's what Todd says."

"Why the hell would you do that? It was just a dream, one dream. Wait until you have recurrent nightmares before running to the head doctor. Once those guys get their hooks into you, they'll never leave you alone. You'll become their latest guinea pig." Abruptly Jennifer stood and walked off.

Surprised and confused, Dave watched her go. Clearly Jennifer was not in favor of his decision to seek professional help. He shook his head and muttered, "You were the one who mentioned the infirmary psych services on the first day we met."

∽∾∽

The next day following afternoon biology lab, Dave headed for Firestone Library. His dream was still with him, and he wondered if it was truly different from those connected with Scott's death. Maybe it was something else, a prediction of what would happen—that would make it precognition—or knowledge of something that had already happened.

That notion grabbed him, and he realized something else about the dream. He was certain it occurred near his old home in New York. He used the Firestone Library computer to search for Upstate New York stories on the Associated Press database. The carnival killing popped up with just enough detail that he had to have more.

When he phoned home, his mother answered on the third ring.

"David, what a surprise. Are you all right?" Chella Austin said.

"Yeah, I'm fine," Dave lied.

"Are you sure? You sound upset."

"I just thought I'd check in, and I need a favor for school. Can you send me today's editions of the papers? You know, the first sections."

His mother hesitated. "Why do you want them?"

"I'm doing an assignment on how different communities cover news differently. Since I know central New York, I want to compare those papers to the big city ones in the library."

Again, Chella seemed to wait a bit too long before responding. At last she said, "I'm not senile yet, and I can still detect a cockamamie story when I hear it. You've heard about the Cazenovia murder, right?"

It was his turn to hesitate. "Yes, I have."

Chella sighed. "I have the newspapers here. As soon as your father has had a chance to read them, I'll mail them."

"Great, Mom. And thanks. I'll let you know when they get here."

❧❧

Two days later, he had copies of *The Cortland Standard* and *The Binghamton Press*. His mother had been sending the former to him every couple of weeks to keep him connected to his hometown. He always consumed stories about murder—those were in the Binghamton paper—with a focus that bordered on obsession. The carnival incident was the front-page story in both the Cortland and Binghamton papers. Dave stared at the Cortland Daily headline.

CARNIVAL WORKER SLAIN.

Chilled, Dave read that the young victim, only seventeen, had been found in the woods alongside the carnival site. The boy had been hit in the head and dragged into the trees where he'd died from repeated blows to the head and face.

The reporter then blabbed a detail he probably wasn't supposed to have, let alone print. A jagged, bloody shard of rock was found next to the body, and the writer suggested it was the murder weapon. Motive was unknown, and police were questioning carnival workers.

Dave read the story twice, feeling dread. He should feel distant, uninvolved. The crime didn't happen on campus or in the town of Princeton. Not even in Norwich. He didn't know the victim.

It was unfortunate and heinous, but what did that have to do with him?

He sat back and closed his eyes, letting his mind wander, trying to quell his fear. He felt the same sensation that hit him when, as a high school freshman, he'd spent a day in the library examining microfiche of the Norwich newspaper. He found the story about his brother's and Carter's murders and finally steeled himself to read it. No one had given him details of the tragedy, an understandable caution for an eight-year-old who remembered nothing of that day. But he had to know the facts, no matter how gruesome. The newspaper said that two boys in a field were attacked and killed, for no apparent reason. Both victims had been disfigured by repeated blows.

Dave jerked, his body shaking. Two puzzle pieces fit together—his fear and the carnival killing. He feared the carnival murder because it was like his brother's and Carter's—the same modus operandi. Repeat criminals tended to do things the same way, picking the same types of victims, the same locations, the same way of entering. Didn't Ted Bundy pick similar girls? Didn't Son of Sam Dave Berkowitz choose the same locations where lovers parked? Didn't Gary Ridgway, the Green River Killer, prefer strangulation? If it was the same MO, could it be the same killer?

Dave re-read the paragraph on how the carnival worker had died. The phrasing about repeated blows to the face, even after the victim was surely dead, was exactly what had been written about his brother's death.

One other detail finally hit him. Shocked, he realized he'd dreamed about the carnival murder on the same night it happened. He'd gone to sleep before midnight and the kid was killed just after midnight. It wasn't precognition he was afflicted with. It was co-cognition.

Chapter 23

Chance Encounters

October 1993, Norwich:

Ten years after the murders of Scott Austin and Carter Shuman, Ed Malone was no longer a family-blessed dairy farmer, but even without lowing cows to rouse him at dawn, he still breakfasted at the Bluebird Restaurant, the only place in Norwich with real made-to-order morning fare. On this Sunday morning, maybe thirty hours after the carnival slaying, he parked his pickup near the downtown restaurant and stepped out into a brisk breeze that threatened early snow. Freezing temperature and frosted grass made him shrink, tortoise-like, deeper into his sheepskin coat. Again he pondered what kept him in central New York when he could be doing odd jobs just as easily south of the Mason-Dixon Line.

Sidewalks were deserted as the occasional Sunday car and truck passed on Broad Street, the state highway connecting Binghamton to Utica. Orange banners on lampposts sported red, brown, and yellow leaves that announced the fall season. Malone figured he'd find similar decorations in warmer places.

The killing in Cazenovia consumed his mind. He knew the victim from his job at the carnival, just as he'd known Scott Austin and Carter Shuman. A not-so-clever mind could see the similarities of the murders. Malone cringed before a hideous, evil force at work, something even the dumb cops might see. But it probably had been a mistake trying to explain that to the deputies. It probably made him look guilty and goaded them to grill him for hours. Why was he near the crime scene? What was he doing all Friday night? When did he get there and when did he leave? What did he see, hear, sense, think? Being drunk and not having a clear memory had not helped get them off his ass.

He peered through the fogged plate glass of the restaurant window. Corn stalks and three pumpkins as big as medicine balls clustered before a sign touting pumpkin and mincemeat pies. Black and orange crepe paper strands framed the half-wall decoration: three Halloween masks—a witch, a skull, and a half-melted, green face. In the restaurant, men in jeans and plaid shirts perched on counter stools. He didn't recognize anyone, but then he really had no friends. Not that he gave a damn. It wouldn't be the first time he ate alone.

Movement on the right caught his eye. In the booth closest to the window sat a thick-armed fellow studying a newspaper. He wore a short-sleeved polo shirt, inappropriate for the weather, and did not stop reading as he poked a forkful of scrambled eggs into his mouth. Malone knew the guy.

He entered, greeted by warm moist air and odors of bacon, sausage, and ham. Plates clattered over conversations. He'd hesitated long enough to catch the attention of the girl at the counter, who seemed about to speak, but he waved her off and slid into the front booth across from John Redford.

"Mornin', John. Been back for a couple of years, haven't you?" Malone's words were rushed.

Redford slowly lifted his head and focused on the uninvited visitor. His green shirt had a lizard on the pocket, the sleeves stretched over large biceps. His slack face tightened, the eyes narrowed, and his tall forehead wrinkled. He grasped the edge of the table with fat fingers and made a slight movement as if to leave. "Do I know you?"

"Maybe. I know you."

The waitress banged down a mug and poured coffee. Past her prime, she wore her brown hair in a bun and seemed more ornery than usual. "How ya doin', Ed. How are all the little demons?"

Malone glared at the woman. She pulled a pad from a front pocket and a pencil from the hairball and stood waiting. Malone ordered poached eggs with scrapple and rye toast. She grabbed the coffee pot and charged toward the kitchen.

"I see you're reading about that murder," Malone said. "Pretty ugly."

Redford pushed the paper to the wall and lifted his coffee mug. He sipped, set the cup down, and thumped his index finger on the headline. "Not so much ugly as scary. I'll bet the carnival guy was plenty scared." He glanced at his half-eaten breakfast, at the paper, and then slowly, as if he'd searched for a way to avoid the task and failed to find one, at Malone. He shook his head, moving a lock of red hair on his forehead. "I don't know you."

Reggie Peckrough, another regular, entered and glanced around. Malone knew the guy and always thought he was a peacock, strutting and posing. Today he seemed different, as if he didn't want to be seen. He kept his head down as he headed to a booth across from Malone and Redford.

Malone lowered his voice. "You knew Scott Austin." It was a statement, one that caused Redford to flinch. "I had a farm near the Austins and often saw kids horsing around in the back fields. And I saw you there. You were big then, hard to miss, and you're even bigger now."

"What if I did? That was years ago. Why do you care?"

Malone answered with a question. "Does that story in the paper remind you of anything? Does it ring a bell? "

Redford forked a chunk of egg into his mouth and drank some coffee. He shrugged. "Should it?"

"The carnival killing didn't happen far from Norwich. Seems a bit like the murders of Scott and Carter, doesn't it?"

The door opened and a swoosh of cold air accompanied a new customer, a large man dressed in a dark blue pin-striped suit, a blue button-down oxford, and a blue tie. Jim Caruthers glanced around before heading for a table. His eyes swept past Malone and Redford, and he frowned. He gave no greeting and went to the back of the restaurant.

The psychiatrist's reaction meant nothing to Malone. He'd only been a sporadic patient over the years and wouldn't be surprised if the man didn't recognize him. The doc had never been much help. *Treated me like I was nuts. Just couldn't accept that evil, maybe from the damn mushrooms, could infect people, just like it had the wolf. Now look what's happened.*

Malone turned back to Redford. "Well, I felt real sorry for the Austins and the Shumans, losing their sons, and then never knowing who did it. You were in the papers, because the cops found you huddled in a ditch near the murders. The story didn't give your name, just called you a juvenile, but in a small town, word gets around. The cops thought you might be a witness. Or maybe more."

The waitress put a plate in front of Malone and refilled his coffee. Malone stabbed his poached egg and dipped toast in the yolk.

"I don't remember any of that," Redford said. "I've been away."

"Yes, you have. They took you to that hospital after they found you. I had a janitor job there for a short time. Even talked to you."

Redford wrinkled his brow. "Oh yeah. I remember you. I thought you were a patient, always talking crazy about burning things."

"Didn't the doctors there help you remember anything?"

Redford shook his head. "They kept asking, but I don't remember how I got into the ditch."

"But before the ditch?"

Redford closed his eyes and didn't answer.

"Did something happen before the ditch?"

"I didn't want it to happen. He made me."

"Who?"

"I don't know." Redford's tone flattened. "They gave me medicines so I wasn't so angry and wasn't scared. I stopped hitting the nurses. I got better. I'm better now, and that's why I'm out. I don't want to think about it."

Malone finished his eggs, not sure he believed what Redford was saying. Across from their booth, Peckrough leaned closer. Silence stretched for a minute as all three diners sipped coffee.

"Where are you living?" Malone asked at last.

"In a shack over on River Road. I have some chickens and a couple of goats."

"I used to have chickens before that damn wolf ripped 'em all apart. And killed my dogs. I shot the bastard. Smashed his skull." Malone pulled up his sleeve and pointed to three red streaks on his forearm. "These are the wolf's present."

Redford ran the tip of his tongue over dry lips. "Do they still hurt?"

"It's the memory that hurts," Malone rolled down his sleeve. "Do any of your memories hurt, John?"

"Not anymore."

"You have dreams, right? What do you dream about?"

"About the mushrooms with biting teeth. They were scary."

Malone dropped his fork. He swallowed some coffee and leaned forward. "Mushrooms that bite. How long have you had those dreams?"

"I had 'em every night until they got the pills right. Now I don't dream much."

"Where were they? The mushrooms in your dream."

"In the woods. I'm not sure." Redford wiped his forehead with the napkin.

"Do you ever go back in the woods, John? Do you want to go back?"

Redford hesitated. "No. Why would I?"

"Because you want to see them, don't you?" Malone had often thought of returning to the woods to search for the rainbow fungi. He wanted to go back, but only went once with the gasoline. He stared into Redford's eyes, searching for some sign. The young man seemed to be gritting his teeth.

Malone spread strawberry jam on a piece of toast, thinking Redford wasn't ready for the truth. "I saw you in Cortland at David Austin's graduation. Why were you there, John?"

Redford jerked upright and his eyes darted around the restaurant. "I don't know no Cort Land."

"I saw you there. In the stands on the football field."

"I was never in Cort Land." Redford lowered his head and seemed to study his cold eggs. When he looked up, he said, "Why were you there?"

"We were both there for the same reason, John. To see David Austin. The real question is why we wanted to see him."

"I never talked to David Austin. And I don't want to talk to you anymore."

"Well, finish your breakfast. You and I should discuss this some more. I know something about mushrooms, and maybe I can help you." Malone left a buck on the table and went to the counter to pay. He got his change and glanced back. Redford and Peckrough were staring in his direction.

Chapter 24

Self-Medication

November 1993, Princeton:

For a month, Dave dreamed off and on, a repeat of the dark scene where he witnesses some act of violence, the dream he was sure depicted the killing of the young carnival worker. He used aspirin and alcohol to cope with the headaches that followed.

He'd returned to Cortland for a Thanksgiving feast that included aunts and uncles from his mother's big family. On the day after the holiday meal, he borrowed the car and took a drive, without a specific destination, content to enjoy relaxing views of snow-dusted hills along Route 23. When he discovered he was approaching South Plymouth, a few miles from Norwich, he slammed on the brakes, slid on the ice, and came to a stop on a rare wide flat shoulder. Panicked, he'd jerked the car into a turn and had retreated to Cortland.

In early December, Dave encountered a dream with a new element: the chase. Like the dream that viewed the carnival murder, this one was also dark and in the woods. The story started with his hiding, watching something terrible. Then a black creature came after him. He ran faster and got ahead of whatever it was, but then he stumbled and fell, and the black figure closed the gap. Dave jumped up, ran through brambles, and plunged across rainbow mushrooms that exploded at his legs, arms, and face. Slipping and falling, getting bogged down in bushes, he almost felt the monster's grasp.

The morning alarm wrenched him from the disturbing image. He sat on the edge of the bed, running through his usual serenity routine of slow and deep breaths. As he dressed, he tried to remember the nightmare. He'd had enough psychobabble from Jim Caruthers to accept that the dream could have something to do with the trauma of his brother's murder, but it pissed him off that he didn't quite get it. He downed two aspirin and headed for the dining hall.

A sparse crowd occupied the dining room at seven a.m. Students who were not morning people and who avoided early classes skipped breakfast. Dave, however, liked breakfast, even if getting up early was a pain. After loading eggs, bacon, toast, and coffee on a tray, he noticed Jennifer sitting alone against the paneled wall. She may not have had a class, but she was both an early riser and, despite her svelte form, an eater. Dave settled across from her.

"That bacon can't be good for your arteries," Jennifer said in greeting. Before he could respond, she smiled, grabbed a piece, and popped half of it into her mouth.

Dave frowned and sipped coffee. He moved his plate closer to his chest, silently daring her to try another raid.

"You're quiet this morning," Jennifer said. "Are you okay?"

"I had an interesting dream again."

"Another with the mushrooms?"

"Yes, but different. Still in the woods, but this time I was running from someone, big and dark, someone who wanted to kill me."

Jennifer put her muffin down. "Kill you? That's new. How did you know he wanted to do you in? A little post-dream analysis?"

Dave tried to decide where the killing notion came from.

What came out of his mouth surprised him. "Because he hit the boys." He had not realized until now that there were victims or that they were boys. Maybe he was projecting into the dream what he'd heard and read about his brother's murder.

Jennifer snatched another broken piece of bacon and ate it, donning an aura of innocence. "Well, dreams aren't something I have, so they don't interest me. I'm an economics or arts or history or literature or pottery major."

Dave took the hint and changed the subject. "If it's economics, you will surely want to know that fungi are one of the most widely distributed life forms on the planet and play key economic roles in making beer, wine, and cheese. They're essential for conditioning the soil for crops. On the other hand, they are a constant threat to our way of life due to crop infestation and livestock disease. Keep that in mind."

"Still obsessed with fungi, I see. What does that have to do with pottery?" Jennifer eyed a gaggle of entering students, one of whom waved. She waved back.

The greeting came from a tall blond guy Dave didn't know. "I see mushrooms in my sleep so I've grown fond of 'em."

A loud laugh accompanied three oversized guys in sweatshirts who plowed through the door and made their way to the cafeteria line where they began clanging silverware onto trays.

"The jocks have arrived," Dave said, thankful that the meaty guys had not waved. "Big and noisy."

"With glorious glutes," Jennifer said.

"Women are so shallow. Don't be a slave to your hormones," Dave said in a superior, reprimanding voice.

After he'd polished off the rest of his eggs and toast, Dave took his tray to the return window, and Jennifer followed, dumping her yogurt container and the muffin wrap in the trash can.

As the background noise of trays, china, and silverware

rumbled louder, they grabbed their backpacks and headed out into still-chilly morning temperatures, turning toward Nassau Street.

The overcast fall sky gave Dave something else to talk about. "This cold air has a smell of snow to it. The squirrels are busy hustling acorns. As if they expect them to disappear under the white stuff."

Both Dave and Jennifer shared childhood memories of frozen winter precipitation measured in feet. They each boasted of building bigger snowmen and being the best snowballer of the gang. She'd skied, but not as avidly as Dave, who started skiing in first grade in Norwich and continued through high school in Cortland. Heaps of snow filled him with wonder—at least until he had to shovel it—and he missed that kind of winter. The threatened snow would be the first of the season in New Jersey, and he imagined how Princeton gargoyles looked frosted in white.

Jennifer adjusted her black scarf. "So what will you do, Dave?"

"That black goes well with your auburn hair, but the orange clashes." He pointed to the ridiculously large orange "P" on the end of the scarf.

"About what's bothering you."

"I'll drop in at Health Services about the headaches."

"They'll deliver you to the shrink. To help you remember the thing you imagine is in your head, even though you went through all this with the guy from Norwich, the one who wouldn't leave you alone."

"I did. Without success. When my brother died, I ran into the backyard blubbering. I had no memory of where I'd been or what happened. I still don't. Dr. Blue said he thought I was suppressing something. Maybe he was right."

"If you've been suppressing it for this many years, it must be terrible to remember. If you let some shrink pick your brain open, you could be worse off than just having an occasional hyperactive dream."

"Easy for you to say. You're not the one with the

dreams. I'm supposed to remember something. If I can ferret out what it is, my dreams and fears and headaches will vanish. It's as simple as that." He spoke with more bravado than he felt.

"You watch too many movies," she said. "What if it turns out that you witnessed your brother's murder? Do you really want to remember that?" Jennifer grabbed his arm. "There's something else, donkey. What if your memory IDs the killer? What then?"

He shrugged his shoulders. "Guess I'd have to tell the cops."

"Who will crap all over your memories."

"Not if I point them in the right direction"

"And point the murderer at yourself."

That afternoon, Dave re-read the Norwich paper's account of the murder of the carnival worker and visited Firestone Library to see if there was anything new from Associated Press. A sheriff's deputy remembered a dark pickup near the carnival at closing hour, one creeping along in a thirty-five-mile-per-hour zone. He didn't get the license plate and couldn't say who was driving, whether it was a man or woman. The Cortland paper mentioned another detail: the victim was a loner without relatives. That fact probably allowed reporters to again mention the mutilation of the young man's face—what the hell, there was no family to complain. Dave was sure this killing was like his brother's, as if he'd seen them both.

Then it happened, a strange, never-before thing: he was crying. It started with a heart pain, a stab of memory: his once happy and annoying big brother alive one moment and then gone forever. The heartache blossomed into physical pain, a crushing pressure on his chest, and he gasped, sobbing. Surely he had cried for Scott before. Hadn't he?

He spent the next hour in a daze, walking and thinking, eventually reaching the University Chapel. He sat on the stone steps for ten minutes and almost entered. Instead, he wandered to the rear of Nassau Hall and checked the stone plaques commemorating ivy plantings by classes past. As he crossed the grass of Cannon Green, he kept his eye out for mushrooms. In front of the oddball Greek temples beyond the Green, he sought wisdom that didn't come. Giving up, he headed to Blair Arch. A cold breeze kicked leaves around the wide cavern leading to the stairs where twenty-fifth reunion classes always had their pictures taken. He counted the steps descending, had a moment of panic when he saw the crowd coming out of the U-Store, turned and recounted steps as he climbed back to the arch.

He passed in front of the magnificently hideous Alexander Hall and walked the path behind Nassau Hall. He crossed Cannon Green diagonally and followed Elm Drive past Dillon Gym, encountering no one he knew and making it to his room. Todd was off somewhere. Dave sat at his desk and opened his chemistry text. He read for ten minutes, lowered his head to his arms, and dozed.

芻芻芻

The end of the semester brought a dream with a twist. Dave was pounding mushrooms with a rag, smashing at biting mouths on their caps, scattering bloody fungal pieces away from his arms. The dark figure came from the woods behind him, and Dave fled, forcing leaden legs to keep moving as the creature came after him, gaining and gaining…

He woke an hour after the dining hall had closed and decided to get a burger on Nassau Street. After splashing cold water on his face, he headed out but never made it to food. He wound up on Prospect Avenue at the club he'd most likely be joining during his sophomore year.

No one challenged him as he filled his cup at the untended tap. He'd downed six cups before a member noticed his wobbly walk and the slop of beer down his shirt and cut him off.

Around ten o'clock he stumbled out of the club and turned away from campus. He wound up in an athletic field edged with trees, a mini forest of pines. Lamps in an adjacent parking lot illuminated a cluster of toadstools at the base of a small tree. Breathing faster, he began stomping on the white caps, squishing the mushrooms beneath his sneakers. Again and again, his foot came down until he fell, banging his head on the tree.

He lay there stunned, trying to figure out what he was supposed to do. He had to get up and return to his room. Or he could just go to sleep. But he hadn't put on his winter jacket, just a sweatshirt, and the cold forced him up. He struggled to his feet, head spinning, and the six beers on an empty stomach burbled up over the crushed mushrooms.

When Dave managed to find his way to his room, Todd was studying. His roommate looked David over. "You look like hell and you smell worse. You barfed on that shirt, didn't you?"

Dave looked down at his stained shirt. "By Jove, I think you're right, Todd old boy."

Todd got up and grabbed Dave by the sleeve and led him to the bathroom. "Get the hell in the shower. Maybe it will fix your drunken head and shitty smell. Rinse the shirt. I'll get your shorts and a tee." He stood, arms folded, while Dave stripped and got under the water.

When they were both back in the room, Todd said, "Didn't you say you had a bio test tomorrow? I don't suppose you studied for it. You can't be a boozer and a student, Dave."

"Right. Student or boozer. Boozer or student. Not both. Right." Dave examined his top bunk calculating how he might get into it.

"So what about the test?"

"Hey. No problem. I'll get up early and go over the notes. It will be about fungi and I'm quite the expert on the little buggers. Kingdom Mycota. Class Basidiomycetes. Hallucinogens. Shell, coral, and bird's nest fungi. Rusts and smuts. I've always liked smuts and sluts." He climbed onto the window ledge and fell into the bed. "Set my alarm, will you? I need to review those sluts. I should ask Jen to be a slut."

Chapter 25

Second Year

Fall 1994, Princeton:

Dave's freshman year didn't end well. Coping with dreams, fears, headaches, and binge drinking, he failed to complete some work for the second-semester chemistry course. For his head problems, he'd considered seeking help, but Jennifer's denigration of psychiatrists stopped him. Deep down, however, he suspected he should see someone, maybe even Jim Caruthers. He squelched the idea, thrusting it deep into some brain dustbin reserved for unacceptable, uncomfortable constructs.

After finals, he stayed on campus to study with a chemistry prof and make up work. Summer in Princeton was quite pleasant—uncluttered walks, the hum of mowers, erudite quiet—and had the advantage of easier beer than in Cortland. Far easier, once he found a grad student who provided a polished, fake ID.

Jennifer had taken a summer job in her hometown, and he missed her. Their parting in May was cool—she didn't like his drinking or flunking or mental issues or all of the above—and she offered only perfunctory replies to his notes. He called once when she wasn't in, so he left a message, but she didn't call back. He had an impulse to borrow a car and drive to Guilford to find her, but his studies and the lack of a vehicle kept him in Princeton. Just the thought of returning to central New York, however, had produced a new notion he couldn't seem to shake: there was something in Norwich he needed to see.

With willpower and adequate time, he fixed his chemistry problem and even had the chance to catch up on reading in several other subjects. His parents rewarded this success with the gift of a cell phone. He felt happy for the academic success and because, during the three months of summer, he did not dream.

ぐぬぐぬ

As a sophomore, Dave moved into a two-bedroom suite in 1903 Hall. The large central room featured a brown sofa with a defeated look, a chewed up coffee table, and battle-weary, thick-cushioned chairs. A television and a refrigerator made it the perfect recreation center. He shared the quad with three friends, one of whom was Todd Jensen.

Another was Colin Painter, a small guy with an innocent smile that belied his personality. He hailed from Chicago and had a Princeton alumnus physician father. There was no doubt that the son was headed for medical school, and his courses included many on Dave's schedule. Dave latched on to Colin as a compadre, someone with similar thoughts on most topics and the same irreverent attitude.

The fourth roommate was Arthur George Peron V, known as Jabe, a giant who used his speed and size to play football, but who still knew his way around a tennis court. He hailed from South Carolina and considered Yankee accents as "foreign." The real test of his patience, however, was his roommates' sense of humor, especially that displayed by Colin and Dave.

"Do you get how sophomoric your lame humor is?" he'd once asked, shaking his shaved head in disbelief and disapproval.

"But we are sophomores," Dave answered.

Jabe frowned. "That is no excuse. Your inane banter just proves I'm the real Princeton student. Old Nassau only let Colin sneak in on coattails of his alumni father. Dave must have been picked to fill some quota for rural bumpkins. Todd, I'll admit, is a hard worker, as am I. We earned our way, in contrast to you less qualified comedians."

"Bull. Legacy students lived with big pressure to get in," Colin said. "We coped. We rose to the top. We are the real Princetonians."

Jabe snorted.

"But you may be right about Dave," Colin added.

Dave adopted a stupid look and bowed.

The four made excellent roommates because they were also friends. Dave had made the connection between booze and academic trouble. Accordingly, he started the fall semester with two aims: to buckle down on books and to curb his drinking.

The resolution held until, in his sober, clear-headed state, he dreamed again.

Not far into the semester, Dave woke screaming, "No, no. Let me go." The scream woke Todd, who rolled from the lower bunk and grabbed his shoulders.

"Austin, wake up," Todd yelled. "You're dreaming."

"I have to get away," Dave flailed his arms, catching Todd on the side of the head and backing him off.

Jabe rushed in from the common room and grabbed Dave, holding on until he really was awake. "What the hell has gotten into him?"

"It's the dream that scares the shit out of him," Todd said.

Dave stopped struggling. "You can let go now. I'm awake."

Jabe released his grip. "Is this the same dream you whined about over beer at Tiger Inn?"

Dave rose from the bunk. "Same dream, but this time I was being bitten, by little rodents. Or maybe they were mushrooms with teeth. But the scary part was human. Someone had me."

"I told you to get help last year," Todd added.

"Holy shit," Jabe said. "You mean this has been happening for a year?"

Since the spring of freshman year, Dave, once sufficiently drunk, told whoever was present, including his current roommates, the story of his murdered brother and his dreams. They knew that the killer had never been caught.

Dave grabbed his bath bag and descended into the bathroom where he found Colin shaving. His roommate finished the job and leaned against the toothpaste-dotted basin.

"Was that you yelling as I left the room?" Colin asked.

"Yeah. Dream."

"Recurring dreams usually mean something serious is bubbling in the subconscious. My dad said more than once that the subconscious has to come out, to get to the surface."

"Where it does what?" Dave fiddled in his bath bag. "Thanks, Dr. Colin. You can send me a bill."

"I'm serious about this, and you should be too. It may only take a session or two with the right professional, but it should be done."

"It'll take more than that. I've been in the clutches of a psychiatrist for years. He's had his multiple sessions."

"This was the same dream?" Colin asked.

"Related, but different. Someone had me and I was struggling to get away."

Colin watched Dave's reflection in the mirror as if the image might reveal what was messing his brain. "A different dream may mean a different mind, one now ready to get help from a professional."

"I suppose—"

"Damn," Colin interrupted as he made the logical leap. "You know something about the fucking killer, don't you?"

"Where the hell did that come from?"

Colin stroked his chin as if he'd suddenly grown a beard.

"The great Doctor Freud said, 'Dreams are often most profound when they seem the most crazy.' You exhibit selective amnesia. That's a device the brain comes up with to protect itself from some painful memory. Of course, I haven't quite gotten my MD yet, so you should get this information from someone qualified. Make an appointment, Dave. For your own good. My service will be added to your tab."

c∽e∽

For two weeks after getting Colin's advice, Dave downed three or four beers every night after dinner, ignoring his resolution to stay sober. Over his third beer at Tiger Inn, he tried to figure out what to do. Although Caruthers said Dave was keeping something secret, the doctor hadn't harped on dredging up old memories. Now his dreams were changing and his headaches were worse. *What the hell. Being sober didn't keep the scary dream at bay. But you know, Davy Boy, the booze won't do it either.*

What really bothered him about the dream was the fear, the frickin' fear that lasted and probably caused the headaches. If he didn't have the fear, he wouldn't have to drink. It pissed him off that sobriety hadn't squelched the dreaming. Maybe Dr. Colin was right—that all it would take to feel normal was a session or two with someone competent. Did that mean that Caruthers wasn't?

Dave wished Jennifer weren't playing whatever game she had going with him. They'd caught sight of each other, but she'd not stopped before disappearing into McCosh Hall along with a couple of hundred others. He could find out where she was rooming—but he didn't. One part of him wanted to talk to her, to discuss his dream and Colin's orders, but another part was ashamed to show her that he was still a defective misfit, one seriously considering seeking help. Besides, she would pooh-pooh the idea of seeing a shrink. She always had. Usually women were all in favor of men getting medical help. It gave them a chance to cluck like mother hens and say, "I told you so." *Make up your own mind, Austin. Act like an adult.*

かかかか

Late in November, on a day when wind was stripping the last leaves from the trees, Dave hid under the hood of his fleece and darted between gothic and not-so-gothic buildings on an indirect path to McCosh Health Services. The red brick building was surrounded by snow-dusted blacktop with parking spaces.

He lurked, hood up, near a rhododendron until no one came or went and then slithered inside. He found a foyer with a door marked "Reception" in the rear. Beyond that sat a smiling woman who waited for the opaque door to close before greeting him.

Dave indicated he had a history of upsetting dreams and was having problems with headaches. She handed him a clipboard with a two-page medical questionnaire and sent him into an adjacent room where he checked boxes for several minutes. After handing it back, he returned to the room and waited until a different middle-aged woman with a friendly but no-nonsense face called him. Her pale skin and all-white shirt, pants, and sneakers made him think he was in the hands of an attendant from heaven. She took him to her office, sat behind a spartan desk, and checked his paperwork.

"You indicated you drink occasionally, Mr. Austin. More than once a week?"

Dave fidgeted. "Yes."

"Every day?"

"Yes."

"What's your choice of drink?"

He wondered what form of alcohol—beer, wine, or the

hard stuff—was more forgivable and picked beer.

The woman scribbled, nodded, and switched topics. "So you've seen a psychiatrist off and on for ten years. Can you tell me the reason?"

Dave sucked in a big breath and let it out slowly. "I witnessed my brother's murder and apparently blocked it out."

The nurse studied him for several seconds. "I am so sorry to hear that. And your chief complaint is this fearful dream—"

"That I think is related."

"Any other physical symptoms?"

"Headaches."

"I see. You were right to come in. Dr. Ellington is our psychiatrist, and tomorrow is her regular day. I'll have a staff physician check your medical history."

Dave went back to his magazine and waited. The nurse returned with a sheet, the doctor's request for baseline lab values. "Any problem with needles?"

Dave shook his head. He didn't like needles, but what he really hated was blood.

"The doctor will check you over after we get this chem panel."

She led him down the main hallway and introduced a lab tech. The girl pointed to a chair and pulled on latex gloves. She wrapped a rubber band on his arm and told him to close his fist. He did so and studied the ceiling.

As the tech drew blood into a tube, Dave closed his eyes and kept them closed until the woman slapped a plastic strip in the crook of his arm. He went back to the waiting room and sat for forty minutes reading issues of *US News & World Report*. Finally he was escorted into an office.

An ancient, overweight man in a white jacket introduced himself as a doctor and proceeded to scan the medical history forms. He checked heart, lungs, and blood pressure. He went over the details of the headaches, including the possible connection to dreams. Finally, he pronounced Dave free of any signs of a purely physical problem and recommended he come back the next day for a follow-up with the staff psychiatrist who would have the lab results.

The nurse reappeared. "We need a summary from the psychiatrist who treated you. Can you provide his contact information? You'll have to sign a release-of-records form."

Dave scheduled a morning appointment with Dr. Ellington for the next day. He signed the release form, wrote down Caruthers name and phone number, and took a lollipop from a glass bowl.

Outside, Dave kept his hood up even though the wind had died and sun splashed the slate paths. He hurried to 1903 Hall, happy not to encounter anyone. No one was in the dorm room to question him. Even though his roommates had urged him to visit the campus infirmary, Dave did not announce his appointment when they showed up later. He wasn't sure why.

That night he slept without dreaming.

Chapter 26

Theresa Ellington

November 1994, Princeton:

Dave showed up early for his appointment at Health Services. Again the receptionist waited for the door to close before she took his name and directed him to a new room to await the doctor. No common place existed for students to sit, probably a nod to medical confidentiality on a gossip-prone campus.

The space had a second door, a pair of plastic chairs, and a small wooden table with picked-over magazines—*Time, Sports Illustrated, US News and World Report*. Two walls held prints. Dave leaned over to read the identification plaques on the frames of Henri Rousseau's *Tiger in a Tropical Storm* and of Eugene Delacroix's *Tiger and Snake*. He sat and was just getting engrossed in an article on college basketball when Dr. Theresa Ellington opened the second door. She introduced herself, shook his hand, and led him to her office.

Ellington was small and neat, about five feet tall, a good-looking brunette in her forties with wire-rim glasses and a pageboy haircut that suited her friendly oval face. Quite a contrast to Jim Caruthers, who was big and casual. Her office was also different. Caruthers's messy desk held a ship model, a Paul Bunyan bobble head, and a jar of lollipops.

Ellington sat behind a wooden desk that held nothing but a brass banker's lamp, a blotter, a pad, and a folder. Caruthers was all about the color blue. Here the theme was brown: dark paneling, a patterned brown carpet with swirls of red, and a large Matisse reproduction, something with a vase surrounded by fruit with a red-brown background. Dave settled into a chocolate leather armchair.

Ellington flipped open the folder, picked up a paper, and examined it. "I've studied your file, and I think you were right to stop in. Repeated headaches and vivid dreams can be debilitating, and you shouldn't have to put up with that when you're trying to do college work. How are you feeling today, David?"

"It's Dave, and I'm feeling well. No dream last night." His anxiety receded.

"Yesterday's examination and lab tests indicate you are in good physical health. Nothing in your history says otherwise."

"That's good, right?"

"Exactly. But lack of a physical cause for your symptoms directs us to the psychological. I phoned Dr. Caruthers, and he faxed a summary of his findings. You've suffered a serious tragedy in the murder of your brother and his friend, and you've blocked out those memories. Does that sound right?"

"Yes, Dr. Caruthers said that years ago when I first saw him."

Ellington checked something on her pad. "He speculates that you may have witnessed the attack and have suppressed the memory, a type of amnesia called psychogenic or dissociative amnesia, the result of a traumatic event. In this case, seeing your brother killed. Do you have any memory of that today?"

"No I don't, but..." Dave gazed out the one window that framed a lone pine tree. "Well, pieces of what could be memories come out in dreams."

"That's possible. Not remembering is the brain's defense

mechanism, which could weaken as you've gotten older. At any rate, there seems to be no organic reason for the amnesia. Dr. Caruthers's summary suggests that you have coped very well, and he chose no further treatment." Ellington removed her glasses and leaned back. "The fact that you are here now indicates something has changed."

"I guess," he said, wondering if this was the guinea pig trap Jennifer harped on.

"This sort of amnesia is akin to trying to keep a beach ball under water. The ball wants to surface, and so does the memory your amnesia is hiding." The doctor replaced her glasses and put the paper back in the folder. "It may be that your symptoms are caused by the struggle to remember. Tell me about the dreams."

He squeezed the arm of his chair, leaving finger indentations in the leather. "Well, the dream takes place in a field and then in woods…"

When he didn't continue, Ellington asked, "Is this a place you recognize?"

"Near where my brother died. But that doesn't bother me. It's the fear. Maybe that's why I drink."

"Could be. What else about this dream?"

With Ellington listening and probing what he recalled, Dave related various elements of his dreams—being chased, a dark figure, mushrooms. He also mentioned the recent dream that he suspected was quite different. He ended with "I feel I should be remembering something more."

Ellington brought her hands together as if she were praying. "Of course. Let me tell you how psychogenic amnesia works. The memories are in your parietal lobe, which stores visual and auditory images, but the recovery process is controlled by other structures like the hippocampus. That's what's blocked."

"So?" He sat forward. "I have to get to the bottom of it. I can't function like this."

"We have to uncover what you know. The memory may be upsetting, but until it is on the surface, you can't deal with it. The good news is that there are techniques to elicit a blocked memory. It may take some time and won't be easy. Are you willing to try?"

Dave hesitated. *Am I willing?* "I guess I am."

"Well, I see no reason to start from scratch. Dr. Caruthers has done all the things I would have done before moving on to what I'm about to suggest. It is a form of relaxation therapy in which we get you into a state where your mind can move into forbidden areas and bring them to the surface."

"You mean hypnosis?"

"Not exactly, but akin to it. You'll be fully aware all the time, just relaxed. Before we get to that, however, I'd want to make sure I understand your dreams. There seem to be multiple dreams that may be related to each other and to your brother's death. They are certainly related by your fear reaction."

Dave nodded. "The place is mostly the same, except for the last one, but new elements pop up. The location is near where my brother and I used to play and near where the murders took place. I never doubt that. Then there are just plain crazy images that can't be real. They can't be memories."

"Let's set aside the most recent dream and focus on the others. Twice you've used the word 'near' to describe where the dream site is in relation to the murder site. Why is that?"

"The dream sometimes starts in a grassy field, but winds up in the woods. My brother was killed in a field near the woods."

"Okay. And the unreal images? What are those?" Ellington added to her notes, her eyes moving between the patient and the pad.

"The toadstools. The moving, biting, red, blue, green, and orange toadstools. Like some kind of rodent fungus. Crazy stuff."

Ellington adjusted her glasses. "Dream distortions reflect

the brain's attempt to present disjointed thoughts and events in understandable images. Even if they aren't exactly true, they could be related to something that is."

"What about the color? I thought dreams were in black and white."

"The idea of only black and white dreams is a misconception. We dream in color but, because they fade quickly, we remember in black and white."

Dave considered that for a moment and then asked, "Could these be hallucinations?"

"Good question. Hallucinations are perceptions in the absence of stimuli, but they occur in the awake state. They can be caused by drugs—LSD and psychedelic mushrooms are well known hallucinogens. Even alcohol and caffeine. The person is awake and often aware they are seeing what isn't there."

"So there really were mushrooms connected with my brother's murder?" he asked.

"You've mentioned woods. Mushrooms often grow in damp woody places. You talk about a dark figure. Is it a person?"

Somewhere a door slammed. Dave brought his knuckles to his mouth, thinking. "There was no person at first. But in a recent dream I saw a big dark figure chasing me."

"Only one?" Ellington asked.

"Yes."

Ellington closed the folder and sat back. "The story seems to be getting more complete. Perhaps it's time to give you help with the memory. Why don't we get started?"

During the next ten minutes, Ellington invited Dave to lean back in the reclining chair and asked him to imagine himself back in time. She spoke in soothing tones that guided him, quite relaxed, back to his Norwich house, first in the back yard, and then up the hill beyond his house. He was told to feel safe, and it worked. Ellington, in a gentle voice, took him to his dream and asked what he could see.

"I see my brother and Carter. They are on the ground,

not moving. I touch Scott but nothing happens. I scream and run."

"Everything is all right, Dave. You are safe. What else do you see?"

Dave hesitated, taking deep breaths. "Not something I see. Just know. There was someone else, but he's disappeared. It's…it's Scott's friend, John Redford." The name came out with a croak, and Dave sat up and began to sob.

Ellington put her arm around him and said nothing until the crying subsided. "Think about John. How do you know he was there?"

"John is waiting when Scott and Carter and I get to where we want to set off the fireworks Carter took from his brother. Or maybe he comes after us. They are setting off fireworks and I get to watch. Suddenly John is gone."

"Where does he go?"

"I don't know. Somewhere. We go after him. And then I…" Dave's voice faded and his body became rigid.

"It's all right, Dave. What did you do?" She got him to lean back.

"I don't remember anything except running." Dave panted with his eyes closed. "I—no—no—I can't."

"All right. That's enough." Ellington talked Dave back from his memory with the same soft and soothing voice.

Dave rose and looked around, eyes wide, unsure at first of where he was. When he figured it out, he started to relax. Until the thought struck him that he might have seen his brother killed. "So what am I forgetting?"

"I won't know until you tell me. Whatever the traumatic event is that you are trying to access, you seem to have some anterograde and retrograde amnesia about it. That just means you have a gap both before and after the time Scott died. Some of what you related may not seem quite right to you—at least it doesn't agree fully with what is in Dr. Caruthers's file. But that's not unusual. Accurate memory about what happened to you may come in stages."

Dave agreed to return the next day and left wondering

about the question of accuracy. He was certain that John Redford had been there that day, but he hadn't seen him doing anything. And he was sure he'd seen something else.

Not far from Health Services, he ran into Jennifer. She fell into step beside him.

"Dave, I was planning to call you tonight, but here you are." She pulled off her orange mittens and took his hand in hers. Smiling, she glanced at the building behind him. "You just came from the infirmary. Does that mean that you're having problems with the headaches still?"

The encounter and question took him by surprise. He could hardly deny where he'd been, but he didn't want to talk about it.

Unfortunately, Jennifer could be like a terrier with a pants cuff, so he would have to tell her something.

"I'm healthy as a horse, but my headaches and anxiety might be due to a type of amnesia. Once I've remembered what happened when Scott died, I'll be able to deal with it, and I'll be fine."

Jennifer let his hand go and started walking. Dave followed. Just past the biology building, she stopped and turned to face him. "So did you remember anything?"

"I think Scott's friend, John Redford, was with us at some point."

Jennifer dropped her mittens and stooped to retrieve them. When she stood, her back was to him. "And you believe that?"

"Why wouldn't I?"

"It's just that you were a kid. It was a long time ago. How can you be sure? Maybe it was something you dreamed."

Dave moved beside her, and they began walking again. "No. My dreams never had Redford in them. This wasn't a dream. I was awake in the doctor's office."

"What does it mean? Will you tell someone?"

Dave hadn't thought that far and wasn't sure who she meant. "I don't know."

Abruptly, Jennifer seemed to lose interest. "Want to have dinner tonight?"

This caught Dave off guard. "Sure," he said at last.

"Good. I'll see you at six-thirty." As she moved away with big strides, her fists were clenched.

⁊ଅ⁊ଅ

In an isolated corner of the dining hall, Jennifer steered the conversation back to what Dave may have remembered during his session at McCosh Health Services. Her approach was not specific but general: she attacked the whole concept of psychiatrist-assisted memory recall.

"There really is no evidence that psychiatrists who use techniques to recover memories provide effective therapy. There are objections to all the methods—hypnosis, age regression, guided imagery, whatever. There's always the chance that the therapist has suggested the answer, that the memory is not real."

Dave listened, working on a roasted chicken breast that suddenly seemed too dry.

When he had no response, Jennifer continued, "She used hypnosis, right?"

"More like relaxation," he said and stabbed a red potato.

"Almost the same thing. The American Psychological Association and the Canadian Psychiatric Association both decided that hypnosis should only be used for forensic investigation. They didn't think it has a place in therapy."

"I took Psych One-Oh-One too, and I don't remember hearing that."

"I looked it up."

"Well, in a sense my memory is a forensic one."

A clatter of dishes made them both look at the serving line, where a student was bent over retrieving the remains of a platter. He'd also scattered a salad.

"But your problem is headaches," Jennifer said. "The

memories may be false, the result of suggestion. In your case, your dream is the suggestion. You told the doctor your dream. She interpreted it and led you down that path. Then you elaborated on it. There's no evidence that dream interpretation recovers memories."

Dave ate more potato as he mulled over Jennifer's arguments. He couldn't totally disagree with her concerns, but he knew his memories were real. "The problems with false memories, if I remember the same lectures you attended, mostly had to do with recall of sexual abuse, mostly in females. Suggestion could lead to remembering things that never happened. But this has to do with murder of a family member, one of the categories where suppressed memory is most prevalent. Dr. Ellington didn't do any leading. I just recalled that John Redford was present the afternoon my brother and his friend were killed."

"Well, I have my doubts. And you should, too."

That evening, Dave's dream was a throwback to the earliest one. He was in a familiar field in bright, blinding sunlight. His brother and Carter lay motionless. Another figure, dark and big, with what seemed to be a halo, stood close to him. Dave screamed, pounded on the monster, and ran, clutching something in his fist as he struggled downhill, plunging through the same rainbow mushrooms that exploded at his legs and arms and into his face. Bogged down, slipping and falling, he sensed the killer gaining on him.

Chapter 27

Spring

March 1995, Norwich:

He sat alone in a shabby bar an hour west of Norwich, nursing a shot and chasing the amber liquid with beer. A single hanging flood lamp cast a centered spot of illumination on the brown table. Only his hand entered the light to encircle the pilsner glass on the cork coaster. The rest of the man stayed in darkness, his features hidden by a midnight blue cap pulled down and a murky jacket, collar pulled up. Not that the TV-addicted bartender or the stool birds gave a damn about him. Or that it mattered if they did. He grabbed the whiskey and sipped, letting the burn caress his throat.

Drinking usually quelled his urges. Not tonight. The impulse, more compelling than sex, had hit him in the woods. Over a year earlier, he'd satisfied his need with the carnival guy, and no one had noticed him. The cop hadn't pulled him over, and even if he'd written down the tag number, it would have done him no good. Whatever satisfaction the killer had felt since then had vanished. He needed…something. Not the thrill. A balance, something to even the score, justice. He tasted the last of the whiskey and took a mouthful of beer.

Deep voices rose and fell in another room, and billiard

balls clacked periodically. He glanced at the dirty window. It had grown dark, and he had work to do. He drained the beer, stuck a bill under his glass, and left.

ↄ૭ↄ૭

Tim, a Norwich High School senior, found the forest road outside of Norwich and eased the pickup into ruts littered with fallen branches. The teenager brushed wavy brown hair from his eyes and felt the wheels spin, spitting gravel toward the thick pines. Fields above the road no longer held crops or livestock, and the housing development on the hilltop had stopped growing years back. This was an isolated spot, perfect for a spring party.

Spruce branches, seeking to reclaim the road space, slapped against the truck sides. In the back of the vehicle, Rob, the class clown, held on amidst cases of beer, sleeping bags, backpacks, and a carton with food. Tall and wide, he made for good ballast as he grasped the side of the truck with one hand and a beer with the other. The truck bounced in a dip, splashing beer in his face.

Rob cursed and guzzled the rest. "Slow the fuck down. We're wasting the beer," he yelled into the open sliding window.

Tim eased off the gas and settled in the center of his seat, pushing back against Stephanie who'd shifted into him on the last bump. "Then quit opening them," he yelled.

The truck slowed, passing hemlock and young white pine, as it made its way up the hill. Even at the reduced speed it vibrated, causing Steph, a small curvy blonde, to press against him. He liked it. Warm and soft. But firm.

"How long 'till we're there? How long?" Laura, the other cab passenger, asked.

"Yeah. I gotta pee," Steph said.

Tim grimaced. "A few more minutes. Just hold it. My father will kill me if this thing smells of piss."

"What's so special about this place? What?" Laura asked, adjusting the Yankees cap over her coppery hair.

Rob stuck his arm through the back window, his fist holding a crushed beer can. "What's so special? Christ, what isn't? Dancing midgets, talking bears, this guy who eats with his feet. Flesh-eating squirrels, ghosts and ghouls, you name it. All kinds of stories."

Steph pushed the arm away from her head. "Dancing midgets huh? Is this place safe?"

"Sure," Tim said. "It's a great campsite surrounded by empty fields and spooky forest, with a huge fire pit, logs to sit on, and plenty of firewood. After a couple of beers you won't care where we are." Tim had heard about the site from his buddy, Jeff, who said he had to try it.

He'd met Jeff, a high-school dropout, working in a hunting supply store. They hit it off, and the guy became Tim's booze supplier. Jeff moved on to other jobs: at a gas station, on a road crew, and doing things that had him nervous about cops, all of which made Tim admire him as a rebel. Tim didn't have a phone number or an address for Jeff, but he could always find him sitting on the hood of his gold Camaro in the parking lot of the Cole Muffler shop, a local teen hangout. The place had more cars in the lot after business hours than during.

Once Tim got into Jeff's social circle, he discovered it wasn't wise to ignore the guy's advice.

The road widened and dead-ended. Tim parked and jumped from the cab. "Move your asses and get a fire going. There's drinking to do!"

As Steph darted into the woods for privacy, Rob passed supplies from the back of the truck. Tim, small and wiry, grabbed a couple of sleeping bags in one hand and an unlit lantern in the other, and started along a narrow, pine straw path. Behind him, Rob lugged the tent and a case of beer. Next came Laura, the elf-like girl called Echo behind her back because she always ended her statements with a word or phrase she'd already used. She carried the food. Steph was last, having returned from her call of nature to pick up a backpack and a gym bag.

The group emerged from trees into a grassy area and climbed to the campsite where a circle of rocks and logs marked the fire pit. The site was fairly level, but above it rose a slope filled with trees and overgrown shrubs. Down-hill, beyond a field surrounded by barbed wire, loomed a dark thicket.

Steph put down her stuff, tossed back her long blonde hair, and rotated slowly in a circle. "Holy crap, I know this place. This is where those murders happened. My father talked about it years later at the dinner table."

"Really, at dinner? Really?" Echo said.

Stephanie poked Laura's shoulder. "Detective Parker Holmes called it his toughest case. He talked about it more than once. Made it clear that the unsolved crime bugged the hell out of him. Two boys were killed with rocks. Spooked everyone." She pointed up the hill. "He mentioned an old syrup still. I bet that wood pile is the last of it."

Laura dropped her backpack near a log and sat down. "I kinda remember that story from something my mom said when I was eight. Warning me not to go somewhere. Kinda."

"What difference does it make where or when an old murder took place?" Tim set the Coleman lantern on a stump. He was the ringleader who'd convinced Rob and the girls that it was a time to celebrate the official start of spring by ignoring the cold and staying out. Actually it was a great night for camping—the air was cool, but warmer than usual for spring. Beer, a joint or two, and the touchy-feely game would make it perfect. He really didn't want to spend time on an old police case. "Besides," he said, "you don't know exactly where it happened, and it's ancient history."

"But murderers like to return to the scene of the crime, right?" Rob said, smiling. "To re-live stuff. To feel the thrill again. Better stay close, girls. Real close." He untied the tent bag and spread the contents in the flat area near the lantern. A balled up white sock tumbled from a nylon fold. He sniffed and tossed it back into the bag. "My favorite sock. Been missing since August." He emptied the sack of stakes.

Laura grabbed the hammer and waved the tool at him. "Don't start with your stupid, scary stories. I sure don't want to think about a murderer. Especially him coming back to his spot." She positioned a stake at the corner of the tent site and pounded four times. "No—scary—stories— stupid."

"How do you know the killer was a he?" Rob asked.

"Women kill with poison, not rocks," Laura said, pounding the tent stake one more time. "I suppose in a pinch they could use a hammer to kill."

"I'll protect you, Laura. You can even share my sleeping bag," Rob said.

"Yuk, cooties. I don't like cooties."

℘৩℘৩

He left the bar and stepped quickly to his truck in the graveled lot. Once inside, with the engine running, he had another urge. He wanted to touch the mushrooms again, to see and feel the multicolored caps. With the rain and warmer weather, they'd grown faster than in the past ten springs. This year, there'd be plenty. He'd seen a few there on his last outing, and now there would be more. He knew where the patch of fungi would reappear, as reliable as dandelions. They always appeared near where he'd heard the teens in the store say they'd be camping. He could kill two birds with one stone.

℘৩℘৩

The sun dipped below the western ridge, coloring the sky pink for a moment, and then dusk was upon the teenagers. A band of clouds formed over the same ridge, but the sky over the campsite was clear, and the first stars bloomed in the darkening canopy.

It wasn't really dark, but Tim lit the lantern. As it hissed to life, he opened the valve fully and then pumped air into the fuel chamber. A comforting white light lit the area. The tent was up, the sleeping bags unrolled, and the beer was flowing. As if in celebration, Rob started dancing like a Hollywood Indian. He pranced about the fire in the lantern light, whooping sporadically with his hand held up, forming a bird beak.

"Freaky," Laura said. "You're a freak."

"A free spirit. And that's not all." Rob stopped and pulled a small plastic bag from his pocket. "A couple hits of this stuff, and we'll all be dancing." Rob waggled the bag a few times and then sat down on the log next to Laura. He rolled a joint and lit it, inhaling, and then passed it to her.

Tim took the bag, rolled his own joint, and brought it to life. He sucked and handed it to Steph. Conversation gave way to sweet smoke, the hiss of the lantern, and the chuff and sizzle of the fire.

Laura told a story about her father working as a stage-hand at Woodstock and how he'd made a Christmas tree ornament from a souvenir light bulb. Tim had trouble listening. The dope had hit him harder than he thought it would. The fire danced in his vision, jumping back and forth, making him feel a bit sick. And Laura wouldn't shut up. He didn't really care about her father. He was even losing interest in getting into Steph's pants. She was being a bitch.

Apparently Rob also hated the tale. "That's a bunny of a story, Laura," he said, dropping an empty beer can. "You should tell it more often."

Laura stared. "Screw you. What the hell is your problem, screwball?"

"Nothing." Rob's head shook and his eyes blinked, the black orbs of his pupils reflecting the flickering firelight. "I was just ribbing you."

"Why don't you both cool it?" Steph said. "Don't go and spoil my mellow."

Tim, his head spinning from the weed, stood abruptly, lost his balance, and fell over the log.

"Nice ass plant. Real nice," Laura squealed.

Tim thought of a pig squeaking. He got up without saying a word and went a little ways up the hill. The light had faded to grayness, still bright enough to see the slope leading down to the trees. He gazed into the thicket.

Rob joined him and turned toward the trees, his face changing from weed-happy to perplexed. "I thought I saw something," he said, eyes on the forest. "You said this place was in the middle of nowhere, didn't you?"

"Nowhere, right," Tim said. "No houses, no farms, no teachers, no parents."

Rob pointed beyond the fenced field. "Well, I think we've got company."

"I don't see anything. What do you think you saw?"

"A light."

Steph and Laura had been listening. Steph stared into the trees. "Probably just a reflection of moonlight on something. The weed's playing tricks on you. Or maybe just an ember from the fire."

Clouds had moved in, keeping in the warmth. They parted to expose the half moon that silvered the ground. Tim tried to remember what had been around the area when he'd camped somewhere nearby years back with his father. Not here, but not far away. Only fields, trees, a stream, but no houses close by. He scanned the trees, shrugged, and returned to the fire.

Rob adjusted his cap and came back to sit next to Steph. "It's dope. Not acid. And I didn't see any dancing, pink elephants."

"The light, was it like a flashlight?" Laura asked, her pitch too high.

"I'm not sure." He opened another can and drained half of it. "It wasn't steady like a flashlight but the beam could have been moving between trees. It didn't seem as white as a flashlight. More wispy."

"Maybe it was the Will o' the Wisp," Steph said.

"Will o' the what?" Tim sipped beer, spilling some on his shirt. His hand shook.

"Will o' the Wisp. I read about it in some magazine. People always see these trails of light dancing around over swamps and in the woods. Sort of blue and ghostlike. Used to scare the crap out of people."

"So what is it?" Rob asked.

"Something to do with gas being released I think. Decomposing trees and animals. I don't know why it lights up. Maybe bacteria that glow."

"Sounds spooky," Laura said. "Spoooookie." The last didn't quite make it to humor.

Tim needed to change the conversation before the girls wanted to go home. "Enough of this crap. Let's drink." He fished a can from the case and tossed it to Rob. The girls sipped their beers tentatively, glancing into the dusky trees.

The moment of fear seemed to pass. Until—

Laura jumped. "What the hell! What was that? Hell."

From the dim woods had come a snap. Not loud, but distinct.

"Just a branch falling," Rob said.

"Could be a bear," Steph said. "It's spring and they're awake and hungry."

"Bull. No bear's gonna come near a fire," Tim said, reaching down to add a branch to the flames. "And we need some more wood, something we should have taken care of when there was more light."

"That's why we have flashlights." Rob patted the nine-volt model beside him. "I'll grab a couple of big logs before we get too buzzed. We'll be in no mood to leave the fire after that."

"There's plenty of light with the moon," Steph said, slipping on a hooded fleece. She aimed her own light into the brush. "We girls can go up the hill. I see some good-sized branches there. You guys go down to the trees and find some logs that won't burn fast. I'm cold."

"The walk will warm you," Rob said. "You realize you're sending us in after the bear."

"It was probably a squirrel," Steph said. She followed a slow-moving Laura into the gloom of the slope.

Tim sure as hell didn't want to go down the hill. He was born to supervise. "I'll stay here. To guard the beer and the girls. If you need help, give a yell." He saluted with his can, happy to let the muscled guy bring firewood.

Rob frowned at the departing girls. "Don't go too far from the fire. And watch where you step."

Chapter 28

Slaughter

Rob reached the rusted barbed wire that separated the field from the forest. Moonlight bathed the field, but the trees inside stood in inky stillness. He was still within calling distance of the campsite and, after swinging the flashlight beam back and forth, yelled to Tim, "I don't see any logs on the edge. I'll go in a bit."

A dozen paces into the woods, he found a four-inch diameter log as long as his leg. The outside was firm, and he figured it, and another like it, along with the wood already at the campsite, would keep them warm until they piled into the tent and used each other for heat. He picked his way farther and came to the edge of a wet sunken area, dozens of feet across. Another good-looking log lay on the slope, and he bent to grab it. He stopped when he saw the colors caught in the flashlight beam.

"What the hell are those?" he asked out loud.

A cluster of quarter-sized mushrooms glimmered shiny greens and pinks. As the flashlight moved, reds and yellows burst from the periphery. He eyed the display in silence, feeling isolated.

He answered his own question, again speaking aloud. "Toadstools, I guess. Pretty wild. Like nothing I've ever seen." He bent and plucked off the cap of the largest mushroom and cupped it in his hand. When he turned the umbrella upside down, black powder puffed from the dark webbing underneath. He dropped the fungus and stood up. "I thought you guys grew only during the summer." He bent and grabbed another mushroom with a bright orange cap veined with blue streaks. "I wonder if you'd burn."

A twig snapped behind him, and he stiffened, aiming the light through the trees. "Tim, that you?" When there was no reply, he answered himself. "Just a branch. Stop imagining things, you idiot."

The flashlight beam reflected from a black swirling mist that seemed to move toward him. He thought first of fog, but realized it was too dry. *Maybe just my imagination.* "Just grab the friggin' logs and get back to the girls and the beer."

He hefted the chunk of wood and started walking to the fence.

The dark-clad man heard Rob's monolog and saw his flashlight as he entered the mushroom area. He killed his own penlight and moved closer, using large trees as a shield, and watched the speaker, a boy in his mid-teens, head toward him carrying two logs. Smiling, he opened the Buck knife.

ᘒᘒ

Relaxing by the fire, Tim snarfed another beer, feeling mellow and quite content to sit while others poked around for firewood. He downed the last swallow as the girls returned, dragging several limbs, each inches thick.

"So you sent Rob in alone to get wood," Steph said, handing him the camp saw. "Your turn to work."

Tim groaned and rose with exaggerated slowness. He accepted the tool, feeling a bout of dizziness and guilt, for he hadn't thought of Rob or of how long he'd been gone. The idea of sawing wood was as appealing as a ten-mile jog, but he deserved the punishment. Rob was overdue. He trimmed the wood into two-foot pieces and threw four onto the guttering fire. Embers flared, and the wood caught, but the flames hardly widened the circle of growing gloom.

"Where is he?" Steph asked and kicked a rusty beer can. "He should have been back by now. Did he get lost?" She stared down the hill.

A breeze swayed the treetops, and high branches creaked. From some distant place came a sound that Tim couldn't identify. He dropped the saw and waited for what he knew was coming.

"I heard something," Laura said. "That way. I heard it." She zipped up her fleece and, holding a flashlight in front of her, faced the woods where Rob should be.

"I didn't hear anything," Steph said. "What did it sound like?"

"A yell. Maybe human. Could have been a yell."

"Oh, God," Steph said. "We should have gathered wood earlier. It's really dark in the trees." She turned to Tim. "You have to check it out."

Tim stared at the black stand of trees and it struck him: he knew them. His friend Arachnophobic Arnie had told him about fleeing from the area, screaming about spiders, claiming the little bastards, quick as the wind, had attacked him, trying to skitter into his ear and lay their awful little eggs. At first Tim blamed the movie *Star Trek 2, The Wrath of Khan* where an extraterrestrial bug crawled out of some poor bastard's ear. But Arnie hadn't seen the movie.

Arnie didn't forget the spider thing. Months later, he broke his ankle and was sitting outside with his cast. Suddenly a few spiders—probably just babies—emerged from under the chaise lounge and headed for the cast toe hole. No reason to panic. Just brush the little fellas off. With his mouth forming a silent O, Arnie jumped up, threw himself into the pool, and sank. It had taken two people to fish him out, and drugs to control the panic.

The woods had changed Arnie, who was pretty much a tough-ass before his experience. Tim was convinced something spooky lurked there. Now he had to go after Rob. His stomach churned, and his mind rebelled, but he'd run out of excuses.

"Move your lazy butt," Steph said, her hands on her hips, like a teacher confronting laziness.

"All right, already. Maybe we should all go down there and find out what's holding him up."

"You go. I'm not scrounging around," Laura said. "At least get closer and yell so he'll hear you."

Tim wondered who she was trying to convince. "All right. Keep the fire burning." He went to his pack and fished out a heavy-duty flashlight. With his back to the girls, he felt for the pistol that Jeff, his Cole Muffler buddy, said he needed.

Tim made sure the safety was on and shoved the weapon down the front of his pants, covering it with his sweatshirt. With his hand on the handle, he headed for the woods, fumbling his way over the barbed wire fences. At the edge of the trees, a cool breeze swept across his neck.

Minutes passed. Steph paced, stopping at every turn and peering into the gloom. Laura added the rest of the wood to the fire. She poked at it and then sat hunched forward, her sweatshirt hood up. More minutes crept by. Five, then ten.

"What could be keeping them?" Steph asked from the ridge. "Are they doing this on purpose? Playing some trick?"

Before Laura could answer, they heard a distant pop. Then another.

"What was that?" Laura stood and threw back her hood. "A firecracker? What?"

Steph stopped moving. "Gunfire."

"Do you even know what a gun sounds like? Do you?" Laura said.

"My father is a cop."

From afar, a light beam danced briefly against tree trunks and high limbs. Abruptly it disappeared. The girls heard thrashing sounds, snapping branches, and maybe grunts. Then a clear and unmistakable high-pitched scream. Followed by disturbing silence. A gust of wind, strong enough to bend saplings, pushed the girls toward the forest.

"Should we go to them?" Laura asked, her voice breaking. "Maybe they need help. Maybe we should go down there."

Steph shook her head. "Shit, no. What the hell can we do? My father says the best defense is to run." She grabbed Laura's sleeve and started pulling.

"Defense against what? We don't know there's any defending to do."

"We have to get help." Steph's voice had risen an octave. "Now, before whoever's down there finds us. If that was a gun we heard, we'd be stupid to go near it without a weapon."

"Maybe's someone hurt," Laura said. "We don't need a weapon to help someone who's hurt."

"Those were gunshots, you idiot. We need to get our asses out of here." Steph grabbed Tim's pack and dumped it on the ground. The truck keys jangled and she grabbed them. Pointing the flashlight toward to path, she started toward the truck. "Stay close."

Laura glanced down the hill and followed.

ↄ৯ↄ৯

An hour after the girls had made it out of the area, Parker Holmes, Steph's father, and two county deputies were searching the woods for the missing boys. It didn't take long to find them. Rob and Tim were close together, throats slashed. Both boys had been repeatedly struck in the face with something large and blunt. Features were obliterated, but the post mortem injuries had not bled. The victims were naked from the waist up, their chests scarred with triple tracks, as if a small rake had been dragged across the nipples and navel. These scratches, too, were bloodless.

The state police arrived an hour later. When the medical examiner moved Tim's body, they found a handgun. Further searching that night and the next day did not produce the missing shirts.

Chapter 29

Crisis

March 1995, Princeton:

Dave coped well from Thanksgiving to March, even though his several sessions with Dr. Ellington did not uncover new memories or new detail in those he did have. He still had dreams, but they were not as frequent or as harrowing. Academically, he was at least surviving. Socially, he was still hanging with Jennifer, more as a friend than as a love interest. His interest was there, but hers had cooled, at least to his male way of seeing things.

On a Saturday morning that welcomed the onset of spring, he woke from a new dream, another one of those in which he was a witness, not a participant. His arms and legs ached, as if he'd spent the eight hours in his bunk running. He stretched to ease the tightness in his calves, then raised and lowered his knees. At last, he climbed to the floor, ignoring the dull ache across his forehead. He tried to put the dream out of his mind as he spent the day studying, but the images haunted him. Only after he did some serious drinking that evening did he forget what he'd seen.

When he finally got to sleep after midnight Saturday, the dream was there again, a repeat of the one he'd had the night before, the one that made no sense and which he'd labored to ignore. He woke Sunday morning with an even clearer picture of what he was seeing. In the vision, he was the impotent witness watching a big man kill. His silent screaming did nothing to halt the carnage, and he woke as the murderer finished with the second victim. Aside from the fact that he was only a floating observer, this couldn't be a vision of his brother's murder. The victims were bigger than his brother and Carter, and agitated girls talked nearby.

How could he ignore the potent dream twice?

Standing, he remembered something else, maybe the real reason he was frightened—the killer knew him. There was no doubt in Dave's mind that the killer in his dream was the one who murdered his brother years ago. Of course the beast would recognize him. The killer knew exactly who Dave was.

The quad was quiet because, as usual, Dave was the last to rise. With muddled thinking, he wandered through the rituals of bathroom and dressing.

He made his way through the heart of campus to his eating club for Sunday breakfast-brunch. Though he wasn't really hungry, he needed company.

Past venerable dormitories and the art museum, he reached McCosh Walk, feeling better the longer he wandered. Perhaps his attempt to not think left room for the unexpected. Spring was winning the battle against winter brown. At Prospect House, the president's residence, green buds filled trees, golden forsythia erupted from corners, and yellow dandelions claimed the lawns. Groundskeepers had heaped mulch around trees. Dave saw forest duff and shuddered.

He ignored the occasional student walking in the opposite direction and crossed Washington Street. His path took him past the Wilson School of International Studies whose many vertical white columns further raised his spirits. A couple hundred yards down Prospect Street he came to his eating club, Tiger Inn. Future members had been invited to sample the Sunday fare.

No Frisbee players occupied the front lawn. Inside, the

smell of bacon had managed to overcome that of stale beer. A murmur of conversation led him toward the dining room.

Few college students relished morning conviviality, and his club seemed to select against morning risers. Those who'd managed to stumble in formed islands of disheveled hair, glum faces, and squinting eyes, as social as lone bull elephants on the Serengeti. Dave deposited his backpack at the table where his roommates were eating.

A senior girl sat at the next table, hidden by sunglasses, nursing a coffee, and reading a paper. She'd celebrated her twenty-first birthday with bacchanalian fervor the night before and was paying the price. A trio of silent lacrosse players ate Danish. Two students with visiting parents had wisely positioned them at a distance with their backs to the morose scene.

Dave approached the stack of trays, took one, and grabbed coffee and juice at the beverage station. He added a plate with eggs and sausage and joined Todd and Jabe who were working on hash browns, bacon, and too-yellow scrambled eggs. Neither greeted him.

Todd poked at his eggs and observed, "Brunch is a pleasant-sounding concept, more pleasant in theory than in practice."

"My soul remains hungry," Jabe said and shoveled in the last of his potatoes. His appetite never entirely waned. "As will yours, based on your breakfast selection."

Dave sat, hearing the clack of careening pool balls and occasional whoops drifting down the staircase of the entry hall. In the front room, speakers sprayed soothing Haydn, a selection offered as penance for the previous evening's raucous rock. He took a deep breath and decided not to mention the dream, not to think about it.

Despite his hangover, Dave recalled the admonition to enjoy "the best years of your life." Reconstituted eggs were a small price to pay for the shelter of college life. Jabe and Todd babbled about something, but he tuned out the conversation.

The rustle of a newspaper at the next table caught his attention. Birthday girl held a New York paper with short stories and lots of photos. A big picture of two young men was on the front page. Dave's peace and idle musing vanished when he saw the headline.

MURDER RAMPAGE IN UPSTATE NEW YORK

He froze, his fingers squeezing the plastic cup until it splintered, spilling the remains of his orange juice.

"What the hell?" Jabe said. "Are you all right? You look like you've seen a ghost."

Dave wiped his hand and stood, continuing to stare at the headline. "Could I borrow that first section, please?"

"You can have it when I'm through with it," birthday girl said.

He remembered that she'd boasted that boxing was her favorite sport and feared she could do what she damn well pleased. At first, she didn't take her eyes from the paper. But when Dave bent to read the story below the headline, she looked up, probably to tell him to get the hell away. Apparently, his face changed her mind. "Here." She handed him the whole paper, grabbed her cup, and double-paced away.

He folded the paper and walked off. The club's Green Room, a lounge with green leather recliners, was empty. The wooden floor creaked as he passed through sunbeams streaming from the large muntined windows, setting dust motes tumbling. He sank into the first chair and closed his eyes. Distinguished alumni watched him from portraits on the mahogany-paneled walls.

The headline said upstate New York, but that was a huge area from Buffalo to Albany. The murder site probably had no connection to him. If he hadn't had the dream, it wouldn't have occurred to him that the story was relevant. But he had to know what happened and where.

When he gathered sufficient courage, he willed his eyes,

first to open, then to see the paper, then to read. As he did, heart thumps started. He stared at the name of the town: Norwich. The letters branded his retinas. A painful name, designating the town where he'd encountered evil, a place where creation seemed amiss. The events of that summer so long ago flooded back, not the details of what happened on the hill, but the aftermath of loss and pain. The memories always danced at the edges of his thoughts, eager to break in and take over. Like a stalking, jealous ex-lover obsessed with possession, refusing to let go. He put the paper down, unable to read more, unsure he could handle any details.

His stomach tensed with pain, and the pain became nausea. His emotional brain took over. More information was unnecessary. A new murder in the same town was a coincidence. Or the work of Satan. It made no difference. He should walk away.

His rational brain fought back. If the details of this murder were different, it was of no importance. But if the details were the same, his psyche might be forced to remember and his amnesia would vanish. He brought the paper up.

Double murder made the story front-page material. Teenage victims, well-liked and respected high school seniors, kids on a spring overnight camp-out meant a story that fed the presses. He read interpretively: two boys and two girls, probably drinking, smoking dope, and groping.

Nothing out of the ordinary. The boys had disappeared hunting for firewood and, when the girls heard a shot, they fled. That was all that the police would say officially, but some reporter had a source with a mouth that confirmed the booze and marijuana. Hardly surprising. Faces of both boys had been disfigured.

He stifled a scream. The article reviewed each teen's background, focusing on school activities. There were quotes from teachers, coaches, and friends, expressing shock and dismay. Nothing substantial. The reporter had done his best to dig up as much detail as possible in the short time before the article went to press.

The location shocked him—his hometown—and the mutilation of the victims stunned him. Then came anger. The reporter hadn't mentioned the similarity to a crime in the same location years earlier. Maybe that would surface later. Maybe the cops didn't want that out, although anyone who lived in Norwich would know. Or would they? Was he oversensitive? He tried to stand, felt lightheaded, and sat back down, his mind fighting the conclusion he didn't want to believe: his dream was about these killings. He denied that conclusion.

There could be no connection between his dream and this story, or between the murders of his brother and Carter and these two boys. Completely unrelated. He had dreamed of two victims, but that was because the human mind liked to embrace pairs of things. Or maybe it was trios.

But the faces of the victims had been destroyed, the same gruesome detail in the killing of the carnival worker the previous fall. That victim was a young man, and he'd been killed by repeated blows to the head. Did that include the face? Were those blows part of what killed him or were they post-death mutilation? Didn't that make a trio of murders, all with the same details?

He walked shakily toward the stairs and thought of another connection between his dream and the story: he'd heard girls' voices and there were two girls who got away.

The newspaper article did not pinpoint exactly where the bodies had been found. And Norwich was a town surrounded by forests and fields. All much alike. A local paper would have more details, including the exact location. Maybe even a map. He needed details.

He climbed to the second floor, his thinking jumbled, ignoring the club member who passed him. In the back hallway, he steadied himself against the wall, and then entered the computer room. A desk and chair, a monitor connected to a PC, and a printer occupied the space. He powered the system.

The University LAN might block porn sites, but a newspaper site would be no problem. He sat, startled by the squeak of the chair's wheels.

He signed in with his University ID and password. The system rejected him. He tried again and was denied again. He knew he had only one more chance before being locked out for an hour. Willing his fingers without the tremor, he typed, one finger at a time, his user name and password. This time it worked. The browser home page presented the University mascot, a tiger with penetrating yellow eyes. He used a news database to search for the terms "Norwich" and "murder" and found several hits. He hesitated to click on any link, but the need to know, to be sure, propelled him. If anything, the computer room was warmer than the dining room, but Dave felt chilled.

The first link was a summary from Associated Press that gave less information than the newspaper article had. The second link was to an article in a Syracuse paper. He read, his hand tapping on the desk. The initial paragraphs were no more detailed than those in the downstate paper: a loose account of what might have happened, who was involved, and how the bodies were found. He clicked on a link to follow the story for more detail.

There was a miniature map with an instruction to click to enlarge. His breath caught and his stomach tightened. This would answer his question. This would be enough. Just knowing where everything had happened. All he'd have to do was click on the map, enlarge it, and it would show where the killings took place—a location well away from his old house he hoped. Somewhere he had never been and would never go. With the cursor over the map, his finger hovered above the mouse button. He closed his eyes, the thump of his heart matching the tapping of the fingers of his left hand. His right index finger inched downward, and he heard the click of the mouse. At the same time, the computer whirred slightly as it retrieved the requested page.

His eyes remained closed, but images played in his mind. He saw himself with Scott lighting fireworks. The picture his brother and the scratching brambles came to him. Events of that afternoon coursed through his head in no particular order. One second, he was crashing back through the yard gate, tears streaming down his face, his mother and father trying to understand what had happened. The next second, he was stealing the matches off the mantel—he didn't know why. Then his father doctoring his wounds. Utter joy about the fireworks. Terror moments later.

He opened his eyes. His chest tightened and then felt hollow as if his heart had skipped—not a beat, but just skipped out. The enlarged map was a simple rendition of the highways surrounding Norwich. Route 23 was clearly marked, meandering through a valley and off towards other small towns. The red star on the graphic gave a much more precise location for the crime. Dave glanced at the scale of the map. It left little question where death had struck.

He knew what it meant. The man who murdered his brother was a serial killer and still lived in upstate New York, in or near Norwich.

Dave put his finger to the screen and slowly traced it along the highway east from Norwich. His finger moved lightly, coming to a stop on the rural road he had lived on. The red star was no more than a few miles from his house.

"The Sugar Shack," he breathed, his voice quivering. Memories came flooding back now even with his eyes open. He could picture the teenagers in the same spot, the crumpled Sugar Shack eerily preserved in its constant state of decay. The visions became mixed with those that had plagued him from his dream, the sense of larger victims, the dark threatening figure of the killer.

He shook his head to clear it, trying to understand what the hell was happening. It was one thing to slowly remember and dream about his brother's murder. But why should he dream about the murder of these boys, even if they occurred in the same place?

Then it struck him. He'd fallen asleep early on Friday,

not long after dark. His dream occurred when the murders were happening.

Dave's belief in science couldn't include distance cognition. He had to put that aspect aside—if it were true that he had somehow sensed the recent murders, he'd let a neuroscientist tell him how that could be. He focused on the idea that his brain was trying to remember something about his brother's murder. At least that could be explained. His repressed memories were fighting to surface.

He sent the article and the map to the printer. As the printer hummed in the corner, he considered what his dreams might be telling him. The mushrooms must exist in the area where the attack occurred. Sometimes the killing took place in the forest and sometimes in an open field. What about the cloth he saw in several dreams? Was that significant? It had to be. Something he would have to remember. He shut down the computer, clicked off the monitor, and stared at his reflection on the blank screen.

He had to understand the person in his dream. All he learned from his dreams was that the man was big and dark. There was also one dream about a halo—could that be hair? And a brimmed hat. At least one dream left him with the creepy feeling that the killer knew him. Then he remembered John Redford, the other boy present that day. Could that be who chased him? John was big for his age. But that made no sense. Redford was only a boy, a thirteen-year-old. The idea struck, clear and compelling. To free his memories, Dave had to go back to the site of his brother's murder, and he had to talk to John Redford.

Chapter 30

Plan

Colin watched his roommate during the week after he'd acted weird at brunch. Normally talkative, Dave became a zombie. He said little, ate alone, avoided Jennifer, and disappeared until after ten at night.

On Friday morning, Colin jogged to Lawrenceville and back, part of his conditioning routine preparing for med school and beyond. In anticipation of his career, he'd begun dealing with people in a diagnostic and prescriptive fashion, and Dave was a ripe target. Colin had recommended the campus psychiatrist. The sessions helped, even without unearthing repressed memories. But Dave stopped the visits. Maybe it was time to see the doctor again.

When Colin got back from his run, all his roommates were still in bed. He heard Dave moan, but that was not unusual, so he ignored it. He showered and went for food.

He was still eating when Todd and Jabe arrived at Tiger Inn. "Where's Dave?" Colin asked.

"Dave is up," Todd reported. "He rose after I made no effort to keep quiet as I dressed."

"Hell, you turned on the radio," Jabe said. "On purpose. Got me up, too."

"So how did he seem?" Colin took a bite of toast.

Todd and Jabe looked at each other before Todd spoke. "No change. Still quiet as a Basenji. Like he's trying to figure something out and doesn't want to be interrupted. When I asked if he wanted to catch some breakfast, he mumbled he'd eat later."

Colin stood and downed the last of his coffee. "I'll check on him."

∽∾∽∾

Dave was not in residence when Colin returned to the quad. With at least three hours reading to do, he pulled out a book and sat in front of the TV watching sports news. He was beginning to feel seriously guilty about the procrastination, when Dave rushed in, crossed to his room, and slammed the door. Rustling sounds and slamming drawers followed. *Now what?* He ignored the Syracuse-Providence game highlights and knocked on the bedroom door.

"What?" Dave asked, his tone matter-of-fact.

"May I enter your kingdom?"

Dave opened the door. Colin eyed the unchanged décor, posters of hairy-chested Jim Belushi in an *Animal House* toga and a dreadlocked Bob Marley smoking a cigar-sized joint, and Todd's contributions of Matisse and Picasso prints. The corkboard held a Playboy calendar, still showing September's Playmate-of-the-Month.

"You do realize that September was six months ago, right?

Dave continued stuffing clothes into a black tote bag whose soccer gear had been dumped on the floor. A long, orange sock lay on the lower bunk.

"Todd won't like that stinky sock on his bed."

Dave ignored the remark.

"So what are you doing? You look like shit, and you're making a mess."

"Gotta go somewhere." Dave pulled underwear, tee shirts, a pair of jeans, and a sweatshirt from a drawer and crammed them into the nearly full bag.

"Got time for a brew?"

No answer.

"Where are you headed? And why in such a hurry?"

"You wouldn't believe me if I told you," Dave said. "You'd think I'm an idiot."

"I already think you're an idiot. Go ahead and tell me."

Dave shook his head. "Just something I have to check out."

Colin left and came back with two beers. He thrust a can in Dave's direction.

"I shouldn't," Dave said. But he took the offering, popped the lid, and downed half the contents. "Maybe that will settle my nerves."

"Your nerves need settling?" Colin threw the mud-stained sock toward a corner clothes heap and sat on the lower bunk. "Talk to me, man. We've been friends since freshman year. I already know you're a nut job. Nothing you're gonna say will change that. Unless you tell me you want to quit drinking. That would be crazy."

Dave closed his eyes and leaned his head against the upper bunk. "I've got to go home. For my peace of mind."

"To Cortland? In the middle of the semester?"

"Not Cortland. Norwich."

Colin wondered what the hell Dave could be seeking in a place that held so much sorrow. "That's no longer your home."

Dave filled his lungs and exhaled slowly.

"So why are you heading to Norwich?"

Dave fished a pair of shoes from the closet. "You remember how effed up I was the other night when everyone was partying out on the lawn? Well, I never said why. You know about the dreams, the dread. Something new has come up."

"What?"

"I dreamed of new murders in Norwich. As they were happening. Last Friday. Again on Saturday."

"Like a premonition? Is that what you're saying?"

"A premonition involves seeing things before they occur. This was an at-the-same-time vision."

Colin considered the notion. "Interesting. Co-cognition. Like a twin seeing from afar what a sibling is experiencing. Even knowing the exact moment of a sibling's death."

"Maybe." Dave zipped closed the sports bag and steadied himself with a hand on the bed. He pulled a crumpled sheet of paper from his pocket and handed it to his roommate.

Colin scanned the printout of the *Syracuse Post-Standard* web site. "Surely this is a coincidence. Murders do happen, even in the same town more than once. Your dream was probably based on something you heard or read."

"Couldn't have been. I went to bed early last Friday after several Jack Daniels. It happened on Friday after I zonked."

"Still could be a coincidence. You've been dreaming about murders for years."

"I was asleep early on a Friday night—truly a rare event—when it goes down. Is that a coincidence?"

"Yes," Colin said with more conviction than he felt.

Dave met his roommate's eyes. "But I dreamed of two older victims, mutilated just like what was done to my brother. And the location is the last straw." He pulled another piece of paper from his back pocket.

Colin eyed a black and white map with a few roads and a centered dark star. "What's this?"

"Where these two teenagers were killed. Where my brother died. Or mighty close to it."

"You can't know that. How accurate could this be? Hell, the area shown is large, and there's no detail. The police probably wanted to keep the detail fuzzy."

Dave's shoulders slumped. "I spent the week asking myself the same questions, raising the same points, trying to convince myself it wasn't true. I know it's the same spot."

"So what? It's not like we're talking the middle of nowhere here. Just a camping spot a few miles out of town. A bunch of teens got drunk and ran into foul play." Colin went to Dave's desk and deposited the papers. "Besides, didn't you say when you were drunk that some guy named John Redford went nuts and probably killed Scott?"

"I don't remember saying that."

"That guy's still in a mental hospital, right? He couldn't have anything to do with these new killings."

Dave grimaced. "I think I saw him at my high school graduation."

Colin walked slowly from the bedroom, circled the common area, and came back to Dave. "You imagined him. Why would Redford be there?"

"Don't know. Why do murders with the same pattern go down in the same spot in the same small town?"

"Thousands of murders occur each year," Colin said. "Eventually two will happen in the same spot, especially if you wait twelve years. That's the definition of a coincidence, something totally random that seems too improbable to be random. It's also why the Law of Large Numbers explains dreams. If six billion people dream more than one dream each night and some see an airplane crash or train mishap or boat sinking, there are enough disasters in real life that a dream will coincide with an event. As for murders in Norwich, you're already so deeply involved—"

"Exactly—"

Colin made a stop sign with his hand. "Nothing good will come of poking around back there."

"I've never gone back." Dave's voice was a whisper. "After my brother died, I never went back up that hill. I went to stay with my grandparents. My parents dealt with whatever they had to deal with. The next thing I knew we were packing to move to Cortland. I never went back to the Sugar Shack."

"It's just a heap—tetanus waiting to happen."

"I want to see John Redford, if I can find him, and walk the area. In all the times we went up to the Sugar Shack, we only went into the little forest below the Shack once or twice. Just ignored it like it wasn't even there. I think it repelled us. If some memory is trying to surface when I dream, the forest may trigger its recovery."

Colin clamped his head with his hands. "Based on that theory, you intend to drive your ass all the way back to Norwich, probably stealing Todd's car, seriously pissing him off. The dream stuff—magical toadstools, murderous trolls, and clowns—don't exist. Just trees. And you won't get near a crime scene roped off with yellow police tape—"

The phone rang. Colin went into the common room to get it. "It's for you," he called. "It's Jennifer."

Dave took his time and, when he took the receiver, acted as if he'd picked up a gym weight. "Hi, Jen. What's up?" He listened, nodding. "I know we haven't gotten together this week. I've been real busy. But I can't do anything until Sunday. I have a paper due and haven't started it, not even the reading."

Colin cast his eyes to the ceiling.

"Right, I'm really inundated," Dave continued.

Colin heard rumbling from the phone as Dave stood listening for more than a minute.

"Okay. I'll call you Saturday evening to let you know how I'm doing." Dave paced in a small circle. "I'll pick someplace and call you…Great…Bye." He gently deposited the phone on its cradle and went back to his room. A moment passed and he yelled, "Damn, I shouldn't have said that."

Colin entered the bedroom. "So you can't even tell your girlfriend."

"I'm not sure she's my girlfriend." Dave fished in Todd's desk for the Pathfinder keys. They were in their regular spot because Todd was obsessive-compulsive. The keys disappeared into a pocket.

Back in the common room, Colin went to the fridge and extracted another two beers.

"You know you're ruining my fucking Friday. I was all fired up to watch some b-ball tonight and get a little liquored. It was setting up to be a great day. And now this."

Dave took the beer. "I'm sorry."

"Todd will kick my ass."

"Tell him you were unconscious." Dave stared out the window into the courtyard where slate paths crisscrossed the greening grass and bud-laden branches swayed in the breeze.

"Oh that's good. I let you go off on a wild goose chase into the forests of upstate New York, and I tell Todd a lie." Colin flopped on the couch.

"Tell him you told me not to go, and I ignored you," Dave said, still staring out the window. "That's the truth."

"Why don't you hold off a bit? Give it a few weeks. Wait until break. A few of us will go with you. We'll make a little trip out of it. Maybe cruise up to Montreal. I hear there are more strippers than pigeons up there."

Dave laughed. "Not Montreal again. Just because the rugby team brags about lap dances doesn't mean they happen." The smile vanished. "I've got to go now."

"Shit." Colin drank some beer. "Then let me come with you. We can split the driving."

"This is something I need to do by myself."

"What about classes? Where are you planning to stay?"

"This won't take long. I'll be back tomorrow or Sunday. I won't miss any classes. I'll find a Motel Six."

Colin sniffed. "You really don't want me to come, do you? Okay. At least tell me what your plan is. That way I'll know when to get worried." Colin waited, but Dave didn't answer. "You don't have a plan do you? You're just thinking to hop in a car and drive north."

"I'll figure it out on my way. For twelve years that afternoon has consumed me," Dave slipped on a fleece. "I play it back over and over again. I want to know what Redford was doing. What could I have done differently?"

"You were eight years old. A kid. You could only run for your life."

Dave picked up the gym bag and walked into the hallway. "There has to be some reason why I dreamed about these new murders in the same place." He pulled the door closed behind him.

Colin watched Dave from the window, unable to fit the facts into some rational, logical story. He reread the newspaper account of the slayings and shook his head. The dreaming might be a sick brain trying to heal itself. But this crap about seeing crimes as they were happening. That made no sense. Neither did hallucinations and psychedelic patterns in the forest. Similar murders in the same place were hard to dismiss as mere coincidence, so he could understand Dave's thinking.

Should he let anyone know what Dave was doing? He'd have to tell Todd the car was gone. Club members would ask where Dave was, and a yarn about studying wouldn't fly. Better to say he wasn't feeling well. Had a touch of the flu—that was always lurking on campus. He'd have to stick with the lie Dave had made up for Jennifer, but what if she showed up to check on him? That would be a problem.

He'd opened his book and started reading when another stark thought struck: the murderer was still in Norwich, and Dave was heading straight toward him.

Chapter 31

Dave marched down Elm Drive to the south parking lot, trying to analyze what he was doing. Colin thought his dreams were caused by drinking more than a few before he went to bed. Even if drinking stimulated the dream, it didn't account for how he could see something as it was happening. If that was the truth, he had to understand it.

When doubt threatened to turn him back, he counted his steps past gargoyles on stone-faced dorms. He crossed the street twice to avoid oncoming students, hoping he didn't meet anyone he knew, and jumped when he heard a familiar female voice. But when he turned around, Jennifer wasn't there. If she had been, he would have blurted out what he was doing and why. She would have tried to talk him out of it and was far better at persuasion than Colin.

A train whistle distracted him. The Dinky, the small train that ran between the Princeton Station and Princeton Junction, was beginning its trip, as reliable as—

The analogy that came to mind was his dreams.

His stride lengthened and became faster in the large lot where Todd always parked. He scuffed on loose gravel past the first ten rows occupied by University vehicles and employees' cars and discovered the Pathfinder two dozen rows farther on. Todd's golf clubs were in the cargo area, and for a brief moment, he considered dropping them off at the dorm. Instead, he gunned the engine and headed out.

Driving on the graveled lot made him think how the Norwich partying kids had reached the camping site. Must have driven in because the newspaper mentioned that the girls had escaped in a truck. That meant they used a route different from his neighborhood, which had no road connection to the Sugar Shack.

A kiosk guarded the junction of Elm Drive and Faculty road. A security guard with a paperback came out as Dave careened toward him. The man's slow-it-down hand signal got Dave's heart racing. He hoped the cop was one of the nice friendly greeters he was supposed to be. All he needed was more questions. The guard waved with a book that appeared to be the Dean Koontz novel Dave had just finished. He liked Koontz and hoped he continued to write.

Distraction from the guard was brief, replaced by the thought as he headed for Route 206 that Colin had been right. Dave lacked a plan. But he'd spent hours with maps of upstate New York, his finger tracing the lines of small rural routes that crisscrossed the area like spider-webs. One road came close to the Sugar Shack. All he wanted to do was visit the site and see, with his own eyes, what was there. Maybe he'd park near his old house and walk, taking the path he'd crashed down panicked and in tears a dozen years back. That was his plan.

As Dave gassed up an hour from campus, his anxiety peaked and again he considered and rejected the notion of turning back. The ride gave him time to decide what he would do, and, by the time the Pathfinder crossed into New York from Pennsylvania hours later, he'd settled into a hazy, passive state, driving on autopilot.

He took the two-lane Route 12 north from its junction with I-81, passing herds of cattle nosing around hay bales, freshly plowed fields ready for corn, and farmhouses ever in need of paint. North of Binghamton, three out of four plots were farms. Each with a run-down barn that reminded him of the Sugar Shack, whose ruins, he hoped, might jog his memory. If that didn't work, he'd just head back to school. Now, the closer he got to Norwich, the more stupid his plan and the whole idea seemed.

Not much had changed along Route 12. Cows that probably still outnumbered people stared as he passed. Horses in shaggy winter coats watched as he slowed behind a tractor. The animals seemed to know he didn't belong. Finally the driver waved him around. Gripping the wheel, Dave accelerated over the yellow line and passed, escaping the accusing stares of cows and horses.

Oxford, a hamlet just south of Norwich, had a reduced speed limit. Dave kept the Pathfinder at the posted speed. Getting a ticket from a cop whose hobby was targeting cars with out-of-state plates would cost money he didn't have.

He spotted a filling station and decided to buy a local map. "At least I'll know where the hell I'm driving," he said aloud. "That'll be step one. Step two, I'll find my old house and park. Step three…"

He quieted as he recognized the location. He had driven through this town with his mother. He savored the memory, no longer thinking of step three, trying to bring back where he and his mother had been heading. Had Scott been with them?

A new Mobil station suggested progress and change, proof he hadn't gone back in time. Maybe different people dwelt here now, people who wouldn't know about the Austins. Then again, small towns hoarded memories.

After gassing up, he entered the store. A rack of maps and hiking guidebooks stood at the end of a gum-and-candy aisle. A map of Chenango County provided good detail of secondary and tertiary roads, and he took it to the counter where a man in his forties, still more muscle than fat, wore a name plate that said *Rob Moore*. He eyed Dave a second too long before the greeting came.

"Not from around here, are you?"

Dave wasn't sure how the guy knew that much about a

customer and wasn't about to tell his life story to a store clerk. "Just passing through."

Moore, who must have lifted weights to account for his bulldog neck, pointed at the map. "We've sold a few of those lately. You're too young to be a reporter, right?"

"Not that young, but I'm no reporter. Why?"

"More than a few of them been creeping around because of the murders. Just like those years back."

Dave felt a tremor and closed his eyes for a second. He opened them and spotted a beer cooler beyond the counter and became thirsty. "Let me have a six-pack of Genny." He probably should have asked what murders Rob Moore was talking about.

Moore smiled. "Let me see your ID."

Dave extracted his driver's license from his billfold and passed it over. It contained the correct information, except for the altered date of birth. Moore examined the document with a hawkish stare that made Dave nervous.

"You're David Austin. Of Cortland." More statements than questions. "This isn't bad for a fake ID. I've seen worse. This would work just about anywhere if you weren't dealing with someone who happens to work in the sheriff's office. Used to be the sheriff. Just your bad luck I'm on duty because my manager is sick. I'm the one who trained him to spot bogus proof."

Dave took a step back. *Oh, shit*, he thought.

Moore leaned forward, resting his forearms on the counter. "I was the sheriff when your brother was killed, David Austin. You were eight in 1983. That makes you twenty. Not quite old enough to buy a six-pack." He slid the license forward. "By all rights, I should call this in, but I'm gonna cut you some slack."

Dave sucked in a breath and, as Moore turned to ring up the map, palmed the ID when he laid bills down. He was almost tempted to thank the guy. He didn't.

Moore handed Dave his change and a receipt. "So why are you back here, David Austin?"

"Just gonna visit the area." Dave wondered if that was too much.

"You mean Norwich."

"Yeah."

Dave took a step toward the exit.

Moore's eyes narrowed. "Remember what they say about sleeping dogs."

When Dave left, Moore picked up his phone and punched in the number of a colleague, Jeremy Tucker. Like Moore, Tucker was still a deputy with the Chenango County Sheriff's Office. The call was answered after the second ring.

"Anything keeping you busy?" Moore asked.

Deputy Tucker, who'd helped Moore subdue John Redford years before, answered in a cautious voice, "Not at the moment, why?"

"Good. I have something that you ought to look into. I'd handle it myself, but I'm tied up." Moore walked to the front door and saw Dave parked away from the pumps. "I just ran into someone from the past, David Austin. We last saw him when he was eight, and now he's back."

"Back? Do you know why?"

Moore watched Dave unfold the map he'd bought. "No, I don't know why he's here, but it doesn't take a big brain to figure out that it's tied to last week's murders."

"Okay, so what's the problem?"

"This community has already linked the murders twelve years ago with these and the Carnival killing last fall. They don't need David Austin prowling around to rile them up. And we don't need questions about how we handled the case."

He picked up a five-pack of cigars and put them next to the register. "We did the best we could, and I don't want him here. Just check him out and let him know he should leave." He recited the car description and tag number to Tucker. "Keep an eye on him. I want to know who he talks to."

"How am I supposed to do that?"

A fluorescent bulb over the dairy case flickered and dimmed. Moore glared at it. "Well, figure it out." He ended the call, unwrapped a cigar, and stuck it in his mouth without lighting it. He sat on the stool behind the register and drummed his fingers on the counter. "I wonder if the kid knows something," he muttered. "I never did buy that amnesia crap."

Chapter 32

ave pulled away from the pump and parked. The encounter with former sheriff Rob Moore creeped him out. *What the hell is letting sleeping dogs lie supposed to mean? Aren't I allowed to come back?* He hadn't abandoned Norwich. His parents had decided to leave and never come back. *So why should I feel guilty for returning?*

He shifted in his seat and unfolded the map, rattling the paper. The county was mostly open space crisscrossed by roads that meandered, following creeks and hills. Interstates existed east and west, but here the roads were two-lane affairs. Many sported two names, a local moniker, probably from an early settler, and a government designation. He searched for his old house, first pointing to Decker Road, also known as County Route 370. It bordered Harloff's Creek, a name he didn't recognize. He was looking too far west.

Dave manipulated the map so that downtown Norwich was centered. He envisioned where he'd lived in relation to the town center. Route 23 crossed Route 12 just north of downtown and went east and west. The house was somewhere off that road to the west.

He started the car and pulled out on Route 12. On the empty highway, he wished for more traffic, something to distract him. He passed the sign indicating seven miles to Norwich, twitched, and glanced at the clock. It was too late to tromp in the woods and fields, searching for the Sugar Shack. He'd need time and luck to find the right forest after so many years. Fields sprouted bushes, then trees, and never looked the same. The tree-filled hillsides that framed the valley reminded him of his father's claim that over half the houses in the county burned wood for heat. That was supposed to make stacking firewood easier, to let Dave and his brother know they were part of a large fraternity of wood-burners.

A *Welcome to Norwich* sign appeared and commercial establishments began to sprout along the highway. Then he was on Broad Street, the name given Route 12 as it went through Norwich. It surprised him that so much was familiar: the bridge over the creek that flooded each spring; McDonald's; a wide main street of shops, including a glass-fronted bank; a grocery store set far back with a big parking area; and an Italian restaurant. All vaguely remembered. The movie theater was still in business with a marquee advertising *Nobody's Fool*.

I'm not, he thought.

A park fronted the elegant courthouse, its gilded dome crowned with a figure of the blind but vigilant Justice. *You must have been off duty when Scott was killed.* On the sidewalk, a fellow with a sack was handing out loaves of bread to three smiling women.

He continued north of the downtown, turned on Route 23, and headed west. The route, filled with residences and a Catholic church, turned right at an intersection with a store on one corner. After blocks of houses and a skating rink, it left the city at a bridge over a creek. Beyond that, better houses on bigger lots could be seen. He vaguely recalled it all.

The day was overcast and, when he rolled down his window to look at signs, a chill hit him. Upstate New York was not as much into spring as central New Jersey, something he should have remembered from Cortland. He hadn't brought gloves or hat. That was stupid, but he'd been in a rush. And Colin had distracted him.

Despite the lateness, he felt a strong urge to see his old house and hunt for the Sugar Shack. "It's getting dark. Don't do it," he said aloud.

He'd talked to himself before, when he was drunk and facing difficult tasks—like finding his dorm, removing clothes, and climbing into bed. The self-dialogue helped calm him and sort out possible courses of action.

Red and blue lights flashed and a single yelp sounded behind him. He pulled to the shoulder and watched the patrol car follow. A big deputy took a moment before getting out of the cruiser. *Maybe Rob Moore changed his mind about the fake ID*, Dave thought as the cop stopped to examine the Pathfinder's rear plate. He approached the driver's door, and Dave lowered the window.

"License and registration, please," the deputy said.

Dave panicked. He didn't know where Todd kept the car registration. He fished in his wallet and produced his real license, handing it to the deputy as he mumbled about not being sure where the registration was.

The deputy examined the license and then Dave's face. After too long a pause, he said, "Not your vehicle, Mr. Austin?"

"No. My roommate loaned it to me." That was only a half-lie.

The cop pointed at the driver's side visor where a clip was visible. "See what's beyond the visor."

Dave pulled it down. On the backside was a plastic holder that contained the car registration and an insurance card. He handed them to the deputy who examined the documents and gave them back.

"Where are you heading, Mr. Austin?"

"Nowhere really. Just visiting Norwich. I used to live here and wanted to see the old neighborhood."

"So you'll be leaving soon?"

Dave didn't have an answer for that.

"Probably not a good time to be wandering around. People are a bit on edge after what just happened." The deputy checked the license again. "They sure don't want to be reminded about a similar murder years back. You would be that reminder."

Dave gripped the steering wheel with two hands and stared ahead.

"The neighborhood you want is about a mile and a half in this direction. Make your visit brief and don't wander around." He handed over the license. "By the way, you were traveling a bit fast for this part of Route Twenty-Three. Pay attention to the speed limits. You got to be careful in areas not familiar to you. Drive safely."

Wow. Another cop who happened to know him. That didn't seem likely. Must be one of Rob's buddies. And what about not wandering and being alert for rural, trigger-happy, nervous residents? Almost sounded like a threat. At least, he hadn't been told to get out of town by sundown.

He replaced his license and papers, thinking he'd just escaped again. What if the deputy wanted to call Todd? Then he'd be under arrest as a car thief. Wasn't that a felony and grounds for expulsion from Princeton? He took a deep breath to calm himself. Hell, he didn't even get a ticket. Now he really needed a drink.

The cruiser pulled out and passed. When his heart rate slowed, Dave followed, shoving aside the thought of leaving. This wasn't a Stephen King town where they ate outsiders. It was where he was born and spent his childhood. He recognized the place and had every right to be here. As the odometer clicked off tenths of miles in late-day light, deep-seated memories, sepia-toned miniatures of time and place, surfaced. The farms looked the same. The houses hadn't changed, standing back from the highway with wide deep lawns. Scott had mowed one of those patches.

The highway bent left and a sign announced a hidden drive. He knew that sign, and it had always confused him, because he could never find any drive. As a youth he wished his mother would slow down so he could get a look at it, sure it led to a secret and magical place. When he told his mother of the fantasy, she laughed and explained that the drive was his own road. He never considered it hidden, and there was certainly nothing secret or magical about it.

He found Canasawacta Terrace. Things seemed unchanged—the road still had a pebble-and-tar surface that afforded good traction in the icy conditions he'd known growing up. When he stopped before his old home, he realized time had passed. It wasn't the house he remembered. Instead of white siding with blue shutters, it had red trim. Instead of a tiny ranch with limited landscaping and a pine tree twice as high as the chimney, it had an addition and was decorated with terraced shrubbery and a little fountain.

Dave pictured snow fights with his brother and sledding on the front lawn. He saw Scott throwing tennis balls against the garage door and leaving marks. This had been his house, but his business had nothing to do with the house itself.

A horn tooted. A green Chevy waited behind him. He maneuvered his car to the roadside and waved the vehicle past. The driver pulled beside him and lowered the passenger window. "Can I help you?"

"Just looking at my old house." Dave pointed.

The guy stared at Dave and then his face paled. "You're David, David Austin." It wasn't a question. "I knew your parents. So sorry."

Dave nodded, expecting the fellow to drive off. But he wasn't finished.

"I bet you're back because of the new murders. Bad business. I hope the police find who did this. It could be the same guy, right?"

"I don't know."

"Listen. The killer will think you know. I wouldn't stay here." Shaking his head, the fellow zipped up the window and drove up the road.

Rattled, Dave realized that any hope of sneaking into Norwich to see the site of his brother's death was gone. Three people, including a couple of sheriff deputies, knew he was here. Which meant that others would find out. Hell, it wouldn't surprise him to be interviewed by a local reporter and make the front page of *The Evening Sun.*

He scanned the area to confirm he was alone. Light was fading quickly. Dave felt a need for light and heat and an even greater need for a drink. Not beer. A drink. Whiskey. Jim Beam. He stopped staring at the dark patches that were taking shape around recessed corners of the house and behind bushes. He backed into a neighboring driveway to turn around and regained the highway heading to town. Without much of a plan for the next day, at least he knew what to do tonight. He'd be drinking. And that was enough for the moment. It was a goal.

Chapter 33

Detective

The grocery store he'd passed leaving town also sold liquor. He pulled into the gravel lot and inspected the building, trying to remember it. The corner structure, obviously once a residence, was covered in white aluminum siding and was fronted by a narrow gray deck. A wooden sign called it Disty's. The name fanned a faint memory, probably because he'd been there with his mother or father. He climbed wooden steps, pushed open the glass door, and jumped when an interrupted laser beam beeped his entry.

The proprietor, a pudgy fellow in his fifties with a weighed-down look, smoothed a ring of fuzzy hair around his baldhead and smiled. The man wore a five-o'clock shadow and a frayed apron over a long-sleeved shirt. "Evening," he said, glancing briefly at his customer before returning to his newspaper.

Dave suspected he'd seen a younger version of Disty. His was not a common face—too jowly to be handsome—but one he might remember from long ago. He returned the greeting and went to the booze.

The liquor section featured dark wooden racks on a plank floor. He passed the vodka and gin section. He hadn't touched vodka since the freshman year incident, a vodka-Jell-O party, after which he'd wound up sleeping face down in a field. The wall held a poster announcing Finlandia's win at the Vodka Tasters Choice Awards competition in Elizabeth, New Jersey. The date was 1983.

Dave stared. The wall decoration hadn't changed in twelve years since Scott had died, as if the murder had frozen time. He shook off the image, grabbed a bottle of Jim Beam, and went toward the checkout, where he almost pulled out his real driver's license. The clerk folded his paper and picked up the license with sausage-like fingers. He glanced at the identification and returned it.

"You're a visitor, right?" The man's voice was cheery and welcoming. He rubbed the stubble on his chin. "What brings you to our fair city?"

"A little sightseeing. Used to live around here." Dave added a bag of chips and a bag of jerky to his order and dropped a twenty on the counter.

"Lived here all my life, and I own this store. I'm Disty," he said, warming to the conversation, probably happy to have someone besides Mr. Clean and Mrs. Butterworth to talk to. "How far back?"

Dave hesitated, uncomfortable talking about the past with this stranger, but he was here to gather information, and this guy seemed willing. "I was born here but I left when I was nine, more than ten years ago." He realized that was a mistake, given the fake ID, and rushed on. "We had a house about two miles from here, just off the highway."

Disty's eyes grew larger. "Canasawacta Terrace?"

"Right."

"That's not far from where those kids were murdered." Disty poked at the paper. "Maybe the cops will catch the bastard this time." The warmth of his voice had become heat. "Just like the other murders."

Dave cocked his head as if to make sure he'd heard the words correctly. One of those murders had to be his brother's. Did this guy know something? He decided to play dumb. "There were others?"

Disty gazed at some space beyond his customer and took a deep breath. He slowly brought his eyes back before answering. "Yeah. In 1983. Two young boys. One of them was my son, Carter."

Shock liquefied Dave's knees. He splayed his hands on the counter to steady himself and stared at them.

"You all right?" Disty asked.

Dave raised his head. "I'm Dave Austin."

A compressor rumbled in the corner, struggling to keep popsicles, pizza, and potpies frozen. Outside, a truck passed, shifting gears and accelerating. A throaty, big-sounding dog woofed twice. A siren screamed. Owner and customer stared as if seeking some truth hidden in the past.

Disty melted back onto his stool and broke the silence. "You're Scott's brother. You were there." The man touched his temples and then seemed to suck in extra air. "Why exactly are you here, Dave Austin? It has to do with this new murder, right?" His hand came back to the counter and formed a fist. "Do you know something?"

Dave had returned to Norwich for answers, and the killing of the two teenagers at a site near his house was part of it. Did he know something? Maybe, but it was still hidden. His answer was true, even if incomplete. "I guess curiosity drew me. But why do you say this murder has anything to do with the killing of my brother and Carter?"

"Damn. Even Jacques Clouseau or that *Naked Gun* guy Frank Drebin would see the similarities. First, the location. I bet the crime scenes are no more than a couple of hundred yards apart. Then the victims. Carter and Scott were almost thirteen. These boys were seventeen. Not quite the same, but close enough, at least in the mind of a killer who is twelve years older." Disty banged his fist on the counter. "And the last thing, dammit, is the way the bastard disfigured those poor kids. With a rock. To the face. Like he was trying to obliterate his victims. It don't take no genius to see this is the same maniac."

Dave winced at the double negative, remembering how

he'd struggled in school to overcome the local speech pattern.

Disty wasn't done. "Even Detective Holmes admitted as much to me, though you won't find that in the papers."

"Holmes?"

"Parker Holmes is the closest thing we have to an investigator. He's been around for a long time and worked my son's murder. He means well, but I swear they could've done more to find the creep who killed Carter and your brother."

"What do you mean?"

"They got stuck on the other kid, John Redford, who was found near the murder site. Crazy or acting crazy. Never admitted anything. But the cops thought he did it."

"But no evidence," Dave said, thinking about the face he saw in the stands at his graduation.

"Maybe because the kid was innocent. They should have kept at it. These new murders mean the guy was someone local, and he's still here."

"Or there's a copycat."

Disty drummed his fingers. "Parker claims they ruled that out—probably by some detail known only to them and the killer. Maybe he'll do more now because one of the girls who escaped was his daughter."

Dave thought that over. Perhaps he needed to do more than just visit the Sugar Shack. He should talk to this detective. "Where can I find Holmes?"

Disty had become quiet, as if the memories of his lost son had exhausted him. He made change, slipped the Jim Bean into a brown bag, and answered in a soft voice. "Try the police station. Downtown. Off Main. At the rear of the firehouse."

Dave left, stepping over the laser beam. The cool, late-day air lifted the gloomy blanket that had embraced him. He'd seen a Howard Johnson Motor Lodge off Broad Street. It would be pricier than the motel south of town, but for some reason, he did not want to leave the boundaries of

Norwich. It just felt more secure. At least the motel would be clean, and the towels would be large enough to wrap around his butt. He and Jim Bean drove there directly.

He parked in front of the motel on a narrow strip just beyond the sidewalk. A figure strode by smoking a cigar as Dave grabbed his bag from the back of the Pathfinder. It was obviously a man, based on the muscular build, flat chest, and the five-o'clock shadow. But he wore a white dress and a feminine cardigan. The fellow waved as he passed, and Dave wondered if he knew a younger version of this character.

The Howard Johnson lobby was decorated in light green and gold with chrome-trimmed furniture. If the motel was under new ownership, the ambiance hadn't benefited. The registration attendant, a young male with a goatee and a narrow tie, greeted him.

Dave responded with "Who's the guy with the cigar and the dress?"

"That's Reggie. Been a fixture in Norwich for years. I think he lives on trust money and spends a lot of time walking around downtown. He's supposed to be nice and works at a food pantry. I see him as free entertainment for the rest of us." The clerk ran Dave's credit card and handed over his room key.

Dave wanted to ask more questions, but goatee had one eye on a television in the corner of the lobby. The Celtics led the Knicks by five, and the attendant's attention fled to the game as soon as he pointed in the direction of the elevator.

Dave decided to take the stairs to the second floor to compensate for the intended enjoyment of several bourbons. His room was spacious, with a small couch, coffee table, and a desk. He put his bag on the double bed, grabbed the ice bucket, and headed to the icemaker. The vending machine produced a cola. Back in the room, he enjoyed his first Jim Bean and coke over ice. Followed by a second. His anxiety lessened.

He thought of the recent murders. The teenagers had been smoking pot and drinking before the attack. That probably made them easier victims. Liquor did that. Lowered inhibitions and defenses. But it also soothed, and that was the effect he wanted.

When half the Jim Bean had disappeared, the disjointed images began. Mushrooms, trees, the dark figure, running, the piece of cloth. And the face of John Redford.

☙☙

Dave dragged himself from bed at eleven Saturday morning. The liquor bottle was still half-full, so he didn't feel too bad, and the shower revived him enough to find breakfast. At a restaurant just south of the motel, he devoured a three-egg omelet with sides of hash browns, bacon, and toast. It was way more than usual, but he'd skipped dinner, except for the chips and piece of jerky. The coffee fixed his fuzzy head. At the checkout counter, the pastry display reminded him that his father used to stop there for donuts after church.

He walked from the restaurant to the police station and asked for Detective Holmes, happy to discover that the officer was working on a Saturday. Maybe he was busy with the murders that still occupied the front page of the local paper. The clerk showed him to a small office with a window that looked out on railroad tracks. The man behind the desk was leaning back with his feet up. Perhaps he'd been resting his eyes.

The detective rose slowly and smoothed his tie. Stocky with short gray hair, a florid face, and keen, dark eyes, he gave the impression of moving in slow motion. He offered his hand. "I'm Parker Holmes. What can I do for you?"

"I'm Dave Austin. I wanted to talk to you about an old murder."

Holmes sat back down in the springy wooden chair.

"Would that be the murder of your brother Scott and Carter Shuman?"

It didn't surprise Dave that Holmes had made the connection based solely on his name. If he had worked the case a dozen years earlier and now had a new case with obvious similarities, he wouldn't need much to turn him in that direction. "It would."

"We've already figured these new murders are like your brother's. If there's a connection, we'll find it. I'm sorry we couldn't solve your brother's case, but the file has never been closed." Holmes straightened a stack of papers on his deck, grabbed his mug, and went to the coffee carafe. He lifted the pot toward his visitor.

Dave shook his head, feeling wired from the three cups of breakfast coffee.

Holmes refilled the mug and leaned against the table next to a clothes tree supporting a cap and a yellow jacket. After sipping, he said, "I checked your whereabouts. Princeton, right? It would be the middle of the semester. Why are you here, Mr. Austin?"

"I had to come. I have been having dreams, remembering things about the day Scott died. I had a dream of what happened to the boys just killed."

"A dream? When?"

"The night it happened."

Holmes ambled back to his desk. "You mean after you saw the story on TV or in the papers?"

"Friday night. Before the reports. I didn't see a newspaper account until Sunday morning."

Holmes brought a large hand to his cheek. "I don't know what to do with that. That kind of thing is above my pay grade. But you said your dreams might have you remembering something about the day your brother was killed. We know that you were present—your shoe prints were at the top of the hill. We also know that you blocked out all memories with some sort of amnesia. Are you saying that your amnesia is lifting?"

Dave wished he'd prepared for this conversation. Maybe he could make it seem more substantive, credible, and useful. "I dream of a dark figure who was there, probably the killer."

"We figured there was a killer present," Holmes said, sounding serious. "Do you remember a face? Anything about him?"

"Not really. I see him with his back to the setting sun."

"But it was a man?"

"He was big."

"That would fit with a few partial prints of a man's shoe that may have been left by the killer. Anything else?"

Dave's hand went to the sleeve of the shirt he was wearing. "I remember running with a piece of cloth."

Holmes leaned forward. "Cloth? What about it?"

"It was dark, maybe blue. Maybe from the killer."

Holmes sipped coffee. "Could it have come from your brother?"

Dave had no answer.

"You didn't have anything at your house."

"I must have lost it."

Holmes put his hands behind his head, and leaned back, swiveling the chair to one side. "We scoured that area pretty thoroughly. Found nothing."

Another thought occurred to Dave. "Maybe the killer took it."

A meditative hum came from the detective. "Was there anything special about this cloth?"

Dave closed his eyes and his face paled. "It was dark and I think it had blood on it."

Holmes swung back to face the desk and flattened his hands on the blotter. "So you remember a figure, probably a big man, and a cloth that you had in your hands. Dark, maybe bloody." The detective stopped and seemed to be weighing his words. "Let me ask you something else. We always suspected that there was another boy with you, Scott, and Carter on the hill that day. You didn't remember anyone else back then. How about now?"

John Redford, Dave thought. But did he really know the guy was there? His dreams were mixed up, the way dreams always are. Could he have seen two figures, one the killer and one the playmate? Or were both the same? He thought John Redford was there, but he couldn't be sure and didn't want to make unfounded accusations. "I'm not sure."

"We suspect that John Redford was with you."

"Did you ask him?"

Holmes took a swallow of coffee. "John was found shirtless in a ditch a mile from the scene. Mentally disturbed. He couldn't answer any questions, even after months of therapy. Spent the next years in a mental hospital in Endicott. They decided he was cured enough for release, but he has no memory of the day he was found." The detective frowned. "Another case of amnesia."

Now it was Dave's turn to stare out the window as several notions struck. They already suspected John. Maybe just seeing each other would spark memories for both.

Holmes had continued speaking. "Sounds like you are still reclaiming any memories you might have. That's fine. I want you to give them to me—anything at all—when you get them. Here's my card. Call me. In the meantime leave the police work to the professionals. You shouldn't be involved. We did a thorough job investigating that crime and came up with nothing pointing to the killer."

"Did you have an actual suspect?"

"Yes, but I'm not at liberty to disclose names."

"Did Norwich have anyone who might prey on kids?"

Holmes hesitated. "There was one guy we knew about back then. Had a bit of a record as a teenager. Got off with a warning. Nothing linked him to your brother or the murder."

"What do you mean 'linked'? Are you saying that, like, Scott or Carter was targeted, and the other just got in the way?"

"It's possible, I guess. But no threats were made to any parents," Holmes said.

Dave considered that information. "Do you think the murderer could still be in Norwich?"

"Possible."

"Wouldn't last week's murders make it more like probable?"

Holmes leaned across the desk, pinning Dave with his intense eyes. "You should have considered that before coming. If the killer thinks you've regained a repressed memory that IDs him, then you are a threat to him. You could be in danger. Go back to college and, if you remember anything, don't tell anyone but me."

Dave rose and muttered something in the way of thanks as he backed from the office.

Before he reached the door, Holmes said, "Austin, I'm serious. I can't control who you talk to, but I can give you a piece of advice. Avoid Redford. He may be out of the hospital, but he's not…well, normal. There's something ticking inside that guy. Stay away from him."

Dave walked back to the motel, considering Holmes's statements. Not interfering with the investigation was standard police fare. Warning of a possible threat seemed a bit farfetched, given the length of time that had passed and what he actually remembered. But he needed to do something to force his memories to the surface. That was the whole point of this trip. He would visit the Sugar Shack. And he had to find John Redford.

Chapter 34

A Theory

The demon had emerged a dozen years back when he killed the two boys, smashing away their filthy mouths. Filthy mouths, filthy thoughts, thoughts that would become filthy deeds. His so-called friends had forced him to do such deeds, to touch them and be touched. To be sucked and be defiled. His father had blamed him, and so had his mother, slapping his face, washing out his mouth, and never kissing him again. She should be proud of him for keeping the little bastards from sin. They wouldn't put their mouths in bad places because they had no mouths.

The killer had felt a great release, but he'd made a mistake. The small boy had escaped with knowledge and a piece of evidence. Now he was back. Why? Was he seeking his brother's killer? Maybe it had been foolish to punish the fornicating teens so close to the mushrooms, but the act had drawn the boy back. To be purified and eliminated.

❧❧❧

Malone showed up for his appointment with Jim Caruthers on Saturday afternoon, a time the doctor set aside for low-price or pro bono service to the less well off. Not much had changed in the twelve years of sporadic visits since the wolf incident. The blue chairs in the waiting room were new, but the pictures on the walls were the same. That usually made Malone feel comfortable. He wasn't sure the sessions helped with the real problem, but the doctor listened to him. Even seemed interested and always encouraged him to return whenever he felt out of control.

Like now. After new killings in the same spot where the Austin and Shuman boys had died. Not far from the damn mushrooms. He needed to tell someone what this meant.

Malone followed Caruthers into the office, sat erect in the comfortable leather armchair reserved for patients, and started talking. "The evil is back, and those damn mushrooms are to blame. The killer is possessed and will kill again. We have to do something."

"Slow down, Ed." Caruthers tapped his index finger on a thick manila folder. "We've discussed the mushrooms at length in more than one session. I thought we agreed that the only thing that makes mushrooms dangerous is toxins. Not demons, not evil. Have you forgotten?"

Malone grumbled, removed his baseball cap, and rubbed his head. "I still think they caused the wolf's madness. You've explained that mushrooms have stuff in 'em that affects the mind. I can go along with that, but that just means that some demon plant drove the wolf insane. I don't know how they do it, but they can kill."

"Even hallucinogenic mushrooms have to be eaten to cause visions—temporary visions." Caruthers drew fingers through the short beard he'd grown. The corners of his lips rose slightly as he leaned forward. "So how do you suppose the toadstools have anything to do with the new murders?"

"The toadstools don't have to do the killing themselves. They get humans to act for them. Or animals, like that damn wolf."

"So some human got near the fungi? Who are you thinking of?" Caruthers asked.

"People like John Redford. And David Austin. And who knows who else. People like the murderer the police can't find."

"How about you, Ed? Could they be using you?"

Malone traced his index finger across the front edge of the desk and pointed it, shaking, at the psychiatrist. "Those fungi are still up there. I saw them."

"I thought we agreed that you shouldn't go back there."

"I couldn't help myself. I had to see if they were back. They are, and they're evil. If they'd touched you, you would know."

"Have they touched you?" Caruthers asked.

"Yes. Maybe not on my skin, but they caused that crazed wolf to slaughter my chickens, kill my dogs, and come after me. The evil behind it cost me my wife, my kids, my farm. The same evil somehow killed those two boys years back, and now it has killed two more. We have to do something. This evil can't stay."

Caruthers tented his fingers and lowered his voice. "We have to do something? What do you mean by that?"

Malone leaned back, gripping the wide arms of the chair, and closed his eyes. "They have to be destroyed."

Caruthers wrote something on a pad and tapped the paper with his pen. "Are you saying that will get the evil out of you and the others? How?"

Malone thought the answer was obvious. He opened his eyes. When he spoke, it was in the voice of a parent talking to a stubborn child. "The mushrooms house the demon—"

Caruthers's hand went up. "You mean a chemical."

"That's your idea. I have mine. We will drive him back to hell, and his control over us will end. We all have to be present to see the mushrooms die. When they go up in flames, the demon will leave and take the evil from everyone who's carrying it."

Caruthers's eyebrows rose. "How can you get John Redford there? And David Austin doesn't live here anymore. And what about the others that you don't know, but who you think are infected? You're not being realistic."

"They may not be as bad off as those I know. I figure the evil will drain from all infected, once the demon is driven out, although it may take a while. As for Redford, he and I are friends. He'll come. And Austin is here in town. I will convince him to be there."

Caruthers's chair moaned as he leaned forward, eyebrows lifted. His face took on a seriousness that Malone was sure he reserved for weighty psychological disease. "How do you know David Austin is here?"

"Heard it from Disty Shuman." Malone smiled as if he'd just revealed his secret font of knowledge. "When Austin hears what I have to say, he'll come. We'll do it tomorrow night at midnight. Under the moonlight after the day of the Lord when all that praying has weakened the demon. Then we'll be free."

"Ed, as your doctor, I'm telling you to not do this. It's not safe, and it's not the answer."

Caruthers escorted Malone to the front door and watched him stride down the front walk. His patient stepped with purpose, paying no attention to the blooming daffodils or the yellow forsythia. A breeze swayed the budded trees that would leaf out in a few weeks. In the midst of spring beauty, his patient's paranoia seemed to have flourished. Now he was planning to drag others into his delusion.

The doctor suspected his strong admonition to forget the burning scheme and to leave others alone would be ignored. He'd better check on Malone in the morning and talk to both Dave Austin and John Redford before they were pulled into Malone's plan. But he did not know where either one was. Something else bothered him. If burning was all it took to chase the demon away, why involve others? It was as if Malone had something else in mind, something he didn't reveal.

Caruthers returned to the desk and jotted a note in his calendar book. He pressed the speaker on the phone and dialed, waiting through three rings before it was answered. "Mother, it's Jim. I won't be able to join you for church tomorrow."

"That's disappoints me, Jim. I hope you have a good

reason. It is never wise to put something before your duty to the Lord."

"I know that, Mother. Something has come up that must be fixed, something that requires my professional expertise. Why don't you ask Cantrell to attend the service with you?"

There was a moment of silence. "I suppose I could ask your sister, but tomorrow is Parker's day off and I hate to interrupt that. However, Cantrell did just call to see how I was doing. We had a nice chat, and I could call her back."

"Fine, you should. How are she and Parker?"

"Cantrell said that Parker had a strange visitor a short time ago, a former patient of yours. David Austin. Rather surprising he should suddenly show up, don't you think?"

Caruthers considered the confirmation of Austin's presence and the new information about the visit to his brother-in-law. "It isn't unusual to come back to a town where one spent childhood years. But why did he stop in to see Parker?"

"Cantrell didn't say. But we both thought it strange he would show up right after the terrible killings that reminded everyone of the earlier murders."

"Maybe not so strange. Well, I have to go, Mother."

"Very well. If you can get free, please join us in church."

ↄଓ

The session with Caruthers did not calm Malone. Agitated, he walked to the Pecky Cypress Lounge, sure a drink would help him think things through. The yellow-paneled bar was occupied by a half-dozen patrons, all men, occupying barstools, drinking, eating burgers and pizza, and watching a basketball game on television. Two guys in jeans bad-mouthed each other at the pool table as they competed for the bills held by a third man.

After ordering his food and drink, Malone noticed another patron sitting in a dark corner. John Redford had not greeted him even though, in Malone's mind, they were now friends. Malone had tracked the boy when he returned to Norwich after leaving his mother and stepfather. He'd found him an apartment in a converted garage outside of town. The guy didn't do much and was a creature of habit, so Malone found it easy to show up where Redford liked to eat and drink. It was Saturday afternoon, and this was Redford's favorite bar. Having him here solved one of Malone's problems: he didn't have to see the guy in his crappy garage.

Malone grabbed his draft and plate and carried them to Redford's booth. Without asking, he slid in across from him. "How ya doing, John?"

Redford lifted his eyes from his glass and took a moment, as if he had to process the visual clues to figure out who the visitor was. "Good."

"You don't look so good," Malone said. "Havin' symptoms again?"

"My vision is blurry. Things are tinged with red at the edges."

"Just red?" Malone chomped down on the burger and took a swig of beer.

"Sometimes the other colors pop up. I don't like that. And my blood pounds. Got tingles in my fingers and toes." Redford ran his fingers over his hair.

"So it's still in you." Malone's words were not a question.

Redford squinted and leaned forward. "It's in you, too. You can feel it, can't you?" He laughed nervously and slopped beer. He put the glass down and began rubbing his feet on the floor, adding a scraping buzz to the drone of the television. "You went near them, didn't you?"

Malone wanted to grab the redhead by the neck and smash his forehead down on the table. Having ten witnesses didn't dampen the thought. He grasped the table edge to hide the twitch in his hands.

Redford must have caught the twitch. "Go ahead," he

whispered. "I can see how much you hate me. Go ahead. You think it would be the right thing to do. And I bet that's not the only time you've thought about it. Maybe you were just a little better at stopping yourself before."

Willing control, Malone pushed the aggressive thoughts away. He counted to ten, trying to steady his nerves. "What do you mean?"

Redford fingered the beaded moisture on his glass. "It's making you think bad things." He paused, his tongue flicking over his lips, wetting them and making them glisten in the fluorescent light.

"I know what we have to do to banish this thing," Malone said.

Redford's mouth curved down at the edges. "You mean to get it out of us?"

"Right."

"Good."

"Don't you want to know how?" Malone asked.

"Maybe. But we have to get it out of the other, too."

That excited Malone. "Right. Who?"

"David. He was there. The mushrooms got into him. And he's back. I can feel it."

Malone considered this thought. He knew Austin was back because Disty said so. How could Redford know? Didn't matter. It was just what he wanted, the chance to get them both in the forest. "Listen to me. We have to go back to the mushrooms. We have to burn them. When they die, you'll be better. You want to be better, don't you?"

Redford's eyes widened and his lips compressed. When he spoke, it was a question. "You want to burn the pretty toadstools? To kill them?"

"We have to. And you have to be there. We can use gasoline. Soak them with it. Light it. Destroy them. The evil will be gone. You'll be free."

"And you?"

"Me too."

"And David?"

"I'll get him to come. We'll all be together. Tomorrow at midnight. Just after the Lord's Day." Malone grabbed Redford's hand. "You know where to go. Meet me there. But don't tell anyone."

Redford pulled his hand away and glared at the wiry man across from him. He sucked on his beer and turned to the television.

⁓⁓⁓

Dave had intended to visit the Sugar Shack after seeing Parker Holmes, but the meeting had exhausted him. He returned to the motel, hung a "Do Not Disturb" sign on the door, and slept. He dreamed that he was seated in a cold, gray room, the sort pictured on television as a prisoner-interrogation site, complete with a nondescript metal table and chairs. Dave sat across from a bulky male in white pajamas who watched, smiling.

The man laughed, a sinister cackle lacking mirth. "You can feel it can't you?"

Dave felt his fist rise. If he hadn't fought to position his hands firmly on the table, he knew his fist would have flown to the creature's face.

"Go ahead," Pajama Guy whispered. "I can see how much you hate me. Go ahead."

Dave willed himself to stay calm. The walls of the chamber were bare, but somewhere in the background, he heard a clock ticking.

The fellow leaned his broad face closer. "You are contaminated." He flicked his tongue out, lizard like, over his lips. "Who are you?"

Dave blinked. That was strange. Surely they knew each other, or why was he there? But the creature showed no recognition, his black eyes as dead as a manikin's. If Pajama Guy didn't know his visitor, how did he know Dave was contaminated? And with what? The guy was familiar, maybe from twelve years back, but Dave couldn't quite name him. "You don't know me?" Dave asked.

Pajama Guy dissected Dave's face with a gaze that chilled. "Should I?"

As can happen in a dream, Dave abruptly realized this was the same face he'd remembered in a session with Dr. Ellington at Princeton. It was John Redford. He wanted to ask him what the hell had happened in those woods. But that meant revealing who he was, in effect giving his name. Now he wasn't sure that was wise. Wasn't having a creature's name the key to controlling it? Dave pushed the chair back. He wanted to leave, as if that were an option in a dream.

"Wait," Redford's mouth pursed and his brow furrowed. "Maybe I do know you."

It sounded like a ploy to get his visitor to stay put. Dave wanted to get the hell away, but there was no escape. Scratching sounds began. Redford was dragging his long nails across the tabletop.

"Yes." Redford made the word end in a hissing sound. "You were there. That's why it's in you." His voice was too loud and his hands twitched.

Dave didn't ask where "there" was. He knew. "What's in me?"

Redford grimaced. "You should have come back that day. I could have finished the job."

"What's in me?" Dave noticed a small button near the door. Had it been there before? He wasn't sure. Maybe pressing the button would free him.

"I had a rock for you. But you ran away." As he said the word, Redford began to rock fore and back, acting like a bobbleheaded doll.

Dave closed his eyes for a moment. "Why did you kill them?" It came out of his mouth against his will.

"Why do you want to kill me?" Redford laughed, apparently at nothing. "You want to kill me because you think I deserve it. And you think it would feel good. You think it would be the right thing to do. Do it. Then you can leave."

Dave floated up and above the scene, as if he was listening from a distance, through some sort of fog, watching himself sit and hear Redford's words. He could understand what the man was saying, but it seemed as though he heard only bits and pieces of the words. "Why did you kill them?" he asked again.

Redford laughed. "Did I? It's all so long ago now. How can anyone remember?"

Dave kicked at the table. "I need to remember."

Redford tilted his head and his eyes wandered over the ceiling tiles. "It would be so soon after the last little accident."

That made no sense, but things often made no sense in dreams. Yet Dave felt driven to force sense, to learn something. If it was information about who killed his brother, it wasn't coming from this nutcase, who never answered the question. Was he saying that he killed Scott and Carson? Dave remembered none of that. It didn't feel right.

Redford continued to talk, rubbing his feet rhythmically against the floor. "I knew you went near the mushrooms. I can feel it, just like I know when you're near me. And sometimes I want to strangle you."

"Why?"

"Because that's what it wants me to do. It's what's in the woods, those little toadstools."

The room grew dark and Redford vanished. Dave was transported to a stand of trees where mushrooms exploded into fireworks. The flares grew and he tried to run. He couldn't.

He woke, panting and panicked. Seated on the side of the bed grasping a pillow, he wrestled with the dream's message: Redford was there, and he was a threat. Dave wanted to speak directly with his brother's friend, but he shouldn't. *Fine, I'll talk to someone who knows him.*

Chapter 35

Hospital

Dave rose, splashed water on his face, and decided to walk to Guernsey Memorial Library. He remembered stopping there after school with Scott and wanted to see if a familiar place sparked memories. He could also check on the location and hours of the hospital that had treated and released John Redford.

The stone and glass building stood a block behind the motel. The exterior, landscaped with trimmed boxwoods in mulched beds, seemed the same, except for a mid-sized evergreen on the front lawn. A five-inch, square plaque before the tree contained the inscription: "In memory of our son, Carter." The donation had been made by Disty and Louise Shuman.

Guilt followed by anger washed over him. Why had his parents not done something similar for Scott? But he knew the answer—it hurt too much to even think about the loss. A memorial tree would be too painful a reminder. Instead, they fled.

He entered the library and surveyed the place. A few patrons sat at tables and two women worked behind the desk. One looked up and smiled. Dave tried to smile back and then moved to an array of blond wood tables that seemed too familiar. He identified the table where he and Scott used to sit. They would do homework or, in Scott's case, whisper to girls, until they were picked up after five. He touched the chair his brother had used and stood quietly for a minute before turning away.

He found the collection of phone books in the corner and pulled out the Binghamton directory. It produced the name of the Riverbend Psychiatric Hospital in Endicott. The listing indicated that the hospital had visiting hours on Sunday morning. He wrote the address on a piece of paper from one of the many piles left around by the library fairy. A wall clock read four o'clock. He stuffed the scrap of paper in his pocket. The Sugar Shack would have to wait because he'd missed lunch. Satisfying his hunger seemed like a good excuse for delay.

Shadows stretched from trees and buildings as he strolled through the downtown area to McDonald's. He ordered a cheeseburger, fries, and a soda and sat, trying to envision what he might learn at the hospital. He just wanted to talk to anyone who knew John. His train of thought was disrupted when two families, each with four kids, took the tables on either side of him. The sibling squabbles, an echo of what he'd lost when Scott died, entertained and saddened him. He finished quickly.

On the walk back to HoJos, he sensed being watched, but when he stopped and checked both sides of the street, all he saw were window-shoppers. No one seemed to pay him any attention. He picked up his pace.

಄ಆ಄

Reggie Peckrough had been leaving McDonald's as Dave entered. He'd seen the blond fellow gawking at him in his dress by the motel on Friday. Peckrough had an eye for faces, even faces changed by aging. After the first encounter a day earlier, he was certain he'd seen the gawker before. He chewed on that certainty on the way to his midnight-blue Chevy parked several blocks away.

By the time he put the key into the ignition, he had it. David Austin was back. He recognized him, not as an eight year old, but as the graduation speaker in Cortland, the event John Redford forced him to attend. His return could not be good. Had the murders triggered a memory that pointed the finger of guilt at someone? Peckrough was familiar with that finger—he'd been a suspect in the old murders, and the police had hounded him.

The bastards would still be making his life miserable if they had anything concrete to go on instead of just his sexual orientation and his record. In his teens, he'd been accused of lewd and lascivious behavior with a minor. As far as he was concerned, it was a trumped up charge over an incident that was just normal curiosity. But he had the label and was grilled more than once after the Shuman-Austin murders. Unfortunately, he could provide no alibi for the time of these killings. Just as he had no alibi for Friday night of a week back. That would come out when the police got around to him. Now that he'd decided to cross-dress just to shock the uptight community, they'd have even more reason to persecute him.

Peckrough suspected the cops had nothing more on last week's killings than they had on the first murders. Unless Austin knew something. Peckrough wanted to know why Austin was here.

❧❧❧

On Sunday, Dave rose early and skipped breakfast, intent on getting to Riverbend before visiting hours ended at twelve-thirty. He checked with the front desk for the best way to Endicott. The clerk directed him south on Route 12 and west on Route 17. Outside, the Pathfinder windshield was covered with frost that he had to scrape. A car idled at the end of the lot as he cleared his windshield. Maybe that was the way to handle frost—just wait it out and let a warmed engine take care of it—but he didn't have the patience. He made a circle on the rear window and got back into the SUV. As he pulled out of the parking lot, the car that had been idling followed.

Dave drove with the heater on, but still shivered. It had nothing to do with the drinking the night before—he hadn't had that much. Maybe it was fear. Fear that he wasn't doing the right thing. Fear that Holmes was correct. Fear that he was poking his nose into police-business and attracting attention to himself. Attracting the killer.

As he drove south, he fiddled with the radio, switching between stations whenever advertisements came on. He wanted music, not words. Occasionally the news would sneak in between songs, and he found himself listening to local news about traffic accidents, bar fights, and even a shooting when police had answered a domestic violence call in Binghamton. Other people's problems did not distract him. He wanted to talk to someone at the hospital about Redford's condition. And then maybe he'd find and talk to Redford. If that was safe.

Dave arrived at the outskirts of Endicott in just over an hour. It had warmed to near forty. He pulled over at the first gas station and asked the attendant if he knew the location of a psychiatric hospital. The guy stared, mouthing the word psychiatric with apparent difficulty. Fortunately, a customer overheard the exchange and gave him directions, enough to get him to the point where he started seeing signs for the facility. He turned onto a road that plunged into woods. A dark sedan followed. By the time the road intersected the main drive of the hospital, the car had disappeared.

A thread of black pavement snaked through a row of mature oaks, mowed lawns, and well-mulched bushes for a half mile. It ended at a brick guardhouse in front of a ten-foot high fence topped with concertina wire. Dave pulled behind a car and eyed the dashboard clock. Nine-thirty. Plenty of time.

The guard, a fireplug sort, finished questioning the driver of the stopped car in front and went back into the shack. He emerged, gave some directions, and the car went through the opened gate. Dave pulled up.

"Your name, sir." The guard had a pen and notebook in hand.

"Good morning," Dave had been thinking so hard on what he had to say that he missed the question entirely.

"Your name?"

"Dave Austin. David Austin."

The guard didn't seem to care. "Can I see your license, please?"

Dave pulled out his wallet and handed over the license, the real one. Fireplug jotted down the numbers and handed it back.

"And who are you here to see, Mr. Austin?"

When Dave didn't answer, the guard developed a frown. "Well, I'm not sure," Dave said. "I wanted to see the doctor who treated a former patient, John Redford. Or anyone on staff who was involved. I knew him when we were kids."

"Are you expected?"

Dave glanced at the guard's nametag. "No, Officer Sanders. Look, I'm a friend of John Redford," he lied. "I just want to find out if there was anything I should know before I contact him. Any precautions. It would only take a moment of the doctor's time." That, of course, sounded like something a rational person would handle over the telephone. For the first time, he realized that he wanted more—the chance to experience where John had been held.

The guard's face seemed to soften. "John Redford, eh? Hold on a minute, please." Office Sanders walked back into the guardhouse and picked up the phone. Dave blew out the breath he'd been holding.

The officer spoke for less than a minute. He came out and went to the rear of the SUV to record the license plate number. Then he slipped back around to Dave's side, taking time to check the back seat. He handed over a plastic-coated badge and a blue sheet. "You're lucky. Normally I couldn't let you in, but Dr. Rahman says he wants to meet you. Wear this visitor's badge and follow this map. Drive straight until you come to a T-intersection. Take a right and that will take you to the main facility. There will be another gate but they'll wave you through. Park your car in the visitor lot to the right and check in with the front desk."

When the gate lifted, Dave drove forward at a sedate speed, passed the second gate, and found the parking lot. Before him stood a redbrick, four-story structure with white cement windowsills and lintels. Bars on the windows gave it an ominous, foreboding mien despite the manicured and landscaped lawns around it. Nothing was planted against the building. A plaque indicated that Riverbend had opened thirty years earlier, before Dave was born.

He entered an elevator-sized space between two doors. The sole decoration was a sign advising visitors to wear their badges at all times. Above the inner door was a camera. He smiled at it. A buzz and click allowed him to enter.

The lobby's tile floor was chocolate swirled with ghostly white that made him feel as if he were walking on the surface of a murky pond. A beige couch, matching armchair, and an empty oak coffee table stood in one corner. In another corner was a desk with a sign indicating someone would come to get him.

He sat and studied the walls with murals of desert southwest scenes. One featured a sunset over a flat mesa. Small cactuses, some round, some flat like pancakes, cast small shadows in the foreground. Farther back stood a large, pole-shaped cactus with an arm bent at the elbow. Two red brick ruins with pieces of dark pottery dominated the second painting. He stared and realized a rattlesnake was hiding in the shadows. The artists were different, but the color schemes matched perfectly. The theme hardly seemed in tune with the gray skies of upstate New York. Maybe they were meant to soothe and distract.

He felt himself sucked into the desert, drawn by a bright pink area in the pueblo portion. He approached the piece, and the color changed from pink to red and then to purple. It shimmered and the colors took the shape of a mushroom.

"Mr. Austin?"

He twitched and turned. A female in a brown guard uniform watched him. The brunette had a pretty face under shoulder-length hair, and her eyes smiled behind gold-rimmed glasses.

He went to the desk. "Yes?"

"You asked to speak to someone who knew John Redford?"

Dave nodded.

"Dr. Rahman happens to be on duty this weekend. He will see you. I'll accompany you to his office. You'll want to leave your car keys here and anything else that might set off the metal detector." She handed him a plastic tray.

Dave dumped in his keys and six quarters. He felt for his phone and realized he'd left it at Princeton.

"I knew John," the woman said. "Probably everyone on staff who has been here long enough did. He was a patient for years. Do you mind if I ask what your association was?"

"I'm sorry. My association?"

"I mean, are you related?"

"No. I'm a friend, a childhood friend. I was passing through the area and wanted to find him. I thought it might be wise to talk to someone who knew him before he was released."

The guard removed her glasses. "I see. We keep records of all visitors, of course. John didn't have many. You never stopped in while he was a patient, right?" She tapped the register as if it might contain his name from years before.

Dave tensed. "No. I mean yes. That's right. I've never been here before. But I knew John many years ago. He and I grew up together."

The desk phone rang. The brunette answered it. "Yes, Doctor." She stood up. "Follow me."

The officer pointed Dave through a metal detector in a hallway at the rear of the lobby. He got a green light, and she punched numbers into a keypad before a metal barrier. It opened, and they proceeded down a cream-colored corridor that turned twice before ending in several closed doors, each with frosted glass and a nameplate. The nearest belonged to Abul Rahman, MD.

Dave entered to find a short man with caramel skin and black hair. He wore a button-down shirt and tie under a white lab coat.

"I'm Dr. Rahman," he said, extending his hand.

Dave introduced himself and sat in the chair in front of the doctor's desk.

"I understand you knew John Redford," Rahman said.

"He was my brother Scott's friend. My brother was murdered, and John may have been a witness. I want to talk to John, but I thought it wise to find out how he might react."

Rahman took his time before responding. "So you were the younger brother who witnessed the murders. I hope that you have recovered from that trauma. Did you have therapy?"

"Yes, with Dr. Caruthers in Norwich."

"Yes, I know Jim. He referred John Redford to us. How are your memories of the event of, what, twelve years ago?"

"I'm still recovering memories. That's why I want to see John. To see if that helps me."

Rahman stared a beat before answering. "I understand. But I can't tell you anything about a patient, so I don't know how I can help you."

"Can you at least confirm that he was well enough to be released?"

"He was released."

"Which you wouldn't do if he were still in need of treatment—"

Rahman held up his hand. "I sympathize with your desire to know how to approach John, but I really cannot discuss a patient. You are correct that a patient wouldn't be released if he or she still needed in-patient treatment. But remember that there's such a thing as out-patient treatment." The doctor studied his visitor before continuing. "Why would you think seeing John would spur memory of your brother's murder? It's my understanding that there's no evidence that John was present."

Dave considered whether he should reveal that he harbored half-memories, including one of John. Wasn't that the reason he was here? "I was present when my brother was killed, and I have suppressed all memories of that event for years."

"Not surprising. And now?"

"Now I am beginning to remember, mostly in dreams. In one of those dreams, I see John."

Rahman brought his hand to his chin. "If he was present and if he has any memories of the event, they are distorted. I wouldn't advise raising the subject with him."

"Why?"

Rahman seemed to be assembling the right words. He looked down at a file on his desk before he answered. "It might not be safe."

The doctor stood, signaling the meeting was over. They emerged from the office just as a tall black man in a white uniform was passing. "Ah, Harold," Rahman said. "Would you escort Mr. Austin out?"

"No problem," Harold said.

As Dave shook his hand, Rahman said, "Be careful with Mr. Redford."

Harold wasn't young, but he still had the thick arms that might be useful for handling unruly patients.

When they had moved away from Rahman's office, he said, "We've had only one patient named Redford that you need be careful with. Would you be looking for John Redford?"

"Yes. I'm a friend from way back. Did you know him?"

"Sure. Saw him most every day, good ones and bad ones. He was hard to forget. Went through years of talk-therapy and drugs, but never really came around. He believed stuff, weird stuff, but he learned to keep quiet about it."

"So he was pretty normal when released?"

They rounded the bend in the hallway that took them toward the lobby. Harold slowed their pace and glanced behind them. "I'm not saying that. As Dr. Rahman puts it, 'When a patient hasn't addressed the real issues that brought him here, he may not be normal even when released.'"

"What does that mean?"

"He never got to the root of his problem, which may have been his involvement in a murder. So, you could say there are unresolved issues. You never visited him, right? I'd have remembered because his only visitors were his mother, his sister, and a coach."

Dave considered that information. He had not been aware that John played a sport or had a sibling, but an eight-year-old might not tune in on or remember stuff like that, even if he'd heard the older boys discussing it. "Where is his mother now?"

"Don't rightly know."

When they reached the lobby, Dave said, "Well, I guess I'll be careful when I see John. But I have to talk to him."

Harold touched Dave's arm. "You should know that John can be violent. He attacked a medical student about a year after he was admitted. The guy worked with John as part of his training and didn't follow all the safety procedures required for dealing with unstable patients. John wrapped the fellow's own jacket around his neck and choked him. No real harm, but John ran off and later denied having anything to do with the student. And there was another incident they hushed up."

Dave didn't know what to make of that tale. It sounded as though Harold had a good imagination and liked to talk, but did he mix fact and fiction? "If John had any propensity for violence, Dr. Rahman would not have released him—"

"Wasn't Rahman's idea to release John Redford."

Chapter 36

Jennifer

Princeton:

On Sunday morning, Jennifer jumped from bed, went to her desk, and booted the computer, drumming her fingers as she waited for the desktop to appear. When it did, she downloaded email and saw nothing new from Dave. She wrapped her knuckles on the desk. Dave hadn't communicated by email or by phone, something he promised to do during their brief Friday call. Nothing. As if she didn't matter. He was up to something, and she intended to find out what. In a face-to-face meeting.

She showered and dressed, imagining his litany of excuses: he forgot, he had his project, he was trapped in the bowels of Firestone Library, he had a new girlfriend. She grabbed a book that was due back at the library and, in a grim mood, marched to Dave's dorm at an hour when most of the campus was still sleeping off the effects of Saturday night.

When she pushed the quad door open, it bounced off the bookcase behind it and made enough noise to wake Colin. She wasn't surprised to find him sprawled on the couch. He'd probably been up at six as usual for his run and then made the mistake of resting on the couch before seeking breakfast. And wound up falling asleep.

Jennifer stomped into the room and growled, "Where is he?"

Colin focused. "Who might ye be seeking, fair maiden? A dragon-slayer? A king to grant your wish? A priest to hear your confession of debauchery?"

"Where's Dave?" Jennifer dropped her book near a brown leather recliner that seemed to be functioning as a trashcan. She stopped herself from rushing into the room shared by Dave and Todd. Instead, she swept an empty Burger King bag and newspapers onto the floor and sat. The rest of the common room seemed relatively neat. A few empty beer cans graced the coffee table and sweat socks were balled at the foot of the couch.

"Not here." Colin remained prone, rolled to his side, and faced the back of the couch, apparently signaling that the conversation was over.

Without rising, Jennifer leaned toward the couch and sniffed, catching the usual aroma of spilled beer. For what seemed like the millionth time, she thanked God she hadn't been born a boy. Not that girls were perfect, but even the most intelligent of men seemed to have an affinity for porcine behavior and mulishness. She rose, came closer, and leaned her head near Colin. "You mean he's not in the quad, right?"

Colin grunted.

"All right, where is he? It's a simple question. I expected him to call last night to give me a progress report, maybe to arrange dinner tonight. He never called. Then I didn't see him on the street. Where'd he go?"

"I don't know anything," Colin said into the back of the couch. "And even if I did, I am bound by the doctor-patient privilege." He put a throw cushion over his head.

Jennifer punched him in the shoulder. "Where is he?"

Colin flinched but was saved from having to deny knowledge again by Todd's entrance. He thumped from the bedroom in boxers and a tee shirt, a highlighter gripped in one hand. "That's a good fucking question. Without asking, the asshole took my car, the one I was supposed to drive to a volleyball game this morning. I was supposed to take Jabe, who had to find another ride at the last minute. Your boyfriend left campus Friday around noon."

Jennifer raised her brows and then frowned. "Friday? But we talked on the phone."

"He left right after," Colin said in a muffled voice.

"To go where?"

Colin moaned and burrowed deeper in the couch.

Todd bounced the highlighter off Colin's back. "What's worse, this jackass lets him do it and then doesn't tell the car part of the story until this morning, after Jabe and I hiked all the bloody way down to the parking lot with the spare set of keys."

"I forgot." Colin's muffled words came from beneath a pillow. "I explained what happened in our earlier painful discussion. I'm sorry and wish you would fuck off."

Jennifer wasn't sure if Colin was sorry about the car or about having been caught trying to keep Todd in the dark. She felt no sympathy either way. "Where'd he go, Todd?"

"Ask Dr. Nutface." Todd grabbed his highlighter. "He's the genius who handed the guy a few beers and then sent him merrily on his way in my car. If you're lucky to have him as your neighbor later in life, he will give your house keys to a bum on the street." Todd glared at Colin as if searching out a vulnerable spot for attack.

Jennifer grabbed Todd's shoulder. "Calm down. You guys have been sharing your vehicle all semester. I'm sure that some of the sharing was done without your permission. And Colin couldn't have stopped Dave if his mind were made up. I want information. When I have it, you two can rip each other apart."

When she had Todd's attention, Jennifer continued. "So Dave had some errand to run that required driving. And he didn't want to discuss it with you. And he's been gone almost two days."

Todd shrugged.

She turned to the couch-burrowing Colin. "Speak. He's made his getaway, so you can breach privilege. Where did he go?"

Colin murmured something. Jennifer picked a magazine from the coffee table, rolled it up, and swatted his shoulder as one would a misbehaving dog. Or pig.

Colin sat up. "That's assault. There's a University code against that."

She rapped the magazine against her hand. "And that's not an answer."

"You are quite alluring when filled with righteousness," Colin said.

Jennifer lifted the weapon. "Where?"

"He just needed to take a trip this weekend. That's all. It was something important."

Jennifer's eyes narrowed. "What was so important? And where did he go to deal with it? And when did he say he'd be back?"

Colin, still in running shorts, pulled a blanket up and scooted away from his interrogator. "He went to check on something he saw in the paper. There was a headline that caught his attention—"

"Headline? About what?"

"Murders in Norwich. I don't know why, but he thought it might be important to him. So he headed to upstate New York. But he should be back in a few hours. He's probably on the road as we speak. So don't worry about it."

In fact, her initial anger at such stupid, typical, male behavior was becoming worry. "So he just suddenly decides to drive over two hundred miles chasing a newspaper headline that you can't figure out the importance of. And you didn't think to ask for more details, or heaven forbid, try to stop him."

"I did try to stop him," Colin said. "No use. I think he had some notion that visiting Norwich might help trigger some repressed memory. Just by being there."

"I hope he remembers that car-theft is a felony." Todd

went toward his room and stopped at the door. "And to top it off, Colin drank all my beer last night. So I got nothing when I got back from the library."

And the beer is probably more important than the car, Jennifer thought. She turned her attention to Dave's logic. Allowing a location to spur a memory actually made sense.

"I tried to talk him out of it," Colin said. "I invited him to hang out and drink beer with me—"

"So he could be soused and smash up my car after he'd stolen it?" Todd called from his room.

"No. So he would settle down and talk. He was all worked up, and there wasn't much I could do to get him to relax. He said he had to go to New York, to walk around in the woods near Norwich. I offered to go with him, but he wanted to do it alone."

"If all he planned to do was stand in the woods and then return, wouldn't he be back by now? It's not a day-long drive," Jennifer said.

"He must have found something. At any rate, I'm sure he'll feel like a complete ass when he gets back. Then you can all tear into him instead of me." Colin rose from the couch and backed toward his room.

"What were the specifics in the article?" Jennifer asked.

"Two teenagers were killed," Colin answered. "Apparently near the place Dave's brother Scott died. He had a map from the paper, and said he needed to go there."

Jennifer held up her hand. "Wait a minute. Is Dave saying that the murders are related? Just based on location? That seems a stretch."

"More than that. The victims were mutilated."

Jennifer's hand went to her mouth.

Colin scratched his head. "He wanted to check it out. Said that he could do this on Saturday and would be back today or would call."

"Has he called?"

"No, but today isn't over, so we have no cause for worry."

"What if he doesn't get back tonight?" Jennifer asked, frowning. "When are you gonna start to worry?"

Out of Jennifer's reach, Colin said, "Too soon to be concerned. He knows how to drive. He has a credit card. He'll call." He pushed open his bedroom door. "Wait, I have a copy of the newspaper article." He disappeared and came back out with a piece of paper.

Jennifer snatched it, scanned the contents. "Have you called him?"

The silence answered her question. She went to the quad phone and dialed Dave's cell phone. After a few seconds a ringing sound came from the bedroom.

Todd emerged carrying the cell phone. He shrugged.

"Well, isn't that just ducky? I guess he was in a hurry." Jennifer's voice had risen. "What if the murders are related to his brother's death? Have you considered that the same killer has struck again? Maybe Dave will be in danger walking around in the woods. This is fucking crazy!"

"There's no way the killer would know Dave was back," Todd said.

She pointed an accusing finger. "I can't believe all you're worried about is your stupid car." She turned back to Colin. "And I can't believe you just let him go."

Neither roommate had an answer. Jennifer looked from one to the other, her face wearing a mask of disappointment as if she'd tasted something sour. "Fine. I want to know if he calls, even if it's late. Give me his cell phone. I'll keep it."

Todd handed over the phone then held up a finger. He disappeared into the bedroom and returned with the charger. He handed it to Jennifer.

"If you don't hear from him by tonight, you need to do something."

"Like what?" Todd asked.

"I don't know. Call the proctors. Call his parents. But something. You said he was upset and wasn't acting right.

Friends are supposed to take care of each other. I've got contacts up there. I'll start helping now."

With Todd and Colin standing open-mouthed and speechless, Jennifer left, slamming the door.

Todd and Colin looked at each other, not moving. They could hear footsteps descending the stairs. And then ascending the stairs. The door flew open. Jennifer grabbed her book and left again.

Chapter 37

An Invitation

Endicott, New York:

Dave left Riverbend Psychiatric Hospital with jumbled emotions. The doctor's warning about Redford was the second he'd encountered in less than twenty-four hours. When he'd advised Dave to drop all inquiries into his brother's death, Detective Holmes had been as foreboding as Dr. Rahman. Then Harold said Redford was violent. That should count as the third warning. Damn the warnings. Dave needed information and had to see Redford. If the guy had been released, how dangerous could he be? If the two of them had memories that pointed to the killer, he would let the police handle it while he was back at Princeton.

Sunlight bathed the parking lot as he made his way to the Pathfinder. The temperature had risen and chased the morning chill. *Perfect weather and plenty of time*, he thought, *for checking the woods.* Then he might look up Redford, meet him somewhere in public, and head back to school. He surveyed the building, imagining how it would be to spend years locked up in a tiny room with barred windows and a locked door. Not pleasant. He was about to open the driver's door when something touched his shoulder.

He gasped and fell against the car. When he cranked his

head around, convinced that Redford had tracked him down, he saw that it wasn't Redford. A much older individual, a man with a weathered look and in need of a shave watched him. It took a moment before Dave recognized Ed Malone, the strange fellow who'd appeared mysteriously at his high school graduation and claimed to be near the Austin house just after the murders. Dave hadn't bought his explanation of what he was doing in Cortland.

He tried to breathe normally while Malone, in jeans and a denim jacket, stood there waiting, his eyes dark and intense. A normal guy would have said something. A cloud masked the sun, and the temperature seemed to drop. When the pine trees and bushes rustled in a sudden breeze, Dave shivered. The parking lot was empty. It was just the two of them. The guard shack was out of sight.

"What do you want?" Dave asked.

Malone held out his hand. "Name's Ed Malone. We last met in Cortland. As for what I want, the same thing you want, I imagine."

Dave ignored the paw Malone pushed at him from a dirty sleeve. "What do you mean?"

"We both want it to end. The evil. The killings."

Dave wondered if he could get into his car without shouldering the guy out of the way. Malone seemed strong and could have a weapon. Dave might be able to outrun the guy to the guard shack, but he'd almost been faster in water than on land in high school. That had to be his paranoia talking. Running was an overreaction. "What are you talking about?"

"You're here trying to find out about John Redford. I know him, too. He's told me all about his stay in this fine place. How he had to calm down to fool the doctors. How he stopped talking about the colored mushrooms, the ones he called clown mushrooms."

Dave edged away, not sure what to make of the man's words. He had a wild look, as if he might explode at any moment. "I've got to get on the road. Long drive ahead.

This mushroom crap has nothing to do with me."

"You're wrong." Malone shook a cigarette from half-empty pack, tamped it against his hand, and stuck it in his mouth. "You felt something while those boys were being slaughtered a few days back, right?"

The word "while" got Dave's attention. That implied simultaneity.

Malone's black eyes held Dave's as he lit the cigarette with a sparkly green lighter. He puffed a few times until a blue haze enveloped his head. "You heard me. You sensed the killings. Why should that be? Give that some thought."

Dave's breathing became shallow as his mind raced over the implications of Malone's statement. His ears warmed and he squinted. He had dreamt about the killings, apparently as they were happening, but how could this guy know?

"I felt it, too," Malone said. "So did John. We're all connected because of the damn mushrooms."

Dave reached for the SUV door handle and thought of bolting, but his mouth began working without his mind. "I knew John growing up and just want to see if he's all right. That's the only reason I'm here. Didn't know he'd left." As the lie passed his lips, he squeezed his eyes shut and frowned.

Malone took a deep draw on the cigarette and allowed the smoke to pass slowly between narrowed lips. "That's not quite true, is it, Dave Austin? You saw John at your graduation ceremony. I'm sure Detective Holmes told you he'd been released. And you don't care if he's all right. You want more."

Dave remembered the redhead he'd seen in the stands at graduation. He was sitting next to someone, not Malone. Redford's friend had been too young, too nicely dressed. So how did Malone know who he'd seen?

As if he'd heard the question, Malone said, "We were there together. We wanted to check up on you. I knew you in Norwich. I had a farm outside of town near where it happened. Your family moved away after the tragedy, as if they knew they had to get away from the evil. And now you're back."

"Look," Dave said. "I spoke with a doctor about John because I never got to see him face-to-face. I suppose I need some closure."

"Whatever the crap that is." Malone tossed the butt to the pavement and ground it under his boot. "Let's not pull punches. We can't piss around while there's a murderer loose. You and I both know that the killing in the woods years ago just repeated. I will put an end to it." There was vehemence in his voice.

Dave glimpsed movement in the pines beyond the parking lot. He studied the trees as he said, "Not sure what you mean by that, but it has nothing to do with me."

"What if I told you I know who killed your brother and Disty Shuman's boy?"

Dave fell back against his car. No one had ever said he knew the killer. Now this weird guy claimed to know. Would it hurt to hear a theory even if no facts backed it? "Okay. You've got my attention."

Malone lit another cigarette. "It's almost noon. You look like you could eat some, and I'm hungry. How 'bout we talk over food?"

A public locale would be a better place to deal with Malone if he turned out to be as crazy as he seemed. And Dave was hungry. "Sure," he said.

"There's a restaurant just south of Norwich. Called Fred's. On the left of Route Twelve. You can't miss it."

Dave looked around and saw no other car. Did Malone expect a ride? No way.

"My car's on the road. I know how to get through the fence. I'll meet you at Fred's." He crossed the pavement and strode into the pine trees.

If Dave had continued watching the trees a moment longer, he would have noticed a figure dressed in black. It appeared for only an instant and vanished. But Dave was already in the SUV.

ভওভ

Later in Fred's, Malone and Dave sat at a table in a small alcove that gave them privacy. Fred's was a decent eatery devoted to lunch and dinner. It had been a house before it was a restaurant and a bar. The color scheme of reds and browns with large oils of hunting scenes on the walls was a bit somber for Dave's taste, but it suited what they'd talk about. In the next room, a family having an after-church lunch chattered. The men waited for the lunch special, a Ruben.

As soon as the waitress left after serving drinks, Malone started talking about the wolf attack that followed his visit to the woods near the Austin home. "Never recovered from that," he said. "Smacked my wife around and spent the night in jail. My kids hated me, the dogs were dead except for useless Fred the beagle, my wife divorced me, and the insurance company refused to pay for the coop and chickens—"

"What's this have to do with the killings?" Dave interrupted.

Malone held up his hand. "You'll see. The wolf went crazy. After it went near the mushrooms. So did I. I left Norwich for a while. Got into bar fights. Came pretty close to hitting my sister once before her husband threw me out of the house. Even saw a shrink."

"Sorry to hear about that. But you're not making sense."

"Here is the sense. I got weird just like the wolf. Just like the killer. Something happened to all of us."

Dave was ready to bolt when the waitress delivered their sandwiches. He forced himself to be patient.

"One night I argued with a barkeep over the amount she called a shot of whiskey," Malone said. "Got my ass kicked out, and found myself on a curb in the rain."

Malone was apparently not to be deterred from his confession. Dave ate and let him talk.

"I used to fantasize about cracking beer bottles over the heads next to me in a bar. For no reason. Even dreamed about watching trickles of blood run down some other man's face." Malone stopped, as if waiting for a response.

Dave ate.

"What if the killer had dreams like that? And acted on them." Malone pointed his finger across the table. "Do you dream of killing, Austin? Do you?"

"No."

"Maybe you just won't admit it. At least I did."

Dave wasn't sure how this was getting him any closer to the killer. A clatter of dishes inside the kitchen was followed by a muffled curse.

Malone continued his tale. "You don't see it yet, do you? Everything went wrong after the wolf attack. The wolf didn't cause things. Something else did."

"What the hell does this have to do with who killed my brother and Carter?" Dave asked.

"I've spent the last dozen years thinking about it. I've written down every bad thing that happened and its cause. Every feeling of rage or anger. And then I thought through every moment of the three years before that night. Know what I discovered? No bad things, rage, or anger happened before the friggin' wolf."

"What does that mean to me? My brother wasn't killed by a wolf. You'd killed the damn thing by the time it happened."

"Did you know they had a strange death at Riverbend while John was there?"

The comment seemed to come out of nowhere. "Strange?" Dave asked.

"Mysterious. An orderly fell and hit his head at the end of one of the corridors. He was found unconscious. Never came to, and died a day later."

"Could have been an accident."

"That orderly took John from his room to the common areas for group activities. He was a big fit guy."

"So?"

"John's pajamas had a ripped pocket."

Dave's glass rattled against his plate, and he used two hands to set it down. This was the second time he'd heard about John being violent in the hospital. The old guy at Riverbend had talked about a med student who was attacked. No question that John did that. Would Malone tell Dave that Redford killed his brother? "Based on a ripped pocket, you think John killed someone? With this and the assault incident, why did they ever let him out?"

"He was a juvie when it happened and hadn't been drugged properly."

This new information was sensational but didn't say Redford killed his brother. Even if Redford was violent as a patient. "How do you know about this stuff?"

Malone offered a crooked smile, more a grimace really. "I had a caretaker job there for a while. And I talked to John."

"Did you think he was crazy?"

"Still is. But you're missing the point. He's crazy because of what's in him." Malone downed the rest of his beer.

The waitress arrived, and Malone ordered coffee. Dave decided he needed coffee as well.

"I explored the woods after the wolf attack," Malone said. "I found the rainbow mushrooms. Looked like little clowns in the forest with their big puffy caps of orange and other weird colors. If you don't believe in demons and evil, think of mind-bending drugs in mushrooms. That's what I hear from the doc I go to. Indians used hallucinogenic mushrooms around here. Just like these. That's what made the wolf insane. They got into him. If you believe in the science stuff."

After the waitress poured coffee, Dave called for the check. He watched her leave. "And I suppose John ate the mushrooms?"

"Or breathed the black stuff they spew. Maybe he still

has them growing in him like a parasite, changing his brain, making him insane. Making him a killer."

"But the doctor released him."

"John fooled him. They claimed that the orderly's injury was an accident, but I knew John did it. I felt it." Malone swallowed coffee. "The same way I knew that those boys were being murdered Friday back a week."

"So let me understand," Dave said, trying to process what sounded like a mishmash of truth and imagination. "You think we're tied to what happened up in those woods somehow. Whenever something like this happens, we know and react."

"Because the mushrooms infected us all."

"I have to tell you, Ed. Your story is certainly interesting, but I'm not like you. I've never spent time in jail for smacking my wife around. And I didn't put my fist through a wall or get kicked out of a bar." He did however drink himself shitfaced on a regular basis, have insane dreams, fail courses, and steal cars.

"Maybe you've been protected by being farther away. But not far enough that you didn't sense the slaughter."

Dave scanned other diners, dressed in suits and dresses, who had filled up the room. Next to them sat a dapper fellow, the cross-dresser. He was finishing his meal and seemed to have no interest in Dave or Malone.

"You couldn't keep yourself from coming back," Malone said.

Dave wondered what Malone was driving at. "I'm not sure I want to be seen with someone with a theory about fungi-caused murders. You seem to be saying that John killed on Friday night. I assume you haven't gone to the police with this."

"No reason to go to the police. No reason at all. No evidence."

"So what do you want from me?"

"I want you with me when I burn the mushrooms tonight at midnight. It will free us all from this curse. Even John.

He'll become sane. You need to be there."

"Wait a second. If John is contaminated by something from these mushrooms or has a fungus growing in his head, how will burning mushrooms in the woods help?"

"The evil force will be driven out. The source of the contamination will be eliminated."

Dave considered the notion. "So, do it yourself. Why do I need to be there? Why midnight?"

"Because you were a witness to the first killings. You've been scarred by what happened. It still bothers you. You want to expunge the evil. And the demon is weakest on Sunday at midnight."

Dave marveled that this ex-farmer in old clothing would even know a word like "expunge." He'd also used "parasite." Despite a desire to just get away from this guy, Dave found himself asking, "So you want me to meet you in the woods? Why would I do that?"

"Several reasons. John will be there, and you want to talk to him. And I won't tell you who the killer is until tonight. What's more, there's something there you should see. It will explain things. And you will get your memory back."

Dave had intended to go near the Sugar Shack anyway. Maybe this guy knew how to reach it. If so, he could get the visit over with and head back to college. But Malone surely didn't want to just look. He had something more in mind. "What good is looking?"

"Not just look. We have to burn them all. You, me, and John." Malone pulled a piece of paper from an inside pocket. "Take this map." He thrust it across the table.

Dave examined the scrap of paper. It was a sketch of a route that led past his old house and around to the side of the hill where Scott had been killed. A star was labeled "Police" and apparently indicated where the police had been stationed to preserve the crime scene.

"Follow the red line," Malone said. "We meet at the X. At midnight tonight."

Follow the map to the spot marked X, Dave repeated in

his head. It sounded just like hunting for pirate's treasure. He should probably bring a shovel. Did Todd have one in the back of the Pathfinder? Maybe Jason Voorhees in his hockey mask or Freddy Krueger with his bladed fingers would join them. He'd need more than his penknife for those two. What insanity!

"You haven't told me who killed my brother."

"I will tonight."

Dave dropped money on the table. "I'll think about it," he said, meaning he'd already thought about it and found it completely nuts. Without waiting for Malone's response, he walked out of Fred's.

Chapter 38

Helper

Dave drove a roundabout route back to the motel, crossing over the Chenango River, still running high with snowmelt, and turning north on East River Road. He drove past the junctions with Main Street and Woods Corners, continuing to Route 12, and then south back to Norwich, all the while debating with himself whether to risk accepting Malone's odd invitation.

"Stumbling into the woods at midnight with a wacko is stupid," said the cautious angel on his right shoulder.

"But you want to experience the area where your brother was killed," answered the bold angel on his left.

"It might be dangerous," said Cautious.

"The man said he'd show you something," said Bold.

The guardian chitchat didn't help. Dave reached the motel room and flopped on the bed, exhausted physically and emotionally. He tried listing the pros and cons again and got to the third pro—the silliest one about driving the demon from his head—before falling asleep.

The late afternoon sun sent insistent rays through the undraped window to wake him. He came from a dream in which Malone in Klan garb burned large mushrooms. In the vision, Dave was part of a group of naked acolytes—male and female—dancing in a circle, chanting sonorously. Beyond the circle stood a giant. Not the Jolly Green Giant but the Grim Gory Giant—hairy, dark, and threatening—who selected jagged stones from a mound at his feet and killed acolytes by firing rocks to their heads. Malone condemned the beast and forced it back toward a dark pit. The vision ended with Malone uttering a curse, or maybe a blessing, that cast the creature into the abyss. He then threw himself in after it.

Showering, Dave considered another aspect of his problem: that he was nuts. He didn't believe it and ticked off his reasons. Sensing the murders did not seem so crazy, if Malone did the same. Something was wrong about the woods. Believing that didn't make him loony. It was rational to visit the site that might stir memories, to see what Malone wanted to show him, and to find out who Malone thought was the killer. If Redford was there as well, he could see what he remembered about the murders. Two heads were better than one. He flinched when the cliché passed through his mind.

Toweling off, he mulled over what he'd achieved by coming to New York. He was closer to the source of his vision, but from the sounds of it, being close wasn't doing either Redford or Malone any good. He should just leave, go back to school, forget he'd seen those teenagers being slaughtered. But he couldn't forget. His memory needed a jolt. Then he wouldn't act like a cringing, defective basket case.

He had to be in the woods. He would go to the Sugar Shack at midnight.

εɔεɔ

Reggie Peckrough had heard about the midnight meeting from John Redford. He wasn't sure what Ed Malone was doing and advised John to stay away, but all he got in response was a noncommittal stare. That probably meant John would go. Peckrough thought the farmer was off his rocker, but he couldn't use that argument with John because it was clear that the two of them shared the same delusion.

On Sunday evening, Peckrough decided he should watch the proceedings. He knew where the colorful mushrooms were and had observed their recent growth spurt. He spent an hour thinking about his own reaction to the weird fungi as he selected an appropriate outfit. It turned out to be austere and black.

◈◈◈

In Princeton, after the irritating meeting with the roommates where she'd learned Dave had gone to New York, Jennifer had decided it was time to act. She checked the university ride site and discovered a student had posted a trip to Syracuse on Sunday. She called, waking the guy up. He was a senior and actually happy to have a rider—she suspected her gender helped. With her coaxing, he'd agreed to leave within the hour.

◈◈◈

After his nap at the motel, Dave dressed, clicked off the television, and walked from his room to the lobby, and out into late-day sun. The crisp air refreshed him. He checked left and right, expecting to see a police car waiting for him with an officer asking why he was still in Norwich and what he really knew about the recent murders. No cops, no sheriff. Hunger drove him to The Bluebird.

He passed the parked Pathfinder and spied a paper stuck under the driver's wiper. *Shit, a ticket*, he thought. It wasn't. The single sheet of yellow paper contained a message printed in black marker:

I'M BRINGING HIM.
COME AT MIDNIGHT AND SEE. M

Obviously from Malone. The "him" had to be Redford. *Who knows what Malone promised Redford to lure him to the rendezvous? Probably salvation.*

Dave meandered head-down to the restaurant, entered, and found a spot at the counter. He ordered a burger and fries. No new customers came in until his burger was served. Then the door entry bell jingled. A moment later, the whoosh of air from the next stool cushion got his attention.

"Are you just going to sit there and stare at your fries, or will you say hello?" a familiar female voice asked.

Dumbfounded, Dave turned to find Jennifer giving him an intense stare. Her blue sparkling eyes, the eyes he'd loved from the first day at Princeton when he helped her move a carton, held him. She was the last person he'd expected to see.

It took another second or two before any sound came out of his mouth.

"What the hell are you doing here?" he asked.

Jennifer smiled, pulled off an orange knit cap, and unzipped a black fleece. "That's not a very warm greeting. As for why I'm here, I'd say I'm probably saving your ass."

Dave struggled to form words, but was granted a moment to do so by the waitress. Jennifer ordered a burger, fries, and coffee and then turned back to Dave with raised eyebrows.

"What do you think you are saving me from?" Dave said. "No, wait. Tell me how the hell you got here? How did you find me?"

She stole one of his remaining fries, dipped it in a blob of ketchup on his plate, and consumed it. "Saving your ass from whatever stupid thing you're up to. Which I can't wait to hear about. Colin said you were supposed to call Saturday and then changed his story to Sunday. You didn't call. So I found a student who was heading to Syracuse, and I hitched a ride."

"But I could be anywhere."

"True, but you're not hard to trace, despite how crafty you think you are. It didn't take Sherlock Holmes, Hercule Poirot, or Columbo. Once here, I remembered how you babbled about the Howard Johnson Motel and The Bluebird in your reminisces of the old hometown. I recognized Todd's Pathfinder, the one with the Princeton sticker in the rear window, in front of the motel, and I glimpsed a Princeton fleece heading in this direction."

Dave wiped his mouth on his napkin. "You're lucky. What would you do if I wasn't at HoJos, and you did no glimpsing?"

The waitress delivered Jennifer's food, asking if there was anything else either of them needed. Dave ordered apple pie with vanilla ice cream and more coffee. Jennifer decorated burger and fries with ketchup and then sampled the meat, seeming in no hurry to provide information. She slowly wiped her mouth.

"I know someone here who'd probably let me spend the night," she said. "Then I'd track you down using the telephone. There aren't that many motels in Norwich. You'd be in one of them. Unless you were a corpse in the woods."

"Well, I'm fine. I'm not in any trouble." Dave wiped his forehead with the napkin.

"So why are you still here? You're supposed to be back in Princeton today."

Dave glanced at the wall clock. There was almost six hours left until he had to be at the Sugar Shack. The sudden appearance of Jennifer—friend, girlfriend, or would-be-girlfriend—complicated things. "I planned to drive to Old Nassau tomorrow."

Jennifer frowned and shook her head. "That doesn't answer the question. You tell me a bull-crap story, steal a car, and leave without telling me anything, and you expect people to treat that as rational behavior?"

"I told Colin where I was off to. And I forgot about our phone date. I had stuff on my mind. But that was no reason for you to follow me. That's not too rational either."

She sipped some coffee. "What are you doing here? Why are you waiting until tomorrow?"

"You shouldn't be here, though. You have classes tomorrow."

"So do you." Jennifer paused, her eyes intent on the cup of coffee in front of her. "I read the newspaper article. Colin told me what you said. So what's up?"

"Nothing," he sputtered. "Or at least nothing now. Except Colin will get his ass kicked for not keeping his mouth shut."

Jennifer consumed a large French fry and put a small brown one on Dave's plate. "That's to replace the one I borrowed earlier. Colin is already suffering the wrath of Todd over the missing car. He seems very contrite in his what-me-worry sort of way. Don't change the subject. What happened to those teenagers?"

"I don't know," he said. "A brutal murder." He felt as though she was waiting for something more from him.

"So you don't know anything more than you read in the newspapers."

He finished his burger.

"Good," Jennifer said. "Let's drive back to school. You will actually keep your promise to have Todd's vehicle back by Sunday."

"I've got one last thing I need to take care of." Dave started on his pie and then stared into the kitchen area. "You should head back though, now that you know I'm fine. Tell Todd he'll get his car back shortly."

Jennifer poked a finger into his thigh. "One last thing? Like what?"

"Just something I have to see. I'll do it and go back to Princeton. You don't have to wait for me."

"Didn't you hear? I hitched a ride. I have no car, so I can't." She finished her food and stood. "Nobody asked me to come after you, but friends don't let friends go to murder sites alone. I don't know everything that's eating at you, but whatever it is, I don't think this is the place to solve it."

He thought about the woods. "No. It's not."

"What is this thing you have to do? Can we just do it and leave?" She touched his shoulder. "Tell you what. If we can be back in my dorm room by around midnight, I'll let you riffle through my underwear drawer."

"I can't do it, Jen."

"Sure you can. You just open it up and run your hand back and forth trough the black and silky stuff. If you find something you like, you can even try it on if you want."

He laughed despite himself. "Black and silky huh? I always pegged you for a white cotton type."

Jennifer tossed her hair over her shoulder and fingered his hand playfully. "Nope. All black. All silk. And everything is a thong. I even wear thongs in the winter when I'm wearing snow pants. I can't stand panty lines. I'm surprised you never noticed."

"I noticed." He pulled his hand away from under her fingertips. "But I thought you just went commando. How about you stay in the motel room tonight? Tomorrow morning, we can enjoy a pleasant drive back to campus in daylight."

Jennifer stared. "For some reason I don't trust you. Nothing you've done this weekend seems sane. And you keep ignoring the question. What's so important that you have to stay? Colin told me why you came up here, so I won't think you're crazy. But I'm also not about to let you do something stupid. Talk to me." Her hand dropped back on top of his.

He finished the last of the pie, realizing he would blab everything. She had that effect on him. He sighed and stood. "Come on." He slapped a twenty down on the counter, more than enough for the two meals plus a fat tip. Jennifer picked up her bag and followed him outside.

In the half-light of dusk, the air had begun to cool. They walked toward the motel in silence until Dave stopped. Jennifer waited, and he took her hand. "Here is what I found out. I'm not alone in having some kind of vision of last week's killings. A guy named Malone also felt something. He has this weird theory about mushrooms causing a psychological disturbance. Maybe it's not so weird, since I see mushrooms in my dreams. He thinks that whoever killed the boys on Friday also killed my brother and Carter. He even said that he knows who the killer is."

"Who is this Malone, and why would he know anything?"

"He ran a farm near our house. He's lived around here all his life and knows the woods. And he wants to show me something up there. That's what I have to do. Meet him in the woods."

Jennifer looked around. It had turned dark, and streetlights were on. "When?"

"At midnight."

"That's nuts. Surely you don't intend to go traipsing in the woods in the dark to see *something*." Jennifer air-quoted the last. "Don't be an idiot. Just forget it. Let's leave."

They'd reached the motel door. Across the street, the faithful from a Methodist church were leaving after a late Sunday service. The organ was belting out the recessional hymn, the music rising and falling as the door opened and closed.

Jennifer had more to say. "You're not telling me everything. Why would you do what this guy says?"

He took a deep breath. "Malone is a friend of someone who may or may not have been there when Scott and Carson died."

Jennifer stopped, her eyes looking as if she'd just found a giant rat in her closet. "Who?"

"John Redford."

Jennifer shrank back as if she'd been struck. Her hand went to her mouth and a squeak emerged, followed by, "I thought he had an alibi."

"Malone says not. Redford will be there, and I will ask him."

"John will be there?" She seemed to be talking to herself. "Tonight?"

"That's what Malone says. And he's planning to do something to end the evil."

Jennifer grabbed his arm. "Then I'm coming with you."

Chapter 39

Woods

Jennifer decided they needed supplies and led the way across Broad Street to a Walgreens. Behind them, a figure in a dark windbreaker and knit ski cap emerged from the side of the building and followed. He waited until the pair entered the store before doing the same.

Dave went to the household goods aisle. "We're gonna need portable light," he said. "Once I turn off the headlights, all will be black." He grabbed two rubber-coated extra-large flashlights."

"And that's why it's stupid to do this at midnight," Jennifer said, picking up four packs of D-cell batteries. "What difference would having some daylight make?"

"Malone thinks there's something mystical in his choice of the time. You know, the witching hour on the day of the Lord. Apparently, demons are weakest at midnight on Sundays."

Jennifer gave that a full instant of thought. "I'll have to ask a prof in the Department of Religion about that when we get back to Princeton. If we get back." She stopped at the end of the aisle and picked up a water gun. "They seem to have everything here, from screwdrivers to motor oil. For protection, can we pick up a thirty-eight?" Her voice had a higher-than-normal pitch.

"Calm down. This has nothing to do with guns or protection. We won't go near if it looks dangerous." Dave pointed to the snacks display. "Better that we should be well fed."

Jennifer handed the batteries to Dave and selected two Chunky bars and gum. "What did you think of Malone? Did he have it all together?"

"Not sure. He's not entirely grounded."

"Dangerous?"

Dave took a moment before answering. "I don't think so."

Jennifer stopped before a display of ceramic-blade kitchen knives. "Maybe we should buy one of these, just in case," she said. "Says they can cut a penny in two. Should be able to handle a mushroom."

Dave didn't smile. "I just want to see what he has to show me, to find out if it jogs my memory. We'll keep our distance. If he does anything fishy, we bolt."

"What about his knowing the killer? Don't you want to hear his theory?"

"Yes, but he probably accuses Redford. His theory is just that."

The figure in the ski cap stood in the tobacco aisle as the pair checked out. When Jennifer glanced his way, he retreated. Dave paid the bill, and they left.

Outside the store, where it was now fully dark, the temperature had dropped into the forties, and a light breeze had come up. Jennifer zipped up her fleece and raised the hood. She opened one Chunky, broke off two squares of candy for each of them, and consumed hers. Then she pulled a pair of gloves from her jacket pocket.

"How did you know to bring gloves?" Dave asked.

"I lived not far from here—Guilford—remember? Sundown means cold."

They crossed to Howard Johnson's and Jennifer retrieved a small travel bag from the desk. They rode the elevator to the second floor and found the room. Inside, Dave picked up the county map he'd bought at the Oxford gas station and put it along with Malone's diagram on the bed.

He studied the county map while Jennifer unpacked her bath bag and brushed her teeth. The target area was somewhere up the hill behind the old Austin house, but Malone's drawing suggested an approach from the north and west on a path unfamiliar to Dave.

"What if the police are still guarding the crime scene?" Jennifer asked.

"It's been a week. The cops are long gone. Besides, Malone's map shows how to avoid the crime scene. But I guess we should keep quiet."

"No kidding." Jennifer traced the route between the motel and the old Austin house. "Hope the path is well-marked. Even a normal, nonthreatening forest is a danger after dark. This one is unfamiliar and comes complete with a crime scene, hallucinogenic mushrooms, and a fanatic. I'm surprised we don't have to buy tickets."

"This forest isn't exactly unfamiliar. I did grow up here and might remember something."

"That was more than a decade ago. You can't even remember to call me from Friday to Saturday. You remember diddly. That's why you're here—to capture something you forgot, which you hope is more than just bigger and better friggin' mushrooms." She closed her eyes, turned away from him and then back. "You said that John may have been there when your brother was killed. Is that something you're now sure of?"

"We've already gone over all my dreams. It's getting late. It might not be a bad idea to get there early."

Jennifer checked the room clock. "Just a moment. There's plenty of time. So you don't know for sure that John was there."

"No, only a feeling. I dreamed of a big guy standing over Scott and then chasing me."

Jennifer paced at the foot of the bed. "Can you identify him?"

"Let's just go."

Jennifer stood with her hands on her hips and raised her eyebrows.

Dave's forehead furrowed. "I think I saw hair, wiry hair. Maybe hair on his chin."

"Well, that couldn't be John. He was just thirteen at the time."

"I could be mistaken about the beard."

A group of guests laughed their way down the hallway. The window vibrated, marking the passage of an eighteen-wheeler that went through gears as it accelerated from a traffic light. A small dog gave a couple of unconvincing yips that were answered by a deep, no nonsense bark.

"What about that cloth you dreamt about a few weeks ago?" Jennifer asked.

"Nothing new. It was dark blue, could have been black. Maybe it was bloody."

"Did the police find it?"

Dave shook his head. "Not that I heard." He grabbed his jacket. "Let's go."

Jennifer made a dissatisfied harrumph and left the room. She returned with two cans of diet soda, popped the top on hers, and drank. "Is that it? Anything else?"

Dave grabbed the other can and went to the window. He guzzled the soda. "I fell as I ran down the hill. Near some rocks. The killer was after me."

"Was the sun still behind him?"

"We were in the trees."

"So you may have seen his face."

He closed his eyes and tried to picture the dream. As he did so, the image formed and increased in detail. First the dark hair, then the full rounded face, then the eyes, all pupil and no white, and lastly a bit of color. Dave focused on Jennifer. "Yes."

They wore hooded, black fleeces as they headed for the car. The garments provided warmth in the cool temperature and big pockets for the extra batteries.

Two blocks north of the motel, Dave turned onto Route

23 and followed it past Disty's out of the city over Canasawacta Creek where streetlights ended. The occasional glow from houses set back from the road plus a cloud-coated partial moon broke the blackness. Jennifer acted as navigator, and with the help of the flashlight, read a couple of street signs. Dave drove two miles without encountering another vehicle, passed the dead end with the old Austin house, and found the turnoff indicated on Malone's map.

With the moon higher and providing a glow, he took a left onto a blacktop road bordered by featureless farmland. They climbed a hill for a distance in the direction of a far off white light, probably a porch light. Dave thought of it as a guiding beacon—or a warning. He slowed as Jennifer watched the left side for the farm tractor path Malone had indicated. As Dave drove past, she spotted it.

Dave backed up, turned in, and killed the headlights, relying on the parking lamps. The path snaked for several hundred yards and widened. He stopped the car and sat unmoving in the black silence. A wave of nausea hit. Unlike the nausea associated with drinking, this one was caused by fear and uncertainty. What if he'd been wrong and the area around the Sugar Shack was blocked off for police work? Then what? He certainly didn't plan to bust through the police line just to look around the site. The possibility that he'd taken this trip for nothing was sinking in. And, somewhere within, a voice whispered that he didn't need to go to the Sugar Shack.

Jennifer tapped him on the arm. "This is very romantic, but shall we continue?"

"I need to know where we are. Just a friggin' minute."

Twelve years earlier Scott and Carter had been setting off fireworks in the clearing near the Sugar Shack, but nothing bad had occurred exactly there. Dave forced himself to concentrate on elusive memories. They'd left the Sugar Shack and were coming down the hill when it happened. A few hundred yards from the Sugar Shack, down near the edge of the trees, was where the evil struck.

"What's the matter?" Jennifer asked.

You don't need to go to the Sugar Shack. He examined the county map and Malone's drawing. The path he and his brother had taken to the Sugar Shack veered among fields and collections of trees, but Dave was pretty sure that the final result was a straight line. And, while it seemed like a healthy hike when he first followed his brother as a five-year-old, one that necessitated canteens filled with lemonade and a sharpened knife—if your parents allowed you to have one—he didn't think the total distance could have been much more than a mile and a half, maybe two.

"What are you doing? We have to get there by midnight."

Dave used the map light to check the scale on the county map. He marked off two miles, in half-mile increments, on the edge of Malone's notepaper. Positioning the makeshift ruler with one end on his old house, he marked off the distances on the map itself. Two miles west of the house was a road that seemed to dead-end near where the Sugar Shack should be.

"I know where we are," he said, pointing to the map. "We are on this track west of the Sugar Shack. I just don't know why we're here."

"You're here to see what Malone has to show you."

"I guess." Dave knew the goal wasn't to reminisce about sledding in his front yard with Scott or watching his father stack wood. He wanted to know if he was crazy. If he found nothing but mossy rocks, trees, and the dilapidated remains of a maple syrup still, then he was crazy. The paranoia that had gripped him a few nights back would become the ranting of an over-lubricated drunk. He wasn't special, and he didn't have a psychic connection to this place. He was just a crazy boozehound who needed to get his ass back to school before his roommates had him committed, or the University expelled him.

Of course, if he found Malone's clown-forest mushrooms and felt something, then that was paranormal. But he didn't believe in the paranormal. There was another possibility, one that depended on chemistry, biology, and psychology. There could be things about human nature that weren't understood. Things that explained the savage murder of young boys. Experts would cite chemical imbalances behind uncontrollable behavior patterns.

Dave started the car and crept forward. A hundred yards farther, the path into close pines appeared. Night creatures scurried into the undergrowth in front of the car. While a rabbit wouldn't be too much of an issue, a deer could ruin the paint job. The side road was where it should be, and it was blocked by yellow police tape. He parked.

"Now, what do we do?" Dave asked, feeling stupid because this was supposed to be his expedition.

"Malone's map indicates we go down the hill from here. We walk. At least there's moonlight. How far does the map say it is?"

He eyed the map and pictured the scene from long ago. An open field below them on the left may be the field where the bull chased him and Scott. Then below it was the forest where Redford had sought privacy to do his business. He gasped. *That was a new memory.*

"It doesn't."

In a young boy's memory, that forest went on forever. Scott had been adventurous, wanting to explore everywhere, and he and Dave had once walked into a stand of trees farther down the hill. An earthquake had chased them out. They never ventured into the part right below the bull field. That was unexplored territory. John had been the first. It was time to re-enter the trees Dave and his brother avoided.

He turned the interior lights off and eased open the door, signaling to Jennifer for quiet. They shielded their flashlights with their hands and Dave led the way into the trees, a collection of maples, birches, and pines. No single species dominated. He imagined each tree struggling to find sunlight and to block its neighbors from the same thing. Could trees sense other trees? Vines climbed fences as if the barriers were a goal to be reached and conquered. Maybe trees could sense him. What foolishness. A tree was just a tree, he assured himself.

"I have to pee," Jennifer said.

"You gotta be kidding. Why didn't you do that before we left the room?"

She disappeared behind a bush, her shielded flashlight marking her progress.

"I can see where you are."

"I'm not plunging in any farther. Close your eyes."

He remembered John disappearing behind a bush on that evil day. A breeze made the high branches creak. *Nothing sinister or evil in the noise. A tree is just a tree.* With mixed emotions, he hoped memories would come flooding back as soon as he recognized the first landmark.

Jennifer returned, and they moved along the path, stepping carefully, avoiding brambles and tangled vines. Random undulations created little bumps, hidden gulches, and the occasional hill over a boulder.

"How close are we?" Jennifer whispered.

"Not much farther. I expect Malone has a light or has built a fire. We should be able to see that."

"I don't see it, and I don't smell it. Maybe he's just playing a joke on you and didn't come."

"Nothing about Malone was even remotely funny."

They scrambled up a rise, grabbing little saplings to help. At the top was a large flat rock that crowned the hill. Beyond was a thin stand of pines. All the undergrowth was gone, the trees winning the war for space. Dave turned off his flashlight and crawled to the edge of the rock. He peered at the area below, a slope with a bowl-like depression at the bottom. And there, in the middle, was a fire. He could make out two men in the semidarkness.

Jennifer squeaked. "That's John," she whispered.

"The big guy," Dave said.

Malone and another man turned their heads.

"That you, David?" Malone called from below. "Come join us. John wants to meet you."

Dave motioned Jennifer back and hissed, "Stay." He unshielded the flashlight and inched down the slope, ducking low-hanging pine boughs, and slipping on loose duff. He reached the basin, a level area bordered on one side by a scattering of large flat rocks, and stopped near the flames, a dozen feet from Malone and Redford.

"Glad you're here," Malone said. He wore a sheepskin jacket with the collar turned up. His hands were in the pockets. "So you can see what explains the killings, the evil, your visions, my visions. You'll know what has to be destroyed." Malone pointed behind him. "Come closer."

Dave got his first view of the adult John Redford, a husky man in jeans and a lumberjack shirt. He remained silent, standing with his hands behind him as if he were a company bigwig inspecting an assembly line that he secretly feared. Malone waved at him, and he stepped back.

Dave wondered what was next.

"No reason to be afraid," Malone said. "Just don't let them touch you."

Them? Dave scanned the area at the edge of the clearing with the light beam. The ground formed another depression, this one shallow, its surface disturbed by more slabs of rock. Between the chunks of slate and tree trunks were toadstools the size of pancakes. At first the caps seemed white rimmed with red, but other colors appeared. More like a theme park creation inspired by Dr. Seuss than anything from nature.

He felt himself drawn forward into the depression. Heedless of Malone's warning about touching, he reached out, not wanting to touch, just wanting a closer look. Maybe needing a connection.

The crop of fungi seemed to pulse, and new mushrooms appeared, replacing the fallen, dead tree leaves, almost as if the leaves, deciding to be something more, became the mushrooms. Dave stepped on one and slipped, catching himself on one knee and a hand. The hand smashed another fungal mass, sending a puff of black into the air. He rose, wiping his hand on his jacket, and stood breathing way too fast, feeling his head throb and his vision blur. Movement. *What the fuck was that? A rabbit? But what rabbit looks like that?* He caught his foot on a root and stumbled, stepping onto another small mushroom. It smeared into something slick and he lost his balance. He slid down the slope on his butt, crushing several fungi, and coming to rest with his face close to another. Somehow, he'd held on to the flashlight.

Nausea swept over him. He couldn't get enough oxygen, and his heart raced. The red ring on the toadstools began to fade, and the edges of his vision blurred red, as if he could see the blood vessels in his eyes. He scrambled upright, grabbing a tree to steady himself. Smears of fungus body clung to his bare hands and slithered into his shirtsleeves. Mushrooms clustered at his feet. Each time he swept the area with the light there seemed to be more of them, and closer. And they had teeth.

Redford laughed from the top of the slope. "You've got to run!"

Dave wanted to run, but was forced to tread cautiously, using his flashlight to find where to step without crushing another toadstool. Slowly, he grappled his way up the slope. The fungi thinned as he got higher. When he'd regained the top and entered the light of the fire, he sucked in big breaths, feeling a tingle in his windpipe.

Redford laughed again. Dave lectured himself to calmness as his vision cleared and panic faded. He had let his imagination take over. With his head clearing, he glanced back at the depression. The toadstools were still there, but they did not move.

Malone nodded to the depression. "See. There's something unnatural here. Did you feel the pull? Mesmerizing, aren't they? This is what I must destroy."

As he said the last word, his hand came from the pocket. Holding a small pistol.

Chapter 40

Confession

Malone motioned Dave and Redford to move closer to each other. Dave took a spot ten feet from Redford. The fire's light barely reached the edge of clearing, and its heat did little to dispel the cold. Pines formed a black wall on two sides. On the north, the ground rose thirty feet to a rock outcropping from which Dave had descended. To the south lay the fungal depression.

The pistol swung from Dave to Redford like a metronome as Malone spoke. "Fire will destroy those suckers."

"I knew you'd be here," Redford said to Dave.

Redford kept his hands behind him. When Dave saw the thin cord between his ankles, he suspected Redford's hands must be tied. The redhead seemed unconcerned, even smiling. Malone, on the other hand, was agitated.

"Why do you need a gun?" Dave asked, edging away from Redford. "We're willing to help you take care of the mushrooms."

"Not enough. When John was still locked up, I burned every damn mushroom. Nothing left. Not even that nasty feeling you get here. Thought I could be at peace. But when I went to work at Riverbend the next day, there was John, laughing at me. I told him I'd destroyed all his little buddies. He pointed to a red blotch on his arm and said, 'I'll just make more, you dumb fuck.'" Malone's eyes widened, and he shivered, causing the gun barrel to dance. "Fire will destroy the source of the evil. But there's evil inside you."

Redford laughed. "Crazy, Ed. They shouldn't have let you work at Riverbend. You should have been a patient." He seemed to be enjoying himself, despite being tied up and looking at a gun barrel pointed at his chest.

How ironic, Dave thought. *I came to solve a long-ago murder. Now I'm conversing with a mental patient who may be a killer and a crazy who wants to be a killer.* "I called the police," he said, trying to sound truthful, and put more distance between himself and Redford. "They're on their way."

Malone paused as if listening for sirens, but the crisp air was silent. If Dave hoped his police threat would halt Malone's paranoid behavior, he was disappointed.

The guy grimaced. "Then I'll have to speed things up." He pointed to a pile near the fire. "Add some wood to the fire, Austin."

A pile of cut logs—way too many for a campfire—stood next to a five-gallon gas can. Dave grabbed an armful of wood, wondering if Malone intended to set the entire forest ablaze. He tossed them on the fire and ducked as glowing embers scattered. The pieces caught, and the circle of light expanded.

When he returned to his hostage spot, he positioned himself a bit closer to Malone. Fighting the urge to glance toward the ledge above, he wondered if Jennifer were still watching, or if she'd gone to get help. The last thought didn't comfort him, for he might not be alive by the time help came. Why had he brought her here? Why hadn't he driven home after listening to Malone at lunch?

"Do you know why Ed wants to kill me?" Redford's brow was furrowed, as if he was asking one of the deep questions of life.

"No," Dave said.

The question seemed less important than whether he could grab Malone and the pistol before being shot. The man handled the pistol as if he wasn't used to it. Probably more of a rifle guy.

"Why shoot me?" Redford asked. "We're in the dark here. I mean, I could understand if Dave wanted to. He thinks I killed his brother."

Malone aimed the gun at Redford. "You know what you've done. You know what you are."

Redford eyed Dave. "What am I?"

"You're the carrier. You drew David here."

Dave lost the struggle to appear calm. "Jesus, Malone. You can't shoot him here in front of me. What the hell is wrong with you? I don't want any part of this. If the mushrooms were what you wanted to show me, I saw them. I believe you now. Let's get some professional help on this, talk to someone who understands mental effects of plants."

"They're not plants. A Princeton guy like you should know that."

The correction caught Dave. He knew damn well that the fungi had their own kingdom, but why the hell should Malone know it?

"That would make you a witness, I suppose," Malone continued. "But a dead witness. So it doesn't really matter what happens after I end this evil. I'm just taking back my life. I'm sending John and his evil back to the pit."

Dave stepped closer to Malone, speaking softly in what he hoped was a soothing tone. "What if you're wrong? What if the toadstools are only mutant fungi? Just a natural twist of nature. I went down there. Right? I touched them. They didn't hurt me. And there are none popping up near us. Right?"

"That's because he's not letting them." Malone pointed the gun at Redford. "He controls them. If you go near the mushrooms by yourself, you see them move. Then you can't breathe. Not when he's here. He laughs and it stops. Don't you see? He controls it."

That was a new notion, that Redford controlled the mushrooms. *Perfect paranoia*, Dave thought. *If you accept the underlying premise, everything fits.* His mind raced over what he could say to keep Malone calm, thinking, and busy with things other than the gun. "What if it doesn't stop?" he blurted. "What if you still don't have a decent job and money? What if you keep drinking and fighting and getting kicked out of bars? Who will you blame then?"

Malone squinted and grimaced. "You. I'll blame you."

"What the—why me? What did I do?"

Redford, apparently stuck on an earlier comment, intervened before Malone could extend his paranoia to indict Dave. "You imagine a lot, Ed. That burn on my arm at Riverbend was from a light bulb." A gust of wind blew a cloud of embers toward him, and he shuffled to the side.

Dave inched closer to Malone, figuring it might give him a better shot at tackling the guy, if Redford held his attention. All he had to do was wait until the barrel stayed pointing in that direction.

"That's far enough," Malone said, swinging the gun barrel toward Dave. "Stop moving. Time put an end to the clown forest mushrooms. And to the pain up here." He motioned to his own head with his free hand.

Dave imagined Malone would kill everyone, including himself. *The nut job is getting excited, not a good sign.* The fire flared and a plume of embers sprayed at Malone. The man's eyes glistened, and he wiped at his cheek. Was that a tear?

Television drama wisdom said that rule one was to keep the guy with the gun calm and talking.

Dave took another furtive step to his left, putting a bit more distance between himself and Redford, who now stood across from Malone with the fire between them.

Redford laughed again. "Of course, he wants to add murder to the list. He's crazy. Didn't you hear him? Starting fires, killing a wolf, beating his wife. You've been a bad boy. Any other killings in there, Ed?"

Another tear rolled down Malone's cheek, and the gun barrel, now pointed at Redford, shook. "Shut the hell up," he shouted. "I had everything. Everything. And you took it away from me, you bastard."

With Redford tied up, Malone was the threat, and Dave had to jump him. Dave stepped forward. "Look, Ed."

Malone spun toward him. "Don't take another step. I thought you would understand. But clearly you don't."

Dave was sure Malone planned to never leave the mushroom glen. He saw the guy's eyes. He'd have no problem adding another body to the pile. The final scene would just take an extra bullet.

"Okay." Dave held up his hands. "I'm not coming any closer. Take it easy. Tell me this. If Redford is controlling it, or if he is the source, why wouldn't he have saved himself by now? Why wouldn't something come out from behind a tree and distract you so that he could run away?"

Redford smiled and provided the answer. "Because I was waiting for you. It's more fun this way. Way more fun."

Dave jerked around. The sudden movement was a mistake. Malone fired and Dave screamed. Searing pain almost made him black out. He fell, grabbing his thigh.

For a moment, everything was still. Malone seemed as stunned as Dave. Then all hell broke loose. Redford leapt at Malone, snapping the cord between his legs, and smashed his big fist down on the gun, sending it bouncing to the ground. If his hands had been tied, he'd managed to get loose. He used one to crush Malone's nose. The man screamed and fell backward with a spray of blood, smashing a toadstool that hadn't been there a moment before. The red and orange colors exploded around his head and he lay moaning with his hands on his face.

Redford grabbed the weapon and pointed it at Malone. That's when the whimpering began.

"Just kill me. I did it. I killed those boys years ago. And the carnival worker. And the two kids on Thursday. I couldn't help it. I had to do it. The mushrooms made me. Let me die." Malone's sobs became keening.

When Redford aimed in his direction, Dave had a vision

of the closed casket. His mother and father would have to hide him because he was about to take a bullet in the face. They would have to bury their second son. His leg hurt like hell, but he tried standing. He had to make a try for the gun. A sharp pain stabbed his arms and hands, and he grimaced, shaking. Something brown and toothy scurried near him. Dave punched at it, and it crumpled, spraying iridescence. He glimpsed other furry creatures, like reddish brown weasels with black claws, running away.

"Nasty little bastards aren't they?" Redford said. "Those fucking claws hurt. I remember when they got me. I had scratches all over my chest when the deputies found me in the ditch. Never did get a good look at them, though. Always switching back and forth."

With tears on his cheeks and throbbing hands, Dave eyed the gun. Knocking the gun out of Redford's behemoth hands seemed hopeless, and he tried to think of what words might calm the big guy. His mind went blank.

"John, lower the gun. It's all right. Give it to me. Now." Jennifer spoke calmly, authoritatively as she entered the clearing.

John wilted, became childlike, and seemed to shrink. He gave Jennifer the weapon.

She shoved it in her jacket pocket and leaned over Dave who was still clutching his leg. She made him lift his hands for moment to give her a look. "We have to get you to the hospital."

Chapter 41

They left Malone near the dying fire, still moaning and whimpering as they climbed the hill. Jennifer and Redford helped Dave limp to the Pathfinder, and together they got him into the back seat. Dave placed an old soccer towel under his bloody pants leg. Redford rode shotgun, and Jennifer drove, bouncing down the tractor path way too fast, the headlights strobing from sky to trees to ground in arrhythmic madness.

"Smashing into a tree won't get me to the ER faster," Dave said in a weak voice.

"Button it." Jennifer slowed slightly until they emerged from the trees and then gunned it, whipping the truck onto the paved road at twice a safe speed. The white light that had guided them up the hill had disappeared.

Redford had said nothing during the hike to the car. Once they were underway, he began to speak, sounding nervous and not quite rational. "I was afraid he'd get smart and tie me to a tree. But he just used twine on my hands and ankles. Said he wanted me right where he'd found most of the mushrooms so he could finish the job. I should have burned him, the little fucker. Maybe I will. I'll get a kick out of smelling his hair in flames. Have you ever smelled burning human flesh?"

"John, that's enough," Jennifer said.

Redford was able to hold his tongue for about a minute. Then he turned around and gazed at Dave, who shook his head.

"The poor schmucks who lived near the Nazi camps smelled it all the time."

"John, shut up!" Jennifer yelled.

"Okay, okay," Redford said, but he couldn't stop talking. He turned toward the back seat. "How are the scratches?"

Dave was so concerned about the bullet he'd forgotten the scratches on his hands and wrists from the weasel claws. Suddenly the burning seemed more intense, as if something was trying to eat its way deeper. He groaned.

"It's the burning that hurts the most," Redford said. "Doesn't stop either. I still feel it sometimes, gnawing at me. Right down into my bones, it seems. For years. That's a long time to put up with pain that no doc could find a reason for."

"You aren't helping, John." Jennifer's voice was quiet, soothing. "Be quiet and help me find the way. We're getting help, and it will be okay."

Redford stopped chattering. Dave didn't need a sadistic litany about fungi or weasels or everlasting burning. Another question was crying for his attention, but pain kept it out of reach.

Jennifer came to Route 12 and didn't know which way to turn. "Where is the hospital?"

Redford pointed left, and three blocks later they entered the emergency-vehicles-only driveway and parked in front of lighted doors. Jennifer grabbed a wheelchair and, with Redford's help, guided the hobbled Dave into it. She pushed him into a quiet room that erupted when she announced, "He's been shot."

Three women and a man in greens whisked the wheelchair away. After Jennifer watched Dave disappear, she took Redford by the arm and led him toward the desk.

❦❧

In the treatment room, Dave removed his hoodie and lay back on the paper-covered table with his arm over his eyes. A young voice introduced himself as Dr. Sinclair, and Dave gave his name.

Dave pointed to his leg, and the doctor gently probed. When a nurse held up a pair of scissors, the doctor waved her off and told her to just get the jeans down with minimal movement. She removed shoes and pants.

"What happened?" Sinclair asked.

"A guy who shouldn't have had a gun shot me," Dave said, panting. "Maybe accidentally. Hurts like hell."

Sinclair examined the still-bloody gash in Dave's thigh, probing enough to make the patient jump. "Just relax and keep breathing," Sinclair said. "This is only a flesh wound. You'll be fine."

"Let's get this disinfected," the doctor said to his assistant. "And bring me a suture kit." He came back to the head of the examining table. "This will take a few stitches, Mr. Austin. I'll numb you so you don't feel the work."

Dave scratched at his hand and then wiped a tear from his cheek.

The local anesthetic helped and a few minutes later, the doctor announced, "Done. You're lucky it was only a flesh wound. The stitching went well, and you won't even have a scar. We'll give you something for the pain and an antibiotic. You'll have to get the stitches out in a week or so. What's wrong with your hand?"

Dave sat up. "Feels like I've been bitten."

"Take your shirt off."

The doctor examined his hands and forearms. All were an angry red.

"I see scratches and erythema—the redness—but it doesn't look like you were bitten. Do you know what happened?"

"I fell into some big, unusual mushrooms. Squished them with my hand."

"Really. You're the third patient I've seen this year with an unusual rash. The other two had unbroken skin that might have been contact dermatitis, something like poison ivy. They also mentioned odd mushrooms."

"These were colored toadstools."

"Did you see anything unusual beside the color?"

Dave didn't know if he should say more, but when a stabbing pain made him wince, he said, "Yes. I saw the mushrooms move, and some kind of rodent bit me."

Sinclair nodded. "What you describe is similar to my other patients' accounts, even use of the word rodent. Could it have been part of an hallucination?"

"I suppose," Dave said, grimacing.

"Interesting. My other two patients also had mental effects that seemed to be hallucinations when they encountered the mushrooms. Maybe a new kind." The doctor went to a drawer and came out with a blister pack containing a couple of circular, orange tablets. "I have a theory. The mushrooms you touched may contain a chemical irritant and a psychoactive agent. The rash could be caused by both."

"What do you mean?"

"The chemical alone could do it, but I think there's a psychological component. You are clearly agitated and have been stressed. Similar to what I saw with the other patients."

"How can a rash be in my head?"

"It's called somatization, the translation of psychological distress into physical symptoms. There's a syndrome called psychogenic purpura, a skin eruption caused by the mind under stress. This could be like that."

"Getting shot will stir you up," Dave said.

"Right. Well, we will treat the rash with antihistamine. But I think you need something to treat the anxiety." He held up the blister pack. "This is clonazepam."

"What is it?"

"Clonazepam is an anxiolytic, a drug for treating anxiety. Take one of these now. If you still feel anxious and upset in a couple of hours, take the other pill."

❧

Jennifer paced in the waiting room until Dr. Sinclair emerged from the treatment area. The doctor introduced himself and asked if she were a relative.

"Classmate," Jennifer explained.

"I see. Mr. Austin's wound was superficial and has been stitched closed. He's all right and will be ready to go in a bit. I'll give him what he needs for pain management, but he shouldn't be moving around a lot until tomorrow. Now, you'll have to wait for the police. Gunshot, you know."

"Can I see him?" Jennifer asked.

"Sure."

Jennifer found Dave dressed and sitting up, staring at his hands and arms, wearing the now-wet jeans he'd sponged off.

"The rash is better," he announced. "The doc said it could be due to a combination of chemical irritant from the mushrooms and my head."

"Your head?"

"Somatization. Caused by stress, like getting shot, finding out who killed my brother, having an hallucination."

Jennifer held up her hand. "We weren't hallucinating about what went on in the woods."

"Not that part and not you. It's about what I saw when I fell in the mushrooms. Colors, new growth, scratching rodents."

"I'll have to take your word on that. I couldn't see past the edge of the fire area."

"The doc said he's seen a couple of patients who claim to have encountered odd mushrooms and lost it. He thinks there's some new type of fungus in the woods that contains an irritant and a powerful brain-altering chemical. Maybe like LSD. At any rate, something psychoactive."

"Does it go away?"

"He treated the skin and gave me something for anxiety. Also a supply of Demerol for the pain. It seems to be working. The rash is almost gone, and I don't feel any more burning." Dave pointed to his bag of personal belongings.

Jennifer handed it over.

"This is Parker Holmes's home number," Dave said, handing her a business card from his wallet. "Can you call him?"

Jennifer got a groggy Detective Holmes on the line and explained who she was and where. Holmes was none too happy to be awakened by the call. As expected, he strongly disapproved of Dave's actions.

Dave took the phone and gave Holmes the account of how Malone had invited him and John Redford to the woods, tied up Redford, and threatened both of them. He told how Malone had been overcome and confessed."

"Where is Malone now?" Holmes asked.

"We left him next to the fire in the thicket off of Route Twenty-Three. Near last week's murders."

"I'll get the sheriff's office to pick him up."

Dave couldn't guarantee that he hadn't recovered enough to flee, but that was now the sheriff's problem. He didn't voice that to Holmes.

"I'm sure the hospital has already reported this. You'll have to repeat this for the officer who's on the way to the hospital," Holmes said. "Make yourself comfortable in the waiting room. I'll be there."

Dave limped to the waiting room with a bandaged leg, hoping the cop would be quick about getting his statement. He hadn't violated any laws by ignoring Parker Holmes's instructions to butt out and leave town. But it was a small town and maybe that was enough to put him in jail and tar and feather him. Another couple of pain pills and he'd be able to sleep through any torture.

Jennifer had disappeared while he was on the phone with Holmes, so he found a comfortable-looking plastic chair and sat, dosing until she came back five minutes later. He had to be shaken awake.

"Just a little longer, Dave," she said. "Then you can hug a pillow at the motel."

"Where have you been?" Dave asked.

"I told the doc about John's background and behavior, and he invited John to spend the night. For observation and a psychiatric consult tomorrow. I convinced John it would be for the best."

"He accepted your advice? Just like that? Perhaps I've underestimated your super powers."

"You have. I added that he would be safe in the hospital in case Malone wanted to try again to purge the evil from him. That appealed to him."

Parker Holmes, looking disheveled, entered the waiting room with a city policeman. Holmes consulted with Dr. Sinclair before he led the young people down a hallway. They settled in a conference room with a round oak table and four padded chairs. A credenza against the wall held a brass lamp and a bouquet of chrysanthemums and ferns. The walls were beige with a framed picture of a sunset. Dave suspected the space was used to deliver bad news.

Jennifer pulled the gun from her pocket and placed it on the table. The officer, a short, sandy-haired young man, donned latex gloves and sniffed at the weapon.

"Been fired," he said and placed it into a manila envelope. He wrote something on the front and put the parcel into his briefcase. He opened a notebook and was ready to write before Holmes spoke.

"The doctor says you'll live. You were lucky. When guns are involved, bad things can happen. Tell me again how this came about."

Dave related the trip into the woods, the encounter with Malone, the shot to his leg, and John's actions. Jennifer elaborated on Malone's threat to kill everyone.

"You should have followed my advice and left town," Holmes said.

Dave felt exhausted and a bit woozy. Probably due to the hour and to the Demerol. He was sick of being told what to do. He struggled to put together a coherent explanation for his actions. "I needed to hear what Malone had to say and to give the woods a chance to jog my memory. Turns out Malone knew everything."

"You said he confessed to killing at least five people, including your brother? And then he attempted to kill you."

"The other way around," Jennifer said. "I watched the whole thing. Once John punched him and had the gun on him, he cried and said he'd done it all. Malone didn't sound normal."

"So you go into the dark woods where you find both Malone and Redford. Then Malone threatens you and Redford with a gun because you have evil in you and killing you is the only way to save the world. Is that about it?" Holmes sounded tired.

Dave put his hands to his temples. "I'd say that summarizes it. And it solves the murders."

Holmes leaned his head back and examined the ceiling. "We'll check it out. I want you to make a statement to this officer right now while things are fresh in your mind. Nothing elaborate. Just the facts. You'll do that separately. We'll be having a conversation with Mr. Malone as soon as he's brought in. We are quite familiar with him."

Twenty minutes later, Jennifer and Dave were done recording their statements. Holmes walked them out to the parking lot. The air was cold but no longer foreboding. Dave imagined it held the promise of spring.

"You've gotten into enough trouble for one night," Holmes said. "Your statements will be available for signing at six a.m. in my office. You can drop by on your way out of town. Now get some sleep."

Chapter 42

Loose Ends

In the motel room, Dave stripped off the damp jeans and his fungal-ridden shirt and collapsed on the bed. He mumbled something to Jennifer, perhaps a goodnight, and immediately succumbed to a fatigue-and-drug-aided sleep.

After she threw a blanket over him, Jennifer rinsed his pants and shirt and hung them on the shower rod. She sat on the chair near the television and bowed her head in thought for several minutes. Twice she got up, paced, and then sat down for more thinking. Finally, she shed her outer clothes, lay down beside Dave, and joined him in sleep. Hers was restless.

Jennifer woke to find Dave on the chair holding his head. "Is your leg bothering you? It's been four hours, so you can take another pain pill."

Dave's face was a trophy for one who hadn't gotten enough sleep. "My leg throbs, but it's not too bad. I'm just recovering from a vivid dream. A bit disturbing."

"Damn. Another dream? The usual?"

Dave seemed to process the question for a while before answering. "Pretty much. Tell you about it later."

"I'm taking a shower." Jennifer grabbed her small bag and disappeared into the bathroom.

As the water ran, Dave snoozed in the chair. He woke

when Jennifer emerged, ready for travel, and poked him.

"Are you planning to clean up?" she asked.

Dave pointed to his wrapped leg. "I'll just sponge off. When we get back to Princeton, I'll be able to tape plastic over the bandage and shower."

"We're ready to drive back to campus, right?" she said.

"Sure. I'll only be a minute." He disappeared into the bathroom and called out a moment later. "These jeans are still damp. Did you wash them?"

"Blood," she said.

"Now I'll be yucky when we stop at the police station to sign the statements."

"Yucky is your natural state."

"Do we have to drop by your aunt's?" Dave asked.

"No. I'll call her and fill her in on what happened. She won't be happy but will understand."

ↂ

A surprise greeted Dave at the police station. When the detective on duty ushered the pair into a meeting room, Rob Moore was waiting.

"I thought you left the sheriff's office," Dave said.

"I said I was no longer sheriff. It's an elected position. I lost, but I'm still a deputy."

"But this is the city police department. Why are you here?" Jennifer asked.

"Detective Holmes decided to sleep late. He asked me to get signatures on your statements and to be here in case you remembered anything else. It's a courtesy thing, since I was on the team that investigated the first murders," Moore said, turning to Jennifer. He handed them the typed statements. "Read these over and make any corrections. If there's nothing big, just date and initial the margin where you made a change and then sign at the bottom."

Dave and Jennifer read, took pens, and signed.

"So, that wraps it up," Moore said. "Holmes said he'd let you know how things work out with Malone. He's in the hospital at the moment and not very coherent. We found him being tended by Reggie Peckrough, not far from where you left him, and Malone didn't resist. Seemed dazed. Peckrough says he's a friend of Redford's and was concerned about the midnight gathering."

The deputy rose and gathered the signed statements into a folder. He smiled, looking quite different than he did in the convenience store: more official and even friendlier. A lot more benign than when he'd eyed Dave and warned him to let sleeping dogs lie. "Have a safe trip back to Princeton."

They were almost out of the building when Dave stopped. "Go ahead to the car. I'll be right there."

Jennifer shrugged and went out. Dave returned to the room to find Moore sipping coffee.

"What?" Moore said, surprise on his face.

"There was something else. Not about what happened last night, but something I remembered about my brother's murder."

"Does this change the statement you just signed?"

"No. It's about the killings twelve years back. I remember I had a cloth in my hand as I ran down the hill away from the killer."

Moore seemed confused. "You never said anything about a cloth twelve years ago."

"I remembered it recently," Dave said, deciding not to mention his dreams.

"Recently. Right. Where did this cloth come from?"

"I ripped it from the murderer's shirt."

Moore's eyes grew big, and he leaned across the desk. "Really. And where is it now?"

"When I was fleeing from the killer that day, I fell and, when I got up, the cloth was gone. I dropped it."

Moore frowned. "That whole area was searched pretty well, including your path away from the murder site. There was no cloth. I helped, and we never found anything like a piece of shirt. Where exactly did you lose the cloth?"

"That's the new thing I just realized. Where I fell. In the patch of mushrooms. That's where I dropped the cloth."

"Where you were with Malone."

"Yes. That's why I remembered. Being in that spot must have brought it to the surface. It could still be there covered with leaves, or maybe in a hole. There's a cavern under the flat rocks lying around. I think I dropped the cloth into a hole. Even after twelve years, some part of it may remain."

"Unless an animal took it." Moore leaned back and turned toward the window. "You didn't say anything about it in your statement. When and how did you get this memory?"

A direct question meant he had to tell the truth. "It came to me in a dream just this morning," Dave said.

"In a dream? That's not really a memory then. But let's just say that there's something to it. Anything else in the dream?"

"No."

Moore stood up, his six-feet allowing him to peer down across the desk. He leaned forward on his knuckles. Dave felt like a suspect.

"Let me see if I've got this straight," Moore said. "After being shot, getting sewn back together, and taking drugs for your pain, you dreamed about a piece of cloth. Cloth that you think you ripped from the murderer's shirt."

He paused as if waiting for Dave to object or maybe to add something. Dave kept his mouth shut.

"And you imagined you dropped this key piece of evidence somewhere in the woods, in the very place where you were last night, near where you claim to have seen multi-colored mushrooms that bit and scratched you." Moore again stopped to give Dave a chance to comment. "You only remembered it—dreamt it—twelve years after the event. Is that about it?"

Dave nodded. "Well, I'd dreamed about the cloth and

where it came from earlier, but now I remembered where I lost it."

Moore's mouth curved downward. "I'll check this out. Have you told this to anyone else?"

"No."

"Don't."

℘℘℘

Jennifer drove to McDonald's where both consumed the Big Breakfast, neither having eaten in over twelve hours. When they were ready to hit the road, Dave volunteered to drive, arguing that his left leg was the one with the flesh wound.

She gave him the look reserved for when he was being stupid and kept the keys. "You've had two pain pills today. Relax and sleep."

Dave shrugged. He was anxious to put distance between himself and Norwich and suspected he'd be the faster driver. But there was no way Jennifer would let a crippled pill-popper drive.

Dave suggested that they get gas at a Norwich station. While he filled the tank and checked the Pathfinder's oil level, Jennifer made her phone call and bought snacks. She returned as the pump clicked off and pointed at the tires. Two seemed soft, and Dave aired them up. Between the car service and McDonald's, it was after nine before they got underway. They drove south without talking and without the radio. In the silence the question that had almost formed in Dave's mind the night before finally took shape. When it did, he said, "Why did Redford obey you? He acted as if he knew you."

Jennifer stared through the windshield and did not answer immediately. When she did, it was in a soft voice. "There's something I have to tell you. I haven't been entirely honest."

Dave's first thought was that he was about to receive a verbal Dear-John letter when he wasn't even a John. Not that he deserved anything better. Hell, he drank too much, acted like a pig, and dreamt of mushrooms and killers. He even had to see a shrink, for God's sake. Jennifer deserved far better.

After a delay, she continued, "My name wasn't always Ensing. My mother remarried when I was ten, and my step-father adopted me."

Dave felt relief wash over him. He'd been thinking that she preferred the swim-team guy who drove her here. A swimmer, not a dreamer. "So? What's the big deal? Lots of people change their names."

"I used to be Jennifer Redford."

It took a moment for that to register and, when it did, he put his hand on the dash. "Redford as in John Redford?"

"John is my brother."

"Why didn't you just tell me?"

Jennifer sighed. "Because it would appear as if I were stalking you. Because I wasn't proud of a brother who'd been in a mental institution. Because I wanted to see if you remembered anything about your brother's murder that im-plicated John."

"Did you think John was guilty of something? He was only thirteen."

"I told the police that John was with me after lunch that day before he went off by himself. The only reason they had for thinking that John might have been with you was find-ing him hysterical in a ditch a mile away. But that could have happened well after the murders. I realized later that I had remembered wrong: John was gone before lunch. He could have been present when your brother and the other boy were killed."

"So you corrected yourself, right?"

Jennifer shook her head. "When I heard that you didn't tell them John was present, I just decided to keep with my original story. John didn't have to be with you. He needed psychiatric care and not a police-grilling, although he got that as well."

"But you were only eight."

"Even an eight-year-old girl can be cunning. And lie."

"So you didn't want me to see the school psychiatrist because she might bring out some memory that would send the police after your brother?"

"Right. Your dreams keep getting more and more detailed about the day your brother was killed, including seeing my brother there at one point. I have a list of your dreams, and I've given them names. In Dream One, you were alone in a sunny field—I call it Alone. In Dream Two, you felt watched—I call it Not Alone."

"Whoa—you've got a list of my dreams, and you've named them?"

"Yes. Number Three is Carnival, in which you first see a figure and mushrooms. Number Four I call Victims because it was the first one in which you know you dreamed about your brother and his friend and know for sure you're at the murder site. Sound right, so far?"

"I guess. And pretty good names: Alone, Not Alone, Carnival, and Victims. Descriptive. What else? Do you have one named Just Plain Nuts?"

"Dream Five is called Flight. You are running from someone and pounding mushrooms. Dream Six is Clutches because someone has you. The one that really got me is Number Seven, My Brother, where you are carrying something as you flee and you remember seeing my brother there at some point."

"That's right. I see John and fell with something in my hand."

"In Dream Number Eight, called New Murders, you see boys as victims and hear girls. Like Carnival, this one isn't about your brother's murder, but of the recent Norwich killings. Now you tell me you have had Dream Nine. Did last night's dream have anything new?"

"Maybe. I identified the thing I was carrying as part of a

shirt." He was about to tell her more when he remembered Moore's order to keep it to himself. He didn't say that he took it from the killer and knew where he'd lost it.

"So we'll call Number Nine 'Shirt.'"

Dave mulled that over as they covered another mile, passing hillsides with trees still with winter-bare limbs. "Well, all of that is history. Even if John was there, Malone was the murderer. It's just too bad that, if your brother saw something, it may have contributed to his mental problems. He is as much a victim of that madman as Scott and Carter."

When they made it to a four-lane highway, Dave turned around to gaze out the rear window. "I should have cleaned off that mess on the rear window at the gas station."

"Other than a little grime, what's the problem?"

"Nothing." Dave faced forward. "I wonder if the mushrooms caused all my mental problems like Malone said. If the ER doc is right about a brain-altering compound, it could have triggered Malone's paranoia and your brother's problems."

Jennifer considered that. "Let's say that the fungi exude an LSD-like chemical. Suppose it caused hallucinations and made any pre-existing mental condition worse. Malone seems to have had issues all along, and the exposure to the mushrooms could have sent him over the edge, making him into a killer. John was diagnosed at Riverbend with a type of epilepsy. That could have made him susceptible."

It was Dave's turn to think. He closed his eyes.

"What's wrong?"

"Your theory is what's wrong. Maybe not wrong, just disturbing. For me. I had visions of the murders. Does that make me mental?"

"Possibly."

"Thanks." Dave stared into the passenger side mirror. "Can you take it up to sixty-five for a stretch?"

"Shouldn't the driver decide the speed?"

"Be bold. Try the left lane and pass a few cars. I want to

check something. After you've gone a couple of minutes with enough speed to pass Grandma and Grandpa, pull into the right lane and fall back to your favorite pokey pace."

Jennifer bit her lip and took the Pathfinder up to seventy, scooting ahead of a half dozen cars and a J.B. Hunt truck. Then she pulled in front of the rig and drifted back down to sixty-three. Dave continued to study the mirror.

"There. I've driven like an idiot. Enough to attract the attention of Pennsylvania's finest. I don't have a ticket on my perfect record, and I don't want one. Can I drive my own way now?"

Dave pointed to the rear-view mirror. "See that blue sedan coming up on us?"

Jennifer checked both the rearview and her outside mirror. "Yeah. So what?"

"It was there on Route Twelve when we were still in New York. It was there on I-Eighty-One. Now it's here on I-Three-Eighty. And still behind us, despite your reckless piloting. We're being tailed."

Chapter 43

A Gift

When Dave Austin left the police station, Moore thought of what the young man had said about the shirt piece. He recalled the missing garment of John Redford, but knew it wasn't that shirt. With a frown, he dialed Jim Caruthers's house number. Moore had worked with the doc over the years in the sheriff's office. When Moore got Caruthers on the line, the deputy asked for a meeting. The psychiatrist agreed to meet if he could come right over.

Moore found the doctor upstairs in a bedroom with two partially packed bags on the bed. A black cat sat in one of the bags. When Moore entered, it growled and retreated to a pillow where it crouched with large eyes. Moore took a chair far from the animal.

"Thanks for taking a moment to see me, Doc," Moore said. "Looks like you're heading out."

"I'm heading to North Carolina, a combined business-and-pleasure trip. So what can I do for you?"

"I have a question about Dave Austin—you remember him, the boy whose brother was killed years ago? Anyway, he told me something before he left to go back to Princeton with his girlfriend."

"Girlfriend? That's news. I knew he was in town, but I thought he was alone. What's the question?"

"He told me something about his brother's murder that I can't disclose. The problem is it came to him in a dream. My question is how reliable is such a memory? Especially of something that happened so long ago."

Caruthers leaned against a bureau. "A dream that was a memory. About his brother's murder. And you're following up. Have I got it right?"

"That's about it."

Caruthers folded his arms. "I can't tell you anything that would violate patient-physician confidentiality. He was my patient. But you already know that David suffered from amnesia. He could be recovering details of the traumatic event that caused his brain to lose track of the memory of what happened that day. Even if the memory were legit, it wouldn't be worth much in a court of law."

"But I'm asking if it could be accurate."

Caruthers took socks from the drawer and placed them in the suitcase. "Details can be accurate, and they could emerge piecemeal, even in dreams."

"So you're saying his latest memory could point to some fact, and there may be more."

"It's possible." Caruthers refolded a dark blue polo shirt before placing it in a bag. "What I'm saying is that a memory recovered a long time after the actual event can be based in reality. It can be at least partially true. Even if it comes in a dream."

Moore stood. "Thanks, Doc."

"Thank you, Deputy. You just made my mind up. I'd been toying with the idea of stopping at Princeton this afternoon. Now I will. Just to find out what's happening with my former patient—about both his dream and his girlfriend."

A frown creased Moore's brow. "He'll see you, just on the spur of the moment? Do you even know where to find him?"

"We're actually good friends. I've seen him at school a couple of times. I have his phone number and know the area and the campus."

"I hate to impose on you, but now that you've sort of authenticated Austin's memories, I have a couple of important questions to ask, and I'd like to do it in person. I've got the next few days off and could drive down. Could you guide me to him? Just for a short meeting."

The cat growled, and Caruthers gave Moore an assessing look. "Questions? Any chance I could listen in? I'd like to hear about any new memory."

Now it was Moore's turn to hesitate. "I guess. That might make him willing to answer. So we can do this?"

Caruthers nodded and studied his watch. "Let's meet at the train station in Princeton. It's on University Place. I can be there at, say, four."

୧ఎ୧ఎ

As Dave and Jennifer crossed the Delaware River at Stroudsburg and continued on I-80, the traffic in New Jersey increased, and that made it difficult to see the blue car. By the time they turned onto Route 206 toward Somerville, neither Dave nor Jennifer saw the pursuer again. They convinced themselves that it had all been a coincidence, more imagination than reality.

They made it back to campus by early afternoon. Dave waved at the gazebo guard, who gave him a sour look. The man scratched his head and watched far too long as they drove into the south lot.

"The campus security guy seemed to know you," Jennifer said.

Dave shrugged. "He probably just recognized Todd's car. Todd's sort of a scary driver."

They agreed to get together to go over things at five. Dave wasn't sure what had to be gone over, since he really had no problems with her being Redford's sister or her concealing that fact. He understood the desire to protect her brother and found it admirable. Certainly far better than sleeping with the swim team. Jennifer went to an econ lecture, and Dave limped to a German language lab.

He phoned Todd to assure him that his vehicle was back, full of gas, and parked much closer to the entrance of the south lot than when he'd borrowed it. He did not have to explain the bloody soccer towel because Jennifer had been smart enough to dispose of it. Todd made a noise that Dave didn't want to interpret.

☙❧

The language laboratory was completed before four. Dave's leg protested the slow walk back to the dorm, but he figured the exercise was probably good for it. He downed a Demerol, and it had begun to take effect when his cell phone rang. The voice was familiar.

"Hi, David. Jim Caruthers here. Are you somewhere private?"

"Dr. C, what a surprise. Private? I'm walking to my dorm."

"Good. I heard you were in Norwich. Sorry you didn't drop in to say hello."

"I was only there for the weekend, and I didn't have any free time. The trip was very sudden. Good to hear your voice again," Dave said, thinking it wasn't all that good.

"You've had plenty of time to memorize its sound. I just wanted to hear why you returned to Norwich for the first time in ten years. And what you were doing." Caruthers seemed to be rushing, something he never did in psychotherapy sessions. Slow progress meant more dollars.

Dave considered what he wanted to say over the phone. "I was just curious about those teens killed last week. Sure seemed like a repeat of what happened to my brother and

Carter. I wondered if the police had made a connection to Scott's death."

"Find out anything?"

"Only that they have a suspect for the recent killings and for those a decade ago. A guy named Ed Malone. Ever heard of him?" There was no immediate answer, and Dave wondered if he'd lost the signal.

"I know him," Caruthers said at last. More delay like phone interviews between Atlanta and Hong Kong. "Actually, I heard what happened to Ed Malone from my brother-in-law, Parker Holmes. Did you remember anything more or new about the day your brother was killed?"

"Not really." Dave wanted to confess remembering where he might have dropped the cloth on his way to his house. He wanted to say it could have evidence on it that would prove that Malone was the killer. But Moore's warning stopped him. Dave reached the dorm. "Let me get up to my room where reception is better. Hang on."

He entered the room where Todd was reading on the couch. Dave waved at him, and his roommate thrust a middle finger in his direction. Dave ignored the greeting, entered his bedroom, and half-closed the door. "I'm back," he said into the phone.

Caruthers continued. "Say, listen, Dave. You won't guess where I am. I'm headed to North Carolina for some business and happened to pick the coastal route. I came down through New Jersey, and I'm just off campus. I'd love to see you, check on how you are doing. And I have a gift for you."

Caruthers's unannounced appearance on campus was a surprise, and yet it wasn't. More than once during his freshman year, the doctor had shown up at Princeton for a visit. The meetings usually turned out to be mini-checkups, free visits with the psychiatrist. The notion of a gift was new. Dave glanced at his watch. It was just after four and he had to meet Jennifer for dinner. A brief meeting was possible. "Sure. That would be great."

"Can we meet on the fringe of campus? I don't want to park and walk to your dorm. I want to get into Virginia before I stop for the night." Without waiting for a reply, Caruthers rushed on, "How about the lake? By the boathouse. That's private enough for us to talk. I can be there in ten minutes."

Although they'd discussed college choices at length in several sessions, Caruthers knowledge of the campus layout surprised Dave. He certainly hadn't had a clue as to where the boathouse was until he actually visited Princeton before making his decision. He hesitated before saying, "That sounds fine. If you want a place easy to get to and park, that will do. It'll be quiet, since there's never practice on Mondays. See you on the shore in ten minutes."

Maybe he could get some insight from Caruthers about Malone and whether solving his brother's murder might eliminate his anxiety attacks and dreams. All that for free. Plus a gift. He emailed Jennifer that he had to meet an old friend and might be a bit late for dinner. It was a twenty-minute walk to the boathouse, but took only five minutes by bike on pavement. And biking was easier on his leg than walking.

Dave stuck his head into the common room. "Can I borrow your bike, Todd?"

Todd glanced at him with narrowed eyes. "Bike, yes. Car, no. Why are you limping?"

"Long story. Film at eleven." Dave grabbed the bike lock key and left.

∽∾∽∾

Moore had arrived in Princeton way before Caruthers and had spent the time thinking. When Caruthers pulled into the space next to him at the train station, Moore joined the psychiatrist in the latter's car. The deputy watched the train called The Dinky depart as the doc dialed David Austin. A surge of late-day traffic cruised past the line of nose-in cars on both sides of University Place as Dave agreed to meet at Lake Carnegie.

"That's good, Doc," Moore said. "I just want a few moments to ask him some questions without anything distracting. Thanks for keeping my presence a secret. If he knew I was here, he'd get nervous for no reason. I find that the relaxed witness is the most reliable."

"I'm not sure your sudden appearance will be very relaxing. And I do feel uncomfortable misleading a patient in any way," Caruthers said. "But you may be right in this instance. It is even possible that Dave would have refused to come if he thought he had to face more questions. My being there might reassure him. That way, I can give you a concrete assessment about the validity of any memory."

"I'll let you talk to him first and get him relaxed. I guess there's no reason why you can't hear what I have to say. You won't repeat it. How far away is the boathouse?"

"Less than a mile."

"Do you mind if we leave my car here at the train station? That way I won't get lost."

Caruthers started the car, backed out of the spot, and swung around in a U-turn to drive past the WaWa store.

Chapter 44

Puzzle

Relieved when they made it back to campus, Jennifer still felt buoyant after her lecture. She thought over the trip as she made her way to her room. Malone's confession had exonerated John. He was no longer under a cloud of suspicion and was getting psychiatric care. That still left the why of Malone's actions, but maybe the police could find motive when they delved into his background. In time, it would become clear.

Identifying Malone as the murderer had another possible effect. Knowing who had killed his brother would change Dave. No more dreams, no visions, and less drinking. She doubted he was mature enough to actually stop drinking totally, but he wouldn't have to over-imbibe to treat his anxiety. She'd told Dave about her brother, and that cleared up the deception between them. Now, their relationship might grow. That thought made her stop.

Did she want a deeper relationship with Dave Austin? He had a good personality and made her laugh. He was a caring person and seemed to go out of his way to please her. Once he got over his problems from the past, he could be worth knowing. And he was actually good-looking. She enjoyed being with him. To see if liking him grew to even more, they needed time.

As she climbed the dorm steps, Jennifer decided that she

wanted a relationship, but it would depend on his actions.

In her room, she checked email. A new one from Dave said he would be meeting an old friend and might be a little late for their dinner get-together. He hadn't given a name for his old friend, and she surmised that it couldn't be a student. They were all new friends. Her phone rang as she was re-reading the email.

Parker Holmes introduced himself. "I couldn't reach David," he said, "so I thought I'd give you the update. I take it you had no problem getting back to Princeton?"

"No. No problems." Jennifer wondered what Holmes meant by "problem" and thought of the couple of hours they'd spent convincing themselves that the blue sedan was following. That seemed outlandish now.

"Good. There's something David should be aware of. Malone's confession was fantasy. An old timer came in when Malone was arrested. He remembered that, when Scott Austin and Carter Shuman were killed, Malone was in the hospital. The guy had an infected old wound, one he'd gotten from a wolf attack a month or so before. He'd tried to ignore the arm, but finally gave in and let his wife drag him to the hospital, and the doctor kept him there for a couple of days."

"Could the friend be remembering the wrong time?" Jennifer asked.

"Hospital records showed Malone was admitted before the murders and released after. No way he was involved."

"What about the recent murders?"

"Last Thursday, Malone was warming a barstool at the Pecky Cypress Lounge from nine till one. The girls who escaped whatever monster attacked those boys know precisely when it happened. Right about midnight. Malone might have killed that young man who worked for the traveling fair, but he sure had nothing to do with last week's murders. I suspect with some more legwork on our part, he'll be cleared of any involvement in the carnival killing as well."

Jennifer tried to understand what this meant for her brother and for Dave. Her head and heart knew that John was not the murderer, but the message came through loud and clear: there was still a murderer on the loose. She said as much.

"Right. Can you tell David what I've told you? I'm about to leave the office and won't be back for several days. I'll keep trying to call him myself, but this is important, and you may contact him first."

"Okay. I'm about to meet him. Anything else?"

"One other thing. I don't want to alarm you. But the fact that David may have information that could identify a murderer, like his memory of a blue cloth he carried down the hill and of what the killer looked like, means he could be in danger. He should be careful. Not go off by himself."

When the call ended, Jennifer's mind raced. Malone was not the killer. Someone else was, and that someone else would want to stop Dave from remembering any more. What could he possibly recall from so long ago? She had the answer: he'd already pictured a bloody cloth, wiry hair, maybe a beard. Now he said it was a blue cloth. Why did that strike her as so important? Blue cloth, blue shirt, blue jeans, a blue sedan. Dr. Blue. Dave had referred to his psychiatrist as Dr. Blue. But he always described the killer as wearing black. Could dark blue be seen as black by an eight-year-old facing into the sun?

Panicked, she reread Dave's email. He went to see an old friend. Old meant Norwich. She had to find him.

❧❧

Dave reached the parking lot near the boathouse and saw a single car. He parked Todd's bike in a rack on the side of the building and, as he engaged the bike lock, heard a familiar voice.

"Over here, David." Caruthers stood near the shore at an

opening in the bushes, the start of the path that bordered Lake Carnegie. The doctor's hair was trimmed shorter than the last time Dave saw it, and it gave him a military look. He'd removed his goatee and now wore glasses, but the choice of the usual blue outfit—jeans and a polo shirt—made him a familiar figure. He'd gained some weight, especially around the middle, and was probably over two hundred. But he stood six inches taller than Dave, making him seem big and not fat.

"Mind if we stretch our legs a bit with a walk?" Caruthers asked. "I've been driving for a while. That's bad enough, but doing it in New Jersey makes it worse. Just a quarter-mile or so while we talk."

Something in Caruthers's voice sounded odd.

"No more than that," Dave said. "I have a minor leg injury. I'm sure you heard I was shot. The bullet only grazed my leg, but it's sore. I'm supposed to rest it, but a walk is probably good for healing. Increased blood flow or something." Actually, the Demerol was making him feel pretty smooth.

"Sure. This won't take long." Caruthers glanced back at the boathouse and began to walk.

A short way beyond the bushes along a narrow path, it happened. Moore struck Dave across the back of his neck. Stunned, but still conscious, Dave fell.

"What the hell?" Caruthers yelled.

"Sorry, Doc. The plan is a bit different than I led you to believe," a new voice said. "Do what I say, or you'll find out what a small-caliber pistol can do at close range. Get your ex-patient to his feet and move him along. I have something to discuss with him."

The voice sounded familiar to Dave, even in his dazed state on the ground.

"Why did you hit him? Stop this now," Caruthers said.

"Button it, Doc, or you'll take a bullet in the face."

The psychiatrist half-carried, half-dragged Dave farther along the path. After a short distance, Caruthers couldn't hold his tongue. "I don't understand what you're doing. You said you had a few questions. Let's talk about this before something bad happens. We can talk."

"Shut the fuck up, Doc."

Dave could hear the words, but, in his woozy state, they made no sense. The foliage thickened. Eventually, they reached the lake overflow bunker, a cement box with two-inch-thick walls above the water level. The shore-side wall abutted the path.

"Drop him here."

As he was lowered to the muddy path, Dave realized who was speaking. The revelation made no sense. How could it be Deputy Rob Moore? His question was answered by a thump. Caruthers fell, his head bouncing off the drain box, and he landed next to Dave.

"Now we have to do a little work to set the stage for your unfortunate accident," Moore said.

He yanked Dave into a seated position and spread his lips with the mouth of a flask. Moore pinched Dave's nose. "Have a drink, kid. It will relax you."

Dave felt his head tip back and a slosh of high-proof whiskey enter his mouth, gagging him as it went down. He started coughing. When that stopped, he eyed the face over him. No doubt it was Moore.

"Good. You should enjoy hearing the answer to the mystery of your brother's death. I know this has been a burden on you, but now it's over. Dr. Caruthers told me about your dreams. What a shame. They will definitely end now."

Dave squinted and tried to move. Moore leaned on his shoulder.

"Here's what will happen. You and the doctor will get into a fight over drugs. He's been your supplier through the years, and now he wants to stop. Unfortunately the fight will get out of hand. He will hit his head on the cement here and fall into the water face first." Moore stopped and eyed Caruthers. "Well, look at that. He's already hit his big head on the drain box. A little shove and his head will be in the water. You'll try to pull him out and slip, falling in yourself. Too bad you're drunk and stoned. And that bum leg affects your balance."

Dave twitched as the needle pricked his neck.

"There, you nosy, fuckin' bastard. I should have killed you along with your brother. I'd smash your face in right now, but that would spoil the accident scene. I always knew you would remember too much. First the dreams and then the trip back to Norwich. And now the memories while you're conscious. Just couldn't let it alone. Probably egged on by this damn psychiatrist. Who knows what you told him. We'll fix that problem as well."

Stunned and uncomprehending, Dave struggled briefly, but Moore had a strong grip. The drug, whatever it was, acted fast. Only when he slumped did the deputy release him. On the ground, he tried to move, but his body wouldn't obey. He wondered what it would feel like to die by drowning.

"Good thing I ran into the doc," Moore said, pinching Dave's cheek. "We had a nice chat about why you might be back in town. Interesting stuff about those memories of yours. I knew I had to do something about that. What good luck to learn the doc was planning to stop in to see you on his way south. Made the job of getting you alone simpler."

Even through the drug, Dave could hear Moore's voice take on a higher pitch and a faster pace.

"I just couldn't pass up the opportunity to put an end to your damn dreams. Real fine that the doc knows the campus well, especially this nice quiet spot. He was happy to help when I told him I'd like to see you. Now he gets to play a leading role in your accidental death."

Death, Dave thought. He would join his brother. But he'd lose everything else. He'd lose Jennifer. He willed his arms to move, but Moore grabbed him by the hair and shoved the flask in his mouth.

"One last drink, Austin." Moore tipped back Dave's head. "The booze contains these nice pills to help you sleep without any disturbing dreams. No more dreams, no more fear, no more pesky memories. Especially the one about where you left that damn cloth. We don't want that turning up, do we? Now I'll fix the poor, traumatized little boy so he won't have to suffer any more. You'll be what you always wanted to be, a normal fuckin' kid."

Moore stood up and checked his watch. "We'll just give the drugs a few minutes to get into your system. You should be feeling sleepy soon. That's right, just close your eyes and drift off. It will be easier that way. It will be obvious you'd been drinking when you came down here. And taking drugs, too. Your problems just became too much for you, especially after that taxing weekend poking around in the woods." Moore knelt and put two white tablets into Dave's jacket pocket. He poured the rest of the bourbon on Dave's shirt and pants.

"You are one hell of a mess, David Austin. Liquor and barbiturates in your blood, more booze on your clothes, more drugs in your pocket. Your medical history made you a risk for stupid behavior like this, mixing depressants. I'll bet the doctor's notes predicted this. Too bad you fought, and he tripped and hit his head on the drain box there. And then you had the really bad luck of falling face down into the water. What a bummer. Just a few more minutes and you'll finally be cured and ready to face life, to achieve your full potential. Too bad you'll be dead."

Chapter 45

The Lake

Jennifer ran to Dave's dorm, yanked the entry door open, and took the stairs two at a time. She rushed into the room without knocking. The animals that sometimes inhabited the living room were in hiding, leaving behind the usual mess. She found Todd with an open book in the shared bedroom. "Where's Dave?" she asked in too loud a voice.

"Wow, you must really want him." Todd turned with a smile that faded when he saw Jennifer's face. "What's wrong?"

"He may be in trouble. He emailed me to say he is meeting an old friend. It could be the man who murdered his brother and now wants to make sure Dave doesn't remember anything more. Where did he go?"

"Whoa. Slow down. I feel like I missed the last three chapters of the book."

"You did. But you'll have to read them later. What do you know about Dave's whereabouts?"

Todd scratched his head. "I heard him on the phone, but I wasn't paying much attention. The conversation sounded friendly, as if they both came to some agreement. He went on the computer and then dashed out."

Jennifer closed the distance between them and put her hands on Todd's shoulders, shaking him as if he were a stubborn two-year-old. "Think. This is important. Can you remember anything else?"

Todd closed his eyes and said, "Apparently, the caller didn't want to take time to come here. He wanted to meet…somewhere quiet. And Dave said he'd see him in ten minutes. He left here about that long ago."

Jennifer backed away. "What time is it? We have to find him. Name some places Dave would go to meet someone close but quiet. Someplace he could reach walking in ten minutes."

"Not walking. He borrowed my bike."

"All right. Think of where he could get in ten minutes on a bicycle."

Todd focused above Jennifer's head, a sign he was thinking. "If the guy didn't want to come on the central campus, he could have parked on Nassau and met in front of Nassau Hall."

"That's not likely. Finding a spot anywhere on Nassau Street, let alone near the front gate, is impossible at this hour. And that sidewalk is never empty. Where else?"

From the floor below came the sound of Van Morrison's "Brown Eyed Girl." Male voices joined in.

Todd placed fingers on his temples. "Wait. I just remembered. The place was secluded, and there was no practice on Mondays. He might have chosen the parking lot near the stadium. Or the soccer fields. Or the sports complex. That would avoid guard shacks and traffic."

"That's not very secluded," Jennifer said.

Jabe stuck his head in the door, filling the frame with his football physique. He eyes went to Jennifer standing over Todd. "What's the fuss? Your voice sounds pretty excited, girl. And you look like a tiger about to pounce."

"We have to find Dave. I'll give you details later, but he could be in serious trouble with the murderer of his brother. He's ten minutes away by bike at some quiet spot, without people. Near where you can park a car."

"People? That rules out the sports complex," Jabe said.

"And the two other lots. There's easy parking, but joggers, jocks, and Frisbee freaks are always around."

"No, wait," Todd said. "I remember Dave saying 'shore' in his phone conversation."

Colin had joined Jabe at the door. "Was it 'shore' or 'sure?'" he asked.

Todd was up and grabbing a sweatshirt. "He said the shore. It has to be the lake. The boathouse. Let's go."

"Crew doesn't practice on Monday," Jabe said.

Todd and Jennifer ran through the living room and out, followed by Colin, who grabbed jackets from the pile near the door. Jabe came last, not bothering with a jacket. Outside, he took the lead, breaking into a run. The four got inquisitive looks from groups of students as they bounded past. A hound of some sort bounded with them as they raced across Poe field south of campus, but then it spied another dog and lost interest in the humans. The university band members scowled when the runners interfered with the random moves they called a formation. Jabe led them to a shortcut through the woods that took a thousand yards off the bike path Dave would have used.

They emerged from bushes and darted across Faculty Road. Jabe reached the small parking area near the boathouse first. A car was in the lot, but no one was visible, and it was quiet.

"We're wrong," Jennifer whispered, panting. "They're not here. We have to check the other places you mentioned, Todd."

Todd waved her to silence. "Not so fast. That car has New York Plates, and look. There. On the side of the building. That's my bike. He's here."

"Or was." Jabe's breathing seemed unaffected by the sprint. He pointed to the opening in the bushes. "That path goes along the lake. We jog there when we get sick of the football field."

"There's another path on the other side of the building," Colin noted. "I suppose it's more likely they took the path closest to the bike, but we should check out the far one."

Jennifer was ready to run, but Colin put a hand on her shoulder.

"Todd and I will check the other way," he said. "You go with big bruiser guy and do it quietly. If this old friend is up to no good, he may be dangerous. Our only advantage is surprise."

"We should have called campus security," Todd said. "One of those old guys could go first."

Todd and Colin hurried to the far side of the boathouse. Jabe and Jennifer moved quietly to the mouth of the path near the bike.

"Keep quiet and stay behind me," Jabe whispered. "If there's any trouble, run and get help. No heroics."

They entered the bushes.

ᘓᘖᘓ

Moore held Dave's wrist and eyed his watch as he took Dave's pulse. "Good boy. Nice and slow."

Dave moaned.

"Now, don't be making any noise. Not that there's any-one around to hear you. All you have to do now, Austin, is die. Accidentally, of course." Moore stepped away from his victim, scanned the ground, and picked up an elongated smooth stone about the size and shape of a large cucumber. "This should do the trick. A little tap on your head, maybe some blood, and in you go." He came back to the drugged Dave. "In fact, blood would be good. I'll rub the wall so there'd be no question about how you got the head trauma."

He began dragging Dave to the drainage basin wall.

ᘓᘖᘓ

Jabe signaled halt and crouched. He brought his lips close to Jennifer's ear. "I saw something ahead through the bushes. And I heard a voice. Not Dave's."

The pair inched closer. Jabe got to where he had a clear view of a big man dragging Dave toward the lake edge. He exploded forward, head low as if wanting to sink his shoulder pads into a lineman's chest. Moore caught the motion, dropped Dave into the water, and raised the rock. Just before the tackle, he brought it down on Jabe's head.

But it was a moving target, and Moore was backing up. The blow was no worse, and had no more effect, than what Jabe experienced every time a meaty linebacker got in his way. He barreled into Moore, shoulder to chest. A woof came from Moore as he flew backward, landing half in a small hemlock and half on the path. As Moore tried to rise, Jabe sent a fist across his jaw and flipped him back to front. He stuck his knee in the guy's back.

"Don't move," Jabe growled, "or I'll break your damn neck."

Jennifer pulled Dave from the water. She was feeling his neck and yelling his name when Colin and Todd arrived.

"Is he all right?" Todd asked.

"I don't think he's breathing." Her voice was panicked.

Colin pushed Jennifer aside and flipped Dave onto his back. He turned his head, checked his airway, and began CPR. After ten chest compressions and two lung inflations, Dave sputtered and coughed. Colin turned him on his side and felt for his pulse.

"It's very slow. He may be drugged, but at least he's breathing on his own. We need an ambulance. Jen, go call security. There's a phone on the front side of the boathouse."

Jennifer ran. As she left, the downed killer made his move. Moore was a strong guy and managed to dislodge Jabe and get to his knees. His freedom was brief. Todd, a former high school wrestler, got him in a headlock and held him while Jabe converted his belt to a band on Moore's wrists.

"Good thing you guys came back," Jabe said. "I appreciate the help."

"There were no new footprints in the wet path on the other side, and we were on our way back when we heard noises." Todd released the prisoner from the headlock and stood over him. "I can understand why you needed help. I've always suspected you football players were mostly padding."

Colin checked the inert figure of Jim Caruthers. "Judging by his blue clothing, this must be the doctor. He has a bloody whack on the back of his head, but his pulse is strong."

"A bloody whack?" Todd said. "Is that the best medical term you can come up with?"

"I'm keeping it in simple layman terms. He's been whacked and it's bleeding. Thus, a bloody whack."

Jennifer bounded back. A flock of Canadian geese chose the moment to land nearby with a flapping of wings and triumphant honking. They settled onto the water with awkward grace and sent ripples in all directions. Over their calls, sirens could be heard.

Chapter 46

Goin' Back

Four university security men arrived at Lake Carnegie, followed shortly thereafter by two borough police cars. From one vehicle two young officers not much older than the students emerged. An older plainclothes cop came from the second car. He surveyed the scene before following the path indicated by the campus officer.

At the incident site, the bear-like man introduced himself as Detective Ursinovitch, a name suited to his appearance. Ursinovitch told Jabe and Todd to release Moore and stood by while one policeman patted Moore down and removed the thirty-eight, a black jack, a syringe, and an empty plastic container. He told the two campus men to stay with Dr. Caruthers and Dave, not to touch anything, and wait for the ambulance. He ushered the rest of the group to the parking lot. "Please identify yourselves and tell me what exactly happened here," the bear said.

Todd answered, indicating that all of them, including Dave, were university students. "We just prevented the guy we were holding from killing Dave Austin and his psychiatrist."

"That's the unconscious man, Dr. Caruthers," Jennifer said. She pointed at Moore. "This is Rob Moore. He's a deputy sheriff from Norwich, New York. You have to arrest him."

The cop held up his hand. "Everybody show some ID to this officer. Jack, make sure no one's carrying. Write down the names." He turned to Moore. "You're a deputy? What's your version of what happened here?"

Before Moore could answer, an ambulance arrived, and two uniformed medical technicians got out. They went to Dave and Caruthers. Dave was barely conscious and Caruthers had begun to come around. The EMTs put them in the ambulance and left, siren on.

Ursinovitch turned back to Moore and raised his thick eyebrows.

"I didn't try to kill anyone. I was saving the Austin kid from the doc who seemed intent on drugging him and drowning him."

"That's bull," Jennifer said. "You were trying to kill them both."

"Why don't we just continue this discussion at the station?" Ursinovitch pointed a finger at Jennifer. "Since you seem to know something, why don't you come with me? The rest of you, ride with this officer. You can give your statements at the station."

He directed the officer called Jack to investigate the scene and left with Moore and Jennifer in his car. Moore was in the back seat behind a grate.

єљєљ

At the station, Ursinovitch had Jennifer wait in a separate room while he dealt with Moore. He donned latex gloves and placed on the table the items they'd collected from the deputy.

"Those belong to Caruthers," Moore said.

"The gun?"

"That's mine."

Ursinovitch examined the plastic container that had what looked like pill dust in the bottom.

"I took it from Caruthers after I subdued him," Moore said. "He was in the act of dragging Austin toward the water. I admit I shoved him to get to the kid, and he fell and hit his head on the drain overflow box. I was tending to the boy when the battering ram hit me."

Ursinovitch bagged the items. He told the young cop to call the hospital ER and tell them about the syringe and pill container.

"How about a cup of coffee, Deputy?" Ursinovitch asked. When Moore nodded, the cop left the room, taking the evidence with him. He took the opportunity to check on Jennifer.

"What was the first thing you observed when you and your friend reached the place where Dave was?" he asked her.

"When we got there, Moore was dragging Dave toward the water with a rock in his hand," she said.

Ursinovitch thanked her and lumbered back to Moore. "How did you get to the lake, Deputy?" he asked.

Moore hesitated way too long. "I rode over with the doc. I told him I wanted to ask Austin some questions about a memory he had of the murder of his brother a decade back. I've had my eye on the doc as the murderer and decided to trap him by saying Austin had a new memory, something that would implicate him. The trap worked and Caruthers insisted on seeing his patient alone before he let me near him. I waited in the parking lot for the doc to bring him to me. Now I'm thinking the kid said something the doc wanted to keep secret and that sent him over the edge. When I heard loud voices, I ran to check it out."

The bear leaned back and stared at Moore. "Did Dr. Caruthers know you were a sheriff's deputy?"

"Sure. We both live in Norwich."

"So you're saying he committed this attempted murder within a short distance of a law-enforcement officer."

"What can I say? He went nuts."

Ursinovitch went back to Jennifer. She made it clear that

Moore's action were way more than assault, explaining the connection to Norwich and the murder of Dave's brother. She said Moore could be involved in several murders in New York. Her statement was recorded and signed.

Moore was arrested on a charge of attempted murder, and Jennifer went to find Dave.

෮ඕ෮

Armed with information on the syringe found on Moore, the ER doctor located the needle mark in Dave's neck and the pills in his jacket pocket. Based on the color, shape, and marking of the pills, the doctor identified them as a common sedative and ordered a tox screen.

Sedation certainly fit Dave's symptoms, and he didn't seem to have any other problems. The ER staff monitored him and, by the time the lab identified the barbiturate in the syringe, he had come around enough to recognize where he was. Colin filled him in on how he got there.

The groggy Caruthers was treated for head trauma. He showed no signs of a concussion, but the hospital doctor took him to task for his high blood pressure and a poor lipid profile. He was released after he promised not to drive for twenty-four hours. Todd took him to the Marriott on Route 1, and Colin delivered his car. The doctor handed them a packet of ski pictures to give to Dave, explaining it was the promised gift.

෮ඕ෮

Jennifer called Parker Holmes from her room. "You were right about Dave being in danger," she said. "He was attacked."

"When? How? Is he all right?"

"He suffered some trauma, but he's doing well, thanks to his quad mates and me. Rob Moore, the Norwich deputy sheriff, was about to kill him. When we got there, Moore had him face down in the lake, and Dave wasn't breathing."

"Whoa. Rob Moore? There in Princeton?"

"That's right. He followed us from Norwich. Dr. Caruthers showed up here because he wanted to visit, and I think Moore used Caruthers to get near Dave. You must know the doctor."

Holmes was quiet on his end of the line for longer than usual. "Oh, I know him, all right. He's my brother-in-law. And you're sure Rob Moore was assaulting David?"

"Yes. No question about it." Jennifer sat on her bed and unlaced her sneakers. "He'd dragged him toward the water with a rock in his hand, obviously intending to make sure he didn't survive being under water."

As she kicked off her shoes and loosed her muddy jeans, she told Holmes her theory, including being tailed by the blue car and how Moore's size and wiry hair matched Dave's memories. "Listen, the local cops said Moore will see a judge tomorrow. What if he posts bail? Is there anything you can do? I'm worried he may try to finish the job he started."

"All you have is possibilities. We need facts to charge a man with murder. But I'll give the local cops a call. We have a few facts that may develop into evidence. And I'll have to check into Moore's background. The one thing you haven't explained is the most important."

"What's that?" she asked, wriggling out of her pants.

"Motive." Holmes spoke to someone near him and then came back to Jennifer. "My assistant heard David tell Deputy Moore about a cloth he'd lost running from the murderer in July 1983. He thinks he dropped it near the mushroom grove, maybe in a hole. My officer told the sheriff, who sent men to scour the site where David was shot. They found more than one hole in that depression. In one was a bit of blue rag, apparently part of a tee shirt with an emblem about the Appalachian Trail. And there were stains. It's been sent to the state lab for analysis. If the rag is connected to the

Austin-Shuman murders and the stain is blood, it will probably match the boys' blood, but there could also be evidence of the killer."

Jennifer thought of her brother's shirt, lost somewhere that fatal afternoon. She didn't know the shirt's color, but he had a lot of tees with writing on them. She prayed that, if there was something pointing to the owner of the cloth, it didn't point at John.

ल॒ल॒

With a clear suspect in mind, Holmes was able to generate evidence from all three murders. He phoned the state lab and told them to compare any DNA to Rob Moore's. At the site of the most recent murders, the police found several shoe prints, a large man's size, that didn't match any of the teens' footwear. One had a cut that would uniquely identify it. Holmes sought a warrant to search Moore's apartment, hoping Moore was a packrat and hadn't dumped the shoes.

Thinking of the prints made him remember another clue from the first murders: the black hair found on one of the dead boys. It had been lost somewhere between the sheriff's office and the Forensic Investigation Center of the New York State Police Crime Laboratory System in Albany. It would have been easy for Rob Moore to lose that evidence. And it wouldn't be difficult to see if the deputy had an alibi for the most recent killings. All of this would take a bit of time, but Moore would sit in jail, if the Princeton District Attorney could convince the judge.

It would also give Holmes a chance to find out what could possibly explain how a law-enforcement professional, someone respected, could commit such heinous crimes. He was sure there must be a reason for such evil. It might not be a rational or sane reason, but one that Moore couldn't resist. Holmes wondered if the current sheriff knew something.

Holmes made the call to the Princeton Borough Police Department and laid out why he needed time to investigate. He was directed to the county attorney, who turned out to be sympathetic, especially since only Moore's fingerprints were on the syringe and the pill bottle he was carrying. Moore stayed locked up.

ℰↃℰↃ

After his release from the hospital, Dave returned to Dr. Ellington for another session of not-quite hypnosis. The barrier that kept him from remembering details of what happened years ago on a hot day in Norwich was breached, and he remembered everything: the fireworks, John's presence and his leaving, the murderer's blue shirt, torn and hanging in shreds. He recalled grabbing at the shirt as the killer grabbed him, ripping the cloth in his frenzy, and running off with the piece in his hand. Most importantly, he remembered getting a glance at the killer's face when he fell and dropped the rag into the hole. There was no question in his mind but that Moore was the killer.

A week later, Parker Holmes provided the last piece of the puzzle. Dave was catching up with the reading for a criminal psychology class and wondering why Jennifer seemed to be avoiding him when the detective called.

After confirming that Dave was doing all right, Holmes said, "The shirt fabric we found near the mushrooms contained three hair fibers with the roots still attached. The DNA extracted matched Rob Moore's, at least based on what we found on a hairbrush in his apartment. Specks of blood may belong to your brother or to Carter Shuman."

That notion brought tears to Dave's eyes, and he couldn't speak.

Holmes had more to say. "So Moore has been charged with the murders of Scott Austin and Carter Shuman and is awaiting extradition back to New York. He also owns a black pickup that matches one spotted near the carnival killing in Cazenovia. Inside the pickup we found a tire iron that tested positive for blood. In his apartment was a pair of shoes whose prints match those found at the site of the most recent killings. He'll be charged in those murders."

"But why did he do it?" Dave asked, his voice breaking.

"I didn't worry much about the why in the past, but the longer I've done this job, the more that question intrigues me. Moore's lawyer has released a psychiatrist's report on the man's background, probably preparing for a defense based on his abused youth. There were some disturbing elements in that story. Are you sure you want to hear this?"

"Should I be hearing it?" Dave asked.

"It's the stuff in the papers, thanks to the lawyer. Nothing confidential."

"Tell me."

"His domineering mother was a religious fanatic, and Moore was physically abused by bigger kids as he grew up. It went on for a while. The reporter for the Syracuse paper suggests this is the basis for an insanity defense."

"Might be true," Dave said. "I remember some of the stuff he was saying as he prepared to kill me. It sounded nuts."

"The insanity defense doesn't require that he act like a madman. Only that he failed to know right from wrong and couldn't control his actions. The argument will be that traumatic events in his early life drove him to kill and mutilate."

Dave put a bookmark in his criminal psychology text. "Events?"

"Moore was abandoned by his parents when he was four. They stayed around just long enough to abuse the kid, both with harsh punishments and sexual perversions. The state put him in foster care. When he was twelve, a group of teenagers ranging from thirteen to eighteen, including one living in the same foster home, abused him and carried it a step farther. It was vicious stuff. Apparently, a second victim was forced to perform fellatio. The kid bit Moore's penis and damaged a nerve. The attackers used his shirt to stem the bleeding. Might explain why he collected shirts."

"He didn't take shirts from Scott and Carter."

"Didn't have time. He was chasing you."

Dave's mind went back to the question of motive. "My God. You mean he was punishing random teenage boys because of what happened to him?"

"That may be it. The big damage may have been psychological. The foster mother said both boys were demon-possessed. She whipped Moore and condemned the abuser and the abused. That went on for a year until he was moved.

"He wound up with a foster family when he was a teenager. They eventually adopted him. But the foster mother dished out a lot of guilt, especially over sexuality. No healing under her guidance."

Dave tapped his textbook as he considered the ramifications of what Holmes said. "So what are you saying? That the motivation for killing my brother and four other boys was a sort of revenge? That the mutilation was retaliation for his own mutilation?"

"That's something for a psychiatrist to say. But, if it's true, it doesn't help the victims, and who knows if it helps the survivors. I suppose violence can stem from violence done to the murderer. I can't say what mixed up stuff might be in Moore's head, but it may involve a distorted view of sex. Research suggests childhood trauma could be behind serial sexual murders, especially if enabled by psychedelic mushrooms."

"Was Moore married?"

"No. Some thought he was gay, but now it appears he was just psychologically castrated and physically damaged. All of his victims were males, and the group that assaulted him years ago could have contained boys as young as your brother and as old as the carnival worker."

"So my brother just got in his way? Is that it?" Dave stood and began pacing. A girl's laugh came from the hall.

Holmes hesitated before continuing. "There's one other thing that may explain his attack on your brother. A couple of old residents of the neighborhood where Moore grew up said that they remembered that there was a girl who might have been involved in the incident in which Moore was injured. One of the residents said the girl's name was Mauriano."

"That was my mother's maiden name." Dave stopped pacing. "You're saying my mother was connected to this creep? No way. No fuckin' way."

"There are many Maurianos in this area. Whether it's true or not may not matter. If Moore thinks it's true, he could have killed your brother for revenge."

Chapter 47

War and Peace

Dave hunted down Jennifer and told her the Moore story, omitting any reference to Chella Austin. She accepted the tale without comment. "So what do you think?" he asked when he was done.

"I think that actions have consequences," she said, bowing her head.

"What does that mean?"

She narrowed her eyes. "It means that what you do causes ripples. For you and for others. There's no action that doesn't have effects."

"Why do I have a feeling that we are no longer talking about the murders?"

Jennifer made her meaning as clear as Montana air. "We're not. We're talking about you. The mystery of who killed your brother has been solved. With time, you should recover all the memories that belong to an eight-year-old boy a decade later. It means that you have to change your behavior."

"What behavior?"

"Drinking like an alcoholic."

"That's bull. I'm not one. Enjoying a little alcohol doesn't make me an alcoholic."

"True, but drinking every night, downing enough to make you do stupid things like helping other sots lift and move a VW bug, and consuming quarts every weekend does."

"You're blowing this way out of proportion."

"Fine. Prove you're okay. Go without booze."

"I like booze."

"Either you admit your problem and change, or we aren't friends."

෧෨෧

The two did not speak to each other for the final two weeks of the semester. After working Reunions Weekend where twenty-five thousand alumni and families descended on campus for four days of carousing, Dave and Jennifer left campus without a goodbye.

The ultimatum worked. Once away from the boozy temptations of college, Dave was able to see what he'd become. Without the excuse of dreams, visions, and anxiety—all had ceased after a session with Dr. Ellington—he had no reason to drink himself unconscious. His resolve was strengthened when his mother said that she knew Rob Moore as a teen, but had nothing to do with any attack. Dave didn't quit beer entirely, but got through the whole summer sober. Maybe the most important discovery was that he actually enjoyed being sober.

When the Norwich *Evening Sun* reported Ed Malone's story, it included the odd mushrooms and a local doctor's theory that the fungi could cause irritation and have psychedelic properties. County officials invited Cornell scientists to investigate. The scientists found the mushrooms, confirmed their properties, and collected samples for cultivation and study. Politicians then came up with the money to clear out the mushrooms, on the basis that they were a hazard too near a residential area. The farmer who'd bought the land from Ed Malone was more than happy to remove himself from the fray and to approve the use of fungicide in the glen. Neither the state of New York nor the Environmental Protection Agency were consulted.

Accounts of Ed Malone, David Austin, and John Redford suggested that there might be an exotic animal in the area. Local animal control experts thought it might be some sort of large rodent. Others suggested a fox or badger. No animal showed up during the scientist's expedition. A psychiatrist from Mary Imogene Hospital in Cooperstown opined that the hallucinogenic mushrooms could have accounted for the imagined attacks by ill-defined animals.

Ed Malone was hospitalized for some time and treated for his mental problems, chief of which was paranoia. He was judged unfit to stand trial for assault in the shooting of Dave Austin and the kidnapping of John Redford, but the judge sent him to Riverbend Hospital. He responded to therapy, but was not released. At least the incarceration at this facility left Malone close enough that he might get visits from his kids.

✄৩৫৩

In September, Dave returned to Princeton to start his third year. Todd, Colin, and Jabe were again his roommates, and the four booked a quad suite with a larger center room on the ground floor in 1901 Hall. Most of the furnishings were in place when Dave sauntered in. His friends were sitting around the living room, relaxing, each with a beer. Open windows allowed warm fall air to blow in, along with laughter and music. Since they'd occupied the space for only a couple of hours, a preternatural neatness prevailed, threatened only by a few empty beer cans and a balled-up food wrapper.

They rose to greet him and embraced in a big group hug. Dave started into the bedroom on the left, assuming they'd made the same arrangement as last year.

"The other one," Todd yelled.

Dave plopped his bag in the designated bedroom he'd share with Todd. The space was small, maybe even smaller than last year. He emerged from the closet-like room. "What's up with this? Didn't Todd and I suffer enough last year?"

"You weren't here, and neither was I, when these bullies dictated things." Todd shrugged. "But at least we got a pretty good deal on the great view."

Dave adopted a philosophical attitude. "We spend nine months here. I guess it's only fitting that my sleeping space is no bigger than a womb." With his foot, he pushed another bag toward the bedroom, left it at the threshold, and headed for the hall door.

"Need any help?" Colin offered, lifting his other leg from the floor and stretching out on the couch.

"I'm fine."

"How about a beer?" Jabe asked.

"No thanks. I'm a scholar now. A sober scholar. We only drink moderately after ten p.m." Dave left his three roomies with puzzled expressions.

He returned to where he'd parked the SUV he'd purchased with his parent's help and the money he'd earned painting garages during the summer. It was five-years-old and had already logged over eighty-thousand miles, but it got him from place to place, and he felt more responsible having it.

Todd had threatened to take any vehicle Dave acquired on a crazed trip cross-country. Or at least to the Jersey shore. Just to pay him back for borrowing the Pathfinder.

The car was packed with duffel bags and cartons. Dave pulled a box full of books to the edge of the cargo area. As he hoisted it, a voice startled him.

"Hey, stranger," Jennifer called from across the courtyard.

Dave dropped the box and swiveled, his heart performing a little dance as his tongue thickened. He swallowed, not knowing what to expect.

Jennifer strode closer. "I haven't heard from you in three months. I guess I was really rough on you at the end of May."

Dave found his voice. "You were rough, but fair."

"Sorry," she said, tucking a strand of hair under an orange ball cap.

"Don't be. I needed it. There was a hell of a lot of truth in what you shat all over me. Got me thinking."

"Did it do any good?"

"I haven't been drunk all summer."

She examined him and smiled. "That's wonderful. You look trimmer as well as sober. Are you saying my tirade actually reformed you?"

"That, and the counseling I've had. I am a better man. You look pretty trim yourself. Lots of tennis?"

She swung an invisible racket. "I took a week of tennis camp and will whip your butt for sure."

"Speaking of counseling, how is your brother doing?"

"Well. He's gotten with a good psychiatrist who found that, like you, he was suppressing a memory."

Dave leaned against the car. "About the day of the murders?"

"Yes, but about something else. As for that terrible day, I think the mushrooms and their hallucinogens caused his bizarre behavior. He ran and wound up in that roadside ditch. But his breakthrough deals with something that happened earlier, when he encountered his soccer coach. Apparently, the guy molested John."

"And your brother just kept quiet?"

"He was too ashamed. Remember, he attended a Christian school at the time, and all things about sex were taboo. His brain fixed the problem by repressing the memory."

"So who was the guy?"

"Reggie Peckrough. Actually, a friend of my mother's. He's been in Norwich for years and is well known to the cops. I think he was the cross-dresser you saw outside the HoJos. He came from Auburn where he'd been accused of molesting another boy. They couldn't quite make the case over there, and he fled to Norwich."

"I'm sorry to hear about John's experience. I—"

Jennifer held up a hand, and they embraced.

When they separated, Dave said, "Too bad this didn't come out when John was first hospitalized. I heard that the psychiatrist at Riverbend didn't release him. Do you know who did?"

Jennifer raised her eyes, as if trying to find a memory in the clouds. Finally she said, "I was just eleven when he was released. He'd been diagnosed with epilepsy and was doing well on a drug. I think some administrator decided, maybe for money reasons, that he was well enough to make it on the outside."

"Ah. The golden rule. Them that has the gold makes the rule. But I have another question."

Jennifer folded her arms. "Let me guess. You want my notes from Physical Chemistry for last semester so you can ace it this fall?"

"Well, yes. That, of course. But I wanted to ask you something else."

Jennifer put a hand to her ear and tilted her head. "I'm listening."

A warm breeze lifted her hair. Dave caught her smell and blinked. "I was wondering if you wanted to go to dinner this evening. Just friends. Just dinner."

"Wait a minute," Jennifer said. "Did I just hear a proposition escape from your lips that didn't end with us in bed?"

"Yes," Dave said. "Just dinner. Just friends. To thank you."

Jennifer considered for a moment. "I'll say yes, but I have conditions."

Dave nodded, waiting for her to continue.

"First, I get to order a steak."

"What happened to your yogurt diet?" Dave pulled his wallet out from his pocket, making like he was counting his money. "Okay. I can swing that."

Jennifer smiled mischievously. "Second. This doesn't get you off the hook. I'll take the thanks, but you still owe me big time."

"Meaning I'll be forever in your debt? I can live with that."

"Great. Then my third condition: I'll agree to the 'just dinner' clause, but let's hold off on the 'just friends' thing for right now. We'll see what happens." Without waiting for a response, she turned her back and walked away from the SUV. She glanced back over her shoulder. "I'm in four-oh-one Cuyler. Pick me up at seven."

Dave waved. When he lifted the box again, it felt lighter.

THE END

A. C. Brooks

A. C. Brooks is a successful entrepreneur, business executive, speaker, and endurance athlete. Now living in California, he began his writing career at Princeton University as a weekly humor columnist for *The Nassau Weekly*. *The Clown Forest Murders*, co-authored with R. R. Brooks, is his first full length novel. He opines on the humor of life at www.andhesays.com. When not writing or starting a new company, he can be found competing in ultra races, triathlons, and running seven marathons in seven days on all seven continents in seven days. This epic race, called the World Marathon Championship, will start in January 2018.

R. R. Brooks

R.R. Brooks spent his career doing pharmaceutical research and development. Now living in western North Carolina with two giant cats and a beagle, he's published fiction and nonfiction, including science fiction and fantasy stories exploring strange encounters and issues of doubt and belief. Leo Publishing released his epic fantasy novel *Justi the Gifted* in 2015. His other novels include a science fiction tale (underway) and second fantasy novel (underway). He is a member of the Blue Ridge Writers Group, the Appalachian Round Table, the Brevard Authors Guild, International Thriller Writers, Inc., Goodreads, ReadLocal, and the N.C. Writers Network. He maintains author's pages on Facebook, Amazon, and Goodreads. This is his first mystery novel.